OFF Camera

CHELSEA CURTO

Copyright © 2024 by Chelsea Curto

Proofreading by April Editorial

Copy editing by Britt Tayler at Paperback Proofreader

Cover by Sam Palencia at Ink and Laurel

All rights reserved.

No part of this book may be reproduced in any form or by any electronic or mechanical means, including information storage and retrieval systems, without written permission from the author, except for the use of brief quotations in a book review.

For the girls who feel like they take up too much space.
You don't.
They just don't dream big enough.

(And for the girlies who love the quiet boys with filthy mouths—Reid Duncan is for you).

AUTHOR'S NOTE

Thank you so much for picking up Off Camera! Since this is a book that features social media managers, you'll notice direct message images throughout the story. The images aren't perfect, and done solely for the purpose of differentiating between text messages and public exchanges. If you're reading on dark mode, be aware the text might be too white!

CONTENT WARNINGS

While this book is a romantic comedy, it does contain some heavier topics. I felt it was important to share them here.

-mention of the death of a parent
-mention of a verbal abuse by a parent
-frequent sexually explicit content
-frequent explicit language
-sexism in the workplace (not done by the MMC)

Please take care of yourselves, and know my DMs are open if you want to chat more.

CHARACTER CATCH UP

Off Camera can be read as a stand alone novel, it does mention characters from my other books.

Shawn, who is mentioned briefly, is from Caught on Camera, a friends to lovers, fake dating sports romance and book two in the Love Through a Lens series.

Dallas and Maven are from Behind the Camera, a single dad x nanny sports romance and book three in the Love Through a Lens series.

Maverick and Emmy are from Face Off, a rivals to lovers, NHL teammates sports romance and book one in the DC Stars series. This is my favorite book I've ever written, and I love it dearly!

My DMs are always open on Instagram (@authorchelseacurto) if you have any questions!

@dcfootball

I heard there were copyright issues with that damn song of yours. It would be a shame if we couldn't hear it this year.

@footballindc

Your sarcasm is getting worse and worse as the seasons go on. Do you think you're funny?

@dcfootball

My goal isn't to be funny. It's to bother you.

@footballindc

Well, you're certainly doing a good job. You annoy the hell out of me.

@dcfootball

I'm adding that as a point in my column.

@footballindc

You probably have an actual column, don't you?

@dcfootball

What can I say? I'm a spreadsheet kind of guy.

@footballindc

This might be the first time you've ever confirmed you're a man. Years later, and I finally know.

@dcfootball

Does it matter?

@footballindc

No.

@dcfootball

Good. It also doesn't matter that you're a woman.

@footballindc

How do you know I'm a woman?

@dcfootball

The video you posted of your offensive line yesterday showed your hand at the end. You can see red nails and a bracelet.

@footballindc

Men paint their fingernails too.

@dcfootball

You're right. I apologize for assuming.

@footballindc

I am a woman, but you can go ahead and admit you're obsessed with me. So much so, you stare at the videos I post for hours.

@dcfootball

Blocking you now.

@footballindc

Don't let the door hit you on the way out.

ONE
AVERY

THIS IS the worst first date I've ever been on.

My hopes were low when he picked a dingy sports bar as our meeting spot, but I persevered. I showed up anyway because I'm a nice person who doesn't ghost someone thirty minutes before we're supposed to meet.

Ghosting would've been better than the hell I've had to endure, though. The thin glimmer of hope I had about the night going from *absolute train wreck* to *somewhat salvageable* slowly slips out the window as the man across from me uses his collar to wipe his nose.

"My issue isn't with *women*," Matthew says urgently. He puts his whole chest behind it like he's proud: each word is punctuated. The right emphasis is on the right noun. He reaches for his beer—his fourth, and we've been here less than an hour—and it nearly slips out of his grasp thanks to the wing sauce on his fingers. "It's with women being in places they don't belong, you know? Sports are *sacred*."

No, I *don't* know, but the only way I can get out of this excruciating conversation that's lightyears worse than a lobotomy is to grin and bear it.

"They should get back to the kitchen, shouldn't they?" I ask. His eyes light up like I just hit a home run out of the park. The queen of improv rolling in with the one-liner to end all one-liners. "The quieter the better, I say."

"Exactly." Matthew slaps the table. The last sip of my mediocre white wine sloshes around in my glass. "It's really not that difficult."

I need a stronger drink.

"It's not," I say through clenched teeth.

I wonder if I can use the knife sitting next to my plate to stab him in the jugular.

I could make it look like an accident. I'd feign innocence and claim I was defending feminism.

I doubt anyone would miss the prick.

"How do you feel about dessert?" Matthew licks his lips, and it takes everything in me not to recoil. "Want to split a slice of cheesecake? Or maybe I could put you on the table and—"

"I'm allergic," I almost yell. The lie slips out easily, and I give him a shrug that hopefully looks more apologetic than like I'm plotting his demise. A barstool over the head would also get the job done. "Besides, I should start making my way home—or back to the 1920s."

"No problem. Maybe next time." He taps the check with his sauce-stained fingers and looks at me. "You owe twenty-three dollars."

I bite down on my bottom lip so hard, I'm surprised I don't draw blood.

I have no problem paying for my meal.

I have no problem paying for the *whole* meal.

But after sixty minutes of half-cold mozzarella sticks and enough misogynistic comments to last me a lifetime, I'm *tired*.

Tired of shitty dates and even shittier conversations.

Tired of men who pretend to be interested in the answers I give them while staring at my chest.

Tired of guys who believe women are only allowed to occupy certain spaces in the world.

I don't know when common decency—like holding the door open and not making sexist jokes—became the bare fucking minimum, but *gosh* I hate it here. I'd rather be single for the rest of my life than deal with this shit on a consistent basis.

"Right." I plaster on the smile that won me Miss Florida and runner-up to Miss America. I throw down two twenties and grab my purse. "Thanks for a great night."

"You too, Ashley," he says, and I don't have the energy to correct him. "Want to do it again next week? Back at my place?"

I slide out of the booth knowing full well this dude wouldn't be able to find my G-spot even with a map and step-by-step instructions.

"I'll text you," I lie again, and I don't feel an ounce of remorse.

"Cool." He stands and pulls me into a hug before I can escape. His hand drifts dangerously close to my ass when he presses me against his chest, and I contemplate breaking his wrist. "Looking forward to it."

The only thing I'm looking forward to is a long shower and scrubbing myself from my head to my toes so I can get rid of his slimy touch.

I wiggle free and try my best not to run down the hallway to the bar's bathroom so I can hide out for the next five to seven years.

Or at least until he leaves and drives far, far away.

I lock myself in a stall and lean against the wall, killing time by blocking his number. I make sure to block him on the dating app too for good measure.

Ten minutes later, once I'm sure the douche canoe isn't loitering around anymore, I head back into the restaurant.

As terrible as tonight was, I really don't want to go home just yet. My apartment is too quiet and too empty, and being alone with my thoughts sounds like the worst idea.

Another drink while watching old NBA highlights on the television at the bar sounds much better.

I see an empty spot at the counter and make a beeline for it.

"Hi," I say to the guy to my right, and he doesn't glance up from his phone. "Are you saving this seat for anyone?"

"Nope." He scoots his stool over an inch to give me some space. "All yours."

"Thanks." I slide onto the ripped leather and put my elbows on the counter, grateful when the bartender comes over and lays a cocktail napkin in front of me. "Can I get a double whiskey neat, please? And a slice of cheesecake?"

"Thought you were allergic," the man with the phone says.

I whip my head to look at him.

His thick-framed glasses hide a lot of his face, but I see green eyes and red scruff on his cheeks that matches the hair on his head. An inviting grin pulls at his mouth, and he seems so familiar to me. I'm certain I've seen him somewhere before, I just can't remember when.

"Eavesdropping?" I ask with a quirked eyebrow.

"Hard not to when the dude you were with spent fifteen minutes talking about why the 1920s would've been a great decade to live in," he says.

"You heard all of that?"

"Every word, unfortunately. The whole bar did," he draws out. "Think it took ten years off my life."

"I'd really like to curl up in a hole. I despised that conversation, but I'm an Enneagram two. I'm a people-pleaser. I—I like to be needed and appreciated. It's almost impossible for me to disappoint someone, even if that person is the scum of the earth," I say. "It's a horrible plight."

"Enneagram?" He pushes his glasses up his nose with a long finger. I notice right away there isn't any wing sauce on his knuckles. "Is that an astrology sign? Fire and water, right?"

"Close," I say, even though he's nowhere near correct.

"Are you lying to be nice to me?"

"I am. Fire and water sound more like *Avatar*."

"*The Last Airbender*? There's something I could talk about for hours," he says.

"What about the James Cameron film?"

"I'm not nearly as passionate about that one. Can't get past the blue aliens."

I sneak a look at him. I'm surprised to find him already looking at me, and I take it as an invitation to study him.

He's handsome with sun-kissed skin and freckles across the bridge of his nose. A button-up shirt is rolled to his elbows, and his forearms have veins. His palms are large, and they must make holding things very easy.

He's smaller and less broad than the men I work with on the football field, but I see the hidden curves of muscles hiding under his sleeves.

"How long have you been sitting here?" I ask.

"Long enough to wonder how you didn't commit a murder. You're a nicer person than me."

"I thought about it, but can you imagine the cleanup?"

"Blood, everywhere. And this place is bordering on unbearable as it is." He grabs his drink and cradles it in his hand. His skin is a shade pinker than it was a second ago, and the flush creeping up his neck is cute. "Can't say I'm a fan of bodily functions associated with death."

"Glad to know you aren't going to hack me into a million pieces. You're adverse to the side effects."

"I'll just bore you to death by talking about comic books. They wouldn't be able to pin the murder on me."

"Do you have a favorite?" I ask. "Comic book. Not alibi to get away with homicide."

"*Watchmen*," he answers right away. "It's technically a graphic novel, so I'll also add in *The Amazing Spider-Man: The Night Gwen Stacy Died*."

"I always liked *Kraven's Last Hunt*."

He blinks at me. "You read comic books?"

"Do I not look like I would?"

His eyes roam down my body, and a deep sound tumbles from his mouth. I warm under his attention and play with the cocktail napkin to give my hands something to do.

"Do you want the honest answer?" he asks, and I nod, desperate for it. "You're pretty. *Very* pretty, and also the first woman who hasn't made fun of me for liking superheroes. I'm wondering if my friends put you up to this as some sort of dare, because I'm not sure what the hell I did to have someone as gorgeous as you rattle off comic book titles at me."

I tuck a strand of hair behind my ear. "I have no clue who your friends are."

"Probably for the best."

"Is there bad blood there?"

"None at all. They're way more outgoing and attractive than me. The life of the party. If they were here, you'd want to talk to them instead."

"I don't know about that. I'm having a lot of fun talking to you," I say, and he blushes again. "And I'm sorry people have made fun of the things that bring you joy."

"It's not any worse than what you put up with tonight. You like sports, don't you? Homeboy you were sitting with told you that you don't belong in that world, and that sucks."

"How do you know I like sports?"

"You started talking faster when you pointed out a basketball game was on."

"I didn't know I was so easy to read," I say.

"I'm a good listener," he says.

"You're also a good eavesdropper," I joke, and he smirks.

The bartender sets down my drink and dessert, and I sigh.

"Thank you." I cut off a bite of cheesecake and groan. "Oh my god. This is delicious."

"I'll leave you to it. I don't want to interrupt the best part of your night."

"You don't have to do that," I say quickly. "The cheesecake is good, but talking to you is better."

"You're only saying that because you ate a meal with a dude who once wore Sperry shoes to a black-tie wedding because he was *bros with the groom*. It's not a fair fight."

"You don't wear boat shoes to events where the dinner plate costs two hundred bucks a head?"

"Fuck no," he says. "Crocs only."

I burst out laughing, and it's not the kind of laughter that sounds like a giggle.

It's embarrassingly loud, a full-on cackle that shakes my shoulders and makes me snort. I almost choke on my food, and I grip the counter to stop myself from falling off the stool.

"Sorry," I wheeze. There's cheesecake lodged in my throat, and I chase it down with alcohol. "That's the funniest thing I've heard all night."

"That's just sad." He grins and drums his fingers on the bar top. "But thanks for the ego boost. Sorry you had to sit through such a shitty date."

"Unless you're the one who sent the spawn of Satan here to give me a night of hell, it's not your fault."

"I have more respect for women than that." He takes a sip of his drink. A drop of liquid hangs on the corner of his mouth, and he licks it away. "I, for one, think they shouldn't just be confined to the kitchen. They should be cleaning the living room too."

I elbow him in the ribs. "Asshole."

"I'm kidding. My mother would be appalled if she heard me making a joke like that. I take it back. Please forgive me," he says.

"Apology accepted." My gaze bounces to his phone. It's sitting face up on the counter next to a lime, and a dozen notifications from a dozen social media apps pop up on his screen. "Wow. Someone's popular. Did I interrupt something?"

"Not at all." He turns the phone over with a swift flick of his wrist, and the gesture makes my heart skip a beat. It makes me think he wants to keep talking to me. "It's all work stuff. My job never stops, and it would do me some good to ignore it for a few minutes."

"I can relate. I love what I do, but it consumes my life."

"Hit woman for the CIA?" he asks.

It's an innocent question. One I brought onto myself, but I still pause.

I never tell anyone the real answer so soon after meeting them.

It's always followed by comments and opinions that make my blood boil. And tonight, after I feel like I've already been dragged through the mud, I really don't want to trudge through hell again.

"Marketing," I tell him.

Technically, it's not a lie.

Managing the Baltimore Thunderhawks' social media does involve marketing. Since I took the position a few years ago, I've racked up a million Instagram followers, two million on TikTok, and a half a million more on other platforms.

I work hard, and I'm damn good at what I do, but I know the stigma that comes with women in the sports industry. The questions that follow when I reveal my career and the interrogation I'm subjected to.

How many players have you slept with?

You're probably having an affair with the owner, aren't you?

Oh, you like football? Name the starting lineups from the 1997 Super Bowl.

Being vague makes life easier.

"Really? I'm in marketing too," he says, turning on his stool so he's facing me. "Am I allowed to ask what your name is?"

I open my mouth to answer, but I hesitate. He heard every other word from my conversation with the swamp rat; what are the chances he heard our goodbyes too?

"Claire," I say, using my middle name and hoping he doesn't notice. After too many awkward situations with men tracking me down on social media and flooding my DMs asking for tickets to games, it's become my go-to until I get to know a guy. I've never felt bad about the dishonesty, but knowing I'm telling a half-truth to someone I'm enjoying talking to makes my chest pinch tight. "And yours?"

"Reid," he says. "Pleasure to meet you."

I smile. "I think the pleasure might be mine."

TWO
REID

I HAD plans to head back to my apartment thirty minutes ago, but I haven't been able to pull myself away from this woman.

She's funny. Quick-witted and smart. Gorgeous and a total knockout.

And when she dropped a comic book title into casual conversation like she was talking about the weather?

My heart almost fell out of my chest.

I wouldn't be surprised if I have a dopey smile on my face or big cartoon heart eyes. If Dallas and Maverick, my two best friends, could see me, I'm sure they'd give me hell for grinning so hard.

I don't even care that she probably lied about her name. The silver necklace with the letter A resting against her collarbone tells me *Claire* isn't what she normally goes by, but I don't give a shit.

I motion to her empty glass. "Can I get you another drink?"

"A drink sounds great." She smiles big and bright. There's a dimple on her left cheek. I noticed it the first time she laughed, and it's as distracting as the bright red lipstick on her mouth. "What are you having?"

"Gin and tonic, which I realize isn't as badass as your whiskey neat."

"Thank my father," Not Claire says. "It was his drink of choice, and I've taken it upon myself to carry on the family tradition. At least three fingers. No ice. It's the only way."

"Shit." I run my hand through my hair at her use of the past tense. "I feel like a dick for bringing up a hurtful memory, and I'm sorry for your loss."

"He passed a long time ago. Therapy is a game changer, and I like talking about him."

"Cheers to paying people to sort through our shit so we don't have to do it alone."

"You go to therapy?" She quirks a playful brow. "Care to share what for?"

"My childhood wasn't particularly fun," I say. "My dad wanted me to play baseball. I wanted to sit in front of a computer and learn to code. Add in yelling and being told I wasn't *man enough* because I didn't know how to put on a baseball glove, and there's a lot to unpack."

"Shit," she echoes. "Now *I'm* sorry."

"Call it even?"

"Okay." She smiles again. "If you say so."

The bartender comes over, and we order another round of drinks. Once we're topped off with fresh alcohol, she raises her glass in my direction.

"What are we toasting?" I ask.

"To nights ending better than they started," Not Claire says, and she clinks her drink against mine.

"That's a little premature. I still have time to ruin your evening."

"Not possible." She hides her grin with a sip of the amber liquid. "This is the most fun I've had in a while."

"How'd you end up here in the first place?"

"Dating app fail. You don't want to hear the whole story. I'll sound pathetic."

"Try me," I say.

"One night, I was feeling lonely after a couple glasses of wine and a night out with friends who are in relationships. I downloaded the dating app where I matched with Tweedledee, agreed to meet up with him, ingested mozzarella sticks that I'm sure are going to give me food poisoning, and now I'm here talking to you."

"If you end up with your head in a toilet, I'll hold your hair back," I tell her.

"Go on. Tell me I'm pathetic."

"I won't. I understand the loneliness."

"You do?" she asks.

"Yeah. I used to be the guy who was always in a long-term relationship while my buddies avoided commitment and fucked around. I was even engaged once upon a time. Somehow, in a weird twist of fate, my two best friends are locked down in serious partnerships with women they adore, and I'm the one who is single. I thought I'd be the first one to get hitched. Had my vows written and everything. Now I'm not sure it'll ever happen."

"I don't know about marriage, but it would be nice to find someone to have a decent conversation with. Like this." Not Claire gestures between us. "This is tolerable."

"Every man loves to hear he's tolerable."

She nudges my side and gives me a pretty smile. "You know what I mean. Why couldn't you have been on the other end of the dating app?"

"I don't do dating apps."

"You don't?"

"I like to keep my private life private."

"Do *you* work for the CIA?" she asks.

"No, but I did almost hack into their database when I was a teenager," I say. "How about I tell you one of my bad date stories to make you feel better?"

"I'm offended it took you so long to offer," Not Claire says.

"I was getting back into dating after a breakup, and I had been seeing this girl for a couple weeks. She invited me to her place, and when we got upstairs, she excused herself to the bathroom to freshen up. She told me she started her period and needed tampons, so I said I'd grab her a box from the drugstore down the street." I swirl my drink around in my glass, reminiscing. "So I get there, pay for the tampons, and head back to her apartment. When I walked inside, she was making out with a very naked guy on the couch. At first, I thought it might be a threesome thing, but then I found out that in the fifteen minutes I was gone, her ex-boyfriend had shown up from out of town, begged her to take him back, and ended up bare-assed where I had been sitting minutes before."

"Oh my god." Her eyes widen. "You went out and bought tampons for her and she repaid you by straddling her ex-boyfriend? What did you do?"

"I stood there while she explained what was going on, said, 'I got you regular and super plus.' Then I left. I think they ended up getting married."

"At least someone had a happily ever after. What did you do with the tampons?"

"I put them under the sink at my apartment in case anyone ever needs one. Haven't dated since." I chuckle and take a much-needed sip of alcohol. "Do you feel better?"

"Yes," she says. "Between commiserating over bad dating history, the drink and the cheesecake, I feel like a new woman." She cuts off a bite of dessert and holds the fork out to me. "Do you want some?"

"I'm actually allergic," I say.

Her mouth pops open. "Shit. *Shit.* I'm so sorry. Is it airborne? Through ingestion? Why didn't you say something? I would've—"

Before I can think about what I'm doing or why I'm doing it, I lean forward and close my lips around the fork. She makes a soft sound when I lick away the crumbs, and I wonder how I could get her to make it again.

"I'm kidding," I say. "It's delicious."

"You can have more if you want."

"Only if you—"

A cheer echoes through the bar, interrupting us. I turn my head to the door where a group of women are stumbling through. They're wearing tiaras, sashes, and bright pink dresses. It looks like a bachelorette party, and their high-pitched screams make me wince.

"Did it just get really loud in here?" Not Claire yells, and I nod.

"Yeah." I bend over and wrap a hand around the leg of her stool, dragging her closer to me. "There. Now I'll be able to hear you."

Her thigh presses into mine, and her fingers brush across my knee as she gets settled in her seat. I get a whiff of her perfume when she leans forward. It smells like the rainstorm we had two nights ago, with a hint of honey and pretty white flowers.

Hyacinths, maybe.

I like it.

"Too close?" I ask.

She shakes her head and bites her bottom lip. "Just right."

"Good." I reach past her and grab her drink and plate, moving them in front of her. "You're not driving home, are you?"

"No. I took an Uber in case I needed to drown my misery with a couple of drinks. I might walk back, though. I love DC in the late summertime."

"Are you from the area?"

"No. I moved up here a few years ago when I took a new job," she tells me.

"A job in marketing," I say, repeating what she told me earlier.

I'm not sure she's being honest about her career either.

The woman is gorgeous, with long brown hair that hangs down her back and big brown eyes. Her skin is tan, her smile is soft, and there's this presence about her. Like she can light up any room she's in without having to try. It makes me wonder if she really spends all her time behind a computer in an office.

"When this opportunity came up, I jumped at the chance to accept it. It's a higher profile position than what I was doing before, and I'm good at it," she says, and I admire her confidence.

"How old are you?" I ask.

"Thirty-one. How old are you?"

"Thirty-four."

"What was the Great Depression like?" she teases.

"Someone has jokes," I say.

"Consider it payback for telling me where I belong in the house."

"I deserve that."

The night stretches longer. The bar gets louder, and we inch closer to each other. At one point, Not Claire is almost in my lap, and when she stands up to use the bathroom, I have to rest my palm on her waist so she can slip past me.

"Sorry." My fingers hook in the belt loop of her jeans and give a gentle tug. "I'm stuck."

"It's okay. Close quarters." She folds her hand over mine. I see a tattoo on the inside of her left middle finger. It's a sunflower, and I wonder what it means. She frees me from the denim and smiles. "There we go."

"Thanks. Want me to order you something while you're gone?"

"I think I'm all set," she says, and I try my best not to look disappointed. "But maybe you'd like to walk me home?"

"Yeah." I bob my head. "I'd like that."

"Good." Her eyes sparkle, and she tosses her hair over her shoulder. "Don't make out with any ex-girlfriends while I'm gone. I'll be disappointed."

She heads for the bathroom, and when she turns a corner and disappears down the hallway to the back of the restaurant, I shove my glasses up my nose, confused.

I don't know what the fuck I'm supposed to do now. Do I kiss her? Walk slow so she understands I don't want to say good night yet? Hint that I'd like to come up so we can talk a little more?

I grab my phone. Dallas and Maverick will have the solution. They'll tell me what to do.

There are nearly a hundred notifications on my screen, an alarmingly high number for a Friday night. I see a dozen text messages in the group chat with my friends. Eight alerts from ESPN. A missed call from my boss and an email from Shawn Holmes, the head coach of the DC Titans football team where I work as the social media manager, with three words attached: **call me asap.**

I hit his contact information and tap my foot on the floor.

"Reid," he answers. "There you are."

"Sorry," I say. "I'm out and didn't see your email. What's going on?"

"Busy night over here. We're drafting a press release about a free agent we're bringing in."

"Wait, *what*? A free agent? When did this happen? I didn't know we were going after anyone."

"Surprise," Shawn says. "He had a lot of offers, so we moved fast. He's finishing up the contract right now, and we need to be ready to announce his signing."

"I can be home in thirty minutes, and I'll get something up. Who is it? Must be pretty important if you're working late on the weekend."

"It's Griffin Harrison."

"Shut the fuck up."

"Dead serious," Shawn says. "His parents live in DC, and he's signing a two-year deal with the intention of retiring as a Titans player."

"This is huge, Shawn. He's been with Los Angeles his entire career and is a shoo-in for the Hall of Fame."

"Why do you think I'm calling you? We want to announce it before the Thunderhawks share their latest roster addition. This is a race for tickets, and if we can get our press release out first, we can make the club a lot of money."

"What are the Thunderhawks doing?" I ask.

"Signing Malcolm Jeffries at quarterback."

"The Super Bowl champ from two seasons ago? That's a big move."

"A big fucking move," Shawn says. "There's three weeks until the preseason starts, and this is the most activity we've seen all summer."

"I'll head home right now and get something going." I jump off my barstool and cradle my phone against my ear. I reach for my wallet and see Not Claire's half-empty glass. Regret hits me and I drop my head back, a groan brewing in the back of my throat. "Dammit."

"Everything okay?"

"All good," I say. "I'll let you know when the post goes live."

"Great. Thanks, Reid. Talk to you soon."

We hang up, and I weigh my options.

I can't rush out of here without telling her I'm leaving. That would be a dick move. After the night she's had, I don't want her to hate me too.

I know I *need* to leave, but I really don't want to.

If I work fast, I could get a post drafted in five minutes and send it Shawn's way. A simple caption. A link to purchase tickets. Some fancy fonts and bold letters. It wouldn't be my best work, but it's cruel of the universe to make me pick between my job and the first woman I've enjoyed talking to in years.

I scan the restaurant and spot her heading my way. There's a pep in her step. Her nose is buried in her phone, and the grin she's wearing is bigger than any I've seen from her all night.

A flash of jealousy hits me.

I wonder who has her smiling like that.

"Hey," she says when she gets close. "I'm so sorry, but I need to head out. A work thing came up, which is such a bummer, because I was having a lot of fun with you."

"I was too."

"Maybe I'll run into you at another bar after another shitty date one of these days," she says.

"If you see me wearing Crocs, don't ask any questions," I say.

She laughs and squeezes my arm. "It was great to meet you, Reid."

"You too. Get home safe."

I watch her move through the crowd of people. She looks over her shoulder when she gets to the door, and her gaze meets mine.

I lift my hand in a wave. Not Claire wiggles her fingers then disappears, and I feel like the smallest human on the planet.

@dcfootball

Griffin Harrison has more Super Bowl rings than Malcolm Jeffries.

You called Jeffries 'decorated' in your post. Seems misleading.

@footballindc

I swear to god you exist only to annoy me.

@dcfootball

How am I doing so far?

@footballindc

I'm irritated, so, pretty well, unfortunately.

@dcfootball

I'm so happy.

@footballindc

Don't you have anything better to do with your time?

@dcfootball

Believe it or not, I do. I'm going on Do Not Disturb for the weekend. You'll be stuck talking to one of the interns.

@footballindc

Such a shame. No one is going to miss you.

@dcfootball

Are you sure about that? Last time I was away and left other people in charge, you didn't send a single message to our official account.

Makes me think you like talking to me. This is probably the highlight of your day.

@footballindc

Is it hard to breathe with a head so big? Seems like your ego would take up a whole room.

Sure hope you don't end up with a broken hand so you can't work for a few weeks.

@footballindc

That would be a travesty.

(Sarcasm, by the way)

What, no comeback?

@dcfootball

Sorry. Have to run.

@footballindc

Oh, okay. Yeah. Hope you have a miserable weekend.

@dcfootball

You too.

THREE

REID

"I DID SOMETHING STUPID." I collapse onto the couch in the hotel suite where my friends and I are getting ready for Dallas Lansfield's wedding and stare at the chandelier above me. "And I hate myself for it."

"We don't do self-deprecating in this house, Plant Daddy." Maverick Miller, award-winning hockey player of the DC Stars and an absolute pain in my ass, sits next to me. "Can we get some context, please?"

I roll my eyes at the nickname. "It's woman-related."

"Woman-related? I haven't heard you talk about a girl in years, Mr. I'm-Obsessed-With-My-Phone. Besides your arch-nemesis, of course."

"He loves her," Dallas says, frowning at the bowtie he's trying to put around his neck. "Can't go a day without mentioning her. You missed today's rant, Mavvy. It was good. There was something about—shit. What was it? Authenticity? Algorithms? His face got all red and he kept grumbling under his breath."

I scowl. "Can we not? You're getting married in thirty minutes and I'm in a great mood. I don't want to bring it down by talking about *her*," I say.

My eye twitches at the mention of the woman I've been feuding with via Instagram and TikTok DMs for the last couple of years. I've always loved my job, but lately, the role has evolved into a back-and-forth sparring match with the person behind the Baltimore Thunderhawks accounts.

They used to be an NFL team back in the '70s and '80s before they were sold and moved out west where they've flourished as the Portland Gophers. When an expansion team was granted to Baltimore to replace them decades later, the girl who runs the accounts made a genius move by resurrecting the old theme song that played before games to bring some excitement back to the original name and logo. She created a cult following in the process.

The song has become so popular, fans from opposing teams flood the Thunderhawks posts after a win so they can hear the catchy tune.

I've even heard Maverick humming it when he thinks I'm not listening.

I hate it.

I hate *her*, and I've hated her for years.

She tags the DC Titans account whenever we lose, and every now and then, I'll have a DM from her waiting in our inbox that makes me want to throw my phone across the room.

Any content I post, she repurposes and makes better. She jumps on trends and racks up millions of likes with viral videos while mine don't gain nearly as much traction. It's all harmless fun, but my title of winning NFL Social Media Account of the Year for the fourth season in a row is at stake, and I don't want to lose to *her*.

There's been this temptation over the years to look her up on LinkedIn so I can learn who is behind the account, and curiosity has almost gotten the best of me. I typed *Thunderhawks social media team* into the search bar once. I was seconds away from finding out her true identity before I slammed my laptop shut and walked away.

If I give her that much of my time, if I make it seem like I'm interested in her and give a damn, it means she wins.

The last thing I want is for her to win.

"Sorry." Maverick holds up his hands, but I know he's not actually apologizing. He loves to bring her up and piss me off. "Go on. Tell us about your problem. I'm an expert on relationships and love now. I can help."

"You got engaged to the first woman you've ever dated. That doesn't make you an expert."

"Fine. Figure it out yourself."

"Okay. *Okay*." I blow out a breath. "I met someone last weekend, and we had a good time. I regret not getting her number, because I can't stop thinking about her."

"Why didn't you get her number?" Dallas asks.

"Right after she left for the restroom, Shawn called and told me about the Griffin Harrison signing. When she got back, she said she had to leave. It was quick and chaotic. By the time I realized I should be asking for her number, she was gone." I sigh. "She's gorgeous. She made me laugh, and she even likes comic books."

"Comic books?" Maverick gasps. "You should've taken her to the courthouse and gotten a marriage license on the spot."

"It amazes me how Emmy fell in love with you," Dallas says, and Maverick's eyes turn to hearts at the mention of his fiancée. "I've never met someone so clueless in my life."

"It wasn't just the comic books. It felt like we had a connection, which sounds so fucking lame when I say it out loud."

"It's not lame." Dallas checks his reflection in the mirror and smiles. "You're allowed to like someone, Reid."

"Doesn't matter if I like her. I'm never going to see her again." I stand and grin at him. "Are you ready to get married?"

"Yes. No. I'm freaking out." He runs a hand through his dark hair and gnaws on his bottom lip. "What if Maven realizes she can do better than me? She's settling, for fuck's sake. And I can't get this damn tie on."

A decade of friendship, and I've never seen him so stressed out.

He's a professional athlete, the kicker for the Titans and the NFL record holder for the longest-made field goal. He's usually great at performing under pressure, but right now, I can tell he's panicking.

"Maven loves you," Maverick says, reassuring him, and it's the same thing we've told him in the weeks leading up to the wedding. "You could show up without a tie and she'd be happy. Hell. You could be naked and she wouldn't give a shit. She gets to marry you, and that is what's important."

"I'm not showing the world my dick," Dallas says.

"Such a shame. You have a nice dick," Maverick says, and I snort. "The three hundred people downstairs would probably love to sneak a glance at it."

"Can we stop talking about my genitalia and focus on the real problem? What is Reid going to do about his mystery girl?"

"I bet I could find her on social media." Maverick digs in his pocket for his phone and pulls up Instagram. "This is where I shine."

"Oh my god." I stand on my toes and peer over his shoulder. "Look at all the message requests you have. Are those all from women?"

"Maybe? I don't know." He waves me off. "I don't notice them anymore. I haven't checked my DMs in years. What's this girl's name?"

"She told me it's Claire, but I'm pretty sure she was lying."

"Not starting off on the right foot, man."

"I can't fault her. She sat through a dinner with a guy who

was sexist as hell. She was probably trying to protect herself." I shrug. "I can't shake this feeling I've met her, though."

"Really?" Dallas grabs his tuxedo jacket and shrugs it on. "Does she work for the Titans?"

"No. I can't place her, but I've definitely seen her before."

"Maybe she lives in your building," Maverick suggests. "We can organize a stakeout and watch all the women who walk in and out. You'll be able to tell if you recognize her."

"Your ideas are getting worse and worse. Look, I appreciate the help, but it wasn't meant to be, and that's fine." I grab the bottle of champagne sitting in a stainless-steel ice bucket and pop the cork. "Today is a special day, and we're not going to bring the mood down by talking about my pathetic love life."

"It's not pathetic." Dallas takes the glass I offer him and downs the bubbles in one swallow. "It's just not moving as fast as others."

"It's not moving because it's nonexistent. I've accepted the fact that until I'm ready to step away from this job, a partner isn't in the cards for me." I shrug and sip my champagne. "Work comes first. Relationships come second. It's fine. Really."

"Could you at least put your phone away and try to have some fun tonight?" Maverick asks,. "Make out with a woman you'll never see again. Have one too many beers and wake up with a hangover. Ignore your responsibilities for a couple hours."

"I left my phone in my hotel room. I'm not going to touch it until Monday," I say.

"Thatta boy." Maverick grins and glances at Dallas. "What do you say, buddy? You want to go see the woman of your dreams?"

"Yeah." Dallas's smile turns soft. "Everything is better when Maven is around." He sets down his glass and looks at me. "Do you have the rings?"

"Yup." I pat my pocket where two velvet boxes are tucked away for safe keeping. "Do you have the vows, Mavvy?"

"I've been guarding these with my life." Maverick puts a hand over his chest. Emmy's initials are tattooed on his ring finger, and I smile at how quickly the former playboy turned into a lovesick idiot. He's head over ass for her, totally fucking obsessed, and I almost got whiplash from how quickly he changed his tune about settling down. "This is the most important thing you've ever asked me to do."

Dallas checks his watch and rolls his shoulders. "Let's do this before Mae changes her mind."

"She's not going to change her mind," I say.

"I know we're not in one of those sister-wives situations, but I hope Maven knows she's not just marrying you," Maverick says. "She's stuck with all three of us."

"Poor girl," I say, and he sticks out his tongue. "She should've run when she had the chance. There's still time to save Emmy."

Dallas opens the suite door and steps into the hall. "Y'all can argue about this later. Can you let me marry my girl first?"

"Of course we can." Maverick gives him a salute. "Ready, Plant Daddy?"

"I'll catch up with you in a second. There are smudges on my glasses from when you pretended to be Clark Kent, and I can't fucking see." I wave them off. "Go ahead. I'll be right down."

The door slams shut behind them and I walk to the bathroom, rinsing the lenses and rubbing them dry. I hold them up to the light and squint, making sure they're clean enough so I don't trip down the aisle.

I double check I have the rings one more time and leave the room, heading for the elevators. As I turn the corner, I run straight into something.

A warm, soft something that pulls on my tuxedo jacket and sends me tumbling to the ground.

"What the hell?" I blink and put a hand on the floor, looking at the person underneath me. Brown hair and brown eyes. A dimple on her left cheek and red lipstick on her mouth. "*Claire?*"

FOUR
AVERY

I'VE BEEN THINKING about Reid since I met him last weekend. I wasn't sure I'd be lucky enough to see him again, and now he's on top of me. Close enough so I can smell his cologne and see the flecks of gold in his eyes.

His mouth parts and his hips press into mine. I recognize chest muscles. Lean, long limbs and pure man.

My back arches, desperate to feel more of him. His sharp gaze sweeps over my face, and my cheeks burn when he stares at me and refuses to look away.

I'm clutching the lapels of his jacket like my life depends on it. His right hand grips my shoulder. My leg is almost wrapped around his waist, and one of us has to be the first to break the silence.

"Hi," I say feebly.

"What are you doing here?" he asks, his voice pitched rough and low.

"I'm here for a wedding. I'm friends with the bride."

"What wedding?"

"Dallas Lansfield and Maven Wood. He's a football player and—"

"How the hell do you know Maven?"

"We play on the same recreational soccer team," I say. "Well, played. Life got too busy for both of us, and we aren't coming back this season."

"Holy shit. I *knew* you looked familiar." He's still hovering above me. I'm still touching him. "I went to her first game years ago, and I haven't been back."

I sort through the hazy memories of that afternoon.

The grand gesture Dallas pulled off for Maven. All her friends being there, including *Reid*, who only looked away from his phone long enough to cheer for one of her goals. The way he didn't pay attention to anyone, detached and off in another world.

We didn't speak that day. After, when it was time to celebrate our victory, he disappeared without an introduction, and I forgot all about him. I hadn't given the mystery man a thought until right now.

"Is this one of those Missed Connections on Craigslist?" I ask.

"Probably a lot less creepy," he says. "Our eyes didn't meet while we were both reaching for the soup in the grocery store."

"But what a story that would be. I'm assuming that means you're here for the same wedding. There can't be too many other ceremonies in the same spot."

"I'm Dallas's best man. I won the honors."

"You did? What game?"

His mouth twitches. "Dungeons & Dragons."

I file that under the handful of things I know about him from the short time we spent together. He's smart. Nerdy and quiet until you get him talking about something he's passionate about, then he goes a mile a minute.

"I didn't realize role-playing games were used to determine best man status."

"They are in my friend group." Reid pushes himself off me and stands. He holds out a hand, and I let him pull me up on two feet. "I can't believe you're here."

"Right back at you. This is a surprise. A good surprise," I add.

"Wow." He takes a step back and looks me up and down. It's slow and drawn out, a thorough investigation as he takes his time. His attention snags on the slit of my black dress, the cut in the fabric that comes halfway up my thigh, and he makes a strangled sound from deep in his chest. "You look great."

If he's going to admire me so brazenly, I'm going to admire him right back.

His tuxedo is form-fitting, and I catch the glimmer of cuff-links on his sleeves. He still has that same scruff on his cheeks and jaw, but his hair is less messy than it was the other night. His glasses are the same, and he adjusts them on his nose when I lift my chin.

Lord, he's hot.

My profession awards me the opportunity to be around good-looking men. The multimillionaires who have no shame in spending money on products and clothes that will assert them as best dressed or hottest in the locker room.

I'm the one to capture videos of them shirtless and sweaty, beads of perspiration dripping down the muscles women dream about. One upload to TikTok and it would break the internet. They're all cocky. Sure of themselves. Womanizers who've never had to work to get the attention of a female.

I've already gathered that Reid is different.

He's shy. Hesitant in believing he could hold the titles of good-looking and most attractive. A guy who would rather fade into the background than steal the spotlight.

But *gosh*, he could be the star of the show.

"So do you." I wring my hands together. I've never been so

nervous around a man before, but the intense way he's looking at me makes my words catch in my throat. Pressure expands behind my lungs, and I take a deep breath, trying to steady myself. "It's good to see you again."

He nods, eyes still firmly on mine. "You too."

Silence settles between us again.

I rock forward on my heels and smooth my palms over the front of my dress. I'm tempted to give him more of an explanation about why I had to run the other night. I want to open the door to my life, but I'm not sure where to start.

"Shouldn't you be downstairs?" I finally ask, changing the subject.

"Shit." Reid checks the watch clasped around his wrist. "They're going to kill me."

"I'm sorry for keeping you for so long."

"Don't apologize. If I was going to accidentally assault anyone in the hallway, I'm glad it was you."

A laugh tumbles out of me, light and free. "I'm the one who should be blamed for assault. I was fixing my shoe, and I got distracted."

"Call it even by saving me a dance later?"

"I'd like that," I say. "But I'm disappointed you're not wearing Crocs."

"I'm breaking them out for the reception. Then boat shoes for the after party."

"I can't wait to see the photos in *GQ*."

"Want to go down together?" he asks, then winces. "Sorry. I mean take the elevator down. To the lobby. Where the wedding is happening. I didn't mean—"

"Sure," I say, saving him the embarrassment. "Why not? We're going to the same place."

He rests his hand on my lower back and guides me forward.

His palm is warm on my skin, and the dip in my dress gives him plenty of space to touch me freely.

I shiver at the contact and the soft brush of his fingers along my spine. I boldly lean into him, craving more, and I'm tempted to push him into the elevator and kiss him senseless.

I wanted to at the bar, but I didn't have the chance. Knowing my phone is shut off and locked in my hotel room with an out-of-office message set up, I'm not going to sleep until I know what he tastes like.

The doors to the elevator open, and we step inside. The temperature seems to climb twenty degrees in the enclosed space. When he reaches past me to press the button for the lobby, I wonder what his touch would feel like on my breasts. Trailing down my stomach and between my legs.

"Are you staying here tonight?" Reid asks, and he must be thinking the same thing I am.

"Yeah." I fix the strap of my dress and heat flares behind his eyes as he tracks my movements. "I knew it was going to be a late night, and not having to worry about how I was going to get home sounded a lot easier than trying to fight the crowd for an Uber."

The elevator stops at the seventh floor, and a group of wedding guests file in. Reid nods hello to a couple of them, and he steps closer to me to give them room.

"How many whiskeys is it going to take for you to tell me your real name?" he asks.

"What are you talking about? I told you my name."

"You told me a name. Not *your* name." He taps the chain around my neck and drags his knuckles across the small silver links. "I'd really like to know what I can actually call you. No bullshit."

I swallow and tilt my head back. With my heels on, we're closer in height, and I like that I can look him in the eyes.

"Avery," I say softly.

"Avery," he murmurs, and my name has never sounded so precious before. "It's a pleasure to meet you for real."

"The pleasure is still mine."

When we reach the ground floor, the rest of the guests head into the lobby. Reid sticks an arm out, keeping the doors open, and stares at me.

"I wasn't kidding about that dance," he says, but nothing about it is forceful.

It's almost like he's begging for the chance, and a wildfire sparks inside me.

"I wasn't either. I hope your best man duties go well." I give him a smile I hope is flirty and throw caution to the wind. "Come find me later, Reid. Maybe we can finish what we started the other night at the bar."

FIVE

REID

"DUDE." Maverick elbows me when I make my way to the front of the ballroom where the ceremony is being held. I stand next to him in my designated spot under an arch made of bright pink and yellow flowers and fix my tie. "Where were you?"

"I was talking to someone," I say.

"Who?"

"Remember that girl from the bar? She's here."

"*What*? What is she doing here? Oh my god. Do you have a stalker?"

"I don't have a stalker, you fucking weirdo. She's friends with Maven, apparently."

"Holy shit," he says. "Did you talk to her?"

"I asked her to save me a dance. That sounds really fucking cheesy, but I ran into her and then literally fell on top of her. She looked pretty in her dress and—"

"I have Emmy's handwriting tattooed on my chest. Her name has been my phone passcode since the week after I met her. I'm king of the fucking cheese. You don't have to justify yourself to me. Are you going to invite her back to your room later?"

I burst out laughing. "No way. I haven't been with a woman

in years. My experience before that is limited to two long-term relationships. Spontaneous isn't in my vocabulary."

It's embarrassing to admit that to the man who used to get any woman he wanted. Maverick Miller has game. He winks at someone and their underwear comes off.

I'm the awkward guy who doesn't realize someone is flirting with me until my friends are giving me shit for not getting her number.

And proposing a one-night stand?

Yeah, right.

I'm the furthest thing from impulsive.

I like to think things through.

I'm into logistics. Numbers and data and analytics.

More pragmatic than idealistic, I prefer to look at all the angles of a problem before determining its possible outcomes.

Asking Avery—who I've known for all of five hours—if I can fuck her sounds like a recipe for disaster.

I can think of a million ways it could go wrong: a drink tossed in my face. Getting slapped. Being subjected to hysterical laughter.

The thought of that kind of humiliation makes my skin crawl.

"Here's what we're going to do," Maverick says as the last of the guests take their seats. "After Dallas and Maven cut the cake and have their first dance, you're going to find your girl."

"She's not my girl," I say, and he snorts.

"She's your girl. This is fucking destiny, man. You're going to hand her a glass of champagne and sit with her. I'm going to pay the DJ a shit ton of money to put on a slow song. You'll say something along the lines of, 'So. About that dance.' Then, you'll lead her onto the dance floor, hold her close, and just enjoy the moment, Reid. If it feels right, kiss her. If it doesn't, talk some more and get to know her. You don't know what's going to happen unless you try."

"What the hell? You *are* a relationship expert. When did this happen?" I ask. It's the same thing I would've told him if he were asking me for advice. "I still remember the time you forgot a woman's name eight seconds after she introduced herself to you."

"Falling in love with someone who keeps me in my place helps." His smile is wry. "I think I'm shit at it half the time, but she's sticking around. I must be doing something right."

"You're doing a lot of things right, Mav." I nudge his side, and he beams. "You'd really pay the DJ to play a slow song for me?"

"Of course I would. I did it at the hockey gala last year so I could dance with Emmy. Why wouldn't I do it again so you can have a few minutes with this woman?"

"You're a good friend."

"Call it premature best man duties for your wedding somewhere down the road. Dallas has you. I have him, and you have me." Maverick cranes his neck. The music starts, and the crowd turns quiet. "Which one is she? The one in the second row? Blondes aren't usually your type."

"You're really bad at being discreet, aren't you?"

I search the room, and I spot Avery right away. She's sitting at the back of the ballroom, sandwiched between two women and staring at me.

I check over my shoulder, expecting to find her eyeing Maverick or Jett, the Titans' quarterback and one of Dallas's groomsmen. When I glance back at her, she's biting her bottom lip and trying not to laugh.

And she's still looking at me.

I've never been one for attention, but I like it from her.

"There," I whisper.

"Where?" Maverick asks out of the corner of his mouth when Dallas gives us a sharp look.

"Four rows from the back. Black dress and brown hair."

"That's literally half the women here. Wait. I think I see her. Oh, shit, Reid. She's pretty." He waves, and I bat his hand away. "What is wrong with you?"

"What is wrong with *you*? What the hell are you doing?" I hiss.

"Saying hello because you clearly aren't going to. I'm getting the ball rolling. Setting you up for the game-winning three-point shot. You're welcome."

"Emmy is going to kill you," I say. "And it's going to be fun to watch."

"Bold of you to assume Emmy wouldn't wave too," he says, flicking the back of my head. "Now shut up, Plant Daddy. Our girls are heading our way."

The precession starts with June, Dallas and Maven's daughter and our goddaughter, walking down the aisle. Emmy follows behind her, and Maverick whines when he sees her form-fitting dress and the smirk she tosses his way. Four other women approach the flower arch, then Maven appears at the entrance of the ballroom.

Everyone stands. Dallas covers his mouth with his fist as she gets closer, and a choked sob racks his shoulders.

"God, she's beautiful," he says. "Look at her. I get to wake up to that face for the next fifty years, and I'm going to want fifty more."

"Shit." Maverick drops his head back and sniffs. "Why am I crying? I never fucking cry."

I wipe my eyes. "Because she's perfect for him, and all we've ever wanted is to see Dallas happy."

I'm an only child, and for the decade I've known these guys,

I've considered them my brothers. We'd do anything for each other.

When my ex called off our engagement, they took me to my therapy appointments. Helped me find a new place to live and loaded up the moving truck in the middle of summer without a single complaint.

When Dallas became a father, Maverick and I treated June like she was our own daughter. We were there for every diaper change. Her first steps and her first words. We switched off feeding duty in the middle of the night so Dallas could shut his eyes for twenty minutes. All three of us walked around in an exhausted daze the first two years of June's life, but we'd do it again.

And when Maverick realized he loved Emmy, the first woman he's ever had feelings for, we talked him through the scary shit. Now those two are next to tie the knot, and my god, I've never seen him so happy.

I wasn't sure if the dynamic of our group would change when Dallas and Maven started dating. It was always the three of us, and adding a new person to the mix left room for someone to feel left out.

Maven was the missing piece.

She's compassionate and kind. Funny and light-hearted, but she knows when to be serious. She brings out a side of Dallas that disappeared when he became a single dad trying to juggle all of his responsibilities, and I'll never be able to thank her for breaking him out of his shell.

I love her so fucking much.

It almost feels like she's becoming a part of Maverick and me too. The sister I always wanted but never had. Someone to protect and encourage and cheer on. Another best friend and another person in my corner. A lifetime with her around doesn't feel like enough.

Dallas's shoulders shake when Maven climbs the stairs and reaches for him.

"Hi, honey," he says softly, and she touches his cheek.

"Hi, sweetie," she says. "Are you okay?"

"Better now that you're up here with me."

"I guess I shouldn't tell you about the runaway bride act Reid and I were going to pull, huh?" Maven jokes, and I bark out a laugh.

Dallas looks at me and smiles. "If I was going to lose you to anyone, I'd be okay with it being him."

"Wow," Maverick grumbles. "That's fucking rude."

"You win everything else. Let me have this one," I say, and he rolls his eyes.

Dallas reaches for me, asking for the rings. I shove my hand in my pocket and pull out the boxes, carefully handing them over.

"Thanks," he murmurs.

"Happy for you, man."

His eyes flick over to Maverick, then back to me. "Do I need to put him on a leash?"

I snort. "Don't think it would help. Stop staring at me, Dal. Maven is way hotter, and she's the star of the show."

"Yeah." Dallas smiles. "She is, isn't she?"

They go through their vows; the promises to take care of each other in sickness and in health. They talk about their future; the kids they're going to have and the plot of land they're planning to buy after the football season ends. Neither can get through the words without crying, and there's not a dry eye in the house.

When the officiant announces them as husband and wife, Shawn, Maven's godfather, whoops so loudly, everyone bursts out laughing.

"Congratulations, you two." I kiss Maven's cheek and give Dallas a hug. "Can't wait to celebrate."

"Thanks for standing up here with us, Reid." Maven squeezes my hand, then glances at Maverick. "You too, Mavvy."

"Shucks, Mae." Maverick grins and drops a kiss to the top of her head. "It's an honor."

When I turn and look out at the crowd again, Avery isn't looking at the couple of the hour.

She's still looking at me.

I'm never the guy who gets the girl, but tonight, I want to try.

Spontaneous.

I can be spontaneous.

Just for the night.

THE MAN SITTING NEXT to me won't stop talking with his mouth full.

It was easy to ignore during the salad course when Italian dressing landed on my elbow after a lengthy, one-sided conversation about Civil War generals I did my best to feign interest in.

We've moved on to the cake, though, and the buttercream frosting from the three-tiered lemon and blueberry dessert is one enthusiastic exclamation away from staining my silk dress.

"How do you know the couple?" he asks. Crumbs spew from his mouth and end up on my nose. I blink, horrified. "Are you family?"

I grab a napkin and wipe my face. The woman across the table shoots me a sympathetic glance, and I'm kicking myself for not taking her up on the offer to escape to the bathroom twenty minutes ago.

It's too late now.

I'm on a sinking ship, and I'm going to drown in a sea of regurgitated food.

"Soccer," I say politely.

"Ah, soccer. A great sport. Did you know the rest of the world calls it football?"

"Fascinating."

"What's also fascinating are the rules. You're familiar with the rules, right?"

"They tend to make sure we understand how to play the game before we're allowed to kick," I say.

Something catches my attention out of the corner of my eye. I turn my head and see Reid approaching our table. His jacket is shrugged off and his hair is a little messy.

With his tie half unknotted and the top button of his shirt popped open, he looks relaxed. Loose and laid-back, soft around the edges. Like someone I could have a whole lot of fun with.

"Hey," he says when he gets close.

"Hi." I tip my chin to look up at him. Pink cheeks. Crooked glasses and a grin from ear to ear. There's a smudge of chocolate on his chin, right along the curve of his jaw, and I have no clue how that got there. *Goodness*, he's cute. "How are you?"

"Just fine, thanks. How are you? How was the cake?"

"Probably the best thing I've ever put in my mouth."

"I'm going to hope that means you thought it was delicious," he says. "Otherwise, I'm going to offer my condolences."

I smile. "Definitely delicious."

Reid clears his throat. "About that dance."

"Yeah?" I ask.

The reception has gone on for a few hours, and it's been a blur of toasts, food, and music. Maverick standing on a chair, grabbing a microphone and demanding the couple kiss. A lot of love, enough to fill the entire room.

This is the first time I've seen Reid all night. The drinks are flowing more freely. The music is getting louder. People are starting to turn rowdy, and I wait with bated breath to hear what he's going to ask.

"I was wondering if, uh, I could cash in on that now," he says. His cheeks turn more pink, and I don't think it's the alcohol he's been drinking that's causing him to blush. "Or if you have a piece of paper where I can jot down my name and you'll let me know when it's my turn, that works too."

"A piece of paper? Are we in the 1800s?"

"I don't know." He fiddles with his glasses then his tie. "I'm sure you've been propositioned a dozen times already. Maybe there's a note on your phone with a list of names."

"Not a single proposition. Can you believe it?" I smile at him. "Are you sure you can step away from your best man duties? Tonight is important, and I'd hate to pull you away from your friends."

"They won't miss me. When I last saw Maven and Dallas, they were making out behind a plant." Reid shrugs.

"Okay. Let's dance." I stand and set my napkin on the table. I brush the lingering crumbs off my dress and smile. "That would be really nice."

He offers me his arm. Our sides press together, and warmth radiates from him. I let Reid lead me to the dance floor. When we're away from the table, I sigh in relief.

"Thank you for rescuing me," I say. That guy was getting food all over me."

"He spilled on you?" Reid stares at my dress, at the thin straps slipping down my shoulders and the way the material hugs my torso before fanning out over my hips. "Where?"

"He didn't spill, he spat. There's a drop of steak sauce between my boobs, and it's revolting."

His eyes bounce to the low-cut neckline of my gown and hold for the quickest of seconds before moving back to my face.

"You should've flagged me down sooner. I'm happy to be of assistance," he says.

"You're doing that a lot, I notice. Swooping in and saving the day."

"I don't think I'm doing anything. You're just hanging out with the wrong people." The overhead lighting dims. The atmosphere turns intimate. "Guys who don't deserve your attention," he says, looking at me.

My pulse jumps in my throat. "Who does deserve my attention? Anyone in particular?"

"We could start with men who don't get food on your dress. Followed closely by dimwitted fuckwads who don't want you to talk about things you're passionate about." Reid slides his hands around my waist. His fingers cinch in the soft fabric gliding against my skin, and I let out a shaky breath. "Is this okay?"

I drape my arms around his neck, linking us together like a key in a lock. "Now it is."

We sway to the beat of a slow song then another, lost to the world around us. Each time we rock side to side, I swear we get closer.

"Spit aside, are you having fun?" he asks.

"I am having fun. The ceremony was wonderful."

"Have you met their daughter, June?"

"Briefly," I say. "She seems like a great kid."

"The best of the best. Maverick and I are her godfathers, and I remember the day Dallas brought her home from the hospital. It was pure panic. I don't think any of us slept for a week because we were worried she would stop breathing in the middle of the night or hurt herself. It's funny to see her so old now."

I rest my head on Reid's chest, and his heart pounds rhythmically under his white cotton shirt. I track the beats, and they're as quick as mine. "You've known Dallas a while?"

"Over ten years."

"Did you play football with him in college?"

He bursts out laughing. "Absolutely not. We randomly met each other. He invited me out for a beer, and the rest is history."

"I'm guessing you're also close with Maverick? You guys looked like you were having a good time up there during the ceremony."

"Watching me, were you?" Reid murmurs.

"Hard not to when you're front and center."

You were too difficult to look away from, I think in some deep recess of my brain, but I keep that to myself.

"They're my best friends." He shrugs, and a button presses into my cheek. "I don't see them as superstars. I see them as the guys who get their nails painted because June wants to try out a new color, and the dorks who spend hours playing video games with me. To the rest of the world, they're gods. Athletic freaks of nature with gifts people would drain their entire life savings to have. But with me, they're just the people I can call in the middle of the night if I need to talk."

His right hand moves to my arm and rubs up and down. I sigh and relax into him.

"It's good to have people like that," I say.

"I'm the luckiest guy in the world."

"I wanted to ask you earlier, but we were short on time. Are you here with a date?"

"No," Reid says around a low rasp. "Did you come solo?"

"Yeah." I nod and lick my lips. Desire curls through me like a wisp of smoke. "I want to make sure no one is going to be mad at me for taking up so much of your time."

"Not a soul." He tucks a piece of hair behind my ear and his touch lingers on my cheek. "Can I tell you a secret?"

I nod, desperate to hear what he has to say.

He rests his forehead against mine. I love how close he is. How warm he is, and how he's staring at me like I'm the only person in the room.

"I wanted to kiss you at the bar," he confesses quietly. "I'm not good with spur of the moment things, though. My brain goes into overdrive when I'm thinking about something I'm going to do. I come up with a hundred ways to attack a situation. I'm not one to live in the here and now, but I'm feeling that way again. Like I want to kiss you and get lost for a while."

"You should've," I say, matching his quiet tone. "You could right now, if you wanted."

"I could?"

"You don't strike me as someone who takes what they want." I run my hands up his chest and tug on his tie. "But you can be greedy with me, Reid."

"*Fuck*." The word is sinister, a promise and a plea. "Can I—" He swallows and rubs his thumb down my jaw. "Not here. I don't want people to watch you. To listen to you. If I'm going to be greedy, I want to do this right."

I clench my thighs at his possessiveness. At the thought of what he might be like behind closed doors with his head between my legs.

"What did you have in mind?" I ask.

"Follow me."

He offers me his hand, and I let him lead me past the party guests. My heart races in my chest, a dangerous whirr that only increases when I follow him into a deserted hallway.

"Where are we going?"

"Just... somewhere else. Somewhere I can see you and hear you. It's too loud in there." He turns to face me, and his bashfulness is back. Red cheeks again, downcast eyes. "I have a confession to make, but you have to promise not to make fun of me."

"Oh no. Is this where you tell me your fetishes? That you've had a relationship with an inanimate object?"

"I—*what*?" He pushes his glasses up his nose, and never in

my wildest dreams did I ever think that would be as hot as it is. "Like a refrigerator?"

"I saw it on a show once."

"I have a lot of questions."

"I'm sorry. I... I make jokes when I'm nervous. Jokes that aren't funny," I tell him.

"I make you nervous?"

"It's a good kind of nervous." I step backward until my shoulders press against the wall. "Not a bad thing."

"I'm not sure I've ever made anyone nervous before."

"Are you going to give me your confession? I'm happy to listen to what burden you might be carrying."

His mouth quirks up on the right side, and a lock of stray hair falls across his forehead. "It's kind of embarrassing."

"Performance issues?"

"No complaints from past participants." His fingers dance down my cheek to my neck, cupping the back of my head and rubbing a thumb under my hair. "I've never had a one-night stand. Not that I'm implying that's what this is or anything. I've never kissed someone without knowing what they like, and I—"

"Reid?"

"Yes?"

"Shut up," I say, crashing my lips against his.

SEVEN

REID

I KNEW this woman was going to be trouble, but I wasn't ready for how *good* she'd taste—like a night of poor decisions. Like lemon and blueberry and crisp chardonnay. Delicious and sexy and so far out of my league, I'm still not convinced I'm not dreaming.

I lead her to a corner that's tucked away so we're out of sight. I thread my right hand in her hair and let my left roam down her body. Over her soft curves. Past her waist and hooking under her thigh. I lift her leg so it's wrapped around my hip, and I feel smooth skin under her dress.

Avery kisses me like she hasn't kissed anyone in years. It actually *has* been years for me, but I must be doing an okay job, because she lets out a soft moan. I mark it down as a stamp of approval.

I bite her bottom lip and smile when she grabs a handful of my shirt and yanks me toward her. I move to her neck and kiss the spot below her ear. The spot above her shoulder and the small sliver of skin under the tiny strap of her dress. Her moan is louder this time, like she's fucking *desperate* for me, and that spurs me on.

"You were lying to me," Avery says.

It's all breathless and rough, and when I glance down at her, smug satisfaction races through me.

She looks thoroughly wrecked, and I've barely touched her. Her lipstick is smeared, and the right side of her hair is sticking up. Her pupils are blown wide and she's breathing hard, like she's been running for miles.

I hum when she arches her back off the wall and tips her hips into mine. I should be embarrassed that I'm already hard, but it's difficult to care about anything when she rests her hand low on my stomach and plays with the button of my pants.

"What am I lying about?" I ask.

"Never kissing someone without knowing what they like."

"I promise this is a first-time thing."

"You're very good at it." Her nose brushes against mine and then she's kissing my neck. Sucking on my skin and breathing hot gasps into my ear when she feels my cock straining against my zipper. "Very thorough."

"I told you I haven't had any performance complaints. There may not be many, but all past participants have given me positive feedback."

"What other feedback have they given you?"

"You really want to talk about this?" I ask.

"I don't see why not." Avery smiles. "You're here with me. Not them."

"My hands." The palm on her leg inches higher and disappears under her dress. I stroke the inside of her thigh and she sighs, content. "They like my hands."

"Because you know what to do with them?"

"I like to think I do. But maybe you can tell me for sure."

I gently grab her chin and kiss her again. It's not as rough as the first time, not because I want her any less, but because I want to savor her for a second. I want to get my head on straight so I don't say something that will fuck this up and ruin the moment.

She kisses me back with her lips and her teeth and some incredible thing she does with her tongue that has my hand moving from her chin to the wall to hold myself up.

"Show me," she whispers. "I want to see."

"How much have you had to drink tonight?" I ask.

There's no way in hell this is happening. Not to me.

"Enough to feel weightless. Like I'm floating and everything is nice. Not enough that I don't know where I am or who I'm with." Her palm folds over mine and she drags my fingers up to the waistband of her underwear. "I want you to touch me, Reid."

I think I might be shaking.

I think I might also be leaking in my briefs.

I've had sex before, obviously, but it's always been in a controlled environment with variables I'm familiar with. Women I've spent days getting to know like the back of my hand.

Avery is a wildcard. I don't know if she prefers things fast or slow. If she wants my fingers or my tongue. What gets her off and what she hates.

And... I'm really out of practice.

I haven't touched anyone but myself in *years*. Now the hottest woman I've ever spoken to is asking me to rock her world, and I'm afraid I'm not going to be good enough for her.

"How..." I stop asking my question so I can suck a pink spot on her neck. There's some irrational need pulsing through me to mark her. To show the world that Reid Duncan scored an absolute knockout. "What do you like?"

"I like a lot of things." She guides my hand to the front of her underwear. The material is damp, and I groan, turned on by her being turned on. "I'm going to like anything with you."

I nudge her hand out of the way. I drag my thumb across the

seam of the lace, and she whimpers. "You're already wet. I want —*fuck*, Avery. Can I see?"

She puts her hand on my head and slowly pushes me to the ground. "You can taste too."

"*Fuck*," I say again, because every other word seems inadequate.

I drop to my knees and hike her dress up her legs. I kiss the top of her thigh, the curve of her hip where her underwear sits high on her waist. I'm eye-level with red lace, and there's a little bow right on the front.

I lean forward and kiss the soft material. I put my foot flat on the floor so she can rest her heel on my leg. She wraps a hand around the back of my neck, urging me closer, and I laugh.

"Something funny?" she asks.

I look up at her, and she's watching me. Her nipples are hard, and the left strap of her dress is falling down her arm. I'm so tempted to take the whole damn thing off.

"I like thinking you want me."

"I do want you."

"Can I touch you?" I ask, wanting to make sure we're still on the same page.

"I might kill you if you don't."

I drag the lace to the side, holding her underwear out of the way. I groan when I find her drenched, wet and perfect. I touch her clit and rub a slow, lazy circle. Running my fingers across her entrance, I wonder what she would feel like wrapped around my cock. I palm myself through my pants at the thought of her spread out in my bed, that dark hair everywhere, and Avery hums.

"Someone could see us," I say, but I don't make any effort to move.

"Then you should hurry up or take me to your room," she says.

I grin at her bossiness.

"What if I want to do both?" I slip a finger inside her before she has a chance to answer. I push past my second knuckle, and she whines. "*Fuck*. Look at you."

"That feels good." The tip of her heel rubs against my cock, and I think she just unlocked a new kink. "I can take two or three. I do when I'm home alone."

"*Jesus*, Avery." I move closer and tap her left leg. I'm imagining her touching herself. Using a toy to get herself off. What she looks like tangled in her sheets with sweat on her body and a smirk on that smart mouth of hers. "A little wider. Let me make this good for you."

"Like this?" She moves her foot across the carpet and drops her hand between her legs, holding herself open so I can see even more of her.

"Wow. Yeah. *Yes*. That's, uh, that's perfect. Will you…" I need to take off my glasses, but I can't stop touching her. I can't stop *looking* at her. "You'll tell me if you don't like something? You'll tell me if what I'm doing is getting you off?"

"I promise." As if she's reading my mind, she plucks my glasses from my face and rests them in the neckline of her dress. They look nice there, between her tits, and I wish my face was buried there too. "You'll be able to tell, though. I've had guys make fun of me for being, um, enthusiastic."

"Make fun of you? What do you mean?"

"I can be loud. I… I like to talk and be talked to. I guess some men like their women a little more submissive, and that's not how I am in bed."

My cock aches. I rest my forehead against her stomach and fight back a frustrated groan. "You really are giving the wrong people your attention. I'm here, and I like loud. I like enthusiastic. I want you to tell me what you're thinking, and I want to talk you through it. Would that be okay?"

"Yeah," Avery whispers. "That would be more than okay."

"Good." I nod. "That's good."

I add a second finger and curl them inside her. I can't see her clearly, so I try to gauge her reaction by her sounds. By the way she touches me and asks for more.

Her hips buck forward. I finally, *fucking finally* put my tongue on her for the first time, and I really wish I hadn't.

She's perfect. The sweetest pussy I've ever tasted, and there's no chance in hell I'll walk out of this hallway as anything other than an addict.

"*Reid*," she says, and no one has moaned my name like that before. "I like that. Can you…"

"Do you want more, Avery?"

"*Please.*"

I'd give her anything she asked when she clenches around me like she's doing right now. My credit card. A Rolls-Royce. Every fucking planet in every fucking galaxy.

I'm supposed to be getting *her* off, but every time she moans, every time she pulls on my hair and says my name when I circle her clit with my tongue, I'm close to losing my self-control. I'm close to acting like a man who's never touched a woman before and finishing in my pants, and I need to get her there before I get there first.

"Deep breath," I say.

She stiffens when I push past her entrance with a third finger. I wait, letting her get used to the feel of me.

"It's a lot," she whispers, and I kiss her hip.

"We'll go slow. You let me know when I can move and I'll make you come, all right?"

"If these are your fingers…" She drops her head against the wall. Her chest heaves, and I watch, mesmerized, as she rolls a nipple between her thumb and pointer finger over the thin fabric of her dress. "What's it going to be like when you fuck me?"

"You want me to fuck you?" I ask, unbelieving.

"Obviously." She grinds her hips into my face. "I thought that was implied, given I'm trying not to cut off your air supply while your head is between my legs."

"I don't like to assume things. Leaves room for error. And, for the record, this would be a good way to die."

EIGHT

AVERY

I LOVE when the quiet ones surprise you.

Just when you think you have them figured out, they do something out of character, like get on their knees and eat you out like you're their favorite meal.

Reid is a marvel, some sex-god sent to give me the best orgasm I've ever experienced in my life.

I'm on the cusp of it, so close and racing to the finish line as fast as I can.

"You're dripping," Reid murmurs full of awe and wonder. "Here I was thinking you were a good girl. A woman who'd never agree to let a stranger kiss her in the hallway, let alone get on his knees. But look at you. You're going to come on my tongue, aren't you? You're going to let me taste it."

It's my undoing. That such a soft, sweet man could know the exact words to tip me over the edge to pure bliss is mind-blowing, but I welcome it.

My vision goes white and my mind goes blank. Nothing but total satisfaction pulses through my veins.

I moan, loud and long, a sound anyone could hear if they were around to listen.

I don't care if they do.

I ride the wave, not giving a damn what they might think. I claw at his hair, at the back of his neck and at his shirt, needing to hold myself steady. If not, I'm going to crumple to the floor.

I revel in the scratch of his scruff against the inside of my thigh and the burn it's going to leave on my sensitive skin. In the gentle way he touches me, refusing to let go.

"Make a mess on me, Avery." He continues to work his fingers into me. He doesn't stop. Doesn't let up, and a sob climbs up my throat. "Can I have one more?"

"I can't." My legs shake. A string in me pulls tight, and tears sting my eyes. "It's—*god*. Reid. I'm full. It's too much. I—"

"Just a little more. That felt so good, didn't it? I know you want to come again. Let me be the one to do it. Please."

I do want to come again. I want it more than I've ever wanted anything in my life. When I glance down at him and see the gleam in his eye, the glide of his fingers disappearing in me, I know I'm going to get it.

Faster, I think, but I must say it out loud too because Reid increases his pace. I hear how turned on I am, the arousal he pushes through until I'm crying out, chanting his name like he's a cult leader and I'm a brainwashed follower ready to drop to *my* knees and worship him.

"I've got you," Reid whispers when my foot falls from his thigh. "I'll catch you."

He stands and I all but collapse into his embrace, utterly exhausted. Totally pleased. Thoroughly spent but hungry for more. He rubs my back, soothing circles that have no right to be as tender as they are after we defiled this section of the hallway.

"No one—" I stop to take a breath. "No one's ever made me come twice."

"All that attention, wasted. You need to give it to someone who can read you. Who can tell you have more left in you." Reid kisses my shoulder, and I shudder. "And I'm just getting started with you, Avery."

He bends down and puts my underwear back in place. He smooths my dress over my thighs. I slide his glasses on his face, and he smiles when he sees me.

"What else do you have planned?" I ask.

"We can end the night here if you want. I'll give you my number. Invite you over for dinner later this week. It can be a date." His eyes stay on me, and he licks his lips. I see the remnants of what I left behind glistening on his mouth in the dull lighting. Scorching heat runs through me, and I wonder if I'm burning alive. "We could also forget this night ever happened and go our separate ways. Or, if you were serious about going back to my room, I'll take care of you again. A third and fourth time too, probably. It's up to you. You're in control."

The orgasms have me all confused. I don't know if I want to laugh or cry.

I've never had this kind of control before, and I like the power. I like being the one to decide the path we're on, and I know what I want.

"Your room," I say with as much conviction as I can muster. I think I'm in a daze. Seeing stars and lots of pretty colors. "We're going to your room."

"You sure?"

I brush my mouth against his, smiling when he lets out a shaky exhale. "I want you to fuck me, Reid. I don't want to be good. Not tonight."

"Okay." He clears his throat. "We're going to need to make a pitstop, though."

"Where?"

"The gift shop. Believe it or not, I don't carry around a box of condoms with me."

"Random hookups in hallways aren't your usual MO?"

"No." He touches my neck. My pulse jumps under his palm, and his cheeks flush red. "I don't want to be good tonight either."

"The gift shop, then," I whisper. My heart races in my chest when he smiles at me. "And make it fast."

I'm shaking on the walk to Reid's room.

It's half anticipation, half nerves, and I don't know why.

I'm a sexual woman. I use toys. I'm vocal about what I want and how I want it without feeling any shame or guilt. I've had one-night stands, and, when I was twenty-six, I had a threesome I still think about when I need inspiration to get off.

This feels different.

It's not a relationship—it's far too soon for that—but it's also not a quick fuck with a man I'm never going to see again.

I like this guy. I don't want to slip out of his room after he falls asleep and make an escape.

I'd like to stay awhile.

"How are you doing?" Reid asks, and he must be nervous too.

I squeeze his hand. "I'm great."

When we get to his room, he holds his keycard up to the lock and pushes the handle down. I follow him inside and let the door close behind me.

It's quieter in here than it was in the hallway. There's no thumping music or clinking glasses. He leads me to the middle of the room and squats down, tapping my calf.

"Let me take off your shoes. Your feet must be killing you. These heels are sky high."

"I like wearing heels, but they can be painful," I admit, lifting my leg. He unbuckles the first strap and I moan when he rubs his thumb across the ball of my foot and massages the sore tendons. "*Oh*. That feels so good."

"You make the best sounds." He guides my right leg down and lifts my left, unbuckling the other strap. "I could listen to them all night."

"Good thing we have a few hours," I say, and he stands. I smile at the lipstick mark I left on his neck and unfasten the second button of his shirt. "You know what I like. What do you like, Reid?"

"I like a lot of things," he says, repeating my earlier words.

His breathing hitches when I trail my hand down his stomach and trace the outline of his cock with my fingers. I run over the head and down his length, getting a feel his size.

Big.

"What do you like the most?" I undo the button of his pants and pull the zipper. "Tell me, and I'll do it."

"I want to see you on your knees," he says, like he's not sure if he's allowed to want it. Like it's something forbidden he could never have. "You made a mess on me, and I want to make a mess on you."

I nod, eager for that too, and I tug his pants down his thighs. Reid kicks off his shoes and gets rid of his socks, throwing them at the wall. He steps out of his pants and unbuttons his shirt, letting it fall to the floor and leaving him in a pair of black briefs.

"Can I look?" I ask.

He adjusts his glasses and nods. "As much as you'd like."

I start at his chest and the light dusting of red hair. I move to his stomach and find the hint of abdominal muscles. They aren't cut and defined. They aren't chiseled out of marble like some Greek god. They're barely there and far from the sculpted physique of an athlete.

It works for him, though. Especially with the red hair that

disappears under the waistband of his briefs and gives way to his cock, thick and hard against the dark cotton.

His thighs are next, and I almost burst out laughing when I see butterflies tattooed well above his knee. There's a group of them in different colors and sizes, some as small as a quarter and others as large as a playing card. Pinks and greens and bright blues, it looks like they're flying away, their wings mid-flutter.

"What's the story here?" I ask. I drag my fingernails over the ink and he lurches forward. "A drunken mistake?"

"No. Stone cold sober." He blows out a breath and puts his hand over mine, guiding my touch over the outline of the wings. His skin is warm, and I want to feel the rest of him. "I lost a bet with Dallas. Maverick ended up with a peach on his ass. I got butterflies on my thigh. Figured I shouldn't stop at one."

"I like them." I drop to my knees and kiss the designs. His groan is soft, and I kiss the artwork again. "I've always had a thing for tattooed men." I move my mouth to the front of his briefs, kissing his cock and licking his shaft through the cotton. His hips buck forward, and I chuckle. "Do you like that, Reid?"

"*Yes.*" He works a hand in my hair and massages my scalp. "Do it again. Please."

Inching his briefs down his legs and over the curve of his quads, his cock springs free. I wrap my hand around it, giving a gentle tug.

I spit on the head and rub my saliva down to his base, making it nice and wet. I stroke him, watching his face to see what he likes best, then swirl my tongue over the tip and take him in my mouth. I hollow out my cheeks and suck him down, grinning around him when he yanks on my hair.

"Sorry," he blurts out. "Sorry. I didn't mean to—"

"You can." I put him back in my mouth, closer to having him

hit the back of my throat before I replace my tongue with my hand. "You didn't hurt me."

"If you keep doing that, I'm not going to last."

His stomach muscles flex, and I can tell he's holding back. Trying to restrain himself, embarrassed by how fast he might finish.

"So don't last," I say, slipping the straps of my dress off my shoulders. I've never been so glad to not be wearing a bra. I bring his cock between my breasts and squeeze them together, letting him fuck my chest. "We have plenty of time."

"*Fuck.*"

"We're going to do that, too."

Reid looks down at me, and I've never been so turned on by the sight of a man before. His green eyes are dark and his lips are parted. Ragged exhales escape as he thrusts upward, using me however he sees fit.

"That's it," I whisper, encouraging him like he encouraged me. "That's good. Do you like to be good, Reid?"

"Yes," he pleads, and pre-cum leaks from his cock. "Avery, I'm going to—"

"Go ahead. Make it messy."

He shudders. Warm, thick spurts of cum coat my chest and neck. He groans and rocks forward, large palms on my shoulders and fingers bruising my skin. I use my hand to finish him off before he's whimpering and whispering my name.

"Jesus Christ," he says after a few minutes of silence.

"I don't think he'd approve of what happened in here."

Reid hooks his arm under my elbow, lifting me to my feet. He kisses me, and I wrap my arms around his neck. "Fuck, you taste so good."

"I taste like you," I say, and he blushes.

"Will you stay for a little bit?" He rolls my nipple between his finger and thumb and spreads his cum across my chest. "I want to make you come again."

"Is this a competition?" I sigh when he pinches the pointed peak. "Who can get who off the most times?"

"I'd win. I've gotten you off twice."

"You drive a hard bargain. I can't say no to more orgasms." I grin, taking a step back and unzipping my dress. It pools at my feet and I walk to the desk on the far side of the room, grabbing the menu from next to the hotel phone. "Can we order some food too? I'm starving."

"What?" Reid's jaw is slack. His eyes are drifting down my body. They bounce to my chest and hang there for far too long to be considered anything other than gawking. "Sure. Yeah. That's fine."

"Are you listening to me?" I ask, a hand on my hips.

"No," he admits. "You're hot and distracting. I'm sorry."

"You could come over here and apologize," I suggest. "On your knees, if you want. Since this is a competition and all."

"I'd certainly hate to lose." Reid stalks my way and shoves the pen and notepad off the desk. His cell phone ends up on the floor. The screen almost cracks, but he doesn't seem to care. He backs me up until my ass hits the edge of the wood, and he smiles when I sit and spread my legs. "And I'd love to repent for my sins."

My mind goes blank as he gives me a third orgasm and half of a fourth, only letting me finish when I fumble with the phone and call down an order to room service.

He's leading our game, but I'm still a winner.

I get to be here with him.

"THESE FRIES ARE DELICIOUS," Avery says. She licks a clump of salt off her fingers, and it's downright indecent. "I could eat eight servings."

"Seriously." I pop one in my mouth. "Who knew the steak tartare and roasted chicken breast at the reception weren't going to be filling? I guess it goes to show you money doesn't buy happiness."

"I'm going to do a taco bar at my wedding. A buffet line of everyone's favorite toppings, and they can have as much as they want. They'll be so full, they'll have to be rolled out."

"Planning on getting married sometime soon?"

"Is that not what's happening here?" she jokes, and I laugh.

"I could get behind a taco bar."

"Speaking of weddings, do you mind if I ask you a question?"

"Go ahead," I say.

"You mentioned you were engaged before."

"I was."

"What happened?"

"Ah." I wipe my hands and lean back on the pillows behind me. My skin is prickly, not because I don't want to tell her, but because her opinion of me might change when I do. "Do you want the long story or the short one?"

Avery fixes the collar of the shirt I gave her and shrugs. She crosses her legs and drops her elbows to her knees. "Whichever one you want to tell me."

"Short story: I work too much. Long story: I missed an important event because I was at the office too late, and it wasn't the first time it happened. It was my fault, and I didn't listen to her when she told me what she needed from me in our relationship. I've learned to put some boundaries up in my professional life since then. I shut my phone off before the ceremony, and I'm not turning it on again until tomorrow because this is what's important right now. That's a big step for me."

"It's not easy to admit when you're wrong, and self-awareness shows maturity."

"It sucks to think you're going to spend forever with someone, only for that to change. Things happen for a reason, though. Glass-half-full optimistic bullshit, according to my therapist. What about you? Ever been engaged?"

"That's something I've never been asked by a one-night stand before." She cocks a brow before continuing. "I haven't been engaged. At one point, I thought I might be. But it's like you said: everything happens for a reason."

"What if I don't want this to be a one-night stand? What if I want to see you again?" I ask.

Avery smiles and crawls across the mattress. She slings one leg on either side of my hips. I rest my hands on her bare legs and stroke my thumbs up her thighs.

"I'd like that," she says. "You mentioned something about dinner."

"My place on Tuesday?"

"Sounds perfect."

She leans forward and brushes her nose against mine. Her

lips are an inch away from my mouth, and when I sit up to kiss her, she pulls back and lowers herself onto my lap. She rolls her hips and grinds into my briefs, and I groan.

"Did you not—" I lift up her shirt. My eyes drop between her legs. Wet. Bare. Pink and fucking beautiful. "*Avery*. Where the hell did your underwear go?"

"Seemed silly to put them back on when I knew they'd be coming off." She ditches my shirt, throwing it behind her where her dress sits wrinkled in the middle of the room.

I move my palms from her ribs to her chest, weighing her tits in my hand. My gaze roams down her body, and I'm instantly hard from seeing her completely naked for the first time. I lift her off me and switch our positions, setting her on the mattress and hovering over her.

"Put your arms above your head," I tell her, and she does.

I've never been a dominant guy in the bedroom, but something about Avery makes me want to take control and have her every way I could ever want.

I look at her again, at the curve of her breasts and the tan skin of her stomach. I spend too long staring at her hips, the skin I want to hold on to while I drive into her from behind. She spreads her legs, and I spend even longer staring at the dampness on her inner thighs and the way she squirms on the sheets.

"Do you like what you see, Reid?" she asks.

My cock jumps when she uses my name, and I nod.

I'm a goddamn goner.

Talk to her. She wants to hear it.

"Yeah," I say. "You're perfect, Avery. Perfect tits. Perfect body. Perfect pussy." She inhales sharply, and I stare at her. "What?"

She shakes her head. "Nothing."

"Do you not like that word? I don't have to use it."

"It's more that I didn't expect it from you." She lifts a shoulder in a shrug. "You're a nice guy. You blush, for heaven's sake, which is the cutest thing in the world, by the way. I didn't think you'd have an A+ dirty talk game, and I'm surprised."

"Oh." I push my glasses up my nose. "I can be very direct. I forget that not everyone operates the same way I do and—"

Avery cuts me off with a kiss, shutting me up the same way she shut me up in the hallway. It's rough and hot, and I groan against her mouth. I sneak a hand between her legs and nudge her knees wide open.

"I like logical," she murmurs before biting my lower lip.

I'm going out of my mind. I'm being driven to the brink of insanity, and when she wraps her hand around my cock and strokes up and down in the tempo I really like, I *whimper*, seconds away from begging.

"Hang on." I bend down and suck on her nipple, wanting to torture her like she's torturing me. She moans, and I file that away for later under things she likes. "Need to get you off again before I fuck you."

"You don't—"

"Yes, I do," I say firmly. "Hold onto the headboard, Avery. There you go. That's a good girl."

She squirms again. I also add *praise* to the list, wishing I had a notebook to write all these things down.

I scoot down the sheets and lie on my stomach, gripping her thighs with both hands. I really want to use my tongue and taste her again, but I also want to watch her.

I press a kiss to her hip bone, and she shudders in anticipation. I drag my finger across her entrance and smile when she drops her head back and tips her legs open even wider.

"Needy," I mumble.

That might be my favorite thing about her. How much it seems like she wants me.

It's nice to be wanted.

"And horny," she adds, lifting her hips.

I push two fingers inside her, giving her what she wants. Even though I stretched her out an hour ago, she's still tight as hell.

"*God*," she groans. She grinds against my hand and fucks herself with my fingers. "You're so close to—*oh*. That's perfect, Reid."

I sit up so I can have a better angle and get deeper. I grab one of her legs and wrap it around my waist, curling my fingers and watching her reactions. "There?"

"*Yes*. Fuck. How are you—you found—*god*. Three. I need three. *Please*."

I add a third finger, humming when she adjusts to the stretch more quickly this time, and just when she relaxes into it, I rub a slow circle over her clit with my thumb.

She jolts forward. Her arms almost slip from above her head, but she catches them at the last second. She moans loudly, a sweet sound that makes me rock-hard.

Five more minutes of watching her like this and I could come without even being touched.

"Look at you getting the sheets all wet," I murmur, mesmerized. It's the hottest thing I've seen in my entire life. "You're soaking them, Avery."

"I'm close," she pants. She opens her eyes, staring right at me. "Make me come, Reid. Ruin me."

Ruin her.

I forget about being careful. I forget about being a nice guy. I'd get on my knees and crawl to her if she asked, and I'm not going to stop until this woman is completely satisfied.

I push my fingers back in her, increasing my pace and finding a rhythm with the circles on her clit while also touching her chest. I wish I had a third hand so I could wrap it around her throat, and a fourth so I could cup her ass.

I want things I've never wanted before, all because she's moaning my name.

Talk her through it.

"You're doing so well," I say. Her legs shake, and I know she's close. "Ah, fuck, Avery. I love when you squeeze around me."

"You're enjoying this too?" she whispers.

"You make me feel so good, and you aren't even touching me. Watching you is enough." I kiss her knee, and her breathing changes. Her back arches off the bed, and she cries out. "There you go. That's it. *Fuck.* Look how pretty you are when you come."

She doesn't last a second longer, falling apart piece by piece as her orgasm hits her.

I work her through it, not stopping when she thinks she's done, and coaxing another one out of her. She sobs and turns into a writhing mess of limbs and tears, begging me for more while also cursing me out.

I ease her down gently, kissing her forehead and her cheek and the space above her collarbone as I slow my movements. When I finally pull my fingers out of her, she groans.

I tug on her bottom lip, and her eyes flutter open.

"Hi," she mumbles.

"Hi."

"That was—" She smiles, stuck in a haze, and I'm not sure I've ever seen something so beautiful. "Wow."

"I hope that's a good wow, and not an *I should really get out of here* wow."

"I really *should* get out of here," Avery teases, looping her arms around my neck. "But I want you inside me first."

"You sure?"

She nods. "I'm sure. I haven't been with anyone in a year. When I was last tested, there was nothing to report."

"It's been, ah, a little longer for me," I admit. I pull off my glasses and set them on the nightstand next to the condoms I bought. "Three years."

Avery blinks. "You're telling me you did *that* to me and it was your first time in *three years*? Are you a goddamn wizard?"

"That's the character I sometimes use when I play Dungeons & Dragons. Supreme magic-users." I blush and rub the back of my neck, knowing I need to stop talking. I'm trying to keep this woman around, not scare her off. "Sorry. Thanks, ah, for the compliment. I also don't have anything to report from my last test."

"That's good," she murmurs. She moves her hands to the waistband of my briefs and looks up at me. "Can I take these off?"

I swallow. My throat is dry, and every nerve ending is awake. It's like I've been electrocuted, and if this is how alive I feel just from her teasing me, what is it going to be like when I fuck her?

Heaven, probably.

Heaven, definitely.

"You can," I say.

Avery yanks my underwear off in one motion. "God, you're so big. You're going to fill me up, aren't you?"

I swallow again.

I've never been with someone so vocal. Someone who is so open about telling me what she wants, and I love it. It strokes my ego and makes me feel like I'm some woman-pleasing sex aficionado, when really, I think I'm flying by the seat of my pants.

I push her legs open. "That's the plan."

"You might not fit."

"I know you can take it," I tell her. "And I'll go slow."

Mirth flares in her eyes. Grabbing the box of condoms, I tear it open and pull out a foil packet. I slide it down my hard length and line up with her entrance. I drag the head of my cock through her, teasing her, and she grabs my hip.

"Fuck me, Reid," she whispers, and I nod.

I push inside her and groan. Her breath stutters and she clutches my forearm.

One inch.

I'm only one inch deep, and I'm already well and truly fucked.

TEN

AVERY

REID PUSHES INSIDE ME, and I can't breathe.

Air is stuck in my lungs. My vision is blurry at best, and I wonder if this is how I'm going to die: with a beautiful man putting his dick in me.

What a way to go.

"*Fuck*," I gasp. I think I might black out from the overwhelming sensation. "I can't—"

"We're barely halfway there," he grunts. There's sweat on his forehead, and I wipe the perspiration away with my thumb. His fingernails dig into my skin, and I wonder what kind of marks I'll have tomorrow. "I need you to take a deep breath, baby. Can you do that for me so I can make this good for you?"

Baby.

It's been years since someone used such an affectionate word with me, and my heart skips a beat.

Goddamn him for making me emotional and horny at the same time.

I inhale and try to relax. I nod and let him know he can keep going and he rocks his hips, almost fully buried in me.

"More," I groan. "I can take more."

"You can take all of it, can't you?" Reid runs his hand up my leg and presses down on my stomach. He thrusts forward, and his groan matches mine. "How are you this tight?"

"Tight for you," I say like an idiot. Like he cares about who I belong to. Like tonight will have any meaning five years down the road.

"That's right." His voice changes. It gets an octave deeper. More possessive, and when he leans over and pushes in all the way to the hilt, there's fire in his eyes. "Mine."

"This..." When he touches my clit, I'm electrified. When he moves to my throat, I'm incinerated. "Best I've ever—"

"Me too. I'm not sure I can—"

"I can't either."

We both let out a quiet laugh, and I lose myself in him. In the bleariness of being so full and so stretched, but also like I need more. Reid gives me what I want, driving into me until I don't know where he ends and I begin.

Sex has never been like this before. I doubt it'll be like this ever again. All-consuming and earth-shattering. It's not just fucking but like our bodies are connected, and I'm not sure what that means.

"Avery. I—tell me what you need to come, because I'm really struggling to keep it together here," he says around a strangled grunt. "And you have to go first."

"I like your selflessness." I smile when he pinches my left nipple. "I'm right there. Right—"

Reid slams into me, and I tremble. The pressure inside takes over. White-hot euphoria pulses through me, and I see stars.

I'm greedy, ravenous, taking everything he gives me until his legs shake. Until his fingers wrap around my neck, the soft pad of his thumb pressing into my windpipe and the feral grin he gives me when I don't ask him to ease up.

His shoulders tense. His eyes lock on mine for one second

before he drops his head back and groans. I feel him pulse inside of me, emptying himself, and never has a man been more attractive.

I did that.

I stroke his arm and coax him through it, watching as he falls to pieces through soft groans and whispers of my name.

"Am I dead?" Reid pants, putting one hand on either side of my head as he calms down. "I think I might be dead."

"I'm heading that way too." I close my eyes and blow out a long breath. "Maybe we're both in heaven."

"I definitely am. I'm still inside you, and you're fucking nirvana."

He pulls out of me and ties off the used condom, dropping it to the floor. He grabs his glasses and shoves them on his face, flopping onto his back and draping an arm across my chest.

"Ah. There you are," he says.

"Can you see without them?" I ask.

"Not really, but I can see enough."

I tap my fingers on my stomach and stare at the ceiling. I don't know what the next part of our conversation should be.

Thanks for the great sex?

Were you serious about dinner?

Want to go another round? Maybe I can bend over the bed this time.

"So." I brush away the hair matted to my forehead and cross my ankles. I need a shower. I should probably put some clothes on, but I'm bone-achingly tired. "What's up?"

Reid laughs, a deep rumble that shakes the bed. "Wow. I was thinking I'd be the one who made this weird because I don't know what to say to people half the time, but you're handling it just fine for me."

"Asshole." I roll onto my side and prop up on an elbow. I

look down at him and find his eyes closed. "What do you have going on this week?"

"I'm going out of town on Thursday, and I'll be gone through the weekend," he says.

"Doing anything fun?"

"Do you consider kissing people's asses fun?"

"I mean, I'll try anything once."

His smile is devastating. "I don't like big group things. Tonight was fine because I was with my friends and celebrating something important to me. But three days of shaking people's hands and pretending like I'm interested in the things they have to say gets really old, really fast."

"What would your ideal day be if you could do anything you wanted?"

"You don't want to hear this answer. I'm not ready to give up this cool guy persona I've got going for me."

"Do I think you're cool?" I ask, squealing when he rolls me on top of him, his hands a welcomed weight on my hips.

"I'd start with a game of Dungeons & Dragons. Then I'd go to the comic book store and make sure I'm not missing out on a new edition of my favorite series. I'd probably play *Call of Duty* with my friends and we'd lose. They're better than me, and I really bring the team down."

"You can't be that bad."

"Twelve-year-olds wipe the floor with me. When they shoot and kill me in the game, they make all these comments about my mom."

"Oh, to be young again," I say.

His thumb brushes along my ribs. "If I was really lucky, you'd be there. And I could fuck you everywhere I wanted."

"Do you want to fuck me in a lot of places?"

"The list in my head is growing by the second. My living

room. Against the window. The shower." He pauses before saying, "Tell me about your ideal day."

"You're going to think I'm stuck-up."

Reid frowns. "Have people called your ideal day stuck-up before?"

"Maybe."

"Attention. Me." He traces the underside of my breast. "Not them."

It's hard to pay attention to anything when he's touching me like *this*.

"First, I'd go and get my hair done," I say.

"Is brunette your natural color?"

"Mhm. I went blond once in college and then decided to try pink in my mid-twenties. Neither was a good look. I'd also get a manicure and pedicure. Then I'd watch a sports game at the bar with a bunch of fans and yell until my throat was sore. After, I'd sneak into your apartment and surprise you on your bed while reading a comic book."

"Naked, hopefully," he says.

"In a Chewbacca onesie," I say.

"You know the way to a guy's heart. Where in that day is you being stuck-up?"

"I don't know. When I spoil and pamper myself. When I want to look and feel good."

"There's no shame in doing things that make you happy."

"I'm glad you think so."

His mouth twists. I think he wants to ask another question, but he shifts gears. "What are you doing this week?"

"The first couple of days should be quiet with work, but the last half of the week is going to be busy," I say.

I'm already picking out the outfits I need to bring to next weekend's NFL conference and creating a checklist in my head. There's my keynote speech I have to review and flashcards to put together. A suitcase to pack and content to schedule. All of that seems inconsequential right now, though, when I'm looking down at him.

"You're free Tuesday, though?" he asks, hopeful.

"For dinner with you?" I smile. "Yeah, I am."

"Good. That'll be fun."

I climb off him and curl up at his side. He wraps his arms around me and pulls me close. I sigh, content, and dance my fingers across his collarbone.

"Thank you for making tonight fun," I whisper. His grip on me tightens, and I relax into the feeling of being safe. A spot I'm not familiar with, but I'd like to get to know. "I thought the cake might be the shining moment, but you swooped in there and stole the show."

"I told my friends about you." He pauses and huffs out a tired chuckle. I think he might be half asleep. Delirious and on the cusp of dreams. "Fuck, that sounds creepy."

"You were writing my name in your diary, weren't you? Playing MASH and using me on your lists of wives."

"We're probably going to end up living in a shack. I'm sorry about the hole in the ceiling," he says.

"I'll decorate and make it nice. What did you tell your friends?"

"How I was kicking myself for not getting your number at the bar. And then you show up here tonight, and... I don't know. As someone who likes routine and order and hates being surprised, I'm beginning to think I might need to start going with the flow more often. Especially if that means I'll get you as a result."

"The last wedding I went to, my boyfriend at the time made out with a bridesmaid," I say. He loosens his hold so he can scoot across the sheets and look down at me. His eyebrows wrinkle and his mouth droops to a frown. "I know, I know. Trust me, I learned my lesson, and you helped me break my bad wedding streak."

"What else was included in the streak?"

"The time before that, the groom showed up in Crocs and really killed the vibe."

He laughs. "Did that douche from the other night try to message you after your stellar date?"

I close my eyes and stretch out my legs. "No. He thinks my name is Ashley, so some girl is probably getting harassed via Instagram DMs because he mistook her for me."

"Sometimes I think the bar for my species can't get any lower. Then there's someone like him who reminds me women's standards for men are in the depths of hell."

"Deeper." I yawn. "All the way down in Treachery."

"You're a Dante fan?"

"I took AP Lit in high school like everyone else. I retained about eight percent of the material."

"That's seven percent more than me." He rests his palm on my stomach and drums his fingers on my hip. "You can stay here tonight if you want."

"I might have to. The last thing I want to do is put that dress back on, and I don't think walking down the hall in a T-shirt that barely covers my ass is proper wedding attire."

"It's past midnight. The time for proper wedding attire is long gone. God knows what you'd see if you went out there now. Dicks, everywhere, probably."

"Guess I have to stay put, then. It's safe here." I open one eye and look at him. He's already looking at me, and it makes my insides warm. "What?"

"Nothing. Just—" Reid shakes his head. "You. This. Stuff like this doesn't happen to me. It happens to my friends, and..." He trails off. "It feels like I've been dreaming for the last two hours."

"It feels like that for me too," I admit. "I really would like to stay, if that's okay. I'll leave in the morning before you need to check out and—"

He draws me close to him and kisses me. It's tender, nothing like what we did earlier, but in the moment, it's perfect. When he pulls away, he sighs into my hair. I can feel his contentment too, and we don't have anything else to say.

The night spirals to morning in a blur of hands and tongues. Of hour-long naps and being woken up with the hot press of his mouth against my shoulder blade. Of one shower then another, sharing bits and pieces of ourselves—physically and emotionally—until the sun starts to rise and my body sags with exhaustion.

I rip off a piece of paper from the notepad on the floor and give him my number just as the clock turns to six. A swarm of butterflies flutter in my chest when he cups my cheek and kisses my forehead, a hickey on his neck and a pair of boxers hanging low on his hips.

"I'll text you," Reid says, leaning against the door. His eyes are heavy, and there's still a smudge of lipstick on his neck. He tries to hide his yawn, fighting off the tiredness with a lazy smile that breaks free across his mouth. "Soon. After a massive cup of coffee."

"I'll be disappointed if you don't," I say.

"I promise. I swear in the name of boat shoes," he says, and I know it's the honest truth.

I'm not a big believer of fate or divine intervention, but as I head out of his room with my heels in my hand and a final look over my shoulder where I find him watching me walk away, I can't help but think Reid was sent to me for a very specific reason.

I WALK into Dallas and Maven's suite at nine in the morning with a tray of coffee and a box of glazed donuts. I haven't stopped smiling since Avery looked at me over her shoulder while wearing my shirt and sauntered down the hall.

I'm running on two hours of sleep, but there's this restless energy in me. Like I don't want to sit still. Like I could run a marathon and hardly get winded.

I guess having the best sex of his life will do that to a guy.

"Hello?" I kick off my shoes and round the corner into the living room. "Anyone awake?"

Maverick groans from the couch. "What time is it? Where am I? Why are you up so goddamn early?"

"It's morning. That's when people tend to get up. What the hell are you doing here? You have your own room. Was it not nice enough?"

"I'm hungover as shit, and I'm dying," he says. "My room was too far away when I was intoxicated last night. Can we lose the sarcasm, please?"

"That's your own fault. You're the idiot who thought he could outdrink a linebacker who weighs two hundred pounds more than him." Emmy rolls her eyes and throws open the curtains. She looks like she's been awake for hours, and I'd be willing to bet she went on a run before sunrise. "Rise and shine, Miller."

"I don't want to." Maverick falls off the couch and onto the floor. He curls into the fetal position and holds a pillow against his chest. "Save me, Plant Daddy."

"You're on your own." I set the drinks on the table in the middle of the room. Dallas's tie is wrapped around a vase of long-stemmed roses, and I don't want to know what happened in here last night. "I feel fantastic."

"Fucker," he grumbles, and I look at Emmy.

"I'm sorry you have to put up with this."

"It's infuriating how much I love him." She sits next to Maverick on the floor. "Come here, pretty boy."

"Love when you compliment me." Maverick throws the pillow to the side and opens his arms. Emmy nestles in his embrace, and he rests his chin on the top of her head. "Are you going to tell us why you're here so early? And why you're grinning from ear to ear?"

I don't know if I should tell them.

Telling them makes it real. A fever dream I'll forget about one day when I'd like to keep it in my imagination for as long as possible.

But I really want to fucking brag.

"I had fun last night," I say.

"I hope you did. Our best friends got married," Maverick answers. "It was cute and shit."

"My night was fun for other reasons," I add.

"Hang on." He squints at me, last night's alcohol evident in his red-rimmed eyes, then gasps. "Holy *shit*. You hooked up with that girl, didn't you? *Didn't you*? You motherfucker. I *knew* paying the DJ would fucking work. I'm a goddamn matchmaker."

I rub my thumb down my jaw and smile, unable to hide my grin. "It was that girl, and we had a good time."

"A good—oh, you've got to be *shitting* me. Dallas," Maverick yells. "Get your married ass in here."

Dallas slides into the living room wearing only a pair of boxers. He has half a dozen hickeys on his neck. There's Sharpie smudged on the back of his left hand, and there's a bandage around his wrist.

"What happened to you?" I ask. "Please don't tell me you broke your hand doing something stupid like the Cupid Shuffle. The season starts in like, two weeks."

"Matching tattoos with Maven." His eyes bounce between all of us. "What's going on? Why are y'all in my hotel room? Who is watching my daughter?"

"Don't worry about the logistics." Maverick waves his hand. "She's practically a teenager. She'll be fine."

"She is *not* practically a teenager," Dallas answers. "The fuck is wrong with you?"

"Shawn has her," I say, and Dallas relaxes. "I saw them in the lobby when I was getting coffee."

"You know I love June Bug, but I need your attention on me for a second." Maverick snaps his fingers. "Plant Daddy got laid last night."

"*What*? I swear if you touched my sister, we're going to have a serious problem," Dallas says.

"I didn't touch your sister. Remember how I told you about that girl from the bar? Turns out she was at your wedding."

"Hang on." Dallas rubs his forehead, slow to catch up. "What's her name?"

"Avery," I say, and his eyes widen. He loses his footing, and I groan. "Dammit. What does that look mean?"

A sly smile settles on his mouth. "I'm just surprised you hooked up with someone. Did you have fun?"

Avery is the most fun I've had in long time.

Ever, maybe.

I can still taste her on my tongue. I can still hear those breathy moans she let out when I touched her. I can still feel how *tight* she was when I sank into her.

Besides the sexual stuff that felt great after an extended bout with celibacy, it's the other things too. Her laugh echoing in my ears. Her hand in mine. Her sleepy smile when she rested her cheek on my chest.

She's fucking perfect.

I sit in the leather chair in the corner of the room and stretch out my legs. "It was nice to let go for a night. I woke up to seventy work emails, but it was worth it."

"Did you two do much talking?" Dallas asks, and I raise an eyebrow.

"Uh, I mean, it was mixed in there with other things." I pull at my collar, grateful my shirt covers the lipstick she left on my neck. Two showers later, and it still hasn't come off. "It's not like we talked about the economy or where we see ourselves in ten years. But she, ah, used to be blond once upon a time. And she's really nice. Still funny, too."

"I don't think I should be here for this." Emmy tries to pull away from Maverick, but he keeps her in his hold. "Maven and I can get brunch while you all talk about Reid's sex life."

"You can stay, Emmy. I don't care. I'm not sharing any details with these fuckers." I lean forward and grab a coffee. "Avery told me she played soccer with Maven, and I realized that's why she looked so familiar. We haven't met, but we've been in the same vicinity."

"Why does that name ring a bell?" Maverick asks. "Avery. Avery. Do I know an Avery?"

"You've slept with half the city. I'm sure there was an Avery in there," Emmy says.

"I really hope he hasn't slept with her. I could never see her again," I say.

"Here I am suffering, and everyone wants to pile their shit on me." Maverick huffs and reaches for one of the coffees. "Fuck me, I guess."

"Have you met her, Dal?" I ask.

"What? No. Nope. No way. Maven mentioned her before, but we haven't actually met." He rubs the back of his neck and clears his throat. "Are you going to see her again?"

"I invited her to have dinner at my place on Tuesday. I guess we'll see how things go when we're talking and not—"

"Fucking," Maverick finishes for me, and I turn beet red.

"Yes. That." I sip the cold brew and sigh. "I'm leaving for the NFL summit on Thursday, and I'll be gone all weekend. I figured if there was any hope of her not forgetting me, we had to hang out this week."

"What is this summit thing again?" Maverick asks. "I don't get to go to anything cool."

"Because you're paid to hit a hockey puck." Emmy kisses his cheek, and he rolls his shoulders back all proud. "Not to do things like create ad campaigns."

"Thank goodness. That would be boring as hell." He cuts a look at me. "Sorry, Reidy Boy."

"My job is way more interesting than that. The summit is a big conference for people who work for the NFL behind the scenes. Social media managers. Marketing and ticket sales. Ever since Theo Asher from Cincinnati started dating Ella Wright, the world's biggest superstar, we've seen a thirty-four percent increase in viewership in women over thirty-five. There are more sponsorship opportunities and higher ad revenue. Plus, people are buying tickets hoping they'll see her when their team plays Cincy."

"Wow. Women are incredible." Maverick taps Emmy's hip. "A woman in the NHL. More women watching football. I'm all for it."

"It's awesome," I agree. "Next weekend is about how we can continue to increase the visibility of the sport and reach new demographics. There are panels set up for specific work groups. They asked me to give a speech, but you all know I hate public speaking. The less people who know my name, the better."

"You're so good at your job, though," Dallas says. "Social Media Account of the Year. Millions of followers. You should own that shit."

"Yeah, but they only know the DC Titans account. Not me, Reid Duncan, the guy who puts together all the content from either the couch in my living room or my office at the arena."

"Huh. I didn't realize you're never in the stuff you share online," Dallas says.

"Nope. I'm happier off camera where no one can see me," I say. "Hiding in the shadows. Unrecognizable. You don't even hear my voice in the videos."

"I could never," Maverick says. "I want my name in big, bright lights."

"Is that to compensate for something?" Maven asks, appearing next to Dallas in one of his practice T-shirts that hangs down to her knees.

"There's the bride." Emmy jumps to her feet and gives her best friend a hug. "How the hell did you sleep with your hair like that? There has to be a hundred bobby pins in there."

"That explains the headache. I thought it was the bourbon." Maven grins and glances at me. "Where did you disappear to last night, Reid? I wanted to introduce you to someone. She's the librarian at June's elementary school."

"You don't have to introduce him to anyone. Our Reidy Boy

took care of that all by himself." Maverick grins. "Some girl named Avery."

"*Avery*?" Maven repeats. She and Dallas exchange a look, and he gives her a subtle shake of his head. "How did that—but you—*what*?"

"He met her at a bar last week, then saw her again last night. Keep up, Mae," Maverick says. "She reads comic books."

"Now that you say it out loud, I might have made her up." I swirl my coffee around. "There's no way in hell she's real."

"Did you like her?" Maven asks.

"Of course he liked her. They went back to his room and had a grand ole time," Maverick says.

I grab the pillow from behind me and launch it at him. It hits him square in the face, and he yelps.

"Can we not announce it to the entire world, please? Yes, I like her. Yes, we hooked up, but I'm sure she only agreed to have dinner with me so she can let me down gently. The woman is fucking gorgeous. She has no business hanging out with someone like me," I say.

"Hey." Dallas frowns. "You have to stop selling yourself short like that. You're a catch, Reid."

"Lexi, one of the Stars athletic trainers, thinks you're really cute," Emmy tells me. "So do I."

"I'm still here," Maverick grumbles, and we all ignore him.

"Avery wouldn't agree to have dinner with you just to reject you," Maven says. "Her job is demanding. She also travels a lot. It would be good for her to spend time with someone who understands the stress of being in and out of the city every weekend."

"We'll see." I shove my glasses up my nose and shrug. "Last night was nice because I could keep my phone off and focus on her. This time next month we'll be in Miami, and I'll be spending most of my days at the arena filming content with the boys."

"I bet you focused on her," Maverick says, and Emmy leans over to pinch his ear. "What? It was a compliment. You know Reid is a thorough motherfucker. He probably gave her the best night of her life."

"I'm done with you." I stand and grab the box of donuts. "And I'm taking these with me."

"This feels like a personal attack," Maverick says.

"It's deserved," Emmy tells him.

"Guess that means you won't be at dinner on Tuesday?" Dallas asks, bringing up our standing tradition of going to Maverick and Emmy's apartment with the Stars hockey players and hanging out.

I shake my head. "Not this week. I'll text you all when I get back from my trip."

"Have fun." Maven gives me a hug. "And do me a favor."

"Hm?"

"Be open-minded," she says.

"Is this a threesome proposition? I'm flattered, but I—"

"It's not a threesome proposition." She laughs and steals the donuts from me. "A general piece of advice. Before you jump to conclusions and make assumptions, think of all the positive things, okay?"

"I think that's enough, Mae," Dallas says. He lifts her off her feet and throws her over his shoulder. "And I'm kicking y'all out. You have perfectly good hotel rooms. Let me and my wife enjoy a few hours of quiet without you being annoying assholes."

"I'm going to need you to say *my wife* again," Maven whispers, and Dallas grins.

"Out," he repeats. "Reid, stop by when you're home from the conference. Emmy, I'll pay you five hundred bucks to take Maverick somewhere else right now."

"Come on, pretty boy." Emmy drags her other half by the shirt like a dog. "Let's go."

There's pain in my chest as I watch them all. I've never seen so much love in one place, and I can't help but wonder when it'll be my turn for that kind of happiness.

@dcfootball

Did you miss me?

@footballindc

In your dreams.

It was nice to have some peace and quiet around here.

@dcfootball

Good weekend?

@footballindc

Best I've had in a while and it wasn't even because I didn't have to deal with you. How was yours?

@dcfootball

Can't complain.

@footballindc

Are you going to the Leader Summit this weekend?

@dcfootball

@dcfootball

You're going to stalk me, aren't you?

@footballindc

Trying to plan how to make your disappearance look like an accident.

@dcfootball

I'll be there.

@footballindc

Nervous to meet me?

@dcfootball

Why would I be nervous? I don't think about you in my free time.

@footballindc

Really? Is that why you liked a photo on the Thunderhawks' page from two weeks ago earlier this afternoon?

@dcfootball

No clue what you're talking about. Must've been one of the interns with slippery thumbs.

@footballindc

Must've been.

TWELVE
AVERY

ME

Hi!

REID

There she is.

ME

Sorry. I was putting out fires at work.

REID

You don't have to apologize. I understand what
it's like to get busy.

ME

Are we still on for dinner tonight?

REID

We are. Any allergies I should be aware of? Still
have a fake aversion to cheesecake?

ME

And shitty men? Yup!

But no other allergies to worry about. Do you
want me to bring anything? An appetizer or
dessert?

REID

I've got it covered, but thanks for offering.
Come by around 6? I'll send you my address
when I'm home from the office.

ME

Sounds good. Should I wear Crocs?

REID

You should. We can match.

ME

Do you really own a pair?

REID

Guess you'll have to snoop around my place
and find out.

ME

Are you giving me permission to snoop?

REID

I've got nothing to hide.

I already cleaned up the bodies.

ME

Nothing screams 'first date' like murder jokes.

Is it silly to say I'm excited to see you?

REID

Even after the murder joke?

ME

Yeah, believe it or not.

REID

Not silly at all. I'm excited to see you too.

I KNOCK on the door to Reid's apartment at one minute to six, and it swings open.

He's standing there with spaghetti sauce on his cheek. His glasses are foggy, and there's a noodle stuck in his hair.

"Wow. Talk about a warm welcome," I say. "You look like you've been through the wringer."

"I feel like it too. I overestimated my ability to multitask," he says. "I'm trying to do my mom's chicken parmesan and failing miserably. She'd disown me if she could see my kitchen right now. It's a fucking disaster."

"Do you want some help?"

His eyes sweep over my outfit. They start at the yellow tank top and work down to the denim skirt I paired it with. He lingers on my white sneakers and the anklet I looped around my left calf. When he finds the ribbon I tied in my hair to keep it out of my face, he blows out a rough breath.

"I don't want you to get messy," he says. "You look really pretty."

"I like to be messy," I say, and his cheeks flush a dark red.

"Come on in." Reid steps back so I can slide into the foyer. "You can leave your shoes there if you want, or keep them on. Whatever you're comfortable with."

I look at his mismatched socks half-hidden under his jeans. There are penguins riding sleds on the left and tiny snowmen on the right. "I think you might be in the wrong season. It's still pushing eighty degrees outside."

He glances down and chuckles. "June gave them to me for Christmas last year. I grabbed them in a hurry. I am ready for cooler weather, though. I can't stand the heat."

"Really? I love the heat." I kick off my shoes and set them neatly next to a pair of black Converse. "But that's the Floridian in me."

"Were you born and raised down south?" Reid asks, and I follow him to the kitchen.

"I am. I drank orange juice for breakfast every morning and I grew up thinking you had to run in a zigzag line to escape an alligator chasing you. That's a total myth, by the way."

"You learn something new every day. You're probably a terrible driver, aren't you?"

"Guilty." I smile. "Will you make fun of me if I tell you I was also Miss Florida?"

He glances at me over his shoulder. "You were?"

"I paid my way through college by playing a princess down at one of the theme parks outside Orlando. I stayed on that path with pageantry." I shrug and lean against the counter. "It was fun."

"I would've guessed something in modeling or acting. But a beauty queen? That's impressive." Reid bends over the stove and stirs a pot of sauce. "What was your talent?"

"Ballet. I started dancing when I was a little girl."

"No wonder you were so smooth on the dance floor the other night. I can't find a rhythm to save my life."

I laugh. "You did just fine."

"I had a good partner." He gestures to the sink stacked with dishes and the mountain of paper towels sitting on the granite island. "Sorry for the mess. It doesn't usually look like this. I, uh, wanted to do something nice for you, and that something turned into an Italian tragedy, almost-burnt cookies, and flowers that have somehow disappeared."

"This is for me?"

"You said you were going to have a busy week, so I thought

you could take a load off for a while. Dinner and dessert are covered. Well. Hopefully. This place might go up in flames in the next ten minutes and the chicken might be inedible. If that happens, save yourself. Don't worry about me."

I push off the counter and walk over to him. I kiss his cheek. "Thank you very much."

Reid sets down the spoon and slides his hands around my waist. "Is this okay?"

"What, the bomb that went off in here?"

He shakes his head. "Me touching you."

"You touched me plenty the other night."

That blush is back, and he dips his chin. "I meant touching you when we're not in a hotel bed."

"Or a hallway...." I arch a brow, and he grins. "It's more than okay," I tell him, because *okay* seems like a silly word to describe the way my heart is hammering in my chest. "You can keep doing it if you want."

Reid reaches past me. I expect him to lift me up and set me down next to the half-diced onions on the cutting board. I expect him to hike my skirt up my thighs and drop to his knees. I'm surprised when he hands me a bouquet of sunflowers.

"Found them. These are for you," he murmurs. "I picked them up at the farmers' market around the corner. I saw the tattoo on your finger, and I thought they might be your favorite flower."

"It is my favorite flower," I say, touching the petals. "These are beautiful."

"I'll put them in a vase until you head home. Then they're yours."

"Thank you, Reid. That's really sweet of you."

He kisses my forehead, then pulls away, cursing when he spies the sauce boiling over. "Could you grab me a paper towel?"

"I think you're going to need something more heavy duty

than that." I nudge him out of the way with my hip. "I'll handle this."

"Are you sure? Your shirt looks really nice."

"I could take it off if you're so worried about me staining it," I tease, and he fiddles with his glasses.

"You, uh, could if you wanted to. But then you might get burnt, and I'll feel like an asshole. You could also borrow one of mine."

"As tempted as I am to add to the collection of your shirts I have in my possession, I'll be fine." I turn the burner down to low and wipe up the sauce splattered across the cooktop. "How long until everything is ready?"

"Fifteen minutes. Do you want something to drink? I have wine and beer. I also have some whiskey."

"How about a tour first? I ask. "Can I see your place?"

"Sure." Reid motions to the space to the left of the kitchen, a large living room with floor-to-ceiling windows and two leather couches. There are plants everywhere, a dozen varieties arranged in a position where they'll get lots of sunlight.

"Wow. It looks like a greenhouse in here."

"I've always liked plants more than people. These ones are easy to take care of when I'm away for work."

I walk to the large shelf on the far end of the wall. There are hundreds of books stacked up, everything from nonfiction to thrillers to—

"Romance?" I ask. "You read romance books?"

"Yeah. Maverick wanted to start a book club with some of the guys on his team, and Dallas and I joined too."

"And all these men—men who can bench press my body weight and play hockey for sixty grueling minutes—sit around and talk about *romance novels*?"

"Once a month. We try to keep it structured, but most of the time, it turns into a huge debate. There's a lot of yelling. We had to get rid of alcohol because there was almost a fistfight over whether the girl should choose the hero or the villain. Someone ended up with a black eye, and Dallas—who tends to be the most level headed of the bunch—busted his lip."

"Oh my god." I stare at him, flabbergasted. "What the hell are you all debating?"

"Everything. What weapon we would use if we were in the story. Which friend in the group is going to be next in the series. Ranking the sexual positions mentioned on a scale from one to ten. Asking ourselves if we'd want a masked man to chase us through the woods." He clears his throat. "We all signed NDAs."

"Wow." I run my finger down the spines. They're the same books I have on my nightstand, marked up and annotated with some of my favorite quotes and scenes. "I'm impressed. I'm used to people telling me romance books are stupid and I should read something with real substance."

"That's fucked up, isn't it?" Reid says, frowning. "I hate that we live in a world where people like to shit on the things that make other people happy. It's like with my comic books and LEGO collection. Some of the looks I get in the checkout line are so irritating. I'm not hurting anyone. Let me buy them in peace."

"You like to put together LEGO sets?" I ask.

He points to the section of the shelf covered in glass doors. "I've been doing them since I was a kid. It's another thing I got into instead of sports. Helps turn my brain off when it feels like there's too much going on up there. It's also a nice break from staring at my phone for hours on end."

"Which one is your favorite?" I look at the skyscrapers and battleships with tiny flags, wondering how much time Reid spent crafting each structure. "I like this medieval castle."

"That one is cool, isn't it? I put it together last year. Took me about six hours on a rainy afternoon."

"Are those actual dragons in the courtyard?"

He laughs. "Yeah. Maverick added them. Said it made it look *cool as shit*. He's not wrong."

"These are all so neat, Reid."

"Thanks," he says sheepishly. "There's a Millennium Falcon set I really want, but it's hard to track down. They always sell out seconds after they go live."

"That's from *Star Trek*, right?" I ask, and his eye twitches. "Kidding. I know it's *Star Wars*."

"You scared me there for a second. Okay, enough nerd shit. I want you to stick around for the rest of the night, and showing you my comic book collection will send you packing."

"I thought they'd be out here. Where are you hiding them? I want to see."

"They're in my bedroom. Do you really want to see?"

"I wouldn't have said so otherwise," I say.

"Just keep the jokes to a minimum, okay?"

I follow Reid through the apartment. There are pictures hanging on the walls, and I get quick glimpses into his life. There's one of him with a woman who has the same red hair as him.

Another of him, Dallas, and Maverick, their arms slung over each other's shoulders and wide grins on their faces. There's him on a football field, pieces of confetti in his hair and more stuck to his forehead.

It's nice to see him celebrating his friends' successes.

"Do you have any siblings?" I ask.

"No. Only child. What about you?"

"A younger sister. She's in New York working in fashion and merchandising."

"The city that never sleeps."

"Have you been?"

"More than I'd like," he says. "It's not my favorite place in the world."

"What is?"

"Tough question. Seattle is okay. Atlanta in January isn't half bad. Denver is decent."

"You're quite the traveler."

"Work takes me places," he says, opening a door to our right. "I get to go to London next year."

"I love London," I gush, and I step into his bedroom.

It's exactly what I thought it'd look like.

Soft beige walls and a big blue comforter on a king-sized bed. A desk to the right with two laptops and a cell phone on top of a stack of papers. A nightstand with a lamp and a charging cable.

The real centerpiece is the array of comic books displayed along the wall.

Three long, clear shelves are tacked to the paint. Each edition is sitting upright and in pristine condition. Half of them still have plastic wrap on them, and I spot publications that must have cost hundreds of dollars.

"Holy shit. Is that the black cover variant of *Venom #1*?" I ask.

"Okay, seriously." Reid leans against the doorframe and crosses his arms over his chest. I try not to stare at the way the tendons in his forearms flex, but I'm doing a terrible job. "How the hell are you so knowledgeable on comic books? The average person doesn't know shit besides the Marvel superheroes, and you're over here talking about misprint editions. What's your secret?"

"I had a crush on a guy in high school who loved them," I admit. "I made it my mission to know everything about collector's editions, characters, and storylines so I could impress him. He turned out to be a massive douche, and I ended up falling in love with all the worlds out there. Now I read them for me."

"Is it too soon to ask you to marry me?"

I laugh. "Sorry. I have a five-date minimum before—"

I'm interrupted by the shrill sound of the fire alarm echoing down the hall. I jump a foot in the air at the noise and cover my ears. Reid groans.

"I think we might have a situation on our hands," I yell.

"How do you feel about Mexican food?" he yells back.

I grin. "Sounds perfect."

THIRTEEN

REID

I CAN'T STOP LOOKING at Avery.

She has a drop of red enchilada sauce on her chin right under the curve of her cheek, and I'm tempted to lick it away.

It's as distracting as the pretty yellow ribbon she has tied in her dark hair. I don't know if I want to leave it in place or find another use for it.

Probably the latter.

"Not a total failure of a night." She wipes her hands with a napkin and adds it to the pile on the coffee table. "A solid eight out of ten."

"That's almost a C," I say. "What are my areas of improvement?"

"They're all things out of your control. Fire alarms. Smoking chicken. The flames that were coming out of the oven. Good call with the extinguisher, by the way."

"Those are all things in my control." I turn and face her on the couch. "I think I'm screwed."

"The cookies might bring you up to a nine," she says.

"I've always been a fan of finishing strong."

I wonder what I'm supposed to do next.

Kiss her?

Invite her to spend the night?

Drag her back to my bedroom and ask her to read *Planetary: Volume 1* naked and on top of me?

Christ.

Why don't they make manuals about how to handle situations like this?

"Are you okay?" Avery asks, and I reach for my glass of water.

"Wonderful," I say, finishing the drink in two sips. "How's the work week looking?"

"Not bad. I was asked to do a presentation for some people, and I feel a little silly they think I'm qualified for the job." She drags her finger through the sauce on her chin then sucks it clean. It's embarrassing to admit my cock twitches. "It's weird to consider myself successful, and it's even weirder that other people look up to me and try to emulate what I do to be successful too."

I frown. "Someone told you that what you do is meaningless, didn't they?"

Avery blinks. She wrings her hands together and touches her necklace. "What makes you say that?"

"Because I used to do the same thing when I talked about my dad."

She laughs, but there's no humor behind it. It's jagged and sharp. An obvious deflection tactic that's probably worked on people in the past. I know there's more to the story, but I don't push her to tell me.

"It's not really a second date conversation," she says. "It's more like a tenth or twelfth or twentieth date conversation."

I nod, understanding. "We don't have to have the conversation at all. I just want you to know you're not alone."

She blinks and looks at me like I have four heads. Her jaw works and her hair curtains her face, hiding it from view.

"I have an ex," she says. "He works in the same industry as me but in a different role. A role of power. When I started to make a name for myself, he started to pull back in our relationship. There were off-handed comments I was able to ignore. I brushed them off and made excuses for him, but it kept escalating."

I scoot closer to her. "What happened?"

"I don't want to go into detail," she says, and I automatically assume the worst. That some piece of shit asshole hurt her, and now I want to hurt him. "Anyway. That's where the self-doubt started. It's eased up the last few years, and I'm finally happy again. I think about how drastically my life has changed and..." Avery trails off and shrugs. She draws her legs to her chest and brings my hand with them. "Things are good now."

"I think it's really cool you're giving a presentation to people who admire you. I hate public speaking, and I could never be on stage," I say, and she pulls me by the hem of my shirt.

"But why? You'd be such a star."

I sit up on my knees so I'm between her legs. She wraps her ankles around my back and urges me closer to her. I stroke the inside of her thigh and look down, my chest a tangle of emotions when I see her.

Horny. Happy. Sort of embracing this whole "live in the moment" thing. Still questioning how the hell this woman is in front of me, looking up at me like I did something spectacular, like hang the fucking moon.

"That's debatable," I mumble, and she laughs.

"Your best man speech at the wedding was great."

"I took three shots of whiskey before someone handed me the microphone."

"Really?" Her brown eyes flash to the front of my jeans. "Never would've guessed."

"About that." I take her wrists and pin them over her head. "I don't want you to think I'm an asshole or making any excuses, but my job is about to become increasingly busier. I told you it's been a point of contention in my previous relationships."

"You're secretly afraid of commitment, aren't you?" she asks, slipping her finger into my belt loop and giving a gentle tug. "I knew it."

"The opposite actually. I'm not a casual guy. When I date someone, I date them because I see a future with them, not because I want a quick romp in the sheets. I've liked spending time with you, Avery. I also know I'm not going to be able to give you the attention you deserve for the next few months, but I don't like the thought of someone else touching you after I've had you."

"What are you proposing?"

"I don't know what I'm proposing because I don't know how to do anything except buy you flowers and burn dinner. The relationship stuff I don't have time for right now, but wish I did."

"You know how to do a lot more than that. You also know how to make me come. How to make me feel good," she says, her voice wickedly low. "How to listen and how to hold a good conversation. You're very good at a lot of different things, Reid."

"You're just being nice," I mumble. My thumb brushes along the edge of her skirt and over her tan skin. I wonder if she likes to sit outside on warm summer days. I wonder if she drives out to the ocean and basks under the sunshine. "But my ego needs the boost after the dinner disaster."

"So, you're not looking for anything serious right now?"

"I'm not, but that doesn't mean I want to stop seeing you."

"Okay." Avery bites her bottom lip and lifts her hips. Her skirt inches up her thighs, and I see a flash of purple under the denim. Lace, just like she wore the other night, and I have to stare at the ceiling. "Are you thinking a friends with benefits thing?"

"I guess." I slide my hand up her leg. "But I also want to make you dinner every now and then. Read a comic book with you in bed and go get ice cream. That stuff sounds like a relationship, but I need to keep my emotions in check. Just for a few months. Does that make me a piece of shit?"

"No." Avery slips her palms under my shirt and runs them up my back. I shiver at her touch. "It's a good idea. My life is pretty chaotic too, and there are going to be days when I can't answer my phone for hours. I'd never want you—or anyone I was seeing—to feel like they were second on my list of priorities."

"Are you okay with a strictly physical relationship?"

She smiles. Some bright, beautiful fucking thing that makes it difficult to remember *why* I'm going this casual route when I think it would be nice to say *fuck the responsibilities* and spend time with her instead.

"Yeah," she says. "Because I'd really like to have you again."

I grab the waistband of her underwear. I snap it against her skin and smooth over the mark with the pads of my fingers.

"I won't take advantage of this." My voice cracks, seconds away from hiking her skirt all the way up to her waist and asking if I can eat her out. I'd like to live on my knees in front of her. "And we're going to need to have honest communication if it's going to work."

"No sleeping with other people. If one of us feels like the other is getting too suffocating or clingy, we'll talk about it." Her right hand moves from my shoulder to the front of my jeans. Avery palms my cock, and my grip on her leg turns bruising. "Work comes first for both of us. It sounds like we both really like our jobs, and we don't want anything to interfere with our careers."

"Yes, yes, and more yes," I say.

She laughs. "You're not paying attention to me, are you?"

"I promise I am. Jobs. Work. No sleeping with other people. I heard every word." I nudge her thighs wide and get my first real glance at her underwear. "God. Look how wet you are."

"Bold of you to assume this is for you." She dances her fingers up her leg and rests them on her hip. "It could be for anyone."

"Don't care," I mumble. "Just like that I get to see it."

"Such a nice guy." Avery pulls the lace to the side, a slow and torturous sort of hell that makes me want to rip the fabric in two and buy her a new pair. A hundred pairs, if it means I get to have her like this again. "Gosh, I like being your friend."

"I've never had a friend like this. Not as beautiful as you."

"Do you want to touch me, Reid? Or do you want to watch?" she asks.

"I think I'd like to watch," I mumble again. The last strands of my rationality slip out of my grasp. "Please."

And I do watch.

I watch her, a rhythm to her movements. I study the way she touches her body, the things she likes and the things she does more than once. I take mental notes of the sounds she makes, of the soft and sweet hitch in her breathing when she lifts her shirt, no bra, and massages her round tits.

I watch and I watch and I *watch*, folding my large body over her small frame so I can hear every sound, so I can talk her through it, so I can tell her how pretty she is and how much I'd like to see her come undone.

Avery kisses me when she's close, a rough and vicious press of her mouth I swallow down, hungry for *more, more,* and *more.* She begs me to touch her when she's close and I do, my fingers sliding inside her and moving in the way she likes.

And when she falls, she says my name. Again and again she says it—*chants* it—and some primal, possessive part of me that's never existed before rumbles to life in my chest.

She unzips my jeans and wraps her hand around my cock when she comes down from her high, stroking up and down and coating the head with her own arousal and blinking up at me with bright eyes.

I fall too when she puts me in her mouth and sucks my cock, a goddamn headfirst plunge into some unknown territory I've never been before.

This is dangerous.

Stupid, probably, to think I can keep my feelings in check and touch her platonically. Casually.

But fuck, I'm going to try.

She licks her fingers clean and I drag her to my bedroom. I set her out on the sheets and grab a condom from the bedside table, one thought racing through my head when she rides me to oblivion and fucks me like the world is going to end tomorrow:

I'm in big fucking trouble.

@footballindc

@footballindc
What if we sit next to each other on the plane to Vegas and don't realize it?

@dcfootball
You wouldn't be able to tell what I did for a living if you saw me.

@footballindc
You're not 6'4 and two hundred pounds?

@dcfootball
If you're waiting for someone who is 6'4 to show up, you're going to be waiting a long time. I'm barely pushing 6'1 on a good day.

@footballindc
Interesting.

@dcfootball

Disappointed?

@footballindc

Besides having a preseason game and two regular season games against the Titans, I'm indifferent about you. It'll be fun to kick your ass and gloat about it.

@dcfootball

I wish I was as delusional as you. It must make life fun.

@footballindc

You can't see me, but I'm holding up a middle finger.

@dcfootball

Really hoping I can avoid you the next few days. I don't want to be stuck socializing with you.

@footballindc

I'm insulted you aren't dying to meet me.

@dcfootball

You'll get over it.

@footballindc

Have you ever looked up who I am?

@dcfootball

Why would I do that?

@footballindc

I don't know. Curiosity?

@dcfootball

You know what they say about curiosity.
I can assure you, I have no clue who you are.

@dcfootball

Have you looked me up?

@footballindc

I don't give you a second thought.

@dcfootball

Yet here you are, messaging me at midnight, nine hours before my plane is supposed to leave.

@footballindc

Thanks for confirming we're not on the same flight.

@dcfootball

Thank god. I'm keeping my phone off so I can have five hours of uninterrupted rest.

@footballindc

I'll make sure to leave you some fun messages to come back to.

FOURTEEN

REID

VEGAS IN JULY is a horrible fucking idea.

I like winter. Snow and sleet and temperatures below one hundred and ten degrees. Not this heat wave that's taken over the western United States and making my life a literal hell.

I'm drenched in sweat by the time I get to the convention center where the conference is taking place. With traffic and an Uber driver who got lost, there's barely any time to shower and change out of my damp shirt before I'm sprinting downstairs, joining the long line of people waiting to check in.

"Name?" drawls a bored-looking woman when I reach the front.

"Reid Duncan." I push my glasses up my nose and shove a pen behind my ear. "DC Titans."

She flicks through the lanyards. "There you are. Social media."

"That's me."

She hums and hands me the lanyard along with a crisp sheet of white paper. "There's a list of events. The welcome presentation and keynote speaker start in twenty minutes, and attendance is required. After that, what you decide to do is up to you."

"Who is the keynote speaker?" I ask. "It wasn't listed on the website. I've checked the schedule every day for updates and haven't found anything."

"Do I look like I have that information?" she asks. "It's above my pay grade."

"Ah. I see. Thanks for all the help."

I sidestep out of the way and make a beeline for the refreshments table at the back of the room, away from the crowd.

"Duncan!" I hear called out, and I turn around. I see Leo Michaels, the marketing manager for the Cincinnati Renegades, one of our division rivals, waving at me. He pushes through people until he reaches the charcuterie boards and fruit plates. "Dude. Good to see you."

"Hey, man." We clasp hands and bump chests. "I didn't know you'd be here. Thought you got promoted."

"I did. We're short-staffed right now, and I didn't have much of a choice about coming. With our QB constantly in the media, I swear to god my workload has tripled this offseason," he says.

"That's a good thing, right?"

"A very good thing. Our investors are happy as shit, and so is my bank account. But it's trash for my work-life balance. I'm up to my elbows in promotional campaigns and potential sponsorships. I didn't know how hard creating slogans that combine football and pop music would be, and it keeps me up at night. I stare at the ceiling and try to figure out a word that rhymes with *dazzle*."

I laugh. "That's what happens when you go from a big fish in a small pond to a tiny fish in an ocean. When we won our first Super Bowl, I didn't sleep for a week. I'm still lucky if I get five hours a night these days."

"How're your boys feeling about the preseason? Is everyone healthy? I saw Dallas got married. How was that?"

It was a blast. They're all healthy so far, but we know how

that's going to go. The injury numbers are only going to increase if the league starts adding more games. I don't know how Jett made it through eighteen weeks last season. His arm was toast by the playoffs. You all deserved the Super Bowl win."

"Thanks for loaning the trophy to us," Leo says. "I can't believe you all signed Griffin Harrison. The guy's a fucking legend. There's no way you all don't win the NFC."

"I don't know about that. The Thunderhawks snagging Malcolm Jeffries is really going to test us. This is the first season we're playing them, and I'm going to lose my mind if I have to hear that song they use on social media all year."

"Aw, come on." Leo grins. "I love when they play the song. I'll hear it in the tunnel after our own games and know they won. Our guys sing it, and sometimes I think our fans want us to lose just so they can see what video the Thunderhawks are going to use with the music on social media."

I roll my eyes. "Not you too, Leo. The song literally just says *Thunderhawks* over and over. It's not creative, and my goddaughter could come up with something better."

"What can I say? I'm a sucker for good marketing." He claps a hand on my shoulder. "What panels are you sitting in on? We should try to link up for dinner this weekend."

"I'm doing all the social media ones, but I'll probably pop into a marketing seminar so I can hear things from your side. Let me know when you're free, and we can grab a bite."

"Maybe tomorrow. I ran into a woman who's speaking this weekend, and I'm going to see if I can find her later. I want to ask her out for a drink."

I snort. "Bold of you to mix business and pleasure. We know how that ends."

"I'd risk it all for her, man. She's a smoke show." Leo pulls out his phone and groans. "I need to take this. The guy I work with in advertising is up my ass about a new project."

"Do you still have my number?"

"Yeah. I'll holler at you later. Have fun in there."

Leo waves and presses the phone to his ear, disappearing around a corner. I grab a bottle of water then make my way into the large conference room. I find a spot in the back, a chair on the aisle close to the door so I can make an escape, and kill time by catching up on the group text messages I've been dragged into.

PUCK DADDY

Did you make it Vegas okay?

DADDY DALLAS

You have to let us know if they announce anything cool, Reid. I heard a rumor about special uniforms we'll wear on holidays.

PUCK DADDY

Of course they give you special jerseys. You guys only play 17 games and have a damn bye week. Gotta keep the fans interested where they can. Fucking snoozefest.

DADDY DALLAS

I'm sitting two feet away from you and you're going to talk shit, Maverick?

PUCK DADDY

You know I love to talk shit.

Attachment: 1 image

Have fun, Uncle Reid! Wish you were here for our tea party!

I burst out laughing at the picture of Dallas, Maverick, Emmy, Maven, and June. All five of them are wearing fancy hats and smiling at the camera. June is holding up a teacup. Maverick is holding a half-eaten scone, and homesickness hits me.

I travel a lot during the season. I'm on an airplane or a football field more than I'm in my own apartment from August until February, but usually, my friends are with me.

When Maven isn't working as the DC Stars team photographer, she and June are on the sidelines in their Titans gear, chatting my ear off during warmups and helping me pick what music to use over video clips.

Maverick comes to as many games as he can, and when he shows up, he brings half the hockey team with him.

I learned a long time ago family isn't what you're born into. It's the people you pick up along the way. The friends in that photo are my family now, and I really fucking miss them.

ME

Looks like fun. We'll have to have another party when I get home.

PUCK DADDY

Don't make too many friends, Plant Daddy. I don't want to be replaced.

ME

You're number one in my heart, Mav. Don't tell Dallas.

PUCK DADDY

Fucking assholes.

I silence my phone as a round of applause welcomes a woman on the stage in the front of the room. I sit back in my chair and get comfortable, wishing I had brought a pad of paper with me so I could doodle to pass the time.

"Good afternoon, everyone, and thank you for joining us this weekend. My name is Meredith Knowles, and I'm the President of Marketing for the NFL. It's an honor to be joined by you all today. We have an exciting weekend planned, and I hope that when you return to your teams, you'll take home invaluable information that will help lift you to success as we approach the season."

I cross my arms over my chest and hold back a yawn. Meredith goes through the usual rah rah rah stuff we hear at all of these events I've heard a dozen times. My head starts to lull until there's another round of applause and I jolt awake, pretending to clap with the rest of the crowd.

"To kick off the conference, I'm going to turn it over to our keynote speaker. This woman is an icon in our industry, and everyone in this room knows her in some way, even if you don't know her real name. She's revolutionized the TikTok and Instagram game while helping her expansion team earn a record-setting profit. The Thunderhawks are lucky to have her, and we're lucky to hear the insights she's going to share with us. Let's give her a warm welcome."

You have to be shitting me.

I crane my neck, desperate to get a glimpse at the woman who's been tormenting me for years. This is my first time ever seeing her, and I'm on the edge of my seat.

Someone climbs up the steps to the stage, and the blood drains from my face as I recognize who it is.

Brown hair and brown eyes. A bright smile and a soft laugh. That same hand she's using to wave to the crowd was in my pants forty-eight hours ago, and I suck in a sharp breath.

Avery runs the Thunderhawks' social media accounts?

Avery is who I talk to every day?

Avery drives me up a goddamn wall?

What the *fucking fuck* is going on?

"THAT WAS AN INCREDIBLE SPEECH, AVERY," Meredith tells me when I walk off the stage to a round of applause. It's the largest speaking event I've ever done, and their enthusiasm lifts my confidence.

"I'm not sure I'd call rambling about the human connection social media creates incredible, but I'm so grateful for the opportunity. Sorry if I derailed the conversation a bit at the end," I laugh.

"Please. Last year the keynote speaker went on a rant about who would win in a fight, Deadpool or Wolverine. Trust me when I say you didn't derail anything."

I think of Reid and bite back a smile.

I wonder who he would pick. He'd probably have a twenty-minute argument ready to back up his decision. Comic books would be used as references, and there would be a PowerPoint presentation.

He strikes me as a PowerPoint guy. Slide after slide of data and graphs and hard evidence.

I should text him.

I should ask how his trip is going and if he's hanging in there despite all the ass kissing.

Maybe I can ask when he's free again to fulfill the parameters of our casual arrangement. He seemed eager about it when he had his hand between my legs the other night at his apartment. There was a look of wonder in his eyes when he told me how badly he wanted to fuck me.

My cheeks heat at the memory, at the thought of his fingers and warm mouth, and I fan my face to try to cool off.

"I'm glad everything went well," I say. "Thank you for having me."

"You're giving another talk this weekend, right?" Meredith asks.

"On Saturday afternoon. It's a conversation about engaging with fans and learning how to draw a boundary when online discourse turns negative. It's a topic close to my heart, especially for the women in a male-dominated field. The amount of times I've wanted to call out grown men for living in their mother's basements and hiding behind their keyboard while they talked shit would astound you, but I keep it professional."

She laughs. "We call someone out, we're a bitch. We keep our mouths shut, they ask, 'what? Don't you have something to say?' We can't win."

"We really can't. We're damned if we do, damned if we don't."

"Sums up being a woman, honestly."

"Gosh, it's good to see you, Meredith. I'll try to catch up with you later this weekend," I say.

We exchange a round of goodbyes and I make my way for the main hall of the convention center. With nothing on the agenda for the rest of the evening, I'm excited to settle in with some room service. Maybe I'll add a bottle of wine and have a nice night with my vibrator and shitty television.

My feet ache. The new black heels I've been waltzing around

in all afternoon were a bad decision, and my toes are killing me. My social meter is dropping lower and lower as I make my way down the corridor, and I could use a little peace and quiet.

I can feel my smile straining around the edges. I can hear my voice turning less friendly the longer I stand, but I keep going.

Working in pageantry and theme parks prepared me for this. I do the dance I've done for years as I pass people: *Hello. How are you? It's good to see you.* I talk to everyone who stops me, giving them five, ten minutes of my time before I'm handed off to the next person for another round of introductions.

I should love the attention.

Twenty-five-year-old me *craved* the attention, but I know it's not totally genuine. They don't want to get to know me. They only want to pick apart my brain and find my deep, dark secrets, like I wrote a manual on how to be successful at my job when, really, it was a stroke of luck.

I had low expectations when I took the Thunderhawks job. I figured we'd have a losing record for the first five years like most expansion teams do. I thought we'd be at the bottom of the standings, hanging on by a thread with a bench of mediocre players on their last stint in the NFL before retirement.

Then, *the song* happened.

It was a right-place-at-the-right-time moment. I never thought a drunken night out with a Grammy-winning producer from Baltimore who used to go to Thunderhawks games as a kid before the team moved out west would end up changing my life.

After four margaritas and a hundred YouTube listens of the original Thunderhawks' soundtrack, we came up with an idea: a new and improved theme song that was fresher. Poppier. Catchy and recognizable enough where you'd stop scrolling to listen if you heard it playing on your phone.

I posted it after our first win, syncing it to a clip of the guys on the team celebrating by dumping a cooler of Gatorade on their coach, and it became an overnight sensation.

It went viral in a way I'm still struggling to comprehend.

Social media followers flocked in by the thousands.

Our empty stadium began to fill up.

We started to win somewhat consistently, and our second year in the league resulted in six wins. Last year we snagged eight victories, and this year, with a roster full of young talent and players who want to work their asses off, we have a real shot at making the playoffs.

Every video I upload gets millions of views and floods of comments. Other team accounts—the franchises I grew up idolizing—message me regularly, popping in to congratulate me on professional milestones.

I also accidentally ended up in a feud with the guy who runs the DC Titans' accounts, and bugging him to no end might be my favorite part of all this madness.

I don't remember how the feud started, but I do know it's my fault. Something I instigated and *keep* instigating.

It's so damn fun to push his buttons.

There's the constant badgering. The sarcasm he lobs my way and my ability to irritate him with only a few messages.

Through all the back and forth, though, I've found myself wondering what he looks like. Who he is and what his story might be. Does he answer me from his couch? From an office? From his bed?

I've been so tempted to do some digging and figure him out myself. One night, after a glass of whiskey and a Thunderhawks loss, I came close. I had the Titans website pulled up, ready to search high and low until I learned his name.

Then I stopped.

I turned off my phone and walked away.

I remembered he's pretentious and a know-it-all. He can't take a joke, and he thinks everything is about him.

I might hate him with every fiber in my being, but I love him assuming I'm unbothered by him even more.

It's written in the stars. As long as he and I coexist in this wide world of sports, we're going to bicker over menial shit. We're going to argue about trending audio and what filters to use on photos. We'll toss statistics at each other, as if we're the ones on the field making the plays.

Working for rival football teams separated by a highway and thirty-eight miles will do that to you, and any possibility of something cordial ever forming between us closed up years ago.

I shake my head and get rid of the thoughts of him.

This weekend is important.

I have notes to look over. Another presentation to rehearse. Friends to see and networking to do, and I can't get distracted by the bane of my existence who's loomed in my peripheral vision for goddamn years.

He might be lurking around here, sitting in the crowd and listening to my talks, but I refuse to give him the time of day.

The conversation I'm pretending to be involved in stalls, and I use it as a chance to sneak away. I turn the corner for the elevators and let out a relieved breath when I find an empty hallway.

"Avery Sinclair," says a deep voice from behind me, and I swear the next ten seconds happen in slow motion.

I glance over my shoulder. My eyes almost bulge out of my head when I see Reid standing there, his arms folded across his chest and his cheeks a little flushed. Above the collar of his Henley is a light pink mark, the spot my nails dug into when I came on his hand the other night, and my face flushes too.

I turn to face him, trying to get a grasp on the situation unfolding in front of me.

"What—" I stare at him, confused. "*Reid?*"

He walks toward me until he's crowding my space. I take a step back and collide with a wall, immediately thrown back to the night of the wedding. My dress around my waist, him on his knees. The scratch of his beard and his fingers on my thighs.

"What are you doing here?" I ask, and it's barely above a whisper. "Are you—is this a surprise?"

That would be a lot of effort just to see me.

Borderline creepy, too.

I like the guy, but showing up unannounced a week after we started hanging out toes the line of *obsessive* and *get me the fuck out of here.*

"What do you think I'm doing, Avery?" Reid asks.

My brain is trying to figure out his riddle. How does he know my last name? Why is he here?

My eyes bounce to the lanyard around his neck. I see **DC TITANS** and **SOCIAL MEDIA MANAGER** printed on the laminated name tag in a big, bold font, and the earth stops spinning.

My breath gets stuck in my chest. I shake my head, refusing to believe *this man*, the one who stared at me like I was the most precious thing in the world and wouldn't look away, is the same one I've been talking to, been *hating*, for years.

"What the *fuck*?" I grab the lanyard and look at it closely. The letters melt together. My vision turns blurry. This has to be a sick and twisted joke. "You—I—how—"

"I had the same reaction when you walked across the stage an hour ago as the keynote fucking speaker," Reid says.

"Oh my god. This cannot be happening. I liked the you I met at the bar, but I *hate* internet you. You're the biggest pain in my ass."

"The feeling is mutual. How long were you going to wait before you told me what you really do? Before you told me your 'small presentation' was a huge fucking speech for all the important people in the NFL? The commissioner is here, for fuck's sake," he says.

My hands shake. I think I might pass out. I cannot believe this is happening. "Look, I'm sorry for lying. I don't want to make excuses, but I did it to protect myself."

"Protect yourself? I'm not going to stalk you, Avery."

"You saw what happened on my date the night we met. Telling a man I work for an NFL team? Please. I'd either be ridiculed for having a stupid job or put through an interrogation a man wouldn't be forced to go endure."

"Okay, fine, you want to be protective over your career. That's fair. But was this *ever* going to come up?" Reid asks.

"Not after two nights of sex. For the record, I felt terrible lying to you. Not the new you. The old you." I pause and tip my head to the side. "Why did you lie?"

"It's stupid."

"Tell me."

He runs a hand through his hair and tugs on the ends of the strands. "The second I mention my job and the guys I'm best friends with, people don't have any interest in me. They have an interest in all the ways they could benefit by being with me. Marketing is my go-to line until I can vet someone and make sure they aren't spending time with me for the wrong reasons."

"You think I'd do that?" I ask.

"I don't know the first thing about you. Especially now," he emphasizes, and for some strange reason, it stings. "You have been under my skin for *years*. Every time I post something, there you are. Every time I come up with an idea, you one-up me. If I have to hear that damn song of yours one more time, I might scream."

"Maybe you should come up with better ideas or find a new job. I've been kicking your ass for a while now. It's not my fault you're not creative." I flip my hair over my shoulder, and heat flares to life behind his gaze. "As for the song, I'm going to use that as ammunition. I have your cell phone number. I'll send it to you every morning. Every night. It's going to haunt you, Reid, until you realize you're never going to be able to compete with me."

His eyes narrow, and I've really pissed him off. I don't know when we stepped so close to each other, but our chests almost press together. I can feel the warmth of his body, can see the deep green shade of his eyes, can taste him on my tongue; salty, sweet, delicious.

"If you're so sure of yourself, wanna make a bet?" he asks low and rough, and I imagine those words on my neck. On my thighs and my breasts.

Goddamn him.

"Who can make who orgasm faster? I already won that competition, and we're never doing that again," I say.

"You wish we were doing it again."

"In your dreams."

"I propose a friendly wager where we keep our clothes on."

"Pretty sure I'm going to take an hour-long shower when I get back to my room to scrub my body clean of you," I say. "Keeping my clothes on will be easy."

He smirks, and I hate the satisfied look on his face. "You're talking about the times we hooked up an awful lot for someone who wants to get them out of her memory."

"Will you tell me already? I'm walking away in ten seconds."

"A competition to see who can secure the most ticket sales throughout the year. Bonus points for new season ticket holders. And why don't we throw in the title of Social Media Account of the Year for good measure? I know we're both gunning for the accolade."

I hum, intrigued.

He has my interest.

"What's the winning prize?" I ask. "How do I know this will be worth my while?"

"If I win, you have to change your social media handle—@footballindc? Really? You play in *Baltimore*, Avery, and I'm tired of people confusing our accounts."

"I did that to piss you off. Guess it worked." I grin, and he scowls. "What do I get if I win?"

"What do you want?"

I tap my cheek, an idea coming to me. "You have to play the Thunderhawks song on your page during every playoff game and publicly acknowledge you lost a bet."

"Deal," he says.

"You're quick to agree."

"Because it's an easy thing to win."

"Hang on. Before we do some weird blood oath where we vow to destroy each other, can we temporarily pause our feud?" I ask and he blinks, surprised.

"We're making up the rules as we go, so sure. We can pause it. Why?"

There's a question on the tip of my tongue, one I'm not sure I'm allowed to ask. Especially now. But I'm going to ask it anyway. It's my last chance to. "We... we had a connection, didn't we? That wasn't—" I swallow. "That was real, right?"

I'm scared to hear the answer.

I'm not going to be able to turn off my attraction to him overnight. Even with this big revelation, I still want to kiss him. I still think he's a nice guy with a good heart.

He also happens to be the man I've loathed since our very first interaction.

Separating the two is going to be difficult.

Reid's eyes soften, and he looks *sad*. Regretful, if I stare long enough, as if he knows how hard this is going be too. "Yeah," he says, and my traitorous heart leaps in my chest. "It was real. For me, at least."

I rub my thumb over my bottom lip. He tracks the motion, like he's watching me one final time and trying to savor it. "Me too," I admit. "What do we do now?"

The air is thick with tension. The heavy moment breaks, and it feels like I've been holding my breath for days.

"We go to war," he says, but there's far less disdain behind it.

"I hope you're prepared to lose." I step past him. I need some space. I need to get my head on straight. "If you'll excuse me, I have things to do. Speeches to write. Content to post. A bet to win."

"It's going to go as well as your season did last year: well below average."

"Not your best dirty talk, but I'll take it. Good luck. You're going to need it."

"It's going to be like that, huh?" He tugs on my belt loop and spins me so I'm facing him. My hands inadvertently land on his chest, and I look up at him. "You're going to wish you never came to Baltimore when I'm finished with you," he whispers in my ear, and I shiver. "Game on, Sinclair."

Before I have a chance to toss back a rebuttal, Reid is moving away and leaving me breathless, confused, and feeling like I just made a deal with the devil.

SIXTEEN

REID

AVERY

Morning, sunshine.

Attachment: 1 video

Getting warmed up for when I beat you.

ME

You should delete my number.

This won't end well for you.

AVERY

I can always message you on Instagram. Or
TikTok. Or YouTube.

ME

Stalking me, Sinclair?

Fuck, I like knowing your last name. It makes
taunting you even more fun.

Oh, shit. You said you were a beauty queen. I'm
going to look up videos of you in your dresses.

AVERY

Go ahead. I'm not ashamed of that part of my
life, and it was an honor to serve as Miss
Florida.

Just so you know, Duncan, I'm planning on
winning this bet.

Which means I have to play the long game. I'm
going to annoy you until you give up.

ME

You found out my last name, I see. Did you
finally look me up?

AVERY

Yeah, and I should've done it years ago.

Congrats on the Robotics win in tenth grade, by
the way.

I'll be back at lunchtime with another rendition
of the Thunderhawks tune. Tell me, do you
prefer the original or the remix?

ME

You're insufferable. Don't you have a speech to
give?

AVERY

You didn't think I was insufferable the other
night when you were on top of me.

ME

Just like you didn't hate me when I was making
you come.

Funny how that works.

I MANAGE to avoid seeing Avery the second day of the conference.

It takes careful planning, eating lunch in my room and sitting in on a conversation about ticket sales software instead of marketing tips and tricks, but I get through the afternoon without running into her.

I don't know how the hell I missed the signs of her identity. They were all there, right in front of me and bright as fucking day.

The night at the bar when she said a work thing came up.

When she shut down after her date started talking shit about women and sports.

Casually asking about my friends who are athletes without showing any interest in getting to know them.

I'm a goddamn idiot.

It explains why Dallas and Maven acted so weird when I mentioned her name after the wedding. They knew the whole time and didn't tell me.

I'm going to *kill* them.

I shove my phone in my pocket and grab my room key, ready to head to the hotel bar. Six hours of panel discussions, reluctant socializing, a mandatory flag football tournament tomorrow, and a fuck ton of confusing thoughts swirling in my head has me needing a drink.

When I make it downstairs and see the bar empty from any conference goers who might want to chat my ear off, I sigh in relief.

I slide onto a stool at the end of the counter and reach for the drink menu. Before I can even take a look at the specials, a blonde bartender is in front of me, showing off her cleavage, and getting close enough to make me uncomfortable.

"Hi," she says, and I barely look up. "Can I get you something?"

"A whiskey neat, please," I say.

"Rough day?"

"Just a day."

"You don't strike me as a hard liquor kind of guy."

"Guess I'm a man of surprises," I draw out.

"Anything I can do to help?"

"Alcohol would be nice."

She laughs like I'm the funniest guy in the world and heads for the well of liquor bottles. "I have to take care of another couple then I'll be back."

I pull off my glasses and pinch the bridge of my nose. I can't tell if I want to sleep for ten hours or take ten shots. A combination of both would be nice, but with six videos to edit and post and a week to go until our first preseason game, there's not enough time.

This drink will have to do.

A laugh comes from across the bar, and I startle at the sound.

I thought I was in here alone, but when I shove my glasses back on and scan the room, I don't like what I find.

Avery.

Sitting on a barstool, talking to some guy.

Some guy who has a suit with shiny cufflinks and slicked-back hair.

There's something about him I immediately don't like. It's the arrogance, maybe, in the way he talks with his hands and leans into her space. He's dominating the conversation while she's sitting there stone-faced with a stiff spine.

I guess that laugh was fake.

I watch them and try to decipher their body language. Her shoulders are angled away from him. His hand is on the counter and keeps inching closer her. I must watch them for too fucking long, because she turns her chin to the right. Her gaze meets mine, and her mouth pops open in surprise.

I narrow my eyes and pretend to scratch my nose, subtly flipping her off in the process. I expect her to throw some sass back, that same attitude she had when we were texting earlier, but she doesn't.

She blinks then looks away, and I feel like a goddamn creep for intruding on a personal moment.

"Whiskey neat," the bartender announces, grinning when she sets the drink in front of me. "Anything else I can get you, sweetie?"

"I'm all set."

"My name is Dana if that changes."

I lift the glass and take a long sip. It's rich going down, smooth with a hint of spice, and I savor the taste of a drink I hardly ever order.

Tonight seemed like a good night to enjoy it, though, and I'm going to blame Avery goddamn Sinclair.

My phone buzzes, and I'm surprised to see a message from her on the screen.

I turn it face down and stare at the back of the case.

I should ignore it.

I don't have any reason to answer.

We're not friends. She's clearly here with someone else, but there's a pressure on my chest nonetheless, heavy and resolute that won't ease up as I wonder what she has to say.

Hell.

I grab my phone.

AVERY

Stealing my drink order?

ME

Someone has to.

Is that a light beer you're drinking? Disgusting.

AVERY

You say disgusting, I say delicious.

Nice video you posted today, by the way. Too
bad it only got 10,000 likes.

ME

Better than the TikTok you posted last night.
The one that only got, what? Four thousand
views?

AVERY

I'm flattered you keep such close tabs on me.

ME

Like how you're obviously not enjoying yourself
over there? Do I need to intervene?

She types out a response, but instead of sending it, she sets her phone down. She picks up her glass of shitty beer, turns her attention back to the guy still talking her ear off, and ignores me.

I'm not jealous.

That's never been a personality trait of mine, but something that feels a lot like anger courses through me when he touches her arm and leans in close to whisper in her ear.

I finish my drink like it's a splash of water.

"Want another?" Dana asks.

I mull it over.

It would be smart to walk away.

It would be smart to go back to my room and mind my fucking business like I've been doing for years, but Avery looks miserable. My throat is tight, and try as I might to get my ass out of my seat, I can't move.

Maybe I want to be the hero instead of the sidekick for once.

Maybe I want to be the guy who swoops in and saves the day when everything is turning to shit.

Maybe I'm torn up that the woman I had such a good connection with is also the woman who makes me want to pull my hair out.

Maybe I *am* jealous that she's giving her time to someone who's clearly not worthy of it.

Maybe, despite agreeing to a bet and wanting to beat her in this game we've found ourselves in, I still want her to give her attention to *me*.

This is too fucking confusing.

"Sure." I shrug. "I'll have another."

I ignore the smile that gets tossed my way and glance at the television. I don't know how long the two of them sit there talking like they're best fucking friends, but it's long enough for me to sip three whiskeys and a glass of water.

The alcohol goes down easier each round. My head starts to pound. A dull ache spreads across my forehead, and I can't look at my phone without my vision swimming. It buzzes in my hand, and another text from Avery pops up.

AVERY

I didn't know you were a lightweight.

ME

Now who's keeping tabs on who?

AVERY

Hard not to when you're sitting there staring at
the television and looking like a lost dog.

ME

Going to put me on a leash?

AVERY

Depends on if you've been bad.

I blush furiously and gulp the rest of my drink down before I answer.

ME

Didn't want to leave you alone with that prick.

AVERY

I thought you hated me.

ME

Hating you and being a nice guy when you clearly look uncomfortable are not mutually exclusive.

AVERY

Can we pause our feud again? I want to leave, but he won't stop talking.

I'm off the stool before I read the end of her message. I throw down a couple twenties and round the corner of the bar, stopping in my tracks when I see his hand on her leg.

I clear my throat. Relief floods Avery's face when our eyes lock, and she mouths *thank you.*

"Sorry to interrupt." I lean my elbow on the bar. "Can I borrow Avery for a second?"

"She's a little busy, man," the guy says. "You can talk to her tomorrow like all her other fans."

"That wasn't meant to be a question, *man.*" I grab his shoulder and pivot his upper body so he's looking at me. "I'm going to borrow her for a second. A lot of seconds. If she feels like coming back, she will. If not, I'll make sure she gets to her room safe and sound."

"You her boyfriend or something?"

"Or something." My eyes land back on Avery. "Ready?"

"Yeah." Avery shrugs her purse up her shoulder and jumps off her stool. "Nice to see you, Peter. Have fun tomorrow."

The guy looks her up and down, a wolfish glint to his eyes. "You too, Ave. You look good."

Ave.

These two have a history, and I'm not sure I want to know what it is.

She flips her hair over her shoulder as she passes me, and I get a whiff of her perfume. I ignore the glare the douchebag of the century is tossing my way and follow her to a quiet alcove that leads to a patio.

Avery pushes the door open and walks outside. I join her and lean against the railing, unsure of what the hell to say.

Silence hangs between us.

I scuff my shoe on the ground and stare at the patch of weeds trying to grow in the cracks of the concrete.

"Thank you," she finally says.

"No problem."

She rests her elbows on the railing, mimicking my pose. "That's my ex."

"He's downright delightful," I say.

"He normally sends his assistant to these things, and when he found me this morning at breakfast, I dropped my plate of cantaloupe." Avery rolls her lips together and shakes her head. "Anyway. You didn't have to do that, and I appreciate you stepping in."

"Is this the one who was mean to you?" I ask.

"Yeah." She lifts her chin to the sky. "I was so excited about how well my job was going. I was proud of all the things I created, and he hated my success. It was a hard break up."

I glance at her, and I hate how pretty she looks in the burnt orange of sunset. "Did you report him?"

"Position of power, remember?" Her smile is weak, and I've never wanted to fight someone like I want to fight him. "It's why

I jumped at the chance to head to Baltimore. It meant a clean slate and not getting involved with anyone in the organization. I could make a name for myself without being known as the woman Peter dumped—even if most people knew it was because I was becoming too successful."

"Peter." I scoff. "He looks like a Peter."

"Do you have something against Peters?"

"My high school bully was named Peter. They like to make people feel small so they can seem big. That asshole in there was doing the same thing."

"I'm sorry." Her face softens. "That's cruel."

"You have nothing to be sorry for. You didn't stick my head in a toilet."

"No. I'm only going to stand outside your office with a boombox and play the Thunderhawks song on repeat for hours."

"I feel bad for you if that's the best you got. I wear noise-canceling headphones when I'm in the arena. You can play that damn song all you want; I'm never going to hear it, and you're just going to look very, very stupid."

"Guess I'll have to come up with a better idea." Avery taps my foot with hers. "Thanks for pausing the feud for a few minutes. We can resume our hatred for each other tomorrow."

"I plan to show you how much I dislike you during the flag football tournament. Hope you packed your sneakers, Sinclair. I'm going to mop the field with you," I say.

Her smile curls around the edges. I hate that I feel it in the center of my chest. "I might have been a ballerina, but my senior year in high school, I played on the flag football team too. I was MVP."

"That's going to make leveling you to the grass even more fun. I haven't played a day of flag football in my life," I say.

Avery laughs. "Oh, this is going to be fun. If my team wins, you better believe I'm going to post the video of your downfall and share it on social media so everyone can see. I'll tag you so you can repost it, if you want."

"Like I won't hack into your computer and delete the files."

She seems to pause at that, and says, "Can you really do that?"

"Guess you'll find out," I say.

"Maybe you'll find some new material to use while you're sorting through everything." She fixes the sleeve of her blazer and checks her watch. "I need to run. I'm meeting some women for dinner, and I don't want to be late."

"Do you want me to walk you there?"

"And why would you do that?"

"You said we're going back to our disdain for each other tomorrow. You didn't say anything about the rest of the night."

She bites her bottom lip and hesitates. "I think I'm good. Thank you, though."

"No problem. Have fun."

"What are you doing the rest of the night?"

I shrug. "Hanging out in my room and reading. These are the last few days of solitude I'll have before the season starts, and I want to make the most of them."

"This time next week, we'll be one sleep away from the preseason."

"And we both know how fast the year goes from there."

"Mhm." Avery pushes off the railing. "Bring your A game tomorrow for the flag football tournament, Duncan. You're going to need it."

She disappears inside, and I spend way too long staring at the sky.

It's better than the alternative, I guess, which would be to stare at her.

Our history of bickering and arguing tells me I can't have her.

So why the fuck do I want her even more than I did three nights ago?

SEVENTEEN
AVERY

REID

Ready to lose in flag football today?

ME

This feels normal. Why did we ever think we
liked each other?

REID

We did like each other. We just don't like
internet each other.

ME

You're right.

REID

That was fun to hear. Say it again.

ME

Never.

REID

How was dinner last night? Did you get food
poisoning?

ME

Nope. No food poisoning.

REID

Bummer.

ME

How was your reading?

REID

I was asleep by ten. Can't ask for a night much
better than that.

I sent my plan for ticket sales to my boss, by
the way, and he said it looks great.

You don't stand a chance at winning our bet.

ME

Sometimes, the work does what it's supposed
to do all by itself.

See you on the field!

SUNSCREEN. Eye black high on my cheekbones. Mascara and nude lipstick.

I pull my hair into a high ponytail and smile at my reflection.

I love playing sports as much as I love watching them. It's the duality of being a woman; of dressing pretty with our hair and nails done to go somewhere nice then, after, throwing on a T-shirt and tennis shoes, ready to sweat for a couple hours.

We can do both, and it's going to be so much fun to kick Reid's ass while I'm wearing makeup.

Gosh.

Reid.

I've tried to avoid thinking about him, but it's nearly impossible.

The way he jumped in to help with Peter.

How he didn't ask questions and just *did*.

His blush when I jokingly asked if he had been bad—I could see the pink on his cheeks from across the bar.

When I got back from dinner last night, I had to hide my vibrator in my suitcase under a pair of socks so I wouldn't use it to get off to the thought of his hooded eyes and his rough voice saying my name.

I felt safe with him, like I could tell him everything about my past and he would listen without judgment. Like I could explain why I throw myself into work until I'm run ragged and on the brink of exhaustion and he'd understand.

I've never felt that way with anyone before.

Our relationship is complicated now, though. Any future of an us—casually, romantically—has gone out the window, and sharing deeply personal parts of myself doesn't fall into the category of *rival I want to crush like a fucking bug*.

Even if I do still think he's hot as hell.

I grab my phone off the bathroom sink and upload the video I've had in my drafts folder for a week. It's a rapid-fire interview shot in our stadium tunnel, a montage of different players giggling when they see the tiny mic I'm holding and answering the questions I lob their way.

There are four hundred likes within seconds.

Comments start to pop up, and as someone who learned very early in her career to *never* read the comments, I ignore the criticism coming from **@urmomlovesme69**.

A new DM lands in my inbox, and I already know who it's going to be before opening it. It's like clockwork with us; one of us posts, the other messages.

I head to the Titans' Instagram to see if he's lying.

It's flooded with content Reid probably spent hours perfectly curating. Photos from their Super Bowl victory a couple years back. Their new jersey reveal and the schedule drop from earlier this summer. A "day in the life" at training camp and a tour of UPS Field, the stadium where they play, through the eyes of a GoPro attached to the back of a golden retriever.

I know it all like the back of my hand except for the latest post in the top left corner of the page.

The asshole *did* upload a video seven minutes ago, a creative digital time-lapse of all the Titans' logos to celebrate the start of their fortieth season.

Dammit.

Reid rarely posts in the morning.

I'll never tell him this, but he's not the only one who's memorized schedules. When you're in an industry of mass consumption and immediate gratification, everything you share has to be strategic and intentional.

It's obvious he's deviating from his routine—the routine I bet he loves—just to get under my skin, and I'm not going to let him.

I slip my room key in my crossbody bag and head down the hall. I take the elevator to the ground floor and say hello to a handful of women I've met at other leadership conferences, gradually making my way to the lobby.

The rosters for the flag football teams are random, and I grin when I see my friend Erin, a marketing director from LA, is one of my teammates.

"Good morning." She hands me a large iced coffee in a to-go cup. "I thought you overslept."

Nope. Just lounging in bed, not *imagining Reid running his hand up my thighs with that cute smile of his.*

It's difficult to actually hate the guy when I can still remember the orgasms he gave me and how goddamn nice he is.

"Just a few minutes behind schedule." I stifle a yawn to sell the act and sip the drink, grateful for the caffeine. "How are you? When is your flight tomorrow?"

"Early." She groans and fixes her baby-blue tennis skort. "Whoever thought it was a good idea to hold this conference five days before the season is an idiot."

"Agreed. Hey, I need your opinion on ticket sales. What have you found to be the most successful way to get new season ticket holders and fans in the stadium doors?"

"I can't really answer that question," Erin says. "The waitlist for our season tickets is eighteen years. These people are die-hard fans, and it blows my mind they're willing to wait that long to watch the games in the stadium rather than on TV."

"Eighteen years? Holy shit."

"Boston is twenty. No one gives up tickets to dynasty franchises. Even if they die, they just pass them on to a son or daughter in their will and the cycle continues. Why are you asking about tickets? Have I finally convinced you to go into client services and start interacting with people in real life?"

"No." I laugh. "I agreed to a stupid bet with someone. It's kind of a long story. Anyway, our single game numbers are strong, but I need to hone in on the long-term commitments."

"You should think about offering promotions. Our season ticket holders get priority for playoff games. We also offer full-year and half-year plans. The half-year folks don't have access to every game, but they do get to keep the same seats whenever they come to the stadium. It makes them feel like they really belong, you know? And, that way, you can alternate their games with another fans' half-year plan and you've sold both seats for the season."

"Shit." I pull out my phone and type out some notes. "That's brilliant. Thanks, Er."

"We also try to spoil them. VIP tours. Meeting the players and the cheerleaders. Early access to the arena. Dedicated parking. Those are the things that make coming to the game a hassle, and by mitigating those stressors, they're more likely to renew."

"I love all of these ideas. I have a meeting set up with our head of ticket sales when I get home, and I can't wait to run these suggestions by him. This is so helpful."

"Who is your bet with?" she asks. "And what do you get if you win?"

"The guy who runs the Titans' accounts."

"The cute one with the glasses?" she asks, and I nod. "Wait a minute. I thought you two didn't like each other."

"I met him in real life." I blush and tuck a piece of loose hair behind my ear. I can't stop fidgeting, and thinking about Reid is making me nervous. "I also might have slept with him twice before realizing who he was?"

It comes out like a question, like I'm unsure if I straddled his lap and fucked him as the sun started to come up. As if I'm close to forgetting the feel of the smooth plane of his palm against my throat and the low timbre of his voice when he told me he wanted to bend me over the bed so he could watch my ass bounce.

I need to be hypnotized so I can get these thoughts out of my brain. They're not good for my well-being.

"Oh my *god*, Ave. How was it?" she whispers.

Incredible.

Best I've ever had.

"Nice," I settle on, and she bursts out laughing. "It was nice."

"You are such a bad liar. He rocked your world, didn't he?"

"Okay, fine, yes, it was amazing. None of the men I've hooked up with before have known how to use their fingers like *that*. And he talked to me during it, which I love."

"The quiet ones are always the most fun." Erin's eyes gleam, and a smile dances on my lips as she voices what I've caught myself thinking on multiple occasions. "It's like they study up on you and know exactly what drives you wild."

"Yeah." My throat is dry, and I try to swallow. "Exactly."

"Amazing is certainly better than nice," says a deep voice at my back. "Glad to know you enjoyed our time together so much you can't stop talking about me. You're the one who is obsessed, aren't you, Sinclair?"

I spin around. The cup in my hand goes flying. Coffee splatters on everything in a four-foot radius, and *Reid* is standing there, his hands in his pockets and his glasses covered in brown liquid.

I really shouldn't be affected by hearing my last name this much.

"Shit. *Shit.* What are you—how—" I grab a stack of napkins and start to dab his chest before I realize what I'm doing and step away. "Hello."

"If you wanted to touch me that badly, you could've just asked." He pulls off his glasses and wipes the lenses clean with one of the only dry spots on his shirt. "I might have said yes."

"What are you doing here?"

"Meeting in the designated spot for flag football." Reid stares at me. "And listening to conversations about me."

"You weren't supposed to hear that," I say.

"Clearly."

"I'm sorry about your shirt. You scared me."

"I'll announce my presence more loudly next time." Reid takes the napkins I'm holding and uses a clean one to wipe the drops of coffee from his neck. "But for now, I'm leaving."

"It's not an airport," I say, and his eyebrow lifts. "You don't have to announce your departure."

A ghost of a smile grazes his lips. His eyes drop to my throat, to the spot he's kissed and sucked and licked, before bouncing back to my face. "See you out there."

When he leaves, I finally let out a breath and look at Erin.

"This just got interesting," she says.

I tuck a flyaway behind my ear with a shaking hand. "What did?"

"The flag football tournament. We're playing their team

first"—she nods at Reid's retreating form—"and I have a feeling it's going to be a lot of fun."

<hr>

I wipe the sweat from my forehead and stand at the line of scrimmage. When the whistle blows, I take off down the field, catching the toss our quarterback lobs my way. The flag on my left hip gets pulled, and I smile at the guy on the opposing team when the play is ruled dead.

"Nice catch," he says.

"Thanks," I say. "The faster the game goes, the faster I can take a cold shower. I thought my Florida blood was made for this heat, but Vegas in July is a different level of hell. Even with air conditioning in an indoor stadium."

"It's unbearable here." He crouches down and waits for the hike. "I'm up in Minnesota, and I can't wait for winter."

When the ball is snapped, I sneak past him, looking over my shoulder and anticipating the pass. Our quarterback launches the ball—an impressive throw from a guy in stadium operations without any playing experience—and just as I catch it, I run headfirst into something.

"Shit," I exclaim.

Arms wrap around me, enveloping me in a tight embrace I recognize as warm and familiar. I squeeze my eyes shut, anticipating the tumble to the ground. I brace myself, but what should be a hard fall is soft, safe, and I blink, confused.

"Fuck," someone groans.

"Oh my god." I glance down and find Reid underneath me with dirt on his cheeks. Crooked glasses, a lock of hair curling on his forehead. Twisted lips, wrinkles between his eyebrows, and my heart pounds in my chest. "Are you okay? Are you conscious? Did you hit your head?"

"Barely." He opens his eyes and looks at me, his gaze a little rattled. "You're lethal, Sinclair. What is it with you and tackling me? The hallway at the hotel, now this? It's becoming a trend, and I'm not sure I like it."

"It was an accident, I swear. Your lip is busted." I touch his mouth, the split part of skin that's turning red with blood, and he hisses in pain. "How did that happen?"

"You have very pointy elbows."

"And here I thought you were planning on leveling *me* to the ground today," I whisper absentmindedly, my eyes still on his swollen mouth.

"It played out very differently in my head." Reid taps my waist, and the contact is searing. "I know it was an accident. If you were going to take me out, I know you'd be more creative."

"How would you want to go?" I ask. "If you had the choice."

"You're going to use my answer to plot my death, aren't you?"

"I might. Maybe it'll happen in two weeks. Maybe it'll happen in two years. I'm going to keep you on your toes, Duncan."

"It's kind of you to ask my preferred method of demise so I'll be comfortable. Something quick and painless, please. I'd like it if we could stay away from quicksand," he says.

"Quicksand?"

"I'm still fairly traumatized from Robin Williams getting sucked into the floor in *Jumanji*."

"How were we allowed to watch that movie as children?"

"What are you talking about? I watched it last week."

I hold back a laugh and shift on top of him, wiggling my hips and trying to find steady ground. He closes his eyes again, a breath coming out in a strangled huff.

"What?" I ask hurriedly. "Are you in pain? Do you need a doctor? Should we do the concussion protocol?"

"I'm fine. Just—" His throat bobs, and his hold on me eases.

"When you do *that*, I can... I can feel you. And my memory is too good to forget the last time you were on top of me so soon."

"Oh. *Oh.*" My cheeks flame. I can feel him too, between my legs, close to the spot he slotted in days ago. Slightly hard, his long length presses against the inside of my thigh, and I shouldn't like it as much as I do. "Right. That, uh, did happen."

"I'd like for you to get off."

"In front of everyone? Seems a little presumptuous. I'd probably be kicked out of the game. Might lose my job, too. Is that your end goal here?"

"Off me," he mumbles, and it's laced with embarrassment. "But not yet. I know people are watching."

I glance over my shoulder, and our teams are starting to head our way. "Yup. They're definitely watching."

"We'll just tell them you're obsessed with me. It would be the truth," Reid says. "Could you, ah, stay there for a second longer? So I don't look like a total creep? I do know how to control myself, believe it or not, and I'm mortified to be in this position. I just—"

"I know you do," I say, and the tension on his face lessens. "I'm flattered, honestly. Not many girls can say they can turn a guy on by knocking the wind out of him. Are you reciting the alphabet backward?"

"I'm listing gaming systems from oldest to newest. It's working."

"What are you up to?"

"Nintendo 64. 1996. God, I loved *The Legend of Zelda: The Ocarina of Time.* I need to play it again."

I giggle. I can't help it. My shoulders shake, and soon he's laughing too.

"Permission to pause the feud?" I ask.

"Pretty sure it paused fifteen seconds ago when my dick got hard, Avery."

"Do you need more time to... cool down?"

"Christ." Reid laughs again. "No, but I do need some time to move away and change my name. I'm putting this under the newly created list of Things We Can Never Talk About Again. Once there, it's not allowed to be brought up."

"Only if we can add me publicly praising your sex skills to it too."

"That worked in my favor, though," he says, and when I give him a look, he drops his head against the grass. The tendons in his neck strain, and I see the faint remnants of a hickey I left behind earlier this week, the light purple still branded on his skin. "Fine. It's added."

"I can't get off you until you let me go," I say. "You're, uh, holding me pretty tightly, so let me know when you're ready."

He props up on an elbow and glances at where we're joined. His arms around my waist, locking me in. My hands on his chest, bracing myself from collapsing totally onto him. It's a position from the bedroom we're mimicking in real life, but this is more intimate. Sensual, almost, in the way his thumb runs along the waistband of my athletic shorts. In the way it almost feels like he lifts his hips, wanting to be closer to me.

I'm not sure he realizes he's doing it.

"This cannot get any more humiliating." Reid takes a deep breath. "I did that so you wouldn't get hurt in the fall. I wasn't trying to cop a feel or anything like that. I wouldn't—"

"You're more of a drop-to-his-knees-in-the-hallway kind of guy," I tell him, and the pink on his face turns crimson. "This is so not your usual play."

Before he can say anything else, we're swarmed by a group of our teammates. A dozen questions get lobbed our way, and our private interlude is interrupted.

"Are you both okay?" Erin asks, squatting down and checking us for injuries. "That was a hard fall."

"I think we're fine," I say. "I was making sure Reid didn't have a concussion. All is right in his head."

"Debatable," he says, and I smile.

I use his chest to push onto my feet and stand. I brush the grass and dirt off my clothes and offer him my hand. "Ready?"

"Hang on. There's something I need to do first." His lips pull into a grin, and he reaches for me. I don't know why I expect him to thread his fingers through mine in some romantic gesture, but he doesn't. Instead, he yanks the flag off my belt and holds it in the air. "You didn't convert on fourth down. It's our ball, Sinclair. Thanks for the great field position."

I gape at him, and when he pops onto his feet and elbows my side, I'm not sure if I want to murder him or kiss him.

I'm afraid it might be both.

@footballindc

Back on home soil, which means my work of taking you down can really begin.

@dcfootball

Glad to know you weren't really trying before. I was going to be disappointed if that was your best effort.

@footballindc

Which method of communication do you prefer me to annoy you from? Instagram DMs? Text messages? I could probably find a carrier pigeon.

@dcfootball

I don't care how you prefer to annoy me, because I'm just going to ignore you.

@footballindc

You're pretty quick to respond right now.

@dcfootball

Only because it gives me something to think about other than my Uber driver's horrible highway skills.

@footballindc

Desperate times call for desperate measures, huh?

@dcfootball

Something like that.

Are you back in town?

@footballindc

Wait a second. Do you care about my well-being?

@dcfootball

Maybe it's morbid curiosity. Maybe I'm out of my mind.

@footballindc

I took a later flight. I land in two hours.

@dcfootball

You paid for Wi-Fi? You can't stay away from me, can you?

@footballindc

Something like that.

"I'M HERE." I drop my duffle bag on the floor and take off my sneakers. My legs ache from being cramped on an airplane for four and a half hours, and the thirty-minute car ride to Dallas's apartment from Reagan International didn't help the stiffness in my knees. "Where are you all?"

"Living room," Maverick yells. I walk down the hall to find them on the couch playing *Call of Duty*, and neither him nor Dallas look away from the television. "Fucking children. Goddammit. I hate this fucking game. What's up, Plant Daddy?"

"Is June here?" I ask. "Or Maven?"

"Maven is at a meeting. June Bug is with Shawn. He's giving her a tour of the stadium." Dallas tries to look around me, but I step to the side and block his view. "What's going on?"

"We're getting reamed by idiot children," Maverick whines. "Can this wait?"

"When the *fuck* were you going to tell me the Avery I hooked up with at your wedding is the woman behind the Thunder-hawks accounts?" I practically yell, and they both gape at me. I've never raised my voice like this, but I'm so pissed off. So angry about being kept in the dark, yelling seems like the only way to get my point across. "The woman who's been antagonizing me for years is the same one who gave me the best orgasm of my life, and you didn't think this was *important fucking information* to share with me?"

"Oh, shit. That's why her name is familiar." Maverick tosses his controller on the cushions and puts his hands behind his head. "Talk about a fucking plot twist."

"You knew about this?" I seethe, and he gives me a guilty grin.

"Dallas might have mentioned it when he was drunk at the reception. Screamed it at me, actually." Maverick shrugs. "It slipped my mind until now."

I turn my attention to Dallas, the real instigator of this whole fucking secrecy pact. "How long have you known?"

"Known what, exactly?" he asks, clearly playing dumb.

"That Avery works for the Thunderhawks."

His eyes dart around the room and he fixes the brim of his hat. He clears his throat then clears it again, and I know he's stalling. Looking at the ceiling instead of me, he says, "How much are you going to hate me if I say a while?"

"How long?" I repeat.

"Since Maven first joined her rec soccer league."

"That's fucking years!" I collapse into a recliner by the fireplace and bury my face in my hands. "I am so mad at you. At both of you. At all three of you, actually."

"Whoa, hey. I'm an innocent bystander," Maverick challenges. "Don't lump me in with this guy."

"I don't understand what the big deal is. You two had a good time when you hung out. Why does it matter if she happens to be your biggest rival? Can't handle someone better than you?" Dallas teases, and my blood boils.

"The big deal is you *lied* to me," I say. "You know how much she pisses me off. You've heard me complaining about her and you decided to not mention her identity, because, what? This is some joke to you?"

"Whoa." Maverick blinks. "A decade of friendship and I've never heard you so fired up about something."

"Not only is there the lying and blatant disregard for my feelings, but there's also our jobs. Avery and I are working against each other in a small market, and in our industry, you have to be quick on your feet," I say, steamrolling past Dallas trying to interrupt me. "She's annoying as hell with her blazers and short fucking skirts. It's distracting, and I can't afford a distraction right now. I met with my boss last week and he outlined metrics I need to hit this season. I have too much at stake to get caught up with someone like her."

"But—"

"And, because I'm an idiot, apparently, I agreed to a stupid bet with her." I stand up and pace around the living room, an energy buzzing through me. "If I lose, not only am I going to probably be unemployed, but I'm also going to look like an idiot."

"A bet? What kind of bet? Oh, is it a sex game?" Maverick asks. "Emmy and I play those all the time. She usually wins. I guess technically *I'm* the winner, because I'm the one who—"

"Fuck off," I groan, exasperated. "This is important. I really hate that you kept something from me. I don't like having a good time with someone only to find out she's the bane of my fucking existence after the fucking fact."

"We should've taken a shot every time he dropped an F-bomb," Maverick whispers to Dallas. "We'd be wasted right now."

Dallas turns off the TV. "I'm sorry for lying. In my defense, I never thought you two would meet. Meet again, I guess I should say. Did you actually meet the first time years ago or did you only see her from across the field?"

"Is this the time for fucking semantics?" I ask. "I saw her from across the field, and that would've been the perfect opportunity to say, 'Hey. By the way. That's the woman who drives you up a goddamn wall. Make sure to not sleep with her at my wedding.'"

"She's not your type, and I saw no situations where you two would ever be in the same space again. You didn't go to any other soccer games, and it didn't seem necessary to bring it up after the fact. We haven't played the Thunderhawks in the time that she's worked there, so it's not like you'd see her in the stadium. Besides, she's not your usual type. I didn't anticipate you two meeting at a bar and again at the wedding. I thought this was all avoidable, especially because you're never the one to approach women," Dallas says.

"I do *not* have a type," I stress. I rake a hand through my hair, frustrated. Irritated. Confused and goddamn annoyed. "I've never had a type."

"Bullshit," Maverick laughs. "You definitely have a type. You prefer quieter women. The sure things, not the risk takers."

"Avery isn't quiet," Dallas adds. "She's loud and she's spunky and she's this person everyone gravitates toward. If you saw her in a crowded room, you wouldn't look twice at her."

"That's not true." I rub a hand across my chest. I couldn't stop staring at her the night we sat the bar. I couldn't stop staring at her at the wedding, either. "And thanks for confirming you've met her before. Another fucking lie. Is our whole friendship a fucking sham to you?"

"Christ, you're being dramatic. I've spent some time with her when she's hung out with Maven. I think she's a fucking delight, and you did too until you realized who her online persona was," Dallas says.

"I don't understand what the big deal is." Maverick stretches out his long legs. "You like this woman. Who gives a shit who she works for?"

"I don't like her," I say.

"What was that about her distracting skirts you mentioned earlier?"

"This skirt she wore one day at the conference." I stare off into space and scratch my jaw. It showed off her shiny anklet. Her tan legs that looked a mile long under the pleated leather, and the back of her thighs. I imagined pushing her against a wall again. Slipping my hand under the hem of it and finding out what color lace she had on that day. I hate the damn thing. "I couldn't focus to save my life."

"And what color was Emmy's dress at the wedding?"

I squint at him. "Pink, right? No, wait. Dark blue."

"Both wrong. It was green. Point is, you do like this woman. You pay attention to her, and you've talked about her for years. You two have always had a connection, whether it was positive or negative. And then you meet her in person and she's someone you've dreamed about? You can't make this shit up."

I snap my mouth closed, and it takes me a second to come up with a rebuttal.

He's not wrong. I've always felt drawn to her. Pulled to her, in a way. When we spent two, three hours at the bar talking, it felt like I knew her. Like I had known her for a lot longer than the time it took us to sip our drinks.

I guess I have.

We never divulge personal pieces of ourselves when we message back and forth on the official accounts for our teams, sticking to ambiguity and anonymity, but every now and then, small things sneak through.

The casual mention of her favorite cuisine (Thai). Learning she likes to run. Her favorite player on the team (their backup QB) and her favorite holiday (Thanksgiving).

By themselves, it's not enough to figure out who she is. Now though, it makes sense why we had an immediate connection in person; it wasn't our first time interacting.

"Real Life Avery and Internet Avery are two different people," I explain, coming to my senses. "I have no clue how the two can intertwine."

"Do they have to?" Dallas shrugs. "Y'all can find a way to exist as two separate parts."

"I don't know if that's even possible. There's deep-rooted annoyance when it comes to her. I'm not sure I can look past it, especially when she's determined to do anything she can to piss me off. She blatantly told me she's planning my takedown," I say.

"Oh, and you're so innocent?" Dallas asks. "You're probably plotting her demise."

"No." I scowl. "I'm not."

"Sounds like foreplay and flirting to me," Maverick says.

I stop pacing, an idea coming to mind. I glance at Dallas and grin. "I need you to do me a favor."

"I'm not helping you break the law," he draws out. "I have a kid to raise, and I'd like to go on my honeymoon before I go to jail."

"Is getting access to the Thunderhawks' stadium breaking the law?" I ask.

"How am I supposed to get you into their stadium? With the key I have?"

"A signed jersey, actually," I say.

"Why not buy a ticket to their preseason game?" Maverick suggests. "It's on Thursday night, and you all don't play until Sunday. Then you're already in."

"I need access to Avery's office without a ton of people around." Dallas's eyes widen, and I shake my head. "Relax. I'm not doing anything bad, and no one is going to get hurt. I promise I'll behave. It's only rubber ducks, not weapons of mass destruction."

"I don't know who the hell this Reid Duncan is." Maverick stares at me proudly. "But I like him. He's fun as shit. Can I come?"

"Only if you stay quiet," I say, and he pumps his fist in the air. "You're a terrible liar, and I don't want you to give us away."

"I swear." He puts his hand on his heart. "I'll uphold your request, Plant Daddy, and treat this with the utmost care and responsibility."

"Will you sign a jersey for me, Dal?"

"Yeah." He sighs. "Only because I know this is you suppressing feelings for her, not actual fighting."

I snort and pull up the Thunderhawks' website. There has to be someone I can track down to help me out. An impressionable intern or someone who knows the resale value of Dallas's signature.

"She wants to wring my neck. I want to mute her on every possible platform where she has a digital presence and find a way to hack into her computer so I can see all of her upcoming ideas. Not sure that's the best definition of romantic," I say.

"Ah. Young love." Maverick sighs. "Those days were fun."

I roll my eyes.

If there's one thing I've learned to do well, it's keep my emotions in check. Staying balanced and even-keeled.

I might be the guy who loves relationships. The guy who craves a partner and someone to do life with, but that doesn't mean I'd ever fall in love with Avery fucking Sinclair.

That would be playing with fire.

A stupid game with stupid prizes, and the last thing I want to do is burn.

Not when I can win and watch her catch flames on the way down.

I SLIDE into the booth across from Maven and bat away the leaves of a plant sitting on the windowsill.

Plant.

Reid.

Motherfucker.

Do I need to be reminded of him everywhere I go?

I glare at her and fold my arms across my chest. "You have some explaining to do."

She hides behind a menu. "Hi, Ave. Good to see you too. How was your trip? And the keynote speech? I bet you smashed it like the boss bitch you are."

I pluck the list of specials from her hand and drop it on the seat next to me, glaring at her some more. "When were you going to mention Reid, your husband's best friend and the guy I've hung out with three times now, is also the man who works for the DC Titans?"

"Did that not come up?" Maven twists a lock of blonde hair around her finger. "To be fair, I didn't know you two were seeing each other until the morning after the wedding. He mentioned your name, and I didn't tell him who you were."

"Why not?" I press. "You know our history. I've sat in this exact booth and bitched about him being a giant pain in my ass. You're telling me you went home, sat in your living room, and listened to him do the same about *me*?"

"The only reason I kept my mouth shut is because up until two weeks ago, I never thought you two would see each other again, let alone hook up. You and I are both so busy during the NFL and NHL seasons, *we* hardly see each other. There didn't feel like a need to bother you with this trivial knowledge about who Dallas's friends might be. I didn't imagine *this* ever happening." There's sincerity there, in the quiver of her tone and the regret in her eyes. "How *did* it happen?"

I tell her about the date at the bar and sit back in the booth, letting out a sigh. "Throw in the wedding and the flowers he bought me, and I was so caught off guard when he tracked me down in Vegas."

"Reid is an all-in guy," Maven says. "When he likes something, when he truly cares about someone, he'd move mountains to make them happy. He never went through a phase where he slept with dozens of women. He doesn't do one-night stands, and I don't think he's ever asked for a woman's number. When he's committed, he's *committed*, and I promise what he did leading up to this big reveal was genuine. The guy you met is the *real* Reid Duncan. I'm convinced the him on the internet is an act."

"That one-night stand fact got mentioned when he pinned me against a wall." I blush at the phantom touch of his hand under my dress. His mouth on my skin and the look in his eyes when he dropped to his knees. I blow out a breath and fumble with the pitcher of water the server brings over, pouring myself a full glass. "I was impressed."

"You don't have to give me details, but I *need* to know. How is he in bed?" she asks.

I gnaw on my bottom lip. Heat inundates my body, and I'm thrown back to that night.

To both nights.

When Reid got in his groove, he *really* got in his groove. Tender and sweet with surprising forwardness. Hot and heavy with a side of funny and laid-back. Small puffs of laughter as we tried to find a comfortable position, followed by the soft brush of his thumb over the curve of my ass.

"Fantastic," I blurt out, half expecting him to pop out from behind a corner and hear me flattering him again. "He was—" I fiddle with my necklace and ignore the aching sensation in my chest. "The best I've ever had."

It wasn't just the physical act of fucking; it was everything that came with it.

After, when he grabbed a damp rag and cleaned me up.

During, when he asked for permission before trying anything new.

Before, when he took his time, using his hands, his mouth, his fingers to carefully explore parts of my body that haven't been touched in years.

I like that we made mistakes.

I like that it wasn't perfect.

I like that we laughed.

I like that he wanted me so badly, he almost got off from getting me off.

"*Really*?" Maven asks.

"Really," I say.

"I knew it. Emmy, Maverick's fiancée, and I always say we think Reid could be the best of the three boys in bed. He's very thorough, and he gives his full attention to things. I figured that applied to taking care of women too." Her grin is sly and catlike. "I bet he has notes on what you like."

"Oh, he does not. I believe he has notes on how to annoy the shit out of me, though, because he does that way too easily."

"They might not be written down, but he definitely does. If you two hooked up again, he'd do everything you'd want without having to ask. When are you hanging out with him next?"

"Never. The only communication we're going to have is through our official accounts," I say. "And the occasional text to irritate each other."

Maven snorts. "Okay. We'll see how long that lasts."

"It's going to last. Before I found out who he was, we agreed on a friends with benefits arrangement. A mutually beneficial physical and casual relationship where we could put our emotions aside and indulge in each other. We can't do that now. It would be too messy. Too complicated, and I don't want complicated. Work is my number one priority. It's going to stay that way, no matter how good his dick is."

"Interesting how you can't stop talking about his dick," she teases.

"Hush," I say.

My phone vibrates on the table.

Reid's name pops up on the screen, and I'm convinced the bastard attached a recording device to me so he knows when I'm talking about him.

REID

Attachment: 1 link

Spoiler alert: this Buzzfeed article said the
Titans have the best social media accounts in
any major sport.

ME

I'm not clicking that. It's probably a virus to
hack into my phone.

REID

You're starting to catch on, princess. Nice job.

ME

I hate that nickname.

REID

Do you really?

ME

Yes.

REID

Noted. Won't use it again.

Attachment: 1 image

There. A non-virus photo, just so I can say I told
you so.

The picture downloads, and there's a bright laptop screen. Four sticky notes attached to the corners of the computer with numbers on them and a stack of pens to the left of the keyboard. Reid's hand is in the center of the frame, the sleeve of his sweatshirt covering his arm almost all the way to his palm, save for the middle finger he's holding up.

ME

Appreciate the photo evidence.

I'm having lunch with Maven. Please stop
bothering me.

REID

Tell her I'm mad at her.

ME

Tell her yourself.

"Reid is mad at you." I ignore the next two messages that

come through and tuck my phone away in my purse. Out of sight, out of mind.

"He'll get over it." She tosses the menu to the side and reaches across the table. She takes my hand in hers and squeezes. "I'm sorry for not telling you who he was, Ave. It was a shitty thing to keep from both of you. I've always said you deserve to be happy, and I guess I got all caught up in the post-wedding love, you know? Like, now that I have it, I want you to have it too."

"I know, Mae, and I love you for that. But I'm happy. I have the best job in the world. I have good friends. I get to live this life I've dreamed about for years. Every night I go to sleep grateful, and I'm not sure how it's supposed to get much better," I say. "If Reid worked in finance or real estate, or, hell, even marketing like he claimed to, I'd consider giving it a shot. I've been down this road before, and it never ends well. The sports world is small, and I can't put myself in that position again."

"It makes me happy that you're happy." Maven smiles and lets go of my hand. "Am I allowed to say the thing I've been thinking since you all figured out who you were talking to online?"

"You know I'll tell you anything," I say. "What do you want to know?"

"I can't help but wonder how much better the sex with Reid would be now. You all have tension and history. Emmy told me hate sex is the best, and I'm kind of jealous I'm never going to get to experience it."

"Don't be jealous. You have a man who worships you, Mae. You don't want to know the kinds of things that are out there. The alternative is scary," I say. "Besides, I wouldn't know. I'm never going to have sex with that man again."

A string in me pulls taut at the thought of Reid on his knees again.

Being pushed against the shower wall as he looked up at me with a shy smile on his mouth.

Another bouquet and my hands on the headboard as he whispered my name.

I don't like him, but fuck if I don't like the thought of *that*.

@footballindc

@footballindc

Do you like music?

@dcfootball

Is this a Twenty Questions game?

@footballindc

No. Just wondering. Your song choices for your posts are always interesting.

@dcfootball

I like Bowie.

And I'm not embarrassed to admit my goddaughter has me listening to Ella Wright's new album on repeat. I'm a fan.

@footballindc

Glam rock and pop music? Interesting combo.

@dcfootball

What about you?

@footballindc

I'm a big Ella Wright fan. I find her music personal. We're the same age, and we've been through similar life experiences: bad breakups, etc. She's relatable.

@dcfootball

Figued as much.

You've used her music on your last three posts on TikTok.

Have fun losing the season opener tonight. I never thought I'd be actively cheering for the Miami Whales, but here we fucking are.

@footballindc

Can't wait until we win so I can call you every hour on the hour and play our song.

@footballindc

@footballindc
You're going to hate me by morning.

@dcfootball
Already do hate you.

@footballindc
Are you sure about that?

@dcfootball
Pretty sure, yup.

@footballindc
Then why are you still talking to me?

xoxo

REID

"DID you really have to wear all black?" I look Maverick up and down and sigh. "You look fucking ridiculous."

"Of course I had to wear all black. This is a special operation. I couldn't show up in fucking blue." He switches the bag he's holding to his left hand and smiles at the Thunderhawks intern walking us through the stadium. "So, Barry. You like football?"

"Yes, Mr. Miller, sir. I do. I also really like hockey. And basketball too. All sports, I guess. I want to work for a team full-time one day." Barry holds the jersey Dallas signed close to his chest. "My brothers are going to be so jealous I met you. We're diehard DC sports fans. I've been going to Titans games since before I could walk. They didn't have any positions open when I wanted to apply, so I came to the Thunderhawks."

"We really appreciate your help," I say. "Avery is a good friend, and we wanted to celebrate her anniversary with the team by decorating her office before the game."

"I wish I had an office. I clock in and stand in a corner until halftime." Barry leads us down a hallway and turns left. "I still make it fun."

"I bet you do, Bar." Maverick messes up his hair, and Barry

beams. "Now, look. This is a surprise, so can you do us a favor and not mention it to anyone that we were here? It would ruin the dramatic effect, and if there's one thing you need to know about me, it's that I *love* drama."

"Of course, Mr. Miller." He stops us in front of a door and taps his keycard on the reader against the wall. "Take as long as you need. When you're ready to head out, you'll go the same way we came in."

"Do you have a card with your information on it?" I ask. "If you email me your résumé, I can pass it along to HR."

"Wow." Barry pulls a wrinkled piece of paper from his pocket. He jots down his name, number, and email, and hands it to me. "Thank you so much. You two are so nice. Avery is lucky to have such great friends."

"Yeah." Maverick throws an arm over my shoulder. "She really is. Especially Reidy Boy here. He knows how to treat her right."

"I'm going to kill you," I say out of the corner of my mouth, shrugging him off. "Thanks, Barry. We appreciate it."

I open the door and step inside Avery's office. It's small, about the size of my office at UPS Field, and overlooks the twenty-yard line. There's a desk in the middle. Pictures on the wall and a stack of personal development books on a small bookshelf.

I see her everywhere; the cardigan draped over the back of her chair. The vase of sunflowers and lilies. There are fifteen different pens spread out across a planner, and a whiteboard shows all the content she has planned for the next month.

For half a second, I wonder if I'm making a mistake by invading her personal space. I wonder if I'm violating some unspoken boundary in our game by storming into her safe haven and causing chaos.

"What's wrong?" Maverick takes a seat on the leather couch

under the window. A groan slips out of him, and he drops his head against the wall. "Fuck, this is comfy. And she has a blanket too? I wonder if she sleeps here."

My chest pinches tight.

I don't like the thought of her being here alone. Late at night and curled up on a piece of furniture that's too small, even for her. I don't like the idea of her working herself to the bone. I don't like imagining a world where she doesn't take care of herself when the season starts, putting others first instead.

"Nothing." I shake my head and clear the cobwebs. "Okay. We have two hundred ducks, but the goal isn't to hide them all. I've numbered them, and we're going to put a random number in random places. The idea is that she'll think she's found them all, but then the next duck will have an even higher number than the last one. She'll have no clue how many she's searching for, and it's going to piss her off."

"This is a good prank," he says. "How many do you want to put out?"

"Sixty-five. It won't be so obvious at first that she's going to find a ton."

"Are you scared about how she might retaliate?"

I sit in her chair and open a drawer, setting one of the ducks on top of a stack of sticky notes. "I'm absolutely *terrified* of the stuffed animals she could fill my office with."

Maverick and I work in silence. We freeze every time we hear voices outside the door, wondering if it could be her. She could walk in at any moment, and knowing we could get caught makes me hide the last dozen ducks quick as hell.

"Done." Maverick dusts off his hands and fixes his black baseball cap. "It's too bad we don't have a camera set up to see her reaction. What other ideas do you have?"

I arrange her pens and planner back in their original position. "I can't tell you everything. What if she interrogates you?"

"Yeah, because Avery and I hang out all the time," he says dryly. "I would do damn well in an interrogation. I—"

A laugh travels down the hall and interrupts him.

It's followed by footsteps and two people talking, and I panic.

"Shit. *Fuck*. That's her," I hiss.

We hear a muffled, "I'm going to get my water bottle and planner and I'll be right there, Marjorie."

I look around the room, frantic. There's a door to the left of her desk, and I grab Maverick by the collar. I shove him inside the closet and slip in after him, cracking the door just as she walks inside.

It's so dark in here, I can't see a damn thing.

It's small, too, and Maverick and I are practically on top of each other. He pulls out his phone and holds up his screen, looking at me.

Oh my god, he mouths. *What do we do?*

Wait, I mouth back. *She said she's going somewhere else.*

I have to pee.

I narrow my eyes and run my hand across my neck, telling him to cut it the fuck out. He flips me off and I ignore him, peering out the small sliver of space between the door and the door jamb.

I spy Avery on her computer. She clicks into a folder, humming a tune under her breath that sounds reminiscent of "Heroes" by David Bowie. When she closes out of the document, her background comes to life, and it's a punch to the gut.

It's her sitting next to a hospital bed occupied by a man who's the spitting image of her; the same cheekbones. The same wrinkles around their eyes. The same dimple, and I can *hear* their laughter through their matching smiles.

It must be her dad, and suddenly, this all seems stupid as hell.

She powers down her computer and grabs her phone. I

watch her pull up a text thread, and she drums her finger along the curve of the screen, deep in thought. She types out a handful of sentences before she deletes them, stares at the ceiling, then starts again.

Maverick taps my shoulder and points at the door. I shake my head and hold up a finger, letting him know it's going to be another minute.

What is she doing? he mouths.

Texting someone.

Tell her to hurry up.

Avery finally finishes her text and stands. My phone buzzes in my pocket and my heart jumps in my chest. I check to make sure she hasn't heard us and open the message.

> **AVERY**
>
> Does your stadium have headphones available
> to fans?

I frown and type out a response.

> **ME**
>
> What?

Her fingers fly across the screen, and my phone buzzes again.

> **AVERY**
>
> I have someone asking if you all provide
> headphones for fans who might be
> overstimulated, or if they need to bring
> their own.

> **ME**
>
> Why are they asking you?

AVERY

Because I posted about our game against the
Titans next Sunday, and they were curious.

I look out at her again, and she's staring at her phone,
waiting for me to answer.

ME

Oh. Yeah, we do. We also have a sensory room
available for use during games.

AVERY

Really?

ME

It was installed a few years ago. A step in
making sporting events more inclusive.

I've checked it out a few times. It's quieter than
my office at halftime, and there're always
people in there. Wish it was the norm.

I wait for her to lob a witty one-liner back at me. Something
sarcastic and full of sass like she usually does. Her mouth curves
into a soft smile, the hint of her dimple popping on her cheek as
she bites her bottom lip.

AVERY

Thanks.

ME

Yep.

She holds her planner to her chest. When she walks around
her desk, she stops in her tracks and stares at the rubber duck
hiding behind a mason jar that's being used to hold pencils.

"What the hell?" she mumbles, turning the duck upside down. She snaps a photo of it and sets it back down. "Weird."

I sigh in relief when she leaves the office and shuts the door firmly behind her.

"Oh my god." Maverick collapses to the floor. "That's the longest I've ever gone without talking."

"How did you survive?" I ask.

He pushes the door open and gulps down a breath of air. "It was tough."

"She found the first duck. The plan is in motion."

"I wonder how long it's going to take before she realizes it was you."

"Probably not long," I say. "Who else would do this?"

"A secret admirer?" Maverick shrugs and stands. "We can blame the intern. We can say he's obsessed with her."

"You're so fucking weird. I think you're missing a few screws."

"That's fucking rich coming from the guy who spent the last few minutes hiding in a closet for a *prank*. Maybe you're the secret admirer. You're halfway to being obsessed."

"Fuck you. This was stupid, wasn't it? What thirty-four-year-old goes around planting plastic ducks in someone's office?"

"I don't know, man. Probably the same guy who smiled when she found them," he says.

"I did *not* smile," I challenge.

"Sure you didn't."

"You're delusional."

"Don't worry, Plant Daddy." He winks. "Your secret is safe with me."

TWENTY-ONE

AVERY

"THANKS FOR HELPING ME," I whisper to Maven and June as we walk into the Titans' administrative offices at UPS Field. "I've been finding rubber ducks around my office all week and I know it was that redheaded jerkwad. This is payback."

"Don't thank me. Thank Shawn for being my godfather and giving me access to this area. He doesn't know what we're using it for, so let's pretend it's for a good cause," Maven says.

"It is for a good cause," I say. "Men should be put in their place every once in a while. Inconveniencing them is one way to do it, since they're a constant inconvenience to me."

"I can't wait for you to meet Emmy," Maven says. "You two are going to be best friends."

I look around the corner and see the coast is clear. I don't know why I thought I'd find anyone; with only an hour to go before kickoff, everyone is on the field for warmups. The place where I *should* be, but I'm sneaking around in the name of revenge.

Reid fucking Duncan is going down.

Maven leads us down the hall to Reid's office, holding June's hand and swinging their arms back and forth. "How did you get all this cellophane into the stadium? Bags aren't allowed."

"I addressed it to myself and sent it to the stadium last weekend. I put on a Titans polo I bought at the gift shop to make it look like I worked here and picked the box up from guest services twenty minutes ago, passing it off as athletic tape," I say.

"You are *ruthless*. I should probably talk to Shawn about stricter security measures, but I'm freaking impressed," she says.

"Are we going to wrap everything in Uncle Reid's office?" June asks.

"Everything we can touch," I tell her, wiggling my eyebrows. "I want it to take him hours to clean it up."

"He's going to be *so* mad. He hates when his things aren't organized. One time, Uncle Mav put his plants in a different order, and he spent two hours putting them back in place." June grins over her shoulder and looks me up and down. "I like you, Avery."

"I like you too, kid. Thanks for being an accomplice."

Maven opens a door and motions us inside. She locks it behind us, and I survey Reid's office.

"Where should we start?" Maven asks. "I'm a first-time cellophaner."

"The desk. It's going to take the longest." I put the heavy cardboard box on the floor and open it with a pair of scissors, handing them each a roll. "We'll go in opposite directions so there are multiple layers. Makes it harder to cut through."

"Have you done this a lot?" June asks. "You're practically an expert."

"I've been known to TP a house or two in my youth. This isn't much different," I say, and I walk to Reid's desk.

There's a photo of him, Dallas, and Maverick in the corner. All three of them are in tuxedos, devilish smiles on their mouths, and their arms slung around each other. The frame to the left is a group shot with a younger June, and everyone is in Halloween costumes.

"That's when we dressed up like *Frozen* characters," June tells me. "Uncle Reid was the snowman."

"He and Maverick have been in your life a while, haven't they?" I ask.

"Since I was born. I didn't have a mom when I was younger, and when people teased me, I didn't really care. I had three dads, and three is much better than one. Uncle Reid helped me learn my ballet dances."

"He did?"

"Yeah. We practiced in the living room. He's not very good, but he did his best. He even wore a tutu. Uncle Mav took me shopping while Daddy was playing football. We always had fun. Then Mom got here, and everything is even better."

My breath catches as I stare at the photograph. I imagine Reid holding June as a baby, rocking her to sleep and singing her a lullaby. Letting her braid his hair and paint his nails. Being her bonus dad so she never felt alone, and showing up when she needed him the most.

Fuck him for being a nice fucking guy.

"Three is better than one," I agree. "And four is better than three. You got lucky with the best mom in the world, June. She's letting you help me make a mess out of Reid's office, and that's cool as heck."

The three of us work in tandem. We climb over each other, going around and around the metal legs and laminate tabletop until his desk is a mess of plastic.

The chair and computer are next, and it takes two more rolls and Maven wrapping his stapler for us to finish the job.

"Wow." June presses her finger into the wrappings and giggles. "That's going to be hard to undo."

"This is brilliant, Ave," Maven says. "I wish we could watch the game here. Look at this view."

"I wish I could see his reaction." I grab a sticky note from a stack on his bookshelf and draw a heart followed by my initials. I tack it right on his covered computer and step back to admire our hard work. "There. Now it's perfect."

"Guess we need to get going," Maven says. "It's almost game time."

"Can we tell Uncle Reid we need something from his office during halftime so he has to come in here?" June suggests. "Then he can see the damage we did."

"I like the way you think." I ruffle her hair. "Will you film it for me?"

"Duh." June grins proudly and knocks her knuckles against mine.

"I have to run. Duty calls. Text me later?" I ask, and Maven hugs me tight.

"I will. Have fun, Ave. Are you wearing your sunscreen?"

I hug her back. "Yes, Mom. Enjoy your air-conditioned luxury box and pray for me. I'm going to sweat my butt off down there."

I make it to the sidelines after the coin toss. I high-five the Thunderhawks players, going through the special handshakes I have with a few of them, and filming their huddle.

"You seem distracted, Avey baby," Justin Jones, star running back and longtime veteran, says. He rests his elbow on my head and looks down at me. "You good?"

"I'm great." I beam at him. "How many yards do you think you're going to have this afternoon?"

"I hope over a hundred. I played like shit last week and we lost, so I need to make up for it. Just wish the Titans weren't so damn good."

"You and me both," I grumble.

It's our first time playing them, and the possibility of getting blown out frays my nerves.

Our defense takes the field, and I let myself lapse into five seconds of looking for Reid. I do my best to be casual about my search, a quick glance to the Titans' sideline instead of a full-on scan of the stadium, but I can't find him.

He must be hiding somewhere.

I'm going to give him shit for that later.

By halftime, I still haven't seen him, and I don't know if I should be worried.

I don't know if I'm *allowed* to be worried.

We might have different takes on how to do our jobs, but it generally involves being around during gameplay, and he's not here.

When the Titans run back onto the field to start the second half, I make a bold choice and head for Dallas at the fifty-yard line.

"Hey, Avery," he says as I approach him. "What's up?"

"Have you seen Reid?" I ask.

He glances around. "Now that you mention it, I haven't seen him since warm-ups. He said he needed to answer a call, but he never came back."

"Okay. Thanks. Forget I asked."

"He might be in the sensory room. He goes up there some-times," Dallas says.

"Do you think—" I snap my mouth closed and gnaw on my bottom lip. "How much would he hate me if I went up there and looked for him? Probably not any more than he hates me right now, right?"

His smile turns softer. "Take the elevators to the fifth floor. Make a left, then you'll see the door marked on your right."

"Cool. Thanks. Have a good second half," I say.

I follow Dallas's instructions, tapping my foot the whole

elevator ride up. When the doors open and I stand in the empty hallway, I wonder if I'm making a huge mistake. This is something a friend would do, and we are *not* friends.

There's a voice in my head telling me to check on him, though.

Encouraging me to put one foot in front of the other and move forward until I'm knocking and waiting for him to answer.

"Come in," says a muffled voice.

I open the door and find Reid inside. He's sitting on a bench, his shoulders curled inward and head hanging low. His hair is messy, and there's a hint of sunburn on the back of his neck.

"Hi," I say. His spine straightens and he turns to look at me. Eyes a little glazed over, he blinks like he's slow to catch up with who I am and where he is. "Is it okay if I'm here?"

Reid looks back at the wall with a single nod. "Sure."

I step all the way into the room and take the bench opposite him. The last thing I want to do is crowd his space, to make him feel like I'm here to save the day. I smooth my palms over my leggings and cross my feet at the ankles.

"Are you okay?" I ask after a beat of silence.

"I'm fine."

I nod even though he's still staring at the wall, not at me. "Okay."

He sighs, heavy and resigned. "My dad called before kickoff. I shouldn't have answered—I don't normally answer. But my parents are getting older, and I'm afraid if I don't pick up..." He trails off, his eyes shuttering closed. "I hate the guy, but I try my best not to be a total dick."

"I understand," I say, and he cuts his gaze my way.

"You do?"

"Yeah." I fix my ponytail to give my hands something to do. "My dad had cancer. He went in for a routine physical and walked out with a stage four colon cancer diagnosis. He fought hard for a few months, but I missed the call that told me he passed because I was busy with work. I've never forgiven myself."

Reid's eyes hold mine. "How long—"

"Four years ago. A few months before I took my job with the Thunderhawks, actually."

"I'm still so sorry. I'm going to sound like an asshole complaining about my dad when yours—"

"Just because our experiences are different doesn't mean yours is less important."

He rubs his arm, and I have the urge to touch him there. To put a steadying hand on his shoulder so he's not alone.

"Permission for a temporary feud pause?" he asks.

My lips twitch. I like this game we're playing. "Pause granted."

"I talked about my dad a little bit the night we met at the bar. He's been disappointed in me for years. Lately, though, he's in this phase where he's constantly telling me how I've thrown my life away. All the opportunities I've wasted because I want to sit behind a phone and videotape athletes. What I do isn't good enough, and it's never going to be good enough for him."

It comes out in a rush of words.

A tangle of emotions claw at his voice as he squeezes his eyes shut and sighs again.

There's a crack in my heart at the weight he must be carrying. The burdens he holds and the battles he's fighting. The thoughts he might have about not being enough, all because of a career that brings him joy.

"Maybe he's projecting," I say. "Maybe it doesn't have anything to do with you."

"My therapist said the same thing. That might be true, but *fuck*, it hurts to hear how much of a waste of space I am. To hear how much better my friends are than me because they're professional athletes."

I get up and take the seat next to him. Our thighs press together, and he doesn't pull his leg away.

"Have you shown him how good you are at your job?" I ask. "The ideas you come up with and how you're helping the Titans bring in more fans and boost the team's earnings?"

Reid tips his chin in my direction. "Trying to find ways to compliment me, Avery? Two weeks ago, you called my videos boring. Why the change in your tune?"

I nudge his ribs with my elbow. "Don't flatter yourself. We've pressed pause, remember?"

"It doesn't matter how much I'm helping the team make. It could be *me* earning that money. He has no clue how it works; I'm a glorified influencer to him."

"Have you set up boundaries?"

"Yeah. Then my mom gets upset, and I cave. She wants us all to be a family, and the more distance I put between us, the sadder she is."

"You're not in charge of her feelings, Reid. You're in charge of yours. You need to do what makes *you* happy. Otherwise, you're going to be miserable for the next thirty years." I pause and rub my thumb across my bottom lip, a smile forming there. "Plus, I've seen you play flag football. You're shit at it. Staying off camera is better for everyone's health."

His laugh is a deep rumble. Soft, and a sound I hate myself for wanting to hear again. It echoes around us, and I laugh too.

"I'm going to ignore that last comment and pretend you stopped talking twenty seconds ago when you were complimenting me." Reid knocks his knee against mine, and I feel the touch everywhere. "I'm sorry for unloading all of this on you."

"It's okay. It's distracting me from the game." I gesture to the television in the corner of the room. "We're losing, and I always want to turn off the comments when I have to be the one to post the final score."

"I'd be concerned about the people who like to lose." He glances at the screen and snorts. "Dallas has a fantastic leg. I can't keep coming up with captions that praise his kicking ability. I'm out of good ideas."

"Maybe you all should stop being so good."

"Beating you is way more fun." He looks me up and down. "Where did your box go?"

"My box?"

"The thing you were carrying into my office before the game."

"I'm not sure I know what you're talking about," I say innocently.

"You are the least subtle person I know."

"You saw me and didn't stop me?"

"Nah. You looked excited. I thought I'd let you have your moment," he says.

"Oh." A smile breaks free across my mouth. "Okay, so... I kind of turned your office into a cellophane kingdom."

Reid drops his head back and laughs again. Louder this time, and his shoulders shake. His grin is bold and beautiful, and I hate him a little bit.

Goddamn him.

Goddamn him for being attractive.

Goddamn him for being vulnerable with me.

Goddamn him for wearing those glasses.

"Fucking genius. I had that on my list to do to you," he says.

"Sorry I beat you to it. Are you mad?"

"Are you mad about the rubber ducks?"

I've been finding them *everywhere.*

In drawers and under stacks of papers.

In between books on my shelf and in the bottom of coffee mugs.

They keep appearing, and every time one pops up, it feels like Reid is there. Like he's sitting on the couch behind me and watching me.

"No," I say. "I'm not mad. How many did you hide?"

"Guess you'll have to keep looking to find out."

I take a breath. The silence grows thick, and I turn my body to face him. "I didn't know about the call. I wouldn't have—"

"That's not how feuds work, Avery. You have to commit to it. You wanted to wrap my desk in cellophane, so you did. And I'm sure it looks great."

"Want to go see it?" I ask.

His eyes light up, a spark of an ember behind the green. "I'd be honored."

We leave the sensory room and head down the hall. When we get to his office, Reid scans us in, and I follow him inside. He bursts out laughing at the wrap job we did, and I can't help but grin.

"Thoughts?"

"I'm impressed," he says. He pulls a pen from his pocket. He tries to stab the plastic, but it doesn't give. "I'm going to need a knife to get this off."

"I made sure your scissors were inside a drawer. I had to make this as difficult as possible for you," I say.

"I've always loved a challenge."

I stare at him, and he stares back.

The noise from the crowd on the other side of the wall swells to a dull roar, and someone must have scored. We might be in the Titans' house, but Thunderhawks fans showed up strong today. A win in enemy territory would be nice.

A win against *Reid* would be nice.

"I should—"

"Are you—oh. Sorry. What was that?" Reid asks.

"I was going to say I should go. The game and—"

"Right. Yeah." He nods and steps out of the way, giving me a wide berth. "Of course."

"Resume the feud?" I ask.

His eyes bounce to my lips then shift to my neck. "Resume the feud," he repeats.

I don't know how it happens.

I don't know who moves first.

If questioned, I would deny any involvement, but maybe it's me.

Maybe it's him.

Maybe it's both of us, drawn together like magnets, an inevitable pull I can't resist no matter how hard I fucking try.

One minute, we're six feet apart.

The next I'm pressed against his door. His hand is tangled in my hair and his mouth is on mine. He's kissing me like a man starved, and I'm not doing a goddamn thing to stop him.

TWENTY-TWO

REID

IT'S ONLY BEEN a few weeks since I last kissed Avery, but *fuck*, I missed it.

I missed the glide of her tongue against mine. The way she grabs my shirt and tugs on my collar. How she moans into my mouth, a sound that makes my cock jump in my pants.

Fucking Christ.

I lift her by her thighs and push her against the door. I pull back and look at her, her eyes wide and her lipstick smeared. There's a smudge of red on her cheek, and I drag my thumb through it, bringing it down to her chin.

"Tell me to stop," I murmur. She whines, a desperate noise that has me close to losing my mind. "Tell me I should put you down and ask you to leave."

Avery's throat bobs with a slow swallow. "I don't want you to stop," she rasps.

"You don't?"

"No." She shakes her head and lifts my chin with the tips of her fingers. "Remember how I told you to ruin me, Reid?"

"Vividly," I say, and her grin is lethal. A sexy smirk I want to feel on my cock.

"Do it again," she whispers. "Forget the bet. Forget how much we don't like each other. One more time, then we'll go back to not getting along." She rolls her hips, a lazy circle that nearly has me forgetting my name. She's dangerous, wielding too much power. "I'll beg for it if you want me to."

Every rational part of my brain tells me to back up. To walk the fuck away and leave her here so I can get back to my job. Back to my responsibilities and away from the five-foot-five distraction in front of me.

But then she reaches between us. She cups me through my joggers, and I know I don't stand a goddamn chance at winning anything tonight.

"Fuck," I mumble. My nose bumps against hers, and I put a hand on the door. "Want to make you fucking come. Want to watch you."

"I'd like that." Avery tilts her head back, her neck bared and her pulse jumping in her throat. Her thumb strokes down my length and I buck forward, crowding her space. "You know how to make me feel so good, Reid."

"Sofa," I grunt. Pulling us away from the door, I move to the couch, glad she kept it cellophane-free. I set her on the cushions and drop to my knees, making quick work of her high-top sneakers and socks. "Too many goddamn clothes."

"This wasn't part of the plan," she says, and I'm distracted when she takes off her shirt. When she tosses it aside and leaves behind a pink bra, tan skin, and full tits. "I didn't think I'd see you today."

"Now look at you. Who knew the beauty queen was such a needy fucking slut?"

"So what if I am?" Her cheeks blaze, and there's fire in her eyes. "Are you going to do anything about it?"

"A lot of things. Let me lock the door first."

"Do you have frequent visitors during games?" Avery asks, tugging off her leggings.

I pop on my feet and flip the deadbolt. I shove an extra chair under the handle for good measure. I dare anyone to fucking try and interrupt us.

"Consider me extra cautious. I—"

The words die in my throat when I turn around and see her. Legs tipped open wide. Wearing nothing but a pair of underwear, the same pink shade as her bra, which now lies in a tangle on the floor. I wonder how many different varieties she has. Maybe one in every color of the rainbow, and I want to see them all.

One hand sits low on her hip while the other pinches a nipple between two fingers. The palm at her waist curls in the band of her underwear, but I grip her wrist. I shake my head and stare at the damp spot on the front of the lace.

"Leave them on," I say, pulling off my shirt.

She licks her lips when I untie the drawstring of my joggers and shimmy them down my hips. I kick off my shoes, the sneakers lost to the world and a problem I'll worry about later.

For now, I can only look at her. At the flush on her skin and the way her mouth parts when I shove a hand in my briefs and give myself a jerk.

Her eyes roam down my body. There's an appreciative haze behind the brown when her attention snags on my thigh tattoos. The ink she licked and kissed and sucked, and the thought of her doing it again has my grip tightening around my cock.

"God," she whispers, reaching for me. "I like your body so much."

"You do? I'm not built like any of the players and—"

"Come here." She eases my hand out of my briefs and presses my fingers into the seam of her underwear. The fabric is drenched and the soft spot between her legs is ready for me. "Do you feel that? It's because of you. Because I get to be here with you. And I want you to make me feel good in the way that I like. You've been thinking about me, Reid, haven't you? When I'm in my bed and touching myself, I think about you too."

"Do you touch yourself when you're talking to me?" I ask, my voice thick with lust. I have to know the answer. I have to know if she's lying there naked and spread out on her bed. "Do you have two fingers in your pussy when you're telling me how obnoxious I am? Do you use a toy and wish it were me?"

"Yeah," Avery whispers. "Why do you think it takes me so long to answer you sometimes? Because I'm teasing myself. Trying to drag it out so I can come right as you say something to me."

Everything is a blur.

Color sparks behind my eyes.

Liquid heat rolls through me.

I can't think of anything else except this fucking bombshell in front of me, a willing servant to her every ask.

I kneel in front of her and give her legs a gentle tap. She scoots her ass to the edge of the cushions. I rest one of her feet on my shoulder, nudging her legs open even wider. My thumb rubs a slow circle over her clit as I hike her underwear up high on her hips.

Her moan is low and long, a sign that I'm starting off strong.

I've remembered everything she likes.

Every place she likes to be touched, and I imagine I'm there with her in her room.

Sitting and watching her, her back arching off the mattress and sweat on her skin.

Fuck, I like to watch.

"What do you use?" I ask. "What kind of toy?"

"Jealous of some silicone, Duncan?" It comes out fractured, cracking around the edges when I hook my fingers in the lace and pull it to the side. She's just as pretty as I remember. Wet and perfect and fucking ready for me. I lean forward and lick over her entrance. "Oh, *fuck*, Reid."

"How can I be jealous of something that can't do this?" I part her with my tongue. A groan slips out of me when she tugs on the ends of my hair. When her nails sink into my back and urge me closer, leaving little half-moon marks behind as she grinds into my face. "You're saying my name, aren't you?"

"I'd be saying it a lot more if you—*oh*."

I bite her thigh to shut her up and sneak a glance up at her to gauge her reaction. Favorable, I think, based on the way she's panting. On the way she's reaching forward, pulling my glasses away from my face and tossing them to the side.

Fuck 'em.

I'll find them later.

"Open your legs a little wider so I can—ah, fuck, baby. There you go. That's so good."

She melts at the praise. Her knees drop open, and I give her underwear a hard tug. The lace rips in half, and I'm tempted to put the pieces in my pocket for later.

I push two fingers inside her, knowing she doesn't want to draw this out; we both have places we need to be. We both have a goal of getting off, not giving a damn about how we get there.

Avery's face scrunches up in a quick burst of tension before she relaxes, her shoulders sagging and her hips rolling. I don't want her to think she's doing all the work, but I want her to do what makes her feel good. What'll tip her over the edge so I can have her again.

Fuck, the ways I want her.

"Remind me why I don't like you?" She gasps when I swirl my tongue over her clit and she lifts her hips, asking for more. "The details slipped my mind."

"Something about the internet." I add a third finger, vaguely wondering if we could work up to four, and she cries out. Her thighs close around my ears, and suffocation by her pussy sounds like the only way to go. "Can't remember. Don't give a shit. Let me fucking eat, Ave. Please."

I press a hand to her stomach, keeping her in place so I can fucking *feast*.

"I used to hate when guys went down on me." She twists a lock of my hair, and my dick aches. "They never seemed to know what they were doing. You do, though. *Fuck*, you make me feel good, Reid."

"What do you need, Avery?" I ask, sitting up on my knees. "Tell me what you want. You want me to talk you through it? You want me to tell you how tight you feel around my fingers? How I wish I could take a picture or a goddamn video of this so I could get off to it later tonight and tomorrow and the day after that?"

She bites her bottom lip, her eyes fluttering closed and her breathing turning ragged. "I'm close. I—"

I lean forward so I can get deeper in her, hitting the spot I know her toy can't touch. I want it for myself, some jealous rage ensnaring me when she bobs her head in a nod, telling me to keep going. To not stop.

I don't think I'm ever going to stop.

Her satisfaction is the only thing I can think about. When she clenches around me, pre-cum leaks in my briefs. I dip my head and press a kiss to her knee. To her thigh. To her neck and her forehead.

"You gonna let go for me, Sinclair?" I murmur low in her ear.

There's a pain in my chest when our eyes meet. When I see desire there and the way she trusts me. It's quick, a burst of lightning before it's gone and she's coming undone on my hand.

Her words are choked sobs. It sounds like she's saying my name, but I can't be sure. I watch as her body convulses. As her legs tremble and her grip on my hair slackens.

When I know she's finished, when I've gotten everything I can from her, I pull back. I hold up my hand, her cum on my fingers and dripping down to my wrist, and I tap her bottom lip.

"Open," I say, and she does. I press down on her tongue and moan when she licks my fingers clean. "God, you're a vision."

Avery's smile is shy and soft, and I wonder how we got here.

Her, naked and sated.

Me, close to following after her.

The seventy thousand fans on the other side of the wall screaming for their favorite football teams have no clue what just happened in here.

"Pause the feud?" she asks.

I nod and suck in a breath. "Yeah."

Her grin turns wicked. Her nails scrape down my chest to my briefs. "Get over here and fuck me, Reid."

I THOUGHT I was the one running the show here.

I thought I was in control, but when Reid steps out of his briefs and strokes his cock, eyes burning into mine, I think I might have misjudged the power balance between us.

I'm staring.

He knows I'm staring, and I know he knows I'm staring. I can't look away from him though, and a whimper escapes from me when he rubs pre-cum down his thick length.

I yank his wrist and he collapses on the couch next to me in a mess of limbs. I ease him onto his back and throw a leg on either side of his hips, hovering above him and looking down at the man underneath me.

"What do you want, Avery?" he asks, and my name sounds like a wicked sin. "The nice guy you met at the bar? Or do you want me to fuck you like I hate you?"

"You know the answer to that." I lean over and brush my mouth against his. A tease, a taste of what could've been. "I can tell by how hard you are that you absolutely *despise* me."

"We should make this quick," he says.

"That eager to get rid of me?" I put my palms on his chest

and run my fingers through the dusting of red hair. "You sounded like you were enjoying yourself a few minutes ago."

"I am." Reid hisses when I reach down and wrap a hand around his shaft. I sit up on my knees and drag his head against my entrance, coating the tip. His eyes widen. "Shit. *Shit.* Avery. Hang on. Stop."

I wince and pull back. "What did I do wrong?"

"Nothing. *Nothing.* It's not you." He tips my chin so I can look at him. "I, ah, don't have any condoms here. I didn't think I'd need a box of Trojans at work. I've never fucked anyone in my office before."

I glance at his desk. "Even if you had some, they'd be impossible to reach."

"I'm sorry. I didn't think about that before we started."

"What if—" I shake my head. "Never mind."

"What?" He cups my cheek. "Talk to me. Tell me."

"What if we didn't use one?"

"Is that something you'd be okay with? With me fucking you like you were mine?"

"Yes," I say right away. "I've never not used one, but with you, I'd be okay with it. I'm on birth control."

"I'd be okay with that, too." His voice is heavy. Caught in his chest and barely audible. "Have you been with anyone since we last—"

"No. Have you?" I ask, my pulse quickening as I wait to hear his answer.

"Just you," Reid says. "No one else."

I lean forward and rest my hands on the arm of the couch. He takes a nipple in his mouth at the same time he slides two fingers in me, and I groan at the stretch. He doesn't let me sink into the feeling for very long. He pulls out of me and uses my arousal to wet his cock, and I watch him.

"Okay?" I whisper, and he nods.

"Perfect," he answers, looking at me.

I lower myself onto him, just the head first, followed by his first few inches. Our inhales are sharp and jagged, and I brace myself as I sink down, deeper and deeper until our hips press together.

We touch anywhere we can reach. His hand on my lower back. Mine moving to his hair, scratching his scalp as I lift off him then settle him back inside me, the deep satisfaction of feeling so full, so perfect, so *right*; an itch scratched and everything I could ever need.

Our bodies move together. It's not a competition, but a collaboration.

A push and pull to get each other to the blissed-out pleasure we both so desperately want.

Time comes to a standstill, and I ignore everything except *him* and the rhythm we slip into, like we've done this a thousand times.

"Fuck," Reid draws out. Perspiration beads on his forehead when I increase the pace, riding him like my life depends on it. "*Avery.*"

One of his hands sits at the base of my throat, his thumb stroking up my neck. He presses into my windpipe with the slightest bit of pressure, and I groan in pleasure at the feeling of being trapped. Of having nowhere to go but down on him again.

There's too much sensation.

Too much *Reid*, and it's never been like this before.

Not with him.

Not with anyone else.

We fuck like we won't get the chance to again, rough and hungry and on the precipice of something magnificent. In the blink of an eye, Reid flips us, my back landing on the plush leather cushions and his hips between my knees. He lifts my leg over his shoulder and slams back inside me, filling me beyond belief.

There are so many things I want to say, but I can't find the words. They get stuck in my throat when he splays his hand out over my ribs. When he traces the underside of my breast with one set of fingers and traces my clit with the other. When he cants forward, a determined glint in his eyes, and bites my bottom lip.

"Hate sex might be my favorite thing," I pant, and his mouth curls into a grin. "Much better than what we did before."

"You should piss me off more often." He pinches my nipple, twisting it between his fingers until the pain melts to ecstasy. "Stop holding back, Avery. Give it to me."

"You give it to me first," I say, lifting my hips so I can meet his thrusts. He groans, and my grin matches his. "There you go, Reid. That's so good."

"Where—" He swallows and tips his head back. Another low groan works its way free. "Should I—"

"Anywhere." I grip his shoulders and rock him into me. "Wherever you want."

"Fuck. *Fuck.*" He pulls out of me and grips his cock, jerking himself up and down. His other hand fumbles between my legs, circling my clit as he comes on my stomach. "*Avery.*"

Hearing him say my name does me in.

I follow after him, stars in my vision as he tips me over the edge to a second orgasm. My skin is on fire. I'm electrified and alive, and I moan through the bliss his touch brings me.

Our synchronized breaths fill the quiet room, but neither of us move.

We stay like that, touching and toeing the line of euphoria until I open my eyes and find him looking at me.

"What?" I ask.

Reid shakes his head. He sits back on his heels and gently

moves my leg from his shoulder, his thumb pressing into my calf. "Nothing."

It doesn't feel like nothing.

I glance down at the mess he left behind. "Do you have anything I can use to clean up?"

"Yeah." He winces when he stands, trudging naked to the closet in the corner. He flips on a light and grabs a roll of paper towels, ripping off a dozen sheets. "Hang on."

His eyes bounce around the room and he finds a water bottle on top of the bookshelf in the corner. He twists the top off and dumps half the contents on the paper towels, wetting them and walking back over to me. I offer him his glasses and he slips them on.

"Sorry it's not warm," he says, kneeling by my side and wiping his cum away. "Or softer."

I watch him, caught off guard by his kindness. By the care he puts into cleaning me up and making me good as new. "It's probably better than going back to the field looking like this."

"People would certainly ask questions." Reid chuckles out a soft laugh, but his hand stills on my stomach. His eyes fix on my belly button and the top of my thighs, and I squirm under his gaze.

Now that the moment of hot and heaviness has passed, I feel split open and exposed, like he can see my deepest, darkest thoughts. I shouldn't still be sitting here naked and he shouldn't still be staring at me, but he is. He is, and I have no clue what he's thinking.

Does he regret what just happened?

Is he counting down the seconds until I get out of here?

"What?" I ask again, and this time, it's barely above a whisper.

"I'm not allowed to talk about it now," he says.

"Why not?"

"Because it was something I could say when I was inside you. Saying it now would be..." he trails off and runs the paper towel low across my belly. A fresh wave of heat ignites in me with the slow drag of his hand. "It's best I keep my mouth shut."

"You could tell me. If you wanted to," I hear myself say, and his eyes snap to mine. "Until we put our clothes on, it's fair game."

Reid's cheeks turn pink, and he dips his chin. He clears his throat, his touch soft on my skin. He moves to my hip bone, his thumb brushing over the top of my thigh, and I let out a shaky breath.

"I chose the wrong spot," he mumbles, and I sit up on my elbows.

"What do you mean?"

"I should've—" His breathing turns labored. "In you. I should've finished in you. So I could see what you looked like. I've never wanted to before, but you—" He lifts his chin and there's desire in his eyes. Pupils blown wide, his lips part as he looks me up and down. "Sorry. That's way too much information and I—"

"I would've liked that. That would've been okay. I said anywhere. I meant it." I put on my bra and shirt and look for my underwear, finding the pair ripped in half. "I'm not sure how I'm going to explain my forty-five minute disappearance."

"Blame me," he says, searching for his briefs.

"I plan on it. You're entirely at fault for this."

"You kissed me first," he says.

"I did not," I challenge.

"Yes, you did."

"You pushed me against the door."

Reid tosses me my leggings and socks. "Call it even?"

"Deal." I finish getting dressed and glance at him. "I should get going."

"Want me to walk you down?" he asks.

"That's okay. I know where to go. I'm practically an expert now."

"Okay." He slips on his joggers and covers his chest with his shirt. "Thanks, uh, for listening to me. About my dad. I appreciate someone lending an ear. I usually talk to Dallas and Maverick about those kinds of things, but they're a little tied up."

"Don't mention it. I'm not going to go off and tell anyone—"

"I know," Reid says, cutting me off. "I know my secret is safe with you."

"Have fun with the desk."

"Have fun with the—" A chorus of cheers leak into his office. The walls shake, and we look at each other. "Guess that's a sign we have work to do."

"Right. Yeah. I'll see you in a few weeks," I say. "At the next game."

"Mhm." Reid slides his hands into his pockets. "And I'll talk to you in an hour when you're congratulating us on our win."

I huff and roll my eyes, heading for the door. "It's only the preseason. It doesn't mean anything."

"It always means something," he says, and I can't help but hear the implication there. "See you later, Sinclair."

"Later, Duncan," I toss back, escaping into the hall and closing the door to his office behind me.

I lean against the wall when I'm alone and take a deep breath.

That was a colossal mistake.

Something that absolutely cannot happen again.

I only make it five feet down the hall and away from the scene of my crime before my phone is vibrating in my pocket.

I check it, expecting to see a score update or a stream of panicked text messages asking where I went, but it's a message from Reid with a photo attached.

My heart lurches to my throat, and I hesitantly open the picture. It's an image of the heart I drew and put on his computer, with six words attached.

> REID
>
> You must really hate me, huh?

I don't bother replying, hiding my phone and sprinting down the hall.

The Thunderhawks lose by twenty-one, but I can't bring myself to care.

TWENTY-FOUR
REID

AVERY

Are you free tomorrow morning?

ME

For what?

AVERY

I wanted to run something by you. A proposal of
sorts.

ME

You disappear off the face of the earth for the
two weeks leading up to the regular season and
now you want to propose something?

AVERY

Did you miss me?

ME

No. The quiet was nice. Going undefeated in the
preseason helped too. How does your 0-3
record feel?

AVERY

I'm not answering that.

Jumping Joe's at 8?

ME

You're going to kill me, aren't you?

AVERY

I can't tell you all my secrets.

ME

Fine. See you then.

AVERY

Where's your enthusiasm, Duncan?

ME

See you then!!!!!!!!!!!!!!!!

AVERY

Being a smart ass doesn't look good on you.

ME

What is Avery's coffee order?

MAVEN

Why are you asking for her coffee order?

ME

I'm being a nice person. Waving the white flag.

MAVEN

Bullshit. Three nights ago, you complained
about her for twenty straight minutes.

ME

Yeah, because she was annoying me.

Come on, Mae.

MAVEN

She gets an ice blonde roast. Light ice, with an
extra pump of vanilla.

ME

Thanks. Give Dallas a kiss for me.

MAVEN

You boys are so weird.

I DON'T HAVE a lot of confidence in Avery showing up to this meeting of ours despite the fact she set it up.

I haven't talked to her since the preseason game where our teams played against each other, and it's been radio silent on her end too. There hasn't been so much as a snarky comment on one of the Titans' posts, and I'm concerned I did something wrong.

Fucking her in my office was accidental, obviously.

I don't know how or why it happened, only that it did, and it was the stupidest thing I could've ever done.

I'd just gotten the idea of her out of my head, and then there she was. On my couch. Opening her thighs and telling me she thought about me when she touched herself, and I turned into an idiot without an ounce of goddamn self-control.

I saw lace. I saw bare skin. I saw her watching me, and I caved.

Fuck, I wanted her in that moment.

I wanted her more than I've ever wanted anything else.

That had to have been enough.

One final time, and now I can be done with her.

The silence has helped.

I've started to forget about how her hair feels wrapped around my wrist. What she sounds like when she comes apart. How she says my name, that breathy little moan she lets out when she needs more.

I made a vow last night when she texted me that we aren't going to pause the feud again. I can't afford to risk being nice. I'm not going to share parts of myself I like to keep hidden. We can settle into the usual back-and-forth we do so well and go on our way.

That is what works well between us, not some quick fuck without a condom that has me asking myself what the *fucking fuck* I was thinking.

And telling her I wished I finished inside her so I could see what it looked like? So I could watch her walk out of my office with my cum running down her leg?

I'm out of my mind.

This *has* to stop.

The bells above the door to the cafe chime, and I glance at the entrance.

Avery comes waltzing through in short overalls and a yellow tube top that shows off half her stomach. That anklet is still looped around her leg, and I remember how much I liked feeling it against my tongue when I kissed her calf.

She scans the room before her eyes settle on me. Her lips quirk up and she saunters over, all hips and curves and an obnoxious smile. When she gets to the open seat across from me, she sits down. She tosses her hair over her shoulder, and I notice she's wearing another ribbon—white this time. She stretches out her legs, and her knee bumps mine.

"Hi," she says.

"Hello." I slide her drink across the table. "This is for you."

She eyes the plastic cup suspiciously. "What is it?"

"Your usual order. Maven told me what you like to get."

Avery blinks and lifts her chin. She tilts her head to the side and studies me. "Did you poison it?"

"I did. I carry around travel sized cyanide and poured it in there while the barista watched me. She's in on it too. I can't believe you figured it out."

"My favorite." She scoops up the cup and brings it to her mouth. I stare at her ear instead of her lips and do my best to ignore the irritating sound she makes when she takes a sip. "Tastes good."

"So." I scoot back so we're not touching. The less physical contact, the better. I don't trust myself after the last time I saw her. "What's up?"

"I can't believe the season starts tonight. The preseason went by way too fast," she says.

"The rest of the year isn't going to go any slower."

"I know." She looks out the window to her right. She taps her painted nails against her cheek and sighs. "My sleep schedule is about to turn to shit."

"Not that I don't love this awkward small talk we're making, but why did you want to meet up, Avery?" I ask. "We don't have enough common interests to warrant a hang out in our off time."

"That's not true. We both like comic books. And romance novels."

My dick twitches at the thought of her spread out on my bed. A comic book in her hand and a flirty smile on her lips. The sheets pooled around her waist and her perfect tits on display as she reads me page after page from something off my shelf.

I need a lobotomy.

"Literature choices don't make us best friends."

Avery levels me with a look. "We need to talk about what happened in your office."

"It was a mistake. I don't know what—"

"We should do it again."

I squint at her. "What?"

"We should do it again," she repeats, and there's more gusto behind it the second time. "Sex. You and me. Together."

"What—" I take a sip of my coffee to stall for some time. I have no clue what to say to that, and I have to tread carefully. "Why—how—what's your reasoning?"

"We have chemistry. I don't like to mix business with pleasure, but you can't deny that we click in the bedroom. Sex with you is a good way to work out the tension I have from my job—a job that's about to get even more busy and chaotic. Knowing there won't be a relationship that stems from it means I—we— can enjoy the physical aspect without getting attached," she says, and I wonder if she's rehearsed this. "I don't have time to date, but I do have time to get fucked. That's what I want, and I want it with you."

I blink. I think I'm hallucinating. I think I'm having a heart attack. There's no way in hell this woman is saying what I think she's saying.

"We can't stand each other," I tell her. It's the first thing that comes to mind.

"We can't stand each other outside the bedroom. Inside the bedroom, we really enjoy each other. Don't we?"

I blush.

Sex with her the first two times was phenomenal. Out of this fucking world. But in my office was... intense. It was rougher. Hungrier. She asked for what she wanted, but I also took what I wanted. I've never come that hard in my life.

"Yes..." I say cautiously. I feel like this is a trap. A ploy to get me to admit something I don't want to admit. "And you want to do it again?"

"I do. Casually. Like what we were going to do before."

"What do I get out of it?" I ask, and she lifts an eyebrow.

"Is sex with me not enough?"

"It is." I clear my throat. The cafe feels a hundred degrees warmer than it did twenty minutes ago. "What do *you* get out of this?"

"Orgasms with someone who understands my schedule and doesn't expect me to call every night."

"How often?"

"Whenever we want." She shrugs and sets her phone down on the table, tapping the screen. "We're in Georgia next week. I know you'll be in Detroit. We can find time."

"I thought we agreed it wasn't going to happen again," I say. "That it was a lapse in judgment so we could get it out of our systems."

"I don't want to get it out of my system," she says matter-of-factly. "No one's taken care of me the way you do, and I want it again."

I grip the table so tightly my knuckles turn white. She's blunt, just like me, and that's not good for my well-being at all.

"I'm confused. You might be obnoxious as hell, but you're gorgeous and smart. You're talented at your job, and you could have any guy you wanted, Avery. Why—" I swallow again. "Why me?"

"Believe me when I say I've tried to stay away from you. I've tried to ignore you, but I can't help it, and it's infuriating. You're nice and selfless. You're attractive, and you know how to treat a woman. We're up to our ears in work, and I think we both deserve to have a little fun."

I nod like I agree with what she's saying.

I guess she's not wrong.

I've tried to stay the hell away from her too, but I keep coming back.

"We need rules," I say. "Stricter rules than what we were tossing around last time we—"

I think of her on the couch in my apartment. Her skirt hiked up around her waist and her nipples hard against her shirt. The way she fucked herself with her own fingers and let me watch until I was begging to have a taste.

Fucking hell.

"What did you have in mind?" she asks, and I shake my head to clear my thoughts.

"Work still comes first. My job is important to me. There can't be any hard feelings if one of us says no because we're busy. And this can't be because one of us wants to win the bet. It's not allowed to be sabotage or meddling. We're fucking because we want to fuck, not because we want the other to miss a deadline. We leave our jobs out of it."

She nods. "What else?"

"We only sleep with each other. Adding other people to the mix is a headache I don't want to deal with. Also, our dislike for each other stops when we get in bed."

"Or on a couch. Or in a hallway," Avery adds, and I have to take a deep breath.

"Right. Any of those places. No insults. No mean shit. It's not some revenge game we're playing."

"Okay." She smiles. "I like all of those stipulations."

"We leave emotions out of it too. If we're going to do this, we recognize what it is: two adults who want to get off. That's it."

"I know you're a relationship guy. Are you going to be able to do this without falling for me?" Avery asks.

I snort. "I haven't fallen in love with you in the three years I've known you. It's not going to happen now."

"Good." She beams and takes a long sip of her coffee. "Are we in agreement?"

"We're in agreement," I say. "What's your schedule this week?"

"That desperate for me already?"

"You're the one who propositioned me."

"I have a season ticket holder event tomorrow night at the stadium, then a fanfest party on Saturday afternoon. Sunday is a three p.m. kickoff, and next Monday, I was asked to speak at Georgetown to a group of communications majors."

"Is that what you got your degree in?" I ask. Just because we're fuck buddies doesn't meant I can't learn more about her.

She nods. "And sports journalism. I've always wanted to work in the industry, and I knew that was a way to get my foot in the door. What did you get your degree in?"

"Computer programming and software technology. Trust me when I say working for a football team was not on my radar."

"Any regrets?" she asks.

"No. Life has a weird way of figuring itself out."

"I like this. Five minutes ago, we were talking about our rules for being fuck buddies. Now we're getting personal." Avery traces the letters on her cup and smiles. "We're talented, aren't we?"

"I guess we are."

"What's on your schedule coming up?"

"We also kickoff on Sunday, but in the primetime television slot that night. Other than that, it's the usual workload. I do have a charity softball game coming up soon. It's one of the Titans' fundraisers, and I'm going to embarrass myself in front of everyone."

"What charity does it benefit?"

"Give Kids the World. Maverick is a big donor, and he got the Titans to partner with him for an event. Some of the hockey guys will be there, and a couple guys from the DC Dolphins baseball team too."

"How are your ticket sales numbers looking?" Avery asks.

"Good," I say honestly. "Snagging Griffin Harrison was a big pickup for us. After the Super Bowl drought, people think this might be the year we get another ring. It entices them to make a deposit, and it's going to help me win our bet."

"Sorry to burst your bubble, but ours are high too. We're running some promotions, and people are flocking to the box office. I'm going to give you a run for your money."

I'm not sure what else I'm supposed to say. I have things to do and a meeting with my boss in an hour. There's a headache starting behind my eyes. I should probably get going, but I don't know proper protocol for walking away from this sort of thing.

"Are you, uh, going to hang around for a bit?" I ask.

"No. I need to change and head to the office."

"Me too." I smooth my hands over my jeans and stand. "I guess I'll talk to you soon?"

"Yeah." Avery smiles again, and I hate how it nudges its way into my chest. "Want to meet up tomorrow after I'm finished with my event?"

"Tomorrow," I repeat. "I'll have to, uh, check my schedule, but I think tomorrow could work. Or, ah, tonight? If you don't want to wait."

"Do you want to wait?" she asks.

"No." I shake my head, and I don't care how desperate that might make me look. She can have this win. "I don't."

"We can do tonight. Your place?"

"Yeah." I nod. "Sure. You remember where I live?"

"I do. I'll text you when I'm heading over," she says.

"Good. That's good. I'll see you later then."

Her smile stretches to a grin. "Have a good day, Reid."

I drop my drink in the trash and head for the exit. When I look behind me, Avery is watching me. She averts her gaze and stares at her phone when I catch her. I know she's pretending to look busy, but it doesn't matter.

She was looking at me, and that makes me feel like a real smug bastard.

AVERY

Busy tonight?

ME

Yeah. Book club with the guys.

Why?

AVERY

So we can talk about the economy.

Why do you think, Duncan? Should I use the
eggplant emoji so there isn't any confusion?

ME

We had sex three days ago. Can't get enough
of me?

AVERY

I can't get enough of your dick. Not you.

ME

I'll text you when we're finished, but no
promises.

AVERY

Cool.

Before I go…

Attachment: 1 video

We won last night. Time to play the song!

ME

My ears are bleeding.

You have a 1-2 record.

AVERY

So?

Thunderhawks, a oh oh oh oh ohhhhhhhhhh!

"PASS ME A WATER?" Dallas asks, and I scoop out two bottles from the cooler, tossing one his way. "Thanks, man."

I settle on the couch next to him. "Where is Maverick? This is his apartment, and he's not here."

"He said he was on his way up," Hudson Hayes, one of Maverick's teammates, tells us. He shrugs and flips through the book on his lap. "Didn't sound like it was a crisis."

"Sorry I'm late," Maverick calls out, bursting through the front door and appearing in the living room. His shirt is on backwards and one of his shoes is untied. He puts a hand on the wall, panting, and takes a deep breath. "Lost track of time."

"Doing what?" I ask.

"Wedding stuff," he says, but I see the lipstick on his neck. "Emmy and I got caught up looking at dinner menus. That shit is expensive."

"Is that what we're calling it these days?" Dallas snorts. "You have a hickey under your ear, Miller."

"Oh. Whoops." He gives us a sheepish grin and collapses

into a nearby chair. His fingers dance over his throat and he sighs. "I can't keep my hands to myself around that woman."

"We don't need to hear about your sexcapades, Mavvy," Riley Mitchell, another one of Maverick's teammates says. "You're making some of us feel single as fuck, and we just want to talk about the book."

"The book. Right. Yes." Maverick holds up the dark romance novel we read over the course of the month and taps the cover. "Thoughts?"

"I liked it," I say. "Outside of our usual wheelhouse, but I'm a fan."

"It, uh, made me question some things about myself," Hudson admits. He's a quiet guy, someone who's just as talented as Maverick but less boisterous about it. "I enjoyed it, though."

"No shit." Riley clasps his shoulder. "Look at you and Reid stepping outside your comfort zones and liking it."

"I mean, I'm not going to go to a haunted house and ask the guy in the Michael Myers jumpsuit to fuck me, but I'd be down to try a thing or two from the book," I say. I scratch my jaw and tuck my chin to my chest, hiding from their prying eyes.

"Like?" Dallas presses, and he's never one to nudge his way into someone's business.

"I don't know." I shrug. "Tying her hands up? Having my hands tied up? As long as it's consensual and everything. I wouldn't want to use rope. That seems... extreme. I'd have to study the logistics of it first. Extensively. Maybe something small like a shoelace or a—"

A ribbon.

Specifically, the white one Avery wore in her hair a couple nights ago when I tugged her into my apartment and pushed her against the door. The picture we knocked off the wall is still crooked, and I haven't had a second to fix it.

"Why are you blushing?" Maverick narrows his eyes. "You're hiding something."

"I'm not hiding anything," I argue. I grab a handful of pretzels and shove them in my mouth so I don't have to say anything else. The less interested I pretend to be, the less he'll care.

"My favorite part was—"

"Hang on, G. Something isn't adding up here," Maverick says, interrupting Grant, his younger teammate. He pops to his feet and walks over to me. "What the fuck is going on, Duncan?"

I groan and scrub a hand over my face. There's no use trying to hide this from them. They're going to find out eventually.

"I might have stumbled into a frenemies with benefits situation," I grumble, shielding my face with the book. "With Avery."

"Who is Avery?" Ethan, another DC Stars player asks.

"She sounds hot," Grant chimes in.

"So *that's* why you wanted to know her coffee order," Dallas says.

"Your wife is on my shit list for spilling my secrets," I say.

"I *knew* it," Maverick exclaims. "I fucking knew it. You've been staring at your phone nonstop lately. Oh my *god*. You're sending dick pics, aren't you?"

"I am *not* sending dick pics," I say, then I panic. "Should I be sending dick pics? I'm not sure how all this works. What's the proper protocol? We've hooked up a few times and—"

"A *few* times? Look at our Reidy Boy living a double life," Maverick says.

"Can we go back to talking about masked men, please?" I beg.

"Knock it off, Mav," Dallas says, and I shoot him a grateful look. "Show some respect."

"Sorry, man. I didn't mean to force you into telling us," Maverick says.

"You didn't. I kept my mouth shut because it didn't seem like something to make a big deal about. Not when you two are settled down with weddings and engagements. We're having fun, which is something I've never, ever done." I shrug again. "It's different to live in the moment."

"Good different?" Dallas asks.

"Yeah," I say. "I feel like one of you guys."

"You're happy, right?" Hudson asks. "You're not going along with it just because you feel like you have to?"

"No." I shake my head and bite back a smile. It was fun to make Pop-Tarts with her in my kitchen at midnight. To sit side by side on the couch and knock out some work after our home games on Sunday, only shutting my computer down when Avery took off her shirt and straddled me. It was nice to lend her a pair of socks that dwarfed her feet when she said she was cold. Those things make me happy. Happy for now, at least, because the second we're behind our phones, I get her usual snark. "It works for us. We hook up, then after, it's back to business." I cut a glance over to Maverick. "I see why you were fucking giddy the first few months you and Emmy did this. I feel like I'm smiling nonstop."

"That could also be because you haven't slept with anyone in three years. Good sex will do that to you," Maverick says, and the guys all murmur in agreement. "But we'll stop talking about Reid's bedroom habits and switch back to masked men. Now, on the subject of morally gray, I'd argue that…"

The next hour devolves into lighthearted mayhem, each of us making a passionate plea about our opinionated stances and trying to nudge the others to our side. It's always been like this, ever since our first meeting when there were just four of us.

The group has expanded over the last year, with some guys only staying a month or two before they lose interest or leave DC. It comes with being a professional athlete, and it makes me glad I don't have to worry about new cities. New friends or new routines. I can stay here and do everything exactly how I like, exactly how I've always done it.

My attention gets pulled from the discussion on bondage when my phone lights up on the end table. I pick it up and see Avery's name.

There's a photo attached to her message, one that has me stifling a groan with my fist and wishing I wasn't in a room surrounded by my friends.

It's her in a dressing room wearing a piece of lingerie. The straps are falling down her arms, almost hooking around her elbows. The neckline shows off her cleavage and the swell of her tits. The underwear hugs the curve of her hips, and I spot the fingerprints I left behind the other night.

The lighting might be dim.

The picture might be blurry—taken as an afterthought, maybe—but that doesn't stop my imagination from running wild.

From wondering what it would be like to fuck her in front of those mirrors.

How that silk would feel between my fingers and how easily it would rip.

AVERY

What do you think?

ME

Hang on a sec. I'll send you my credit card number.

Buy as many as you want.

AVERY

Do you think you make more money than me?

ME

I hope we're paid the same, but that was a desperate way to say I'd like to see you in one of every fucking color.

Purple is my favorite, though.

My brain is short-circuiting.

AVERY

Good. I hope book club is fun.

ME

Come over after.

AVERY

Now who wants who again?

ME

Please?

I can't think of a more coherent response.

I do want her again, and it's confusing as hell.

She's not part of the routine, an anomaly that's throwing a wrench in my plans of staying focused. Of keeping my eyes on the prize; not just our bet, but the incentives set by my manager too.

How the hell am I supposed to say no to *that*, though?

Guys like me don't get women like her.

Maverick and Dallas and Hudson and Riley get women like her. They breathe, and women fall to their feet.

Me?

No fucking chance.

Every time I'm with Avery, it still feels like a fever dream.

Outside the bedroom, she irritates the ever-loving shit out of me.

She makes me want to pull my hair out and has me furiously

answering comments like my fingers are going to fall off if I don't get to them fast enough.

It's different behind closed doors when we put our phones away.

Work and life get paused when she shows up at my apartment, and I can be someone else for a little while.

The dude who scores a goddamn beauty queen.

AVERY

I should go pay for this before they think I'm
trying to rob the place.

ME

You're too good to do something like that.

AVERY

What if I want to be a little bad, though?

ME

Going to block you now. I don't want to get
hard around my friends.

"You okay, Plant Daddy?" Maverick asks. "You look a little red."

"Fine. Just peachy. It's sunburn. From being outside. In the sun. Warm weather. Climate change." I bob my head and pull on my collar. "You know. Save the turtles."

Dallas smirks. "Let him be, Mav."

"Speaking of sunburn, you all are confirmed for the softball game, right? Our donations surpassed last year, and there's still a week and a half to go," Maverick says proudly. "We're going to have a good turnout."

"Still can't believe you got me to agree to play competitive sports." I stand and tuck my book close to my chest, thumbing through the pages. "But I'll be there."

"I'm a man of many talents," Maverick says. "You heading out?"

"Yeah. I have some work stuff I need to wrap up," I say, and it's the first time I've ever lied to them. "Thanks for another great chat, gentlemen."

I wait until I'm safely downstairs and away from their prying eyes before I read the last message I received. The one from Avery that's been burning a hole in my pocket since she sent it fifteen minutes ago.

AVERY

You'd miss me too much if you blocked me.

ME

I'm heading home.

I know you have an early flight tomorrow, but if you want to be bad, I'd really like it if you came over.

AVERY

Bad, huh?

ME

Sorry. My dirty talking is shit.

AVERY

I think it's perfect.

And I'm already on my way.

REID OPENS the door to his apartment holding a watering can.

I glance at the metal object, then up at him. "Doing some late-night gardening?"

"I forgot to water the plants before I left for work this morning. They probably hate me," he says. He takes a step back and looks me up and down. "You're wearing a coat? It's unseasonably warm out."

"I've been cold today," I say.

"Are you sick?" Reid asks.

"No. I feel fantastic."

"Want to come in?"

"I'd love to." I slip inside and kick off my sandals in the foyer. "How was book club?"

"Masked men. Haunted houses. Bondage." He walks to the living room and I follow behind him, unbuttoning my coat as I do. "The usual."

"And what are your thoughts on bondage?"

Reid glances at me over his shoulder. "Favorable, I've learned," he says quietly, almost like he's embarrassed to admit it. "On a small scale at least."

I hum and lean against the wall, watching him busy himself with the array of plants. He leans over one in a large pot, mumbling something to himself as he waters it then touches the soil.

"Which one is your favorite?" I ask.

"Maybe this one." He points to a plant in the corner of the living room sitting on a stand. "It's a Philodendron Moonlight. Loves indirect light. Very easygoing, which is perfect for when I'm away for a few days for a road game. I follow this guy on social media who has a greenhouse down in Florida and takes care of all kinds of plants, and I've learned a lot from him. I've always been intrigued by botany and..." Reid trails off and looks at me over his shoulder again. "I'm boring you, aren't I?"

I smile and push off the wall. I unfasten the last of the buttons and drop the coat away from my shoulders, revealing the purple lingerie set I bought an hour ago.

Reid sucks in a sharp breath. His eyes bounce to my chest then back to my face. His grip on the watering can slackens, and he slowly sets it down on the windowsill.

"Not at all," I say. "I could listen to you talk about plants all night."

"You've been in my apartment wearing *that* for five minutes, and I'm talking about *plants*?" he asks. "I need to be sedated, and you need to tell me to shut up."

I laugh and stop in front of him. I take his hand and put it on my shoulder, guiding his fingers down my arm then across my chest. His touch is soft, and his eyes stay on mine as I rest his palm on my breast.

"I do love to tell you to shut up, but I've never seen you in your natural habitat. You can keep going, if you want. Tell me more about Philodendrons, Reid."

He shakes his head. His gaze rakes over my outfit, from the lace to the little bows on the hips of my underwear. His attention holds on the cut in the fabric that shows off my breasts, a deep, plunging neckline that pushes them together and gives me cleavage I dream about.

"That—" He licks his lips and hesitantly drags his thumb across the design on my chest. My nipples harden under the pad of his finger, and I arch my back, wanting more. "I like this a lot."

"Do you like the color?" I ask around a rasp.

"Purple," he murmurs, and he dips his head. He licks a slow swipe of his tongue over the path his thumb took, and I moan. "For me?"

"Figured I could use something new," I say. He lifts me off my feet with surprising ease, and I wrap my legs around his waist. I'll never get over how strong he is. "Might as well make it purple."

Reid walks us down the hall to his bedroom, his eyes never straying from my body. It feels like he's studying me, drinking me in, and I don't know why it makes me squirm.

"You're so fucking sexy," he says, low and rough, his lips brushing over my ear. "How am I the one who gets to have you?"

"Luck of the draw, I guess," I tease, and his eyes darken.

He kicks open the door to his bedroom and sets me on the bed. I prop myself up on my elbows and he stands between my legs. I can tell he's hard through the denim of his jeans, the material straining around his cock, and I give him a pleased smile.

"I almost had a situation at book club." He pulls off his shirt and tosses it near his desk. His glasses tip sideways on his face, and he pushes them up his nose. "Because of the photos you sent me."

"Did you want me to stop?"

"No." Reid shakes his head and fumbles with the button on his jeans. "I liked them."

"Do you like this?" I ask, toying with the straps of the

matching set. I drag the left one down my arm and he yanks on his zipper. "Should I leave it on or take it off?"

"Wish there was a way for me to say both," he mumbles, stepping out of his pants and adjusting his cock. "You probably spent a lot of money on it, and I don't want to ruin something so pretty."

"Ruin me instead." I lift my hips and shimmy the underwear down my legs. I fling them at him, and he reaches out to catch them. I open my knees and rest my palm low on my stomach, watching his labored breathing. "How do you want me, Duncan?"

He sets the underwear on his desk, and I wonder if he's going to keep them. He drops his glasses next to the lace and hooks his thumbs in the waistband of his briefs, tugging them down his thighs until his cock springs free.

"Need to fuck you," he says.

I touch my clit, teasing myself. I scoot back across the sheets, and he kneels on the mattress between my legs. He rests his palm on my calf and strokes up and down, staring at me.

"So fuck me," I say, pushing a finger inside myself. I groan at the stretch and drop my head back on the pillows. "Please."

"Such good manners." Reid wraps his palm around my wrist and pulls my finger out. I whimper at the loss, and he chuckles. "Do you want to be bad, Avery? Or do you want to be a good girl and get what you want?"

"Good," I struggle to say, twisting on the sheets. "I want to be good."

"Then open your legs, baby. Let me see how wet you are for me," he says.

Baby.

My skin heats at the affectionate name.

He doesn't use it every time we're together, but when he

does, it sparks a fire inside me. It makes me feel sensual, power-ful, a woman who can have whatever she wants.

With him, I don't have to be professional. I don't have to hold myself to impossibly high standards. I don't have to be careful with my word choice or smile until my cheeks hurt.

I can be depraved, wild. I can crave things others would turn their noses up to. I can be loud, *free.* I can let go and savor the bliss of the pure fucking nirvana he brings me, all while feeling safe. Secure and sexy.

The men I've been with before expected me to act a certain way. They wanted submissive. A follower, not a leader. The quiet, dainty girl who took what they had to offer without making a peep.

Reid is different.

I've never felt more like myself than when I'm with him.

"How wet do you think I am?" I ask, spreading my legs.

I cup my breasts and push them together, a nod back to our first time together. His cock twitches and he groans, the tendons in his neck flexing under the tension in his body.

"Soaked," he says, and it comes out slurred. "Jesus, Avery. You're so fucking beautiful. I could look at you all night."

"Can I have an orgasm first? Then you can look all you want."

"I think that's a fair trade-off." Reid leans forward and kisses me, soft at first, then with more hunger behind the press of his lips. His hand replaces mine, two fingers pushing in me without any warning, and I hiss. "Deep breath, Ave," he murmurs against my mouth. "There you go."

I exhale, my limbs relaxing as he holds himself over me. His free hand rubs a circle over my stomach and I moan, sinking into the sensation as he pulls out of me then presses back in.

"Reid," I whisper, needing him closer. Needing more of him.

I wrap my arms around his neck and yank him to me so his chest is against mine. It's only been a few days since I last saw him, but it feels like an eternity. "More."

"You want to try four, beauty queen?" he asks, teeth grazing down my neck. "To get you nice and ready for my cock?"

"I can do it," I say, and he kisses my throat. "I want to try."

"You tell me if you want me to stop. If it's too much."

I never want him to stop.

"Okay."

"I won't hurt you. I promise."

"I know," I whisper, closing my eyes. "I know you won't."

Reid kisses me again, and I know he's distracting me. Pulling my attention from the inevitable burst of pain I'm going to feel before it starts to feel good. The hand on my stomach moves to my clit and rubs soft, slow circles as he gently works four fingers into me.

My vision blurs, and I cry out. I arch my back off the bed, a deep ache settling low in my belly as he stops halfway inside me and kisses my forehead.

"Okay?" he asks.

"Give me a sec," I pant, and his lips move to my cheek, kissing there too.

Tears sting my eyes, but the longer he waits for me to give him the okay to keep going, the better it feels. The more at ease I am, and the pain subsides. I lie back on the mattress and Reid follows me, crowding my space.

"I could come from this," he tells me. "I've never—Christ, Ave. You're—"

I grab the back of his neck and bring his mouth to mine, kissing him. He whimpers, and I can't help but smile.

"Make me come, Reid. Make me come, and I'll let you come inside me."

"Fucking hell," he whispers, long fingers working me to the brink of ecstasy. "Never heard such a good incentive before in my life."

I'm close, *so close*, and when he moves his wrist and gets even deeper inside me, I detonate.

I fall over the edge, a mess of garbled sounds and his name on the tip of my tongue. I chant it, the only coherent thought left in my brain. When I think I'm finished, tapped out and thoroughly spent, Reid coaxes another orgasm out of me with his tongue. It's quicker than the first, a bolt of lightning that sends me freefalling again, and I can't remember my name.

He doesn't give me any reprieve, though. His fingers slide out of me and I reach for him, desperate for him to fill me again. His palms move to my hips, turning me onto my stomach and lifting me on all fours. I'm a boneless heap of heightened senses and electrified nerves, but he doesn't seem to care that he's doing all the work.

"Are you ready for my cock now?" he asks, his body folded over mine. "Do you need a breather?"

"Fuck me," I whisper, bracing myself for the thrust of his hips. "And don't be gentle."

Reid grunts, a sound of agreement he punctuates with the push of his long length inside me. I gather myself, wanting to make this as good for him as he's made it for me, and I work down his shaft, inch by inch, until we're fused together.

"Goddamn, Ave. Look at you taking all of me."

I rock forward then sink back on him, fucking him how I know he likes to be fucked. His fingers dig into my skin, but he's letting me be the one in control.

We lose ourselves in each other. Maybe it's five minutes. Maybe it's five hours. Time seems irrelevant, because every second with him is complete and total perfection. We find the rhythm we both like, the slam of his hips enough to topple me over, but he's there, an arm around me, keeping me upright.

I hear how wet I am, how much I like being here with him, and I tighten around his cock. Reid groans and his legs tremble, and I know he's trying to hold back.

"Reid," I say, guiding his hand to my neck. He hesitates for a fraction of a second before touching my throat, and I smile even though he can't see me. "What are you waiting for?"

"I. Don't. Know." Each word is emphasized with a thrust, and my breath catches in my chest. "Is it still okay if I—"

"*Yes*," I assure him.

"I've never—"

"Let me be the first," I practically beg, and that unlocks a part of him I haven't seen before.

I can barely blink before he's pulling out of me and switching our positions, my back against the sheets again. I watch with wonder as he lifts my leg to his shoulder and eases back into me.

It's rougher. A man starved and going after what he wants. Nothing about it is nice or kind or sweet. Reid comes undone, his face flushed and his body tensing with every jerk of his hips.

"Want. To. See. You," he grits out. "When. I. Make. You. Mine."

Any other time, it might be romantic.

But not now.

Not with his pupils blown wide and a possessiveness to his words.

Now, it's just fucking *want*.

"Do it," I dare him, and he snaps.

He groans, a sound that echoes off the walls and fills the space behind my ribs. His thighs lock up, and I feel him finish inside me. He gulps down strangled breaths, his shoulders slouching and his eyes closing. I rub up his arms and over his shoulders, touching his neck and his cheek and waiting for him to calm down.

"That—" Reid blows out an exhale and runs a hand through his sweaty hair. "I think I'm dying."

"I've got you," I say gently, and he opens an eye. He glances down at me and groans again.

"Look at the mess I made." He winces when he pulls out of me, then stares between my legs. "That's the hottest thing I've ever seen."

I drag my fingers through his cum then touch my clit, smiling when his throat bobs around a swallow. "I like it."

"You do?"

"Mhm. Do you?"

"Yeah," he says slowly, lifting his chin to look at me. "I do. A lot."

"Want to do it again in an hour?" I ask, and he laughs, collapsing next to me on the bed.

"Might need an hour and a half," he admits. "I think you took years off my life."

"Sorry."

"No, you're not."

"No." I smile and he reaches for me, bringing me flush against him. "I'm not."

"We're going to shower in a minute. I'm going to clean you up. Let you use the bathroom. Hygiene and all of that," he mumbles. "But I want to rest for a second. It's been a long day, and I just got fucked within an inch of consciousness."

"Okay." I close my eyes, exhaustion threatening to overtake me. "Are you going to wash my hair? Rinse me off?"

"Yeah." His breath is warm on my neck, and it's comforting. "Might get on my knees in the shower too. Take care of you again. Maybe twice. Would that be okay?"

I stifle a yawn and curl in closer to him. "Anything with you is okay, Reid."

He hums and takes my hand in his, resting it on the center of his chest. His heart hammers under my palm, and I wonder if he can feel how fast mine is beating too.

TWENTY-SEVEN
AVERY

REID

You forgot something at my place.

ME

What did I forget?

REID

Attachment: 1 Image

Look familiar?

ME

Those aren't mine.

REID

The fuck? Yes, they are. I literally took them off
of you five days ago.

ME

Are you sure about that?

REID

Do you think I have a parade of women coming
through my apartment?

ME

Maybe.

I'm just fucking with you. I wanted to get you
riled up.

REID

Of course you did.

"ARE you sure I should be here?" I ask Maven. I follow her down the hall to Maverick Miller's penthouse and the dinner waiting for me on the other side. "This is a private thing you all do with your family and friends. I'm not a part of that. In fact, I'm Public Enemy Number One. The girl who works for the opposing team everyone hates."

"Who cares what team you work for? You're my friend, and I want you here," she says, looping her arm through mine. My nerves start to fray the closer we get to the apartment, and when we stop outside the door, I dig my heels into the ground. "What's the big deal?"

Reid.

Reid is the big deal.

He and I haven't spent any time together outside his bedroom—or his living room, kitchen, foyer and the wall in his shower—since we started this arrangement.

I'm not embarrassed to be seen with him.

I just don't know how the hell I'm supposed to act.

I don't know which personas we're going to slip into; the ones that hide behind our phones and go at each other's throats with sarcastic one-liners? The ones when we're in his bed and I'm on top of him, his mouth warm on my neck and his hand between my legs? Strangers who pretend like they don't know what the other sounds like when they come?

I hate not knowing what I'm walking in to.

I sent him a message earlier to let him know Maven was

forcing me to tag along so it wasn't a total surprise, but he didn't answer.

I'm not sure if he even read it.

I saw him active on social media, sharing clips from their game last night and a reminder about their charity softball game later this week.

No text, though.

I hate that my chest pinches tight at the thought of him not wanting me here. At worrying if I'm invading his space or taking up too much room in his life. I blow out a breath to steady myself, and I feel like I need to sit down.

"I'm fine." I plaster on a megawatt smile. "Let's eat some food."

Maven walks in without bothering to knock, and I hang back in the foyer as she makes her way deep into Maverick's home. A row of shoes are lined up against the wall, and I spy Reid's black Converse in the mix. The pair he laces up when he walks me down to the Metro when it's late and dark, so I don't have to make the trek alone.

The sight of them loosens the tension I'm holding, and I slide off my sneakers.

"Hi." A tall redheaded woman leans against the wall and offers me a tentative smile. I recognize her from the wedding and a few of the photos Maven has posted online. "I'm Emmy, Maverick's fiancé."

"Hi," I say, smiling back and connecting the dots. "I've heard so much about you from Maven. I'm Avery. Thank you for letting me crash your night."

"I can't believe we haven't met," she says. "You're a lawyer, right?"

"No, I work in social—"

"I'm kidding." She turns on her heel and walks down the hall, motioning for me to follow. I trail behind her, gaping at the artwork on the wall and the decor that probably costs upwards of six figures. "I know exactly what you do. I love him to death, but Reid is fucking insufferable sometimes. I can't believe I don't know your social security number or your mother's maiden name from how much he talks about you."

A laugh races out of me. "I'm glad we agree on the insufferable part."

"Everyone is in the living room, and the food should be ready in a few minutes. Can I get you something to drink? Beer? Wine? Liquor, if that's more your speed?" Emmy rounds the corner into a kitchen made of marble countertops and sleek appliances. She swipes her martini off the island and knocks a grape off the charcuterie board. "Whatever your heart desires."

"Do you have whiskey?" I ask. "I'll take one. Neat."

Emmy reaches for a crystal decanter that might cost as much as my rent. "We're going to get along just fine."

We make small talk as she fixes me a generous pour of the amber liquid. She slides it my way and knocks her glass against mine.

"Cheers," I say, taking a long sip. "Oh, shit. This is the good stuff."

"Don't ever date a man with expensive taste. One minute you're buying brand name olives, and the next he's chartering a plane to Spain just so you can have the freshest pick of them straight from the tree." Emmy hums out something that might be a laugh and drags her fingers across her lips, a reluctant smile forming there. "I love him though."

"When's the wedding?" I ask, staring at the huge diamond on her finger. "Does your hand get tired from carrying around that rock?"

"Next year, maybe. We might elope. Can't decide." She shrugs, unbothered by the lack of planning. "And it does, to be honest. I wear a silicone one when I'm at the rink, and I forget how heavy this is. It's too damn big."

"C'mon, Emmy girl. You don't have to brag about me to our guests," Maverick says, popping into the kitchen and dropping a kiss to the top of her hair. "June Bug is here tonight. Let's keep this family friendly."

She sighs and curls up against him, her cheek in the crook of his neck and a content grin finally settling on her mouth. "Your ego knows no bounds."

"Hey, Avery." He turns his attention to me and smiles. It's intimidating, one only an extremely good-looking man could pull off without looking like a total asshole, and Maverick does it effortlessly. "Feels like I've known you for years, but it's nice to finally meet you for real."

"Thanks for letting me join your dinner. I know I'm not a member of the Stars or the Titans, and I appreciate you opening up your home to outsiders," I say.

"Nah. You're family. Doesn't matter who you work for." He rubs his hand up and down Emmy's arm. "Does Reid know you're here?"

"No." I take another sip of my drink and play with my necklace. I'm going to need more liquid courage to get through the night. "I'm not sure if he knew I was going to be here at all, honestly."

"He knows. He's a little preoccupied right now," Maverick hurries to tell me. "If you go down the hall to the right, you'll find him."

"Is this one of those Naked Man things?" I ask. "Am I going to walk in there and see him posing on a couch with his dick out?"

"I sure as shit hope not," Maverick says, horrified. "That would probably traumatize June Bug."

I burst out laughing and bury my face in my hands. "That

visual is appalling. I'm going to pretend I never said anything and disappear before I make things worse."

"Second door," Emmy calls after me. "The first is a closet."

I pass the noise coming from the living room and make my way down the hall. The walls are covered in photographs and I take my time to look at them. Snapshots of hockey teams. Maverick with a baby June. Maven on Maverick's back, her arms out at her sides and pretending to fly. Maverick and Emmy kissing on a beach. A shot of him, Dallas, and Reid, all smiling at the camera, similar to the one in Reid's office.

They're all so *happy*, with so much love on display, and I think back to Reid telling me about his broken relationship with his dad.

It makes me glad to know he has a support system.

People he can rely on when the going gets tough.

Everyone needs a family like that.

I stop outside the door Emmy directed me to and peek inside. Reid is sitting on a stool and facing a mirror. There are eight braids in his red hair, and I hold back a laugh.

"There." June adds a hair tie to braid number nine and smiles. "You look very pretty, Uncle Reid."

"Thanks, JB." He grabs her by the waist and blows a raspberry on her cheek. "You ready for some dinner?"

"Yeah." She wiggles free from his embrace and adds a headband to his hair. "Did you bring the mashed potatoes?"

Reid laughs and stands. "Of course I did. I can't let you and Emmy down."

I accidentally kick the door and wince at the creaking sound. I try to flatten myself against the wall so he won't see me, but it's too late.

"Avery?" He glances over his shoulder. "Hey."

"Hey. Didn't mean to interrupt. I—Maverick and Emmy sent

me this way, and I can see now that it probably looks like I was spying on you or something."

"Not at all." He kisses June's forehead then reaches for the door, opening it fully. "Sorry I didn't have a chance to answer your text earlier. Work was chaotic with an injury and five different meetings. My phone died after lunch, and I forgot my charger at home."

"Sounds like it's been a day."

"Long. Tedious." He shrugs. June waves hello to me before sprinting down the hall. "Better now, I think."

"The braids help, don't they?"

"The only reason I'm still functioning. Are you hungry?"

My stomach picks that moment to rumble, and I wince. "I am. I accidentally skipped lunch and didn't have time to eat after my run before heading this way."

"How long have you been a runner?"

"Gosh. Almost ten years now? When I stopped dancing, I wanted something that pushed me outside my of comfort zone. Training for half marathons has been a good supplement to that rigorous lifestyle I used to have."

"You'd kick my ass in a sprint." He brushes past me, the sleeve of his green Henley grazing my arm. "Come on, Sinclair. Let's go before there's no food left."

Reid introduces me to the DC Stars hockey players. There are a handful of Titans guys mixed into the bunch, a second-string running back and a defensive tackle I recognize from their roster. They all come up to me and say hello, taking the time to shake my hand and look me in the eye.

Maven blows me a kiss from across the living room and I laugh. She sits in Dallas's lap and he rocks her in his arms, soft and quiet contentment on her face as she looks up at him and whispers something secret in his ear.

Nothing about the night feels awkward, and I'm far from out of place.

Reid and I make small talk here and there between bites of our food, but I talk to everyone else too. I show some of the Stars players the social media stuff I do, and Grant, a cute hockey boy with shaggy dark hair and blue eyes, won't leave my side.

"I'm going to get some fresh air," I tell him, rising to my feet and pulling on the hem of my skirt. "I'll be back in soon."

"Do you want some company?" he asks.

"Grant," Emmy warns. "Stay. Let her have a minute. You all haven't stopped chatting her ear off since she got here, and I don't think she's interested. You're also eight years too young for her and annoying as hell."

I tip my head Emmy's way in an appreciative nod. I slip out the big glass doors off the living room and into the October air, breathing a sigh of relief at the quiet.

I lean my elbows on the railing and soak up the view of the city in the distance. The buildings wink back at me, and the Washington Monument looks small under the night sky. My shoulders sag. My social meter starts to slowly recharge under the stars, and I smile at the half sliver of the moon peeking out from behind a patch of clouds.

"Hey," a voice says from behind me, and I'd recognize it anywhere. "Mind if I join you?"

I glance at Reid, my chin on my shoulder and my smile stretching wider at the sight of him. Hands in his pockets. Socks on his feet and ruffled hair. He's beautiful in the moonlight and I sigh, drinking him in.

"I'd like that," I say, looking back at the skyline so he doesn't catch me staring.

He crosses the balcony in five long strides and leans against the railing. His fingers wrap around the metal and a muscle in his jaw works. I stare at his side profile and wonder what's going on in his head.

"I didn't know if you wanted to be left alone," he says.

"I've been alone all day. This is nice."

"Are you okay with it being me?"

I wonder if that's why he's kept his distance tonight. If that's why he let Grant talk my ear off—because he wasn't sure if I wanted him around.

It's sweet and vulnerable and perfectly him.

"If it can't be Maven or Emmy, you're a good runner-up," I joke, and he smiles.

"How was work?" Reid asks.

"Busy. Shitty," I admit around a tired exhale. I hesitate telling him this next part because of our bet, but it feels like something I need to share. "Our ticket sales have stalled, and I'm at a loss at what else I can do."

"I say this without any disdain behind it, believe it or not, but winning games helps. A three-game losing streak to start the year doesn't typically make people want to splurge on seats." He pauses, tapping his cheek, and I see an ink stain on his finger. Blue, and it makes me curious if he writes all his notes by hand. "Unless they're masochists. Maybe Thunderhawks fans are. They might have to be to like that song."

I nudge his side with my elbow. "Your team was bad once upon a time."

"We were fucking horrible," he agrees. "That was before the TikTok and Instagram boom, and thank fuck for that. I didn't have to see all the mean shit people said. I would've quit other-wise. Now I'm immune to it."

"People do say some mean shit, don't they?"

"Dallas missed a field goal on Sunday, and someone commented saying they hoped he tore his Achilles. Wild how athletes aren't perceived as real fucking people with real fucking feelings."

"Kind of makes me want to go into their office and force them to read mean tweets out loud about their work performance. See how they like it." I sigh and rub my neck, the remnants of an earlier headache stretching all the way down to my spine. "You all get together every week for a potluck dinner like this?"

"When we're in town, yeah. It started with Maverick's teammates, and it's gotten bigger over the years. It's my favorite day of the week," he tells me. "It's nice to have friends you can be yourself around."

"Are any of them fans of comic books?"

"No." Reid laughs, that rumbly noise that sounds so nice. "They don't make fun of me, though."

I hum in understanding. "That's why I've always liked Maven so much. I can scream at the television while we're watching a game and she doesn't bat an eye."

"Women," he murmurs, but nothing about it is bitter. "So goddamn friendly."

The moon gets higher in the sky. Behind us, there's muffled voices and cheering. I wonder if I should head back inside or go home. I don't know how long my invitation lasts, and I don't want to overstay my welcome.

"Work was rough for me today, too," Reid says, breaking the silence. "I don't know if I should be talking about this with you, but you can commiserate."

"I love commiserating," I say.

"We're also struggling with ticket sales. We already have such a loyal following, and finding new fans to reel in is proving to be more difficult than in years past. My boss has been on my ass lately about engagement and fan interaction, but I don't know what the hell he wants me to do."

"We're in the same boat. Algorithms are changing. It's taken me weeks to get consistent views on various platforms when I used to rake in millions after only a few hours. It's so frustrating, but I think we're both doing the best we can." I swallow, and I swear he steps closer to me. "I really liked the text series you did with your players. The one you posted on Friday? That was fun," I tell him. "Very unique."

"Oh. Thanks." Reid's mouth quirks, and I like that hint of a smile more than I should.

"Don't let it go to your head. The rest of your stuff annoys the shit out of me."

"Right back at ya, Sinclair." He glances at me, and the stars look like they're twinkling in his eyes. "Want to come over tonight?"

I should go home.

That would be the responsible thing to do.

I have four emails I need to draft and send to potential sponsors by noon tomorrow. A YouTube video I need to edit and pare down from forty-five minutes to sixteen. DMs from giveaway winners I need to sift through so I can collect their addresses and mail out merchandise.

But that same feeling that struck me the night at the bar when we met strikes me again; I don't want to go.

I don't want to be alone.

I want to be with him.

"Yeah," I say. His pinky brushes against my hip, and I remind myself it would be reckless to kiss him out here. That would make this real, a living, breathing thing that exists outside the bedroom, and that's not part of our rules. "I do."

"Good," he mumbles, voice thick with lust I feel like a blanket around my shoulders. "Been wanting you all day, and I can't wait anymore."

We plan strategic exits thirty minutes later, one right after the other. We walk the fifteen blocks to his place, stopping at a food truck for empanadas and a jar of fresh salsa. When he unlocks the door, his keys end up on the floor and I end up on my knees.

Reid wraps one hand through my hair and curls the other around my chin, our eyes locked as I take him to the back of my throat until he says my name.

Later, after he pulls me apart then puts me back together slowly, methodically, in the perfect way I like, I realize Tuesday might be my new favorite day of the week.

"THE LAST TIME I threw a baseball, I was eight," I say, fixing the brim of my hat. "I'm going to go ahead and apologize for the shit show that's about to happen."

"It's for a good cause." Maverick tucks in his jersey and bends down to lace up his cleats. "Who doesn't love helping charity?"

"I'm all for helping charity, but making a fool of myself in front of five thousand people is going to be fucking embarrassing." I take a sip of my Gatorade, like it's going to make me an athlete. "When I'm slow around the bases, you guys can't make fun of me."

"Dallas isn't fast," Maverick says, clasping my shoulder. "He looks like a baby deer learning to walk when he starts running."

"I heard that," Dallas yells from around the corner. "And I run just fine, you asshole."

"Dad said a bad word." June looks up from her book and grins. "He has to put money in the swear jar."

"You're going to be rich, kid." Maverick lifts her off the couch and spins her around. "I'm going to contribute a hundred bucks to the jar too. Just so you can really earn some dough."

She grins and gives him a hug. "Thanks, Uncle Mav."

"Sorry, JB," I tell her. "I'm not rich like Mavvy, so he'll put in an extra hundred on my behalf. Won't you, Miller?"

Maverick rolls his eyes and digs out his wallet, handing June two crisp bills. "I swear people like to take advantage of me," he grumbles.

"Is Avery coming today?" June asks, pocketing the money. "I liked her a lot and she's very fun. I helped her wrap your office in the preseason. Mom says you could use someone like that in your life, Uncle Reid, so you should hang out with her some more."

My office and the preseason game.

Fucking her on the couch.

Starting this friends with benefits arrangement that's been the best thing of my fucking life.

I never thought I'd be thankful for cellophane, but I might have to buy some stock in their company as a thank you for ensuring I'm perpetually satisfied.

"You little devil. I don't know if she's coming," I say. "It's not her team, so she doesn't have a reason to come."

"Did you invite her?" Maverick asks.

"No. I mean, I guess I did? I told her it was happening and where to buy tickets. But we don't do that sort of thing. We just —" I clear my throat and choose my next words carefully. "Hang out."

He smirks. "Yeah? And how is the *hanging out* going?"

Fucking amazingly.

It's simple and easy, full of mindless need.

Our hands are on each other the second she walks through the door and it feels like we've been doing this for years.

I'm living in a daze or some alternate reality.

It's the only logical explanation for why my three-year slump of only having my hand to get me off is broken by having nonstop sex with a woman so far out of my league.

Avery sent me a photo a few days ago when the Thunderhawks were away in Pittsburgh. It was a half-lit shot from her hotel room, her fingers between her legs and her shirt riding up her chest.

I jerked off to it, some rare bout of spontaneity telling me to record myself and send it to her, and I was rewarded with another photo, closer up, with the words *wish you were here* written under it.

It *works*, and I don't know why we didn't start doing this earlier.

"The hanging out is going very well," I say to Maverick. "We've settled into a groove."

"And how are your feelings for her?"

"You like Avery?" June asks. "Like like her?"

"It's not like that, kiddo. We're... friends. Ah, friendly, I guess is the right way to describe it. She's nice and all, but I don't have feelings for her."

"You need a girlfriend," June says. "Everyone else has someone. Don't you feel lonely?"

Kids and their lack of filters.

"I'm not lonely. I have plenty of things that make me happy. You. Your dad and mom. Mav and Emmy. My job. My LEGO collection and plants. Happiness isn't defined by having a partner, June Bug," I say.

"I know that. Mom tells me I can live alone with ten cats if I want to." June wrinkles her nose. "I don't want cats, though. I want dogs."

"It's a real shame your parents haven't gotten you a dog yet," Maverick says, raising his voice so Dallas can hear him from the bedroom. "You've only been asking for *years*."

"I can't wait until you become a father so I can give you a

hard time," Dallas says, appearing in the living room. He drops some money in the swear jar and kisses the top of June's head. "Go get your backpack, sweetheart. We're heading out in a minute."

June takes off down the hall. When we're alone, Maverick clears his throat. He avoids our gazes and looks at the ground.

"About, ah, the father thing," he says, and we both stare at him.

"No fucking way," I say.

"You're fucking joking," Dallas adds.

"Emmy and I had a long conversation the other night. We've both been back and forth on if we want kids for a long time, and, truly, life with her is enough. I don't need anything else. I wake up every day, happy as shit, and I know I'm going to be happy for the rest of my life. But lately... I don't know." Maverick laughs. He runs a hand through his dark hair, and his palm shakes. "We agree that something is missing. With only two years left on her contract with Baltimore, we're going to start trying for a baby next summer. If it happens, it happens. If it doesn't, we'll keep playing and keep trying."

"Holy *shit*." Dallas wraps him in a tight hug. "Maverick Miller. A fucking *dad*. I never thought I'd see the day."

"That's Daddy to you," he jokes.

"This is awesome, man." I hug him too. "Look at you growing up."

"When is it going to be your turn?" Maverick asks. "It feels weird I'm going through all these life changes while you're single. You're *never* single."

"You had a phase in your life where you had fun with people without caring about the labels. I've never gone through that phase, and maybe now it's my turn. To not think about five, ten years down the road, but just what I'm doing tomorrow."

"Does Avery want kids?"

"No clue. That's not really relevant to our situation," I say.

"When you were dating Sheila, you had that conversation by your fifth date," Maverick says.

"And I ended up with a broken engagement and a canceled wedding. Can you two stop meddling and let me be? I know this isn't who I usually am. I know this isn't who I'm going to be the rest of my life, but I'm having fun right now. We're two consenting adults who know what we want. Who know the rules and the boundaries we've set up, and rely on honest and open communication to keep having fun. Let me fuck in peace. I didn't give you shit when you were going through your playboy lifestyle before you met Emmy."

"Fine." Maverick holds up his hands. "I'll drop it."

"Thank you," I say. "Now let's get the hell out of here so I can embarrass myself."

I hate playing sports.

I always have, ever since my dad taught me how to hold a tee ball bat when I was four years old.

All the other boys are signed up for baseball, he told me when I was in elementary school.

You can't sit inside all day like a fucking pansy, he yelled at me when I locked my bedroom door and pulled out my laptop in middle school.

No woman is ever going to take you seriously if you don't have some sort of athletic accolade under your belt, you goddamn fucking loser, he snarled when I begrudgingly decided to try out for my high school team and got cut the first day.

I tried.

I tried and I tried and I fucking *tried* to be an athlete, but I'm not. I'm uncoordinated and slow and so far from fucking grace-ful, it's hysterical.

I hate standing in the sun.

I hate people watching me.

I hate swinging a bat and missing the ball and being embar-rassed when I'm at the plate.

I hate it all, and even though I keep telling myself this is all for a good cause, my skin is prickly. My motivation is declining with every inning, and I can't get out of here fast enough.

"You good, Plant Daddy?" Maverick calls out as he jogs to first base at the top of the fifth.

I start my trek to the outfield after three strikes and squint into the sun. "Fucking dandy."

We set up UPS Field with a baseball diamond, and Titans fans are out in full force today. They've filled the seats we opened up so they could get a glimpse of their favorite players. There's a signing line scheduled for after the game, and I've already assigned one of the interns to be in charge of filming content for it.

I know they put me out here because I can't catch to save my life, but standing alone and in the heat is not my idea of a good time.

I'm miserable, and I pull off my hat and wipe my forehead.

"Having fun?" someone yells from behind me.

I turn around and find Avery sitting in the row closest to the field. She has on a big sun hat that covers her head and a strappy little tank top that shows off her shoulders.

My throat goes dry at the sight of her.

"Have you been here the whole time?" I ask, jogging her way.

"Yup."

"You aren't melting? You should move to the section in the shade."

"I can't make fun of you from all the way over there."

I snort and put my glove on my hip. "You haven't talked any shit yet."

"Because you haven't done anything impressive. You could at least try to catch the ball, Duncan."

"Want to come down here and show me how it's done, Sinclair?"

Her grin is sly, and I hate that my dick twitches. "Don't tempt me with a good time. I'm a fast learner."

I flip her off and turn back to the field, trying to focus my attention to the game. Dallas strikes out, and Maverick cheers when he's sent back to the dugout.

"Your ass looks nice in those pants," Avery calls out.

"Stop distracting me," I yell at her. "Do you have money on this game or something?"

"On the charity softball game?"

"I don't know."

"Nah. I like seeing you riled up. Is this how you look when you're responding to me online? Red-faced with wrinkled eyebrows?"

I huff and crouch low, watching the next player take the mound. He swings and misses the first pitch, and I sigh.

"I hate playing sports," I admit, and out of the corner of my eye, I see her scoot to the edge of her seat. "I'd much rather be inside playing my kind of games. This is my idea of hell."

"You'd make a good athlete, though. You have very nice shoulders," she blurts out, and I turn to look at her again. "And you're strong."

"Keep your tongue in your mouth," I joke, and it's her turn to throw a middle finger my way. "You don't—"

"Duncan!" Maverick screams. "The ball!"

I look at the infield, trying to figure out what's going on. The batter, a running back from the Titans, is making his way to second base with a surprising amount of speed.

"Reid, the—"

"I see it." I lift my arm above my head and wait for the ball to drop in my glove.

Except, it doesn't.

By the time I realize I'm too far left, the ball is six inches away from my face, and then everything goes black.

I'M on my feet before I can think twice.

Reid is lying motionless on the field, his arms out at his sides and his hat knocked off his head. I charge down the stairs that lead to the turf and leap over the wall. The six-foot drop feels like it takes forever, and when my feet land on the ground, my heart beats wildly in my chest as dozens of players surround him.

"Is he dead? Oh my god, he's going to be so pissed if he's dead," Maverick says when I get close. "How did he not see the ball?"

"He's not *dead*." Dallas squats down and touches Reid's chest, exhaling a sigh of relief. "He's breathing. Thank fucking god."

"What do we do? Do we call an ambulance?"

"I can get one of the trainers. They're—"

"I'm alive," Reid grits out, and my eyes sting with tears. My vision turns watery when he pushes onto his elbows and winces, a nasty mark forming on his face. "This is why I don't play fucking sports."

"Thank *fuck*." Maverick drops to his knees and holds Reid's hand. "Are you ok? What the hell happened?"

"Bad depth perception and a breeze. Should've put me at catcher." He sits all the way up and groans when he finds his glasses broken. "Shit."

"We need to make sure you're not concussed," Dallas says. "You went straight to the ground."

"I'm fine." Reid rubs his forehead and tips his head to the sky. "I know who I am and where I am."

"Still. We're going to have you evaluated. And you're not playing the rest of the game," Dallas argues.

"I should've gotten hit in the face sooner. Would've saved me from this fucking misery," he answers, and I bark out a laugh. Reid cranes his neck and looks at me with wide eyes. "Hey, Sinclair."

"Hey." I slip my hands in the back pockets of my jean shorts, our gazes holding. After three beats of staring at each other, I sniff and dip my chin, not wanting anyone to see me emotional. Not wanting *him* to see me emotional. "What a way to lose an out."

"Figured it was time for me to be dramatic about something in my life." He reaches out an arm, and Dallas helps him to his feet. "I'm fine. Really. I'll pop in with the doctor and watch the rest of the game from the sidelines."

"You're going to have to get cleaned up before that, man," Maverick tells him. "Your nose is bleeding, and we can't scare the kids."

"I can help," I offer. "If you need a hand."

Reid's throat bobs. There's blood all down his chin that's already started to dry. The left side of his face is swelling, and he's definitely going to have a black eye in a few days.

I want to hug him.

I want to put my hand on his chest and make sure he's breathing.

I know he is—he's six feet away from me and holding full

conversations—but I want to check for myself. Just to know everything is okay.

"That would be nice," he says, brushing clumps of grass off his pants. "I can, uh, show you our medical room."

The crowd around us starts to disperse and the fans cheer. He gives a feeble wave to the spectators, and Dallas slings an arm over his shoulder.

"Want one of us to come with you?" Dallas asks under his breath.

Reid shakes his head. His eyes meet mine again, and his smile is soft around the edges. "I'll be in good hands."

"Do you have another pair of glasses at home?" I ask Reid as we talk through the tunnel to the Titans' training room, and he nods.

"Yeah. They're big on my face and look stupid as fuck, but they'll have to do." He stops short of opening the door in front of us and touches my wrist. The brush of his finger against my pulse point is searing, electrifying, and I suck in a sharp breath. "You okay?"

"Yeah. Yup." I wipe under my eyes and smile. There's a smudge of mascara on my thumb, and I hope I don't look like a raccoon. "Can't believe you missed that pop fly."

"The blood doesn't help my case, but I'm fine. Really."

"I know." I bob my head and look over his shoulder. I'm afraid to look at him straight on, because I shouldn't be feeling like this. I shouldn't be worried about his health or if he has internal bleeding. I shouldn't be making a list of the things he might need if he has a concussion, or wondering if he'd be okay with me helping to take care of him. "I'm not worried."

Reid steps closer to me. His cleats knock against my sandals, and I tip my chin back so I can look up at him.

I can't explain what happens next or why, but one minute,

I'm giving him a fake smile, and the next, a sob is escaping from the trenches of my chest.

"Come here," he says gently, pulling me to his body. He smells like sweat and grass and the metallic scent of blood, but I don't care. I melt into his embrace as he hugs me, fingers brushing through the ends of my hair and arms steady around me. "I'm okay, pretty girl. I'm all right."

"I was worried about you," I admit around a hiccup, and it's muffled by the pinstripe jersey that has no business looking so good on him. "One second you were lobbing sarcasm at me, the next you were flat on your back. I didn't like seeing you like that."

"Think you might care about me, Sinclair," he says into my hair, and I'm struck with the sudden and horrifying realization I *do* care about him. "Just a little bit."

"In your dreams, Duncan," I say, even though we both know I'm lying. I inhale a deep breath and he presses a kiss to my hair. To my forehead and the curve of my cheekbone. To the corner of my mouth, and my heart skips a beat. "We should get you cleaned up."

"Whatever you say, Doctor Avery."

I tug him through the door and sit him on a leather table. I find a washcloth and run it under the faucet, wetting it until it's soaked. I stand between his legs, and he rests his hand on his thighs. His chest rises and falls too fast for my liking, and I frown.

"Can I touch you?" I ask softly, because this is different from our normal encounters.

This is intimate, *personal.* Our clothes are on but my body is on fire, aware of every one of his movements.

The press of his thighs. The brush of his fingers over the back of my hand. His exhales, warm on my skin.

"Yes," he croaks, a fractured word I feel in the center of my chest. In the tiny crevice by my heart, the spot that's been empty for far too long. "You can do whatever you want to me."

There might be a deeper meaning there.

Later, when I'm in bed and trying to fall asleep, I'll overanalyze it and wonder what he meant, but for right now, I take him at face value and fall into caretaking mode.

I cup the back of his head, his sweat-soaked hair soft between my fingers. I dab his forehead and his cheek. The ridge of his nose and the line of his jaw. Reid's eyes flutter closed, and for half a second, I wonder if he's asleep.

I like seeing him like this, perfectly at peace and without a phone in his hand. Attentive and present and *here.*

I move the rag over to the cheek that's swollen. His skin is hot to the touch and already tinged shades of pink and red. An expression of pain flashes across his face, but I soothe the sting away with a brush of my fingers, and he melts into me.

I study him, and I'm hit with how beautiful he is. How nice and kind he is, and how willing he is to accept help. The epitome of the perfect man, who one day, when he has the time to slow down and enjoy what's around him, is going to make someone very happy.

I frown again and settle my hand at the base of his neck, clearing the thought away.

"That feels nice," he murmurs. It's hazy, stuck in a fog and probably close to a concussion, but I accept the compliment anyway. How could I not? "Could you follow me around and do that forever?"

I puff out a laugh and rest my forehead against his when he's cleaned up and good as new. "Reid?"

"Yeah?"

"I think I'd like to kiss you right now. If that's okay. If you're feeling up to it."

He hums and opens his eyes. "I'm definitely feeling up for it. Might help me heal even faster, in fact."

I move closer to him, until our chests are pressed together and our bodies almost fuse as one. He lifts his chin, in a dare almost, leaving the ball in my court to make the first move.

So I do.

I kiss him not because we're in the heat of the moment, but because I want to.

Because I *need* to.

"You're beautiful," Reid murmurs, and I tuck it away close to my chest. "Sometimes I still can't believe I get to have you like this."

"In another part of your stadium?" I ask, my lips moving to his neck. I kiss below his ear. Above his collarbone, and I smile when he tips his head back and groans. "It's becoming a trend, I've noticed."

"No." The single word shakes. Turns fraught and hesitant, like he's afraid to admit this next part out loud. "Like you're mine."

A thousand emotions hit me at once, and when I pull back, I see them in his eyes too.

Mine.

It's been so long since I've belonged to someone, but I like how it feels with Reid.

Like coming home after a long day, comfortable and familiar.

A string in me pulls tight, and the six inches between us is still too much. I give his shoulders a gentle nudge, telling him I want him to move back. Telling him I want more, want *him*, and he understands, scooting across the table and dragging me with him.

I throw a leg over either side of his waist and cradle his face in my hands, careful to be gentle because he's in pain. Our kisses turn messier, greedier when he slips his hand under my shirt and I hiss at the cool touch of his palm against my ribs. More desperate when I roll my hips and grind against him, the tight material of his pants leaving nothing to my imagination.

I feel him hard, ready, and when I look down at him, a single question on the tip of my tongue, he grins.

"Fuck me, Avery," he whispers in my ear, licking a hot swipe of his tongue up my neck.

"I only wanted to make sure you were okay," I say, shimmying his pants to his knees, his cock springing free. "I was worried."

"Show me how worried," he says. "Show me you care."

I do show him. With my hands. With my tongue. With the spit I use to rub up his cock then down, getting him wet enough so he can slide into me with one lift of his hips.

It's heaven. The best thing I've ever felt in my entire life, and when he tells me he's close, when he tells me he should probably pull out, I stay firmly in place, savoring the warm release I feel inside me before I follow him over the edge.

Reid looks a little dazed when he comes back to earth, and we get dressed. Later, I hold his hand while the team doctor checks his head, and a sharp pang of happiness bursts through me when I hear he's going to be okay. That he's fine, and he only needs to ice the injuries.

Everything about the afternoon feels different, and I think, maybe days too late, that we might be heading down a road neither of us can come back from.

THIRTY
AVERY

ME

My place tonight.

REID

I finally get to see your apartment?

ME

You sound happier about getting a tour of my place than you do about fucking me on the kitchen counter.

REID

Come on, Sinclair. I can have both.

Dinner? I'll pick something up on the way.

ME

Sure. I'm good with whatever.

REID

I have a meeting until six, then I'll head over.

ME

Thanks for the reminder. I need to talk some shit on your post after your loss on Sunday. Gosh, I can't wait until we play against you next week.

REID

Fuck you.

ME

That's the plan for later tonight.

Hopefully you're willing to lend a helping hand.

REID

And if I'm not?

ME

You can sit in the corner and watch.

"I HOPE MEXICAN FOOD IS OKAY." Reid sets down a large paper bag on my kitchen island. "Enchiladas sounded fucking amazing."

"Perfect." I stand on my toes and grab two plates from the cabinet, putting them next to a dish of queso. "How was your meeting?"

"Not bad. A professional development one-on-one with my boss. Seems like he's changed his tune as far as my performance goes. I had a couple videos go viral in the past week, and merchandise sales are up. We've also secured some large group ticket sales for December around the holidays, so things are looking encouraging on all fronts."

"Still think you're going to win our bet?" I ask, putting a hand on my hip.

Reid crowds my space. He tilts my chin to meet his gaze, and his eyes are dark. "Without a doubt," he says nice and low before he kisses me, and I know it's a promise of what's to come later tonight.

I shiver at the press of his mouth. I hum in appreciation when he lifts me in one easy swoop and sets me on the counter. A knife clatters into the sink, and the bottle of chardonnay I pulled out of the fridge nearly rolls onto the floor.

"Your cockiness isn't cute," I say. "But your new glasses are."

"I bet your wet pussy would tell me differently."

He's right.

My underwear is damp. My nipples pebble under my shirt, and I cross my arms over my chest so he can't see the effect he has on me. "In your dreams, Duncan."

"Trust me, you're always wet in my dreams," Reid says, and I can't help but laugh. "You're also usually naked in my bed and reading a comic book."

He steps back and pops a chip in his mouth, leaving me breathless and aching for him. The asshole knows it, too, because he clamps down on a smile. His attention bounces to the front of my shorts and holds there until my legs open and I rest my hand on my thigh, teasing him like he's teasing me.

"I'm glad to see you're still on two feet after your less than stellar baseball play," I say. "Any lingering pain?"

"No," he rasps, pulling his gaze to the bag of food. He unloads two Styrofoam boxes and sets them on the counter. "I can't believe I haven't seen you since then. How was Denver?"

"Fun. It would be a beautiful place to live. Winning helped, and the guys are finally finding their groove. Malcolm is gelling well with the offense and—" I shut my mouth and giggle at the expression on Reid's face. "You don't care about this, do you?"

"What gave it away?"

"You look like I just started talking about calculus and physics."

"That's not right. If you started talking about calculus, I'd be fucking giddy. I'm a numbers guy, Sinclair. Integrals are my form of dirty talk."

"Sounds like I need to step it up in the bedroom," I tease, and his sharp gaze cuts to mine. "What?"

Reid moves closer to me and cups my cheek. "You don't need to step anything up. You drive me crazy."

"I do?" I ask, and he nods.

"All the fucking time. With your text messages. With your photos. When you're ribbing me on your official account." Reid drags his thumb over my bottom lip. "The things I want to do to this smart fucking mouth."

"What kind of things do you want to do?"

"I'll show you once I get you fed." He squeezes my thighs. "Food first."

We work around each other in my kitchen. I point out where I keep the silverware and he fills two glasses with water. We sit on the barstools and dig in, melting into silence while we eat.

"What are you doing for your bye week next week?" he asks, finishing off his first serving of food.

I lick away a drop of hot sauce from the back of my hand. His eyes follow my movements, and he shifts on his stool. "I have some reading I want to catch up on, and Maven mentioned a dinner with her, Emmy, and a few of the girls who work for the Stars."

"It's cool you all are friends. From what Maven and Emmy have told me, getting close to women in the sports world can be difficult," Reid says.

"Very difficult," I agree. "There are some who are in the industry for the wrong reasons. They want to get close to the players. They want to find a rich husband or boyfriend and think this is the way in. For the most part, though, we all want to see *more* women in our fields. We want to break down the barriers and stereotypes associated with our careers. We want to be valued like our male counterparts." I shrug and inhale half my enchilada. "Sorry. I don't mean to make this a whole feminism thing."

"You're not. It's important to you. And, as someone who's spent their fair share of time with you and would love to see more women in sports, it's important to me too."

"Thanks for being part of the team." I swipe a forkful of beans off his plate. "Do you want a tour of my place?"

"Of course I do. I need to see where you do all your pathetic trash talking."

I laugh and jump off the stool, tugging on his sleeve. "Come on, Duncan."

I lead him to the living room, a smaller space than his and not nearly as nice. I wasn't looking for anything fancy when I moved up here, just somewhere I could make my own.

I think I've done a good job adding personal touches. The shelf shoved against the wall is overflowing with books. The antique lamps and the tables on either side of the couch add a pop of color to the space. The fuzzy blanket draped over the small chair by the window is cozy, and it's the spot I like to sit in and watch the snow fall in late winter.

I've always wanted something to feel like *mine*, and in the last year, this has become more like a home. Less of a spot where I rest my head for ten hours between being at the stadium, game nights and travel days and more like a safe haven.

Reid examines every nook and cranny, and I wring my hands together. I don't know why I've been hesitant to show him my apartment.

In a way, it feels like the next step someone would take in a relationship. Maybe I'm afraid he'll find something he doesn't like and run away. Maybe I want him to feel like he has a place here, a spot where he belongs too.

"I like it," he says after a long stretch of silence. He touches the mason jar of sunflowers sitting in the window and smiles. "It's very you."

"Is that a good thing?" I ask, watching him pick up a framed photo from back in college. He taps the corners and his smile gets bigger. It reaches the crinkles around his eyes and the scrunch in his nose. "Sounds like it could go either way."

I've always been the popular girl. I was prom queen and cheerleading captain in high school. President of my sorority in college and homecoming queen. The one who had dozens of friends and could always find someone to talk to.

In my twenties, that popularity mixed into my dating life. I could score any guy I wanted, and I wouldn't think twice about their opinion of me or how I was perceived. If they thought I was silly for wearing dresses to work and six-inch heels because I liked how they made my legs look, I didn't care.

My confidence with men has wavered in the last few years, though. After my breakup with Peter, I've become unsure of myself. Worried that maybe I'm not enough. Scared to share parts of my life I used to give away freely.

I'm reluctant to tear down my walls become someone already tore them down so aggressively in the past.

Reid is the first guy to be in my apartment, and it feels like that's important.

"It's a very good thing. I can tell so many things about you just from looking around. You like to read and decorate. You get cold easily, so you always need a blanket nearby." His fingers wrap around the crochet project my mom gave me for Christmas six years ago. "I'm glad I get to be here and see it."

"That's where I message you most of the time." I point to the couch, the leather a little worn, but very loved. "There, and my bedroom."

His eyes blaze. "I've been dying to see your room since I got here."

I drag him down the hall, his hand in mine. I like the way his thumb rubs the inside of my wrist. How close he stands to me, as if he doesn't want to be far away, not even for a second.

When we get to my room, Reid doesn't bother to look around. He nudges me to the bed and I sit on the edge of the mattress, anticipation building at the base of my spine.

He bends down to kiss me and smiles when I wrap my arms around his neck. I tug him on top of me until we're a tangle of limbs on the already wrinkled sheets.

Reid holds himself above me on the bed and blows out a breath. "Fuck, I've missed you."

"You talked to me every day."

"Not the same. I don't like going so long without seeing you."

"So don't." I peel off my shirt, desperate for him. "Come by anytime."

"That won't bother you?" He pulls the cups of my bra down and palms my left breast. His mouth closes over my nipple and I sigh, ready to chase the relief I've craved since I woke up this morning. "I don't want to take up too much of your time."

"I—*ah*. It won't be time wasted when I know I'm going to get *this* out of it."

Reid's laugh is a rumble against my skin, and he makes quick work of my lounge shorts and underwear.

His knuckles brush across my entrance, and I know he can feel how wet I am. How ready I already am. The orgasm I gave myself in the shower before he got here did little to fill the void of his touch, and *fuck*, I've missed him too.

"*Shit*, Ave. I love how responsive you are and how badly you want me."

"Yeah?" I wrap my fingers around his wrist, keeping his hand there. His thumb circles my clit, and I groan. "I want you more than I've wanted anyone else, Reid."

He knows my body better than I do at this point. He's an

expert in the things I like and the things I love. It's cruel torture to lie here and let him have his way with me, a demise he's going to draw out to last as long as possible.

Reid moves away from me, and I miss him already. He scoots to the end of the bed on his stomach, his intent clear as he settles between my legs.

He pulls off his glasses and tosses them toward the pillows, not a care in the damn world where they end up. Eyes glinting with determination and lust, a sinful spark behind the green, he grins when he bites the inside of my thigh.

"Going to get you off first," he mumbles. He licks his lips and holds under my knees, his palms smooth and steady. "I like having your cum on my hands and tongue." I drop my head back when he parts me with two fingers. I grin when he groans in delight and curses me under his breath. "Fucking look at you. Dripping already, and all for me."

Two fingers press inside me, stretching me, then three. My back arches off the bed. He bands an arm over my stomach, keeping me in place, and I grind into his face.

"Taking it so well," Reid says, and when he adds his tongue, I moan his name. I grip the back of his head, burying his face in my pussy. "Guess you missed me too."

I've missed you so much.

The words must tumble out of me accidentally in a fog of desire, because his movements slow. His touch goes from rough to gentle, and he kisses the top of my knee.

"I want you inside me," I whisper, hoping to breeze past the admission.

He undresses, discarding his shirt and jeans and the navy-blue boxers I like. There's a hole on the ass, right near the curve of his cheek, and I love that he hasn't bothered to replace them yet.

He lines himself up with my entrance, and I let out a shaky

exhale. He strokes my calf to help me relax, and I nod to tell him I'm ready.

Our groans match when he sinks in me, and no matter how many times we do this, the first burst of sensation is almost too overwhelming.

Reid leans forward, his elbows by my ears and his chest against mine. I feel the sweat on his pecs. The beat of his heart and his hand traveling from my chest to my throat, fingers wrapping around my neck in the perfect way I can't get enough of.

He moves, an easy thrust until he's buried all the way inside me.

My breath catches and he strokes my windpipe up and down, murmuring my name.

This doesn't feel like fucking.

This isn't the game we usually play.

It's tender and gentle and sex in its most real form. Vulnerable. Raw and taking our time.

I want him to stay inside me forever.

I want him to take over my heart and my mind, and when our gazes meet, I swear there are stars behind his eyes.

"Okay?" he slurs, a little drunk on euphoria.

"Perfect." I touch his cheek and he turns to kiss my hand. "It's always going to be okay, Reid. I trust you."

He nods, cheeks pink and breath stuttered. He opens my legs wider, finding a new angle, one he's never reached before.

A moan escapes me, and I'll never get over how *good* he makes me feel.

How full and how perfect, and how sometimes, when he's looking at me like this, I think the moment could last forever.

SEX HAS NEVER BEEN like this.

I know I'm buried inside her and trying not to lose my mind, but it's never been like *this*. Careful and slow. A pressure in my chest when I thrust into her and she whispers my name.

Fuck.

Fuck.

What the fuck does that mean?

Any coherent thought I try to have flies out the window when she pushes her tits together. When she plays with her nipples and moves her hips like a goddamn goddess.

How does this still feel *so fucking good*?

We've been fucking each other for weeks and it still hasn't lost its appeal. I think I want her more now than I did the first and second time we were together, craving her like she's the life-line keeping me alive.

God, the things I want to do to her.

The things I want to try but can never find the time, because I'm too easily distracted. Lost in the world of her tight cunt and the way she clenches around my dick, like I'm her salvation too.

"*Jesus*, Ave. A week and a half without me and you're tight as hell. Have you been using your toy? Have you been fucking yourself to the thought of me?" I ask, my stream of consciousness growing shakier by the second.

"No." She whines when I press on her clit. She cries out when I give it a light slap, and she trembles when I twist her nipples. "It doesn't satisfy me anymore. Not after having you." I grin down at her, smug and proud, and her eyes flutter open. She laughs when she sees the curve of my smile. "That went straight to your head, didn't it?"

"Never going to forget it. Next time I'm over, I want to fuck you with your toy. I think I know all the ways you like to be taken care of, but that'll help me make sure. I don't want to forget anything."

"That—" Avery groans. I'm so close to losing it, and every noise from her is fuel to the fire. Another piece of rationality shredded to nothingness. I've never had any problems lasting in the bedroom before, but with her, it feels like I only have goddamn seconds until I come. "Sounds like a dream."

She's the fucking dream, with her hair spread out on the pillows and her tits lifted up by her bra. I didn't bother to take it off. I want to see the way they bounced when I fuck her nice and hard.

"What do you need?" I ask, and she meets me thrust for thrust. "What do you need to come?"

"Can we try on my side?" she pants. "I like how deep you get that way."

I know it's one of her favorite positions, and we readjust. I hike up her leg and drive into her while my fingers grip her knee. Marking her has become one of my favorite hobbies.

I like finding new places to touch her. New parts of her body I haven't explored that I can claim as my own. The underside of her left ass cheek. Her right hip and her left shoulder in a spot she can hide with her hair.

Avery grabs my ass, letting me know she wants it faster. Harder, and we fall into the pace we know so well. I give her what she wants, the quick snap of my hips and a hand on her neck.

She likes that best, I've learned. I never thought I'd be the guy who wrapped his fingers around someone's throat, but *fuck*, she looks pretty dressed up like this.

"I'm close," she says, telling me what I already know.

Her eyes close, and when I slap her clit again, she jolts to life.

"Keep them open. Want to watch you," I say, and her cheeks color with a deep red blush.

There's another minute where she tries to hold on. Tries to prolong the inevitable and enjoy the ride a little while longer, but I'm done waiting.

I want to feel her on me, and I want to feel her now.

"Reid," she whispers. She squirms on the sheets, a long moan following my name when I touch her nipples. "I'm—"

"That's it, Avery. You can do it," I say, and she topples over the edge.

She twists in my hold, trying to find the best spot for relief, but I keep her pinned to the bed. I work her through the high, only stopping when her eyes glaze over and she rests a hand on my chest.

"Fill me up," she whispers, and *fucking fuck*, I love how direct she is. How she doesn't leave any room for error because she tells you exactly what she wants. "I want you dripping down my leg."

I'm a simple man, and that makes me lose control.

My release hits me, and I groan. My muscles spasm and I see spots in my vision as I spill inside her.

I don't know how long it takes me to calm down, just that I fall onto the mattress and take a deep breath.

"Fuck," I draw out, opening an eye. "You killed me."

"I'll send flowers to your grave." She stretches out her legs and lifts her arms over her head. "Look at the mess we've made."

"*I* made." I reach over and tap her knee. "Open up. Let me see."

This is my favorite part. Avery opens her thighs, and I groan again. I graze over her pussy and the thick liquid sticks to my fingers.

Ruin me, Reid.

I'd like to do that again.

"Do you like what you see?" she whispers, and I bob my head.

I fucking *love* what I see.

It's the most possessive I've ever felt, and a word echoes in my head.

Mine.

For the first time since we started this thing between us, I wonder what it would be like if she were mine for real.

Would we have the same chemistry?

The same tension?

Would we say the same things to each other, or would it get boring after fifty, one hundred, a thousand times?

I don't think anything with Avery could be boring.

"Can I clean you up?" I ask, because I have the urge to take care of her. To make her as good as new.

"I was thinking we could go somewhere like this. Still messy." Avery nudges my hand away and replaces it with her own. "No one would know."

"Next time," I rasp, finding my voice. "Let's take a shower first."

When we climb into her bed an hour later, I pull her flush against me. Her back rests against my chest and her hands find mine. I sigh, content.

We've had a couple sleepovers. There have been a few times

after we've finished where it's too late for her to catch the Metro or an Uber, but it's early tonight. It's barely nine, and I'm not sure if she wants me to stick around.

"I'm tired," she yawns, drawing her knees to her stomach. "It just hit me."

"Go to sleep if you want." I kiss the top of her head. "You don't have to keep me entertained."

"Will you stay? At least for a little while?"

"I'll stay as long as you want." I yawn too and bury my face in her hair. I inhale the scent of her shampoo and smile. "Did you have a good day?"

"Not bad," she says. "The deeper we get into the season, the busier it is at the office. I can't believe we've won three games in a row. I'm posting four times a day on Instagram and three times a day on TikTok, and it *still* doesn't feel like enough."

"Yeah, but it's way more fun when you're posting about victories, isn't it?" I ask.

"Oh, definitely. If we could keep this streak going when we play you all next, I'd be on top of the world."

"Don't get your hopes up, Sinclair. The Titans do their best work later in the season, and the boys are just getting started."

"Could you let me have one thing?" Avery teases. She pokes my side, and I grab her wrist. "Just this once?"

"Nah." I close my eyes. "This is way more fun."

We're both quiet, and I realize how *nice* the moment feels.

Normally we only hang out for a few minutes before we're grabbing our clothes and getting dressed. There's never any lingering, never any cuddling. Not like this.

I wonder what else I can get out of her. Showing me her apartment is a big step, and I want to know more. I want to ask the question I've been wondering since I met her at the bar all those weeks ago.

"Are you asleep?" she asks.

"Close, but not all the way there yet. What about you?"

"I'm awake. You sound like you're stirring up there."

"The wheels in my head never stop." I rub my hand down her arm. "Can I ask you a question?"

"No, you cannot hack into my computer and steal the content I have planned for the next month," Avery says.

"Maybe I've already done that."

"If you had, I would've gotten a text message about the folder I keep all my plans in."

"Well, now I'm intrigued. What's the name of the folder?"

"'If you're Reid Duncan, do NOT click here or the computer will explode.'"

I laugh. "Original. I like it. You get points for creativity, that's for sure."

"Thanks," she says, and I feel her smiling against my chest. "What's your question?"

"Will you tell me about your dad? That night at the bar you told me you liked talking about him."

Avery spins in my hold so we're looking at each other. "What do you want to know?"

"What was he like?"

Her smile is beautiful, pulled from a memory. "He was the best man in the entire world. He was patient. A good listener. He loved my mom so deeply, and he loved me and my sister too. I'm talking daddy-daughter dances. Learning my recital numbers and practicing with me. Taking me to basketball games down in Orlando—that was our thing. It's how I fell in love with sports."

"Really?"

"Yeah. We'd go to games together all the time. We sat five rows up from the court, the first two seats off the stairs. I don't know how he stumbled into the seats, but he did, and thus began my love affair with sports. I have this dream that one day the Orlando Blazers will win a championship, and he'll be there in spirit when I celebrate."

"Did he ever get to see you in action on the sidelines? You said you worked down in Florida before coming to Baltimore, right?" I ask.

"Yeah. I was with a UFL team in a similar role. It didn't have the scope or scale the Thunderhawks position does, though."

"Is that where you met your ex, Peter?"

"Someone is nosy tonight." Avery laughs and rests her chin on my shoulder. "Why so inquisitive, Duncan?"

"Dunno." I shrug. "I know your orgasms like the back of my hand. Figured I should learn a little more about your personal life too."

"If you insist. Peter was the Vice President of Client Services for the UFL team, and we started spending a lot of time together as we brainstormed ways to get fans in the door. Spending time together turned into dating, and I thought we were happy. While I was in my role, our team's follower count quadrupled. I hate using the word *successful*, because it's so trivial and subjective, but I was. That's when Peter started to get frustrated. He was jealous my hard work was paying off, and he started trash-talking me to other people in the organization."

"I bet he loved that you got to give the keynote speech in Vegas," I draw out. "Fucking prick."

Avery shrugs. "I don't care what he thinks anymore."

"Well, that's good."

"Reid." She kisses my cheek, and I look down at her. "Are you jealous?"

"*No*," I say quickly, but it almost feels like a lie. "Okay, maybe I am, but it's because you're this incredible woman, Ave. Not everyone deserves to experience that incredibleness. Attention, wrong people. Remember?"

She's quiet for a minute, and I wonder if I said the wrong thing.

I worry I overstepped a boundary, but then she sighs, and I wait to hear what she has to say.

"Remember how I told you the story about him was a tenth or twelfth date kind of conversation?" she asks, and I nod. "I feel like we're at that point, don't you?"

I swallow.

I wouldn't consider fucking her six ways to Sunday a *date*, but the amount of time we've spent together goes well past twelve dates. It's probably pushing more like fifteen, twenty, and it hits me how close we've gotten.

The parts of ourselves we've shared and the way we can talk without judgment. Me, about my dad. Her, about her past significant others and where she thinks she's struggling in the workplace. There's trust there, and I realize I'm scared to hear what she has to say, because I think I'm going to care a little too much.

More than I should.

More than I'm allowed.

"I shared a few details in Vegas, but I want you to know the whole story. Peter was always strategic. He never hit me. All his abuse was verbal. A backhanded compliment here, an insult there. A disgust for the things I did. One day, we got in an argument. I had a hard time setting personal and professional boundaries back then, so when I say I was constantly on my phone, I mean I was *constantly* on my phone. He came home, saw me doing something on Instagram or TikTok, and he said some terrible things."

I don't know if I want to hear the rest. I already feel sick. I'm already clutching her tighter, as if I'm able to change the past and protect her, but it's a part of Avery's story.

I need to hear it.

"What kind of things?" I ask.

"He called me a whore. He said I was sleeping with the team. That no woman would *actually* want to work in the sports industry unless they wanted to get fucked by a bunch of football players," she admits, a tremble in her voice. "That's the real reason I didn't tell you about my job the night at the bar. I didn't know you, and I was afraid you'd say the exact same thing. And, after only spending a few minutes with you, I knew I'd be really disappointed if the nice guy I liked talking to felt the same way as the person who made me move away from home."

"Oh, sweetheart."

The endearment slips out, but she doesn't seem to mind. She draws a shape on my bare chest, her fingers running through the hair before settling over my heart.

"I haven't dated anyone since Peter. Casual hookups have been easier to manage than the messy side effects of diving into something serious."

"How do you feel about something serious now?" I stupidly ask.

Avery props up on an elbow. Her hair hides her face, and I shift so I can look at her.

"It doesn't seem nearly as scary as it did before," she admits. "Meeting you has reminded me of how much good is left in the world. How much love there is to give and receive. Look at you and your friends. Look at me and Maven, and now Emmy, too. I'm happier than I was back then, and that's a wonderful thing."

Love.

What a silly fucking word.

Could I love Avery?

One day down the road, could I fall for her?

I love fucking her.

I love hearing what witty one-liners she's going to toss my way.

But could I *love* her?

"Thank you for telling me," I say. She tilts her chin and kisses me, a soft press of her lips that has me wanting more. "For trusting me enough to share."

"I've never trusted anyone like I trust you, Reid."

I know that's a fucking important step, but suddenly, talking is the last thing I want to do.

I roll on top of her and her lips quirk up into a smile.

I wrap my hand around my cock, stroking myself, already hard and needing to have her again. Needing to show her all the good thing she should have. She nods, and this time when I fuck her, it's different.

There's a promise behind the thrust of my hips, as if I'm telling her, *You deserve better*.

She answers me enthusiastically, and for the first time since we've been together, I let my emotions sneak through. I treat her like I would if I belonged to her.

I kiss her the way I would kiss her every morning if I woke up next to her, and when she kisses me back, I think she might be doing the same thing.

@footballindc

Did you see the NFL's VP of Marketing will be at the game today?

I'm going to find a way to ask him who's int he lead for Social Media Account of the Year.

And if we beat you on our home turf? it would be electric.

@dcfootball

Social media is only one part of our bet. Don't forget the number of ticket sales is the other half. Get your client services people to print out the data with new account information, and we'll talk.

@footballindc

Fine. Only if you do the same.

@dcfootball
Already have it in my hands.

@footballindc
Did you have something to do with the twenty-five ducks I found in my office? I know they weren't there yesterday.

@dcfootball
I have no clue what you're talking about.

@footballindc
How the hell are you even getting into the stadium? Are the ducks ever going to stop?

@dcfootball
I have friends everywhere.

I might have created an access badge for myself too. It wasn't hard when I got into the Thunderhawks' database.

@footballindc
Wow. You're diabolical.

THIRTY-TWO
REID

ME

My place after the game?

AVERY

Depends if we win or lose.

ME

I'll make sure you win either way.

AVERY

Tempting.

ME

You know where I'll be.

AVERY

Preferably on your knees with your head
between my legs.

ME

My favorite place in the world.

"WHAT ARE YOU DOING TONIGHT?" Dallas asks. He pulls off his helmet and shakes out his hair, the ends of the dark strands already sweaty from his pre-game warmup. "Feels like I haven't seen you in ages. I'm stuck playing *Call of Duty* with Maverick, and you know how competitive he gets."

"Sorry." I unplug my phone from the portable charger I've been using the last hour and slip it in my pocket. "I've been busy with work."

"Is it just work? Or is your attention going other places too?"

I glance up at him. "What do you mean?"

"Avery," he says. "I figured y'all are spending time together."

"Oh." I rub the back of my neck. "We are, but it's only a couple nights a week."

"How's that going?"

"Good. We're having fun."

"I'm glad. You deserve to have some fun, Reid, and I'm glad you found someone you like hanging out with."

"Yeah." I bite back a smile because I *really* like hanging out with her. "Me too. Have you seen her today?"

"I saw her talking with some guy in a suit a little while ago. It seemed like they were having a good time." Dallas shrugs and heads for the water cooler. "They were over by the tunnel."

I narrow my eyes and look in that direction, finding her right away.

She *is* talking to a guy in a suit.

Laughing, too, with her head thrown back and her shoulders shaking.

That's her real laugh, the one she reserves for things that are really, really funny.

It's usually followed by a snort and a hand over her mouth, trying to hide the fact that she's giggling uncontrollably, and who the *fuck* is this douchebag who's taking up her time?

I roll my shoulders and glance at Brandy, one of our interns.

"I'll be right back," I tell her. "Can you make sure you get some video of the warmups and the pregame huddle so we can post it before kickoff?"

"Of course," she says excitedly, and I know I'm going to come back to more content than I could ever need. "Thanks, Reid."

I make my way to Avery. I get stopped a handful of times by people wanting to say hello. Allen, the head photographer, asks me about a player photoshoot next week. Britta, one of the cheerleaders, asks me if we're still on for the feature I'm doing on the dancers tomorrow.

It takes me longer than I'd like to break free from the conversations, but when I finally make it over to the tunnel, Avery is still laughing.

"Hey," I say, and she turns to look at me.

Her smile stretches wider when her eyes meet mine, and she tips her head to the side as she looks me up and down.

"Hey," she answers. "New sneakers?"

"Oh." I lift a foot, showing off the Nikes I bought two days ago. "Yeah."

"I like them." She glances back at the man in the suit, and I *hate* how he's staring at her. "Reid, this is Andrew. This is his first time in Baltimore, and I was explaining some of our traditions to him."

"Nice to meet you," I say, stiffly shaking his hand.

"You too." Andrew doesn't give me more than three seconds of his time before he's looking at Avery again. Stepping closer to her and leaning over her shoulder. "Tell me more about the song, Avery."

"Oh." She brightens and pulls out her phone, tapping on the screen. "I can't take all the credit. I met Rich Royce, the producer of the song, in a bar, and the idea came to us over a pitcher of margaritas. I can't believe how receptive the public is to it, and it makes me happy so many people are cheering for us to win just so they can hear it."

"It's genius," Andrew says, and Avery blushes. "I know the Titans have won Social Media Account of the Year the last three years, but I think the outcome is going to be very different this season."

Avery glances at me and sticks out her tongue. "Hear that, Duncan? Your reign is going to end soon."

"I have a few tricks up my sleeve," I say, sliding my hands into my pockets.

I wish I wore something warmer than loose fitting joggers. I wish I had something more professional on than a white long-sleeved Titans shirt and a backward hat. Avery looks like the picture of corporate America with her nice blouse and pleated slacks, and I know she's making a better impression than me.

"Reid and I have a bet going," she tells Andrew. "We're competing against each other for ticket sales and account of the year."

"Should be an easy win for you," Andrew says. "Just show your face in the videos."

"What?" Avery frowns. "What do you mean?"

"You're pretty. Gorgeous, even. Over fifty percent of the NFL's viewership is male. You want season ticket holders? Show yourself off. Sell yourself as a perk of joining the team's fanbase. You're doing too much right now. Tone it down a little."

"Oh," Avery says softly, and she stares at the field.

"Who cares about the content you're posting? Fans want to see hot women, and that includes you," Andrew says.

My hand flexes at my side. I don't like the direction this conversation is heading, and I want to intervene without acting like some self-righteous bonehead.

"I purposely leave myself out of the videos and photos," Avery challenges. "We all do. No social media manager is front and center. The purpose is to showcase the players. To give fans an insider look into what's happening on the field. It's not a dating app. Or a place to meet women."

"Maybe that should change, especially if they have a pretty face like yours. As for Social Media Account of the Year, well…" Andrew looks her up and down and grins. I hate his teeth. I hate the way his eyes gleam and how his attention hangs on her chest. I hate *him*. "I have a few ideas for that too. Provocative sells. Why do you think the Texas cheerleaders have more Instagram followers than half the teams in the league?"

The motherfucker laugh like he's the funniest guy in the world, and my eye twitches. I glance at Avery, and she's still staring at the field. Her shoulders curve in, and she's hanging her head in a way that tells me she's pissed. Hurt and upset.

"Don't talk to her like that," I say sharply. "You're diminishing her job, and that's bullshit."

"I'm not diminishing anything," Andrew argues. "*My* job is looking at data, and data doesn't lie. Men are going to watch football no matter what. You want more people to come through the doors? Give them a reason besides four quarters of touchdowns."

"Are we ignoring the rise in female viewership?" I ask, folding my arms across my chest. "Thanks to Ella Wright, women are—"

"Oh, for fuck's sake." He laughs, and I'm seconds away from strangling him. Cutting off his air supply and beating him to a pulp, and I've never been in a fight in my life. "Enough about that bitch. Speaking off the record, I hope she and Theo Asher break up. I can't stand seeing her on my television screen every week."

"But you want Avery to show her face?" I ask. "That's pretty hypocritical of you."

"I'm just telling you what the people want."

"Get out," I say, and Avery jerks her neck up to look at me.

"What?" Andrew asks.

"I said, get out."

"This isn't your stadium. You're not the head of security. You don't have a lot of pull here, buddy, and if you want to have a job tomorrow, I'd be very careful about what you say next."

There's a maniacal part of me that has the burning desire to support Avery. I don't want to make this situation about me, but I want her to know I have her back. That not everyone thinks like this prick does.

I want her to know she's valued. She's appreciated, and she's damn good at what she does. Fuck the bet. Fuck the game. This is bigger than that.

"Avery Sinclair is the best of the best," I say, keeping my voice level. "Three years in the league, and she's accomplished milestones others haven't in double that time. She's created a song every NFL fan recognizes. She's cultivated a diverse following of a football team loved by millions. Take a look around, Andrew. You know what I see? I see men. I see women. I see kids and older folks who have waited fucking *years* for the Thunderhawks to come back to Baltimore. *Avery* has had a hand in that. Sure, they still have a ways to go with season ticket holders and loyal fans who are in this for the long haul, but every fucking seat is sold. The stadium is filled. You know why? Because *Avery* comes up with promotions to get people in the doors. She does weekly fan spotlights, telling the stories of people who have been watching football for decades. She documents the charity work the Thunderhawks do. She makes this environment fun. A community others want to be a part of. And if you think telling her to show her face in front of the camera is the *only* way she's going to get fans in the door, you don't know fucking *shit* about how hard she works. That's an insult to the hours she puts in at the office. The late nights when she's awake until three, four in the morning, making sure every single photo she's going to post is fucking *perfect*. She's going to wipe the floor with me this year in our bet, and it's going to be a fucking *honor* to lose to her."

I stop for a breath. I move my attention to Avery, and her bottom lip is trembling. I want to reach out and hug her. Since this clown clearly doesn't value her as a professional, I refrain from pulling her to my chest and telling her it's going to be okay. I'm not going to give him any more ammunition.

"Here." I reach into my pocket and pull out a folded piece of paper. I hand it to her, and her fingers brush against mine when she takes it. "It's our ticket sales numbers so you can compare them to yours. I have a feeling yours are higher, which means you're winning, Sinclair. Congratulations."

I turn on my heel and head back to the Titans' sideline. The roar of the crowd is nothing but dull noise, and as much as I want to turn around and look behind me, I don't. I keep my gaze ahead, staring at the scoreboard.

We might win by fourteen, but after hearing Andrew's shitty comments, it feels a lot like a loss.

THIRTY-THREE

AVERY

IF I STARE at my computer any longer, I'm going to go cross-eyed.

We're not even halfway through the season, and I already feel like I've hit a wall. I'm tired. My feet constantly hurt, and I don't remember the last time I ate a meal sitting down.

From the moment I wake up to the moment I go to sleep, work consumes me. The only break I get from it all is when I tumble into bed with Reid, his hands on my body a welcomed reprieve from the stress of my everyday life.

My conversation with Andrew last week isn't helping either. His words are still echoing in my ears, and I can't get his smug smile out of my head.

I can't get *Reid* out of my head, either.

No one's ever stood up for me like that.

I didn't go to his place after the game, choosing to spend the night alone in my apartment with a bottle of wine. Our communication has been sparse since Sunday, and I know he's giving me space. Giving me time to process what was said to me, but I've been wanting to hear from him.

As if on cue, my phone buzzes. I snatch it up, happy to see a text from him waiting for me on the screen.

REID

How's everyone taking the loss over there?

ME

We're just fine, thanks. No need to rub it in.

REID

How are you?

ME

Tired. Hungry. I haven't eaten lunch yet, and I'm starving.

REID

Want me to bring you something?

ME

You don't have to do that.

REID

I'm in the area.

ME

You're in Baltimore?

REID

No, but I can be. Shawn gave the guys the day off, and I have nothing to do.

ME

Oh.

That's okay. I'm fine. Really.

REID

Stop overthinking it and tell me what you want,
Avery. You need to eat.

ME

Thai sounds good.

REID

Anything in particular?

ME

Surprise me.

REID

I'll call when I'm parking.

An hour later, I'm downstairs waiting by the visitor's entrance when my phone rings.

"Hey," Reid says, breathless on the other side of the line when I answer.

"Hey. I'm inside. Figured I'd escort you up so you can't pull a fast one on me and booby trap my office."

"You want me to stay?"

"Did you only bring food for me?"

"No," he admits. "I grabbed something for myself, but I figured I'd eat in the car. I don't want to interrupt your day."

"Come up. I need a break, and it would be good for me to put my phone down for a minute."

We end the call and he pulls open the heavy glass door, his hair a little windblown and his cheeks a little red. He makes his way through security screening and spots me, lifting his chin in greeting as he shuffles over with two large plastic bags.

"Are you feeding a small army?" I take the bag from his left hand and head for the elevators. "This looks like one of everything off the menu."

"It is. If you don't want to give me detailed instructions, I'm going to interpret it however I see fit." He fixes his glasses behind his ears. "Whatever we don't eat, I'll take around the corner. I saw a guy hanging out with his dog under the overpass, and I figured he might like a hot meal."

"That's Larry," I say. "And his dog's name is Biscuit."

"Larry," Reid repeats with a smile. "You've met him before."

"A few times. He wished me good luck before my interview years ago, and I've always tried to check in on him. Biscuit is his best friend, and he loves peanut butter."

"Does Larry like spicy food?"

"He does. I'm sure he'd be happy with some leftovers."

"I'll make sure to visit him after."

Knowing he has a plan for the extra food makes my skin prickly and warm. It makes my stomach do a summersault and my heart twist in my chest, a dangerous thing.

"That's nice of you," I say quietly as we step into the elevator.

"I try to be a nice guy." Reid shrugs and leans against the wall. He stares at the ceiling before looking at me. "When was the last time you had a real meal?"

"Um." I pull on the hem of my dress, distracted by his attention. "Dinner last night?"

"That sounds like a question, not an answer."

"Dinner," I repeat. "We had a team photoshoot this morning, and there was no time for breakfast. I did have a coffee, though, so I'm not operating on an entirely empty stomach."

"Avery," he murmurs. "You need to take care of yourself. The season is only going to get busier and—"

"I know," I snap, wincing at my tone. "I'm sorry. I'm trying to get better about setting time aside for my meals while I'm at the office, but I'm being pulled in a dozen different directions. It's hard to put myself first."

Understanding dawns, and his features sharpen. Reid hums

and steps toward me. His fingers hook under my chin and he lifts my head.

I'm not sure I'm breathing.

"People-pleaser," he says. My eyes widen, and he blows out a laugh, a puff of air. "I didn't forget."

"I told you that the night we met."

"I have a good memory. Here's what's going to happen: the nights you come to my place, I'm sending you home with left-overs so you have a meal for the next day. The days you're busy and don't have a free minute to order something, I'm going to have food delivered to you. Barry the intern and I are friends, and his job duties now include getting you the food I send."

"But I—"

"You can take care of yourself. I see that. I *know* that. You're a strong, independent woman, Ave, and that's badass. But I'd like to help a little bit. If you'll let me."

The same sensation I felt the other night when he wrapped his arms around me and held me tight settles in me again.

I felt it during the game too, when he went after Andrew.

It's the recognition that, yes, this is physical.

Yes, we fuck anywhere and everywhere.

But there's something else lingering under the surface.

A deeper connection neither of us have explored.

It would be easy for him to brush aside my problems.

Deem them not *his* problem and walk away.

He's not, though.

He's offering me a hand. Figuring out how he can carry some of the load, and no one has ever done that for me before.

"Okay," I whisper. The elevator doors open to my floor, and neither one of us walks out. "You can help."

"Thank you." Reid holds out an arm and gestures for me to go ahead. I slip past him, my shoulder grazing against his chest, and heat radiates from him.

I want him.

I want him so badly I can't think of anything else.

The hunger is gone.

The exhaustion is gone.

All that's left is the desire to feel his skin against mine.

To sink onto him and fuck him until he's saying my name like a goddamn prayer.

"Find any ducks lately?" he asks, and I clear my thoughts.

"One this morning in my closet on a shelf I can't reach. How did you manage that?"

"Maverick. His height comes in handy."

We step into my office. I sit on the couch and stretch out my legs. My stomach rumbles, and Reid gives me a knowing look.

"What? It's good timing." I unload the containers and shake my head at the mess. "This is an alarming amount of food."

"Like I said: whatever doesn't get eaten is going to a good home. I promise I won't waste it. Now dig in, Sinclair. I don't want to hear another word out of you until you've had at least eight bites."

Any retort I have dies on my tongue. I slurp down the tum kea chicken soup and dig into the mixed vegetables next. Ten minutes turns into fifteen, and I didn't realize how hungry I was until I reach a breaking point after devouring half an order of pad se-ew.

"I'm full," I say. "I can't do anymore."

"Thank you for letting me feed you." Reid takes the carton from me, and I blush. His fingers brush against mine, and a jolt of electricity jumps through me. "Take a break."

I drop my head on the pillows, ready for a nap. "This might have been counterproductive. I don't want to do anything else the rest of the day."

"What else is on your agenda?" he asks.

"I'm doing a player profile on Malcolm, so we have an interview scheduled. I also have a meeting with our ticket sales manager this afternoon."

Reid looks at me. "Avery."

"Yes?"

"We need to talk about what happened at the game."

"No, we don't." I stand up and grab the empty containers, dropping them in the trash can and organizing my desk. "I'd prefer to forget about it."

"Hey." He stands from the chair he's sitting in and touches my wrist. "Did I do something wrong?"

I want to laugh.

What Reid did is the furthest thing from wrong.

It was the most selfless thing a man has ever done for me, and I've been grappling with how to thank him. How to tell him how much I appreciate what he did and the things he said.

Thank you for standing up for me to that sexist prick doesn't seem sufficient.

"No." I turn to face him, and he's frowning. "You were... perfect. Wonderful. Every other lovely word you can find in the dictionary? Your picture would be under it. But what happened at the game isn't new. It's something I've experienced for years, and I'm going to *keep* experiencing it. You heard it on my date the night we met. You heard it again on Sunday. My ex used to say shit like that, for fuck's sake. There's a large number of people out there who don't think women belong in this world I'm a part of, and I have to live with that."

"It's bullshit," he mumbles, tugging me to the couch. "Fucking bullshit."

"It is," I agree. "You remember what Andrew said. He told me to tone it down. I'm doing too much. I've always felt like... like I take up too much space. Like my dreams are too big. Like I'm wrong for wanting to be the best in an industry that tries so hard to make me feel small and shove me in a tiny box."

"You don't take up too much space, Avery," Reid says around a shaky breath. "You should take up more. All of it, if you can, and the last place a person like you should ever be is in a fucking box."

I swallow the lump in my throat, and my hands tremble as I rest them on my thighs. "Ever since I've been involved with football, working in the NFL headquarters has been my goal. I considered the Thunderhawks a stepping stone. I figured I'd stay here a few years. I'd build a reputation, then I'd really make a name for myself in New York. I don't think that's going to be happening anytime soon."

"What about a different goal? One that doesn't involve sexist assholes who deserve a trip to HR?"

"I'll dream up something new eventually. Maybe it's here. Maybe it's somewhere else. I don't know yet." I sneak a glance up at him, and he's already staring at me. "For now, this is enough. Our bet is still on, Duncan, and if you think I'm going down without a fight, you have another thing coming."

His lips twitch into a smile. "Did you look at the numbers I gave you?"

"I did."

"And?"

I sigh, defeated. "You're still ahead of me. Yes, you're allowed to gloat, but don't get too excited. We still have a long way to go."

Reid laughs, and the sound makes me the happiest I've been in days. "Are you serious? I thought for sure you would be winning."

"You thought wrong. What happens if one of us wins one part of the bet and the other wins the second part?"

He shrugs. "We fuck, call it even, and try again next season?"

It's my turn to laugh. "You have yourself a deal." My computer pings with a meeting reminder, and I sigh. "I should get going. I don't want to start my afternoon behind schedule."

"I'll clean this up and head out."

"Are you sure? I'm sorry to dine and dash, especially because you drove all the way out here and—"

"It's fine. Really." He scoops up the untouched food and drops it back in the plastic bag. "Go."

"Thank you for lunch. I feel like a new human, and I really appreciate it."

"I'm leaving the soup in your mini fridge so you have something to eat tomorrow," he says, and I nod.

"That's perfect." I stand and smooth out the wrinkles in my dress. "Hey, Reid?"

"Yeah?"

"Thank you for being here. For being there for me at the game on Sunday. For…" I trail off, the words difficult to find. "Thank you for pausing the feud so you could be on my side."

"Ah." He pushes his glasses up his nose. "We never paused the feud. Competition or not, I meant every word."

"You did?" I ask, and my heart thumps in my chest like a metronome.

"You never take up too much space, Ave. Not with me," he says. "I think I'd like you to take up more of it."

When I get back from my meeting, the only trace that Reid was here at all is the single rubber duck sitting on my keyboard, a sticky note with a hand-drawn heart right next to it.

@footballindc

Happy bye week!

Any fun plans?

@dcfootball

A D&D campaign and a trip to the comic book store.

A collector's edition of Watchmen is releasing on Thursday, and I need it.

@footballindc

Do you have any other free time in there?

@dcfootball

Texting you.

THIRTY-FOUR
REID

ME

Sorry. I didn't want any of the interns snooping and seeing our messages.

Come over tonight?

AVERY

I won't land from Seattle until after nine. We're delayed because of a maintenance issue.

ME

What about tomorrow?

AVERY

Girl's night. Hoes before bros, buddy.

ME

Let's do tonight. I don't care that it'll be late.

AVERY

Now who's the needy slut?

ME

Only for you, beauty queen.

IT FEELS good to sit at the table in the dark corner of the tiny bar and sip a beer with my friends. I haven't hung out with Dallas and Maverick in a week and a half, and even though we're an hour past the time I'd prefer to be home and winding down for the night, I can't find it in me to complain.

"We haven't been here in ages," I say. "Thank fuck for the bye week and the one time a season Dallas drinks. You two keep this place in business with your tipping, and I'd hate for it to go under."

"It must be nice to have such an easy schedule," Maverick says. "I'm out here covering four time zones in five days. Busting my ass between Eastern and Pacific Standard, and you all are on a twenty-minute flight to Cleveland."

"You wouldn't last a second in the NFL, pretty boy," Dallas says.

"Hey. Only Emmy is allowed to call me that." He grabs his glass and downs half his drink. "She'll kick your ass if she hears you using her nickname for me."

"How did you get that nickname?" I ask. "Please don't tell me it's some inside joke involving sex."

"Nah." Maverick grins. "I've been ashamed to tell the story, but now that there's a ring on her finger, I think it's safe to say she's accepted the fact I'm never going to leave her alone. She's stuck with me for life. The first day we met, I assumed she was a fan waiting at the arena for me."

"How the hell did you make that mistake?" Dallas asks. "Emmy could kick my ass in an arm wrestling contest."

"It was stupid," Maverick says. "I saw a hot girl and got all flustered. I hit on her, and she didn't like that I didn't know who she was. She told me the only thing she wanted to do with me was kick my ass on the ice, I was giddy she called me pretty, and the name started."

"And now you two are living happily ever after." I lift my

drink his way, and he knocks his glass against my bottle. "How's the wedding planning coming? Have you two locked down a date yet? A venue? Anything?"

"I'm going to have grandchildren before he makes a damn decision," Dallas grumbles.

"Emmy and I hardly get any time together with our travel schedules. When we are alone, I don't want to spend the afternoon we're in the apartment talking about flower arrangements and centerpieces." Maverick shrugs. "It'll happen when it happens. Maybe it won't ever happen. Maybe we'll go to Vegas and do it. Or Mexico. Hell, maybe I'll have an officiant come out when we play against her team next month and we can do it before the game."

"Those all seem tame for you," I say. "Surprised there isn't any mention of fire or something dramatic as fuck."

"Don't give him ideas," Dallas warns, and I laugh.

"Speaking of Emmy, where are your better halves tonight? It's normally impossible to separate you all. I haven't been the fifth wheel in a while, and I kind of miss it. You two don't have nearly as much gossip as the girls do."

"Mae told me they're meeting Avery for some drinks," Dallas tells me. "Girl's night."

"That's right." I remember her telling me about the outfit she was going to wear when she was falling asleep in my arms last night. "The three of them are probably trouble when they're together."

"They could probably take over the world," Maverick says, and he glances over my shoulder with a sharp grin. "And speaking of trouble, look who it is. Jesus, Dal. It's like you and Mae are on the same brainwaves."

I spin in the booth. I follow his line of sight to the door and the three women sauntering inside. Every guy in the bar watches them too, and I swear to god everything moves in slow motion.

There's Maven with her blonde hair. Emmy with her fiery red and Avery with—

Fucking hell.

The wind gets knocked out of me when I see thigh-high black boots and a mini skirt that barely covers her ass. Her top cuts off halfway up her stomach, showing off smooth skin.

I can tell from all the way over here she's not wearing a bra, and she should definitely have a fucking coat on. It's way too cold outside.

My throat goes dry.

Someone says my name, but I'm not listening. I'm too busy paying attention to the way Avery tosses her hair over her shoulder. The glitter on her neck that shimmers and sparkles under the shitty bar lighting. The bright red lipstick on her mouth and how I'd like it on my cock.

"Fuck me," I mumble.

"You're a good-looking guy, but you're not really my type," Maverick says.

"Did you all plan this?" I ask, looking at my best friends. "Is this some purposeful setup so we'd be in the same place at the same time?"

"I swear we didn't." Dallas holds up his hands in innocence. "But talk about timing."

"Timing," I repeat, and I stare at Avery again. She settles on a stool at the bar and chats with the bartender who's giving her a not-so-subtle once-over. I don't like the way his eyes flick to her chest when she leans her elbows on the counter. I fucking *hate* the way he steps closer to her, invading her space. "How do you guys do it?"

"Do what?" Maverick asks. "Pretty broad question there, Plant Daddy."

"Watch other men flirt with your women. Know they're undressing them with their eyes. See them laugh because someone else said something and you wish it were you," I blurt out, and my cheeks heat with a blush. "Hypothetically speaking."

"Putting a ring on her finger helps. It gives a pretty clear *don't even fucking try* message," Dallas says. "I guess I take it as a compliment. They can flirt with her all they want, but she's going home with me. Now, if they ever made her uncomfortable, you bet your ass we'd have a big problem on our hands. I'm not afraid to deck someone in the face if they don't back up when Maven asks them to."

"Emmy tells them to fuck off before they even try to talk to her." Maverick cradles his chin in his hand, a dopey smile settling on his mouth. "I'm the luckiest bastard in the world."

"Is Avery your woman now?" Dallas asks.

"No," I say. Something bitter stirs in my chest with the word, and I narrow my eyes at the guy who takes the seat right next to her. "Definitely not."

"Sounds like you're not sure," Maverick says.

"We're not—there's no label on it or anything. But, lately, things have started to feel different." I glance back at my friends and sigh. "Our arrangement is starting to feel less like a physical relationship and more like..." I shrug and take a long sip of my beer. "More."

"Is that a bad thing?"

"No. Yes. I don't know." I shrug again, because I really don't fucking know. "Maybe I'm being dramatic."

"What's changed?" Dallas asks.

"A month ago, we'd fuck, she'd hang around for a few minutes, then she'd leave. Now we fuck, and I ask her questions about her dad. She sleeps over, and I bring her lunch. I stand up for her when some asshole talks shit to her. I bought her a

Christmas present I think she's going to like. Before, we'd taunt each other on our official accounts and give each other shit. It's all texting now. We keep up with each other throughout the day, and none of our arguments hold any actual heat. I think—" I swallow and pull off my glasses, scrubbing a hand over my face. "I think I could fall for her."

"You got all of that from watching some dude try to talk to her at the bar?" Maverick asks. "That's pretty fucking impressive."

"No. It's not just right now. The last couple of times we've hooked up, it felt like we both had something we wanted to say. Neither of us wanted to be the first to say it, though."

"I've been waiting for this moment." Maverick clears his throat. "Remember when Emmy and I thought we could do the friends with benefits thing and you told me I was an idiot because there's no way to have a friends with benefits arrangement without someone catching feelings? That it's just sex until it isn't because emotions *always* get involved? Surprise, mother-fucker. It's you. You're the one with the feelings, and things are about to get messy."

I play with the coaster sitting on the table and spin it between my fingers. "In hindsight, I recognize this was a really fucking stupid idea." I drop my head back and groan. "What the hell am I supposed to do? I can't go over there and be an asshole. What if she wants those guys to talk to her? She's single and it's allowed."

"Wait, what? You two aren't exclusive?" Maverick asks.

"In the bedroom we are. Flirting and dating other people are gray areas I didn't think to address. I don't want to cock block her because I'm an idiot who broke our rules and now has a crush on her. Besides, it's not like I'm in love with her. I just, you know, don't like seeing other guys talk to her."

"What if she's breaking your rules too?" Dallas asks. "What if she's sitting there wishing you would come over and cock block her? You could be her hero."

Her hero.

I don't know why that makes me puff out my chest. It makes me roll my shoulders back and hone in on her body language.

She doesn't look interested in the khaki-wearing guy who scoots his stool closer to her. She keeps trying to talk to Maven and Emmy, and he keeps trying to talk to her.

That won't do.

"Move," I tell Maverick, and he grins.

"Oh, shit. Is this about to go down?"

"Nothing is going down. I'm only going to say hi."

I climb out of the booth and make my way over to the bar. The closer I get, the more visible Avery's discomfort is. Her lips are in a thin line, and she's glaring at the spot on her thigh where the douche canoe in the polo is touching.

I slide up next to her and block him from her line of vision. Her eyes widen, and relief floods her face. The corners of her mouth turn up in a pretty smile, and she tips her head to the side.

"Yes?" she asks with a curious lift of her eyebrow.

"Reid." I hold out my hand so she can shake it. Her fingers lace through mine and squeeze. "I hear you like whiskey. Neat. Can I buy you a drink?"

"A whiskey neat, huh? I think I'd like that," she says.

"Hey." There's a tap on my shoulder. "Buddy, we were in the middle of a conversation."

I glance behind me and stare at the man. I look him up and down, and when I get to his feet, I laugh.

"Sorry, dude. She has an aversion to boat shoes. It was never going to work out between you two," I say, wrapping my fingers around her wrist. "C'mon, pretty girl. I'm stealing you away."

Avery beams and follows me over to the jukebox. She leans

against the wall and stares at me. "Wow, you're smooth. Thank you for the rescue. I think my IOU list is a mile long at this point. What is it with us meeting in bars surrounded by shitty men?"

"I wasn't interrupting, was I?"

"You think I wanted to talk to that sleazebag? He was telling me how much his watch cost." She snorts. "I prefer the company I'm with right now."

"I didn't like watching you give your attention to someone else. Not when I'm here." I pause before adding, "Not ever."

"I didn't do it on purpose," she says. "I wasn't trying to make you upset."

"I know you weren't. Lately, I think I'd like for you to give your attention to me. Just to me," I say, sharing the thought that's been on my mind all week. "In the bedroom. And outside it too."

She hums and steps closer. Her hand moves to my collar and tugs. "I'd like that," she whispers.

"You would?"

"Yeah. We work well in the bedroom. Maybe we could try... out of the bedroom. Maybe not dating but...going places with our friends? Together? Like tonight. We could've come here together, and it would've been fun."

"Okay." I nod. "So not dating."

"But not *not* dating," she adds before groaning. "I don't know. I like spending time with you, Reid. I'm not saying we need to hold hands or anything like that, but it would stop people from flirting with us when we don't want to be flirted with."

"No one flirts with me," I say, and she laughs. "What?"

"That girl three tables behind you won't stop looking over here. And don't get me started on the one by the bathrooms."

"Sounds like you might be jealous, Sinclair." I reach a hand up and brush my fingers down her cheek. "But you don't have to worry about them. I'm only looking at you. I have been for a while now."

Avery's eyes soften, and I feel her smile in the center of my chest. "I'm only looking at you too, Reid."

"Now that that's settled, do you want to come sit at our table? I'm sure Maven and Emmy have already made their way over, and I'm not letting Boat Bro talk your ear off again," I say.

"I'd like that." She kisses my cheek and tugs on my arm. "Let's go, Duncan. I want to ask our friends their opinions on the Crocs versus Sperry debate."

Our friends.

Like we do this all the fucking time.

She drops her hand from mine as we make our way back to the table so no one asks any questions about our PDA. She sits on the opposite side of the table. We don't touch the rest of the night, but I realize how badly I'd love to do this all the fucking time.

THIRTY-FIVE
AVERY

REID

Are you staying in town for the holidays?

ME

Yeah. We play on the 23rd. There's not enough
time to fly down to Florida then back up. What
about you?

REID

Christmas Day game. First time in history. Have
any plans?

ME

Maven invited me to their place on Christmas
Eve, but I'm not sure I'm going to go. I don't
want to intrude.

REID

It wouldn't be intruding. We'd all like it if you
were there.

ME

Are you going?

REID

Yeah. It's one of our traditions. When Dallas, Maverick, and I realized we all hung around the city for the holidays, we decided to do a Christmas Eve dinner. It used to be Chinese food instead of a nice ham, but we haven't skipped a year yet.

ME

I like that story. Are you sure it's okay if I come?

REID

Positive.

ME

Okay. I have a present for you. It's not big, but I wanted to get you something.

REID

I have a present for you too. Two presents, actually.

ME

Really?

REID

Yup.

ME

I can't wait.

REID

Are you close with your mom and sister? Do you get to spend any time with them this time of year?

ME

My sister is swamped with work during the holidays just like I am. The three of us always do something in mid-January when things settle down. We're going to have to make some adjustments this year, though, because the Thunderhawks might sneak in as a Wild Card team.

I'll FaceTime them on Christmas Day. We usually all bake something while we talk to each other, so it never really feels like we're separated for the holidays.

What about you? Do you talk to your mom?

REID

Yeah. I know she wants me back in Ohio for the holidays, but she also understands why I don't go. She came and visited a few years ago, and I think I'll fly her out again next year.

It's okay, though. I get to spend time with my favorite people, and all is right in the world.

ME

I'm excited to be included.

REID

I'm glad you'll be there.

I LOVE early winter in the mid-Atlantic.

The air is crisp. There's a coolness in the breeze. Everything is lighter and brighter, the slog of summer and fall long gone.

I smile when I step onto the pavement outside my apartment and head for the Potomac, nothing but still silence and a beautiful sunrise in front of me.

These mornings of solitude are my favorite time of day.

I've always been happiest surrounded by friends and family and coworkers. At peace in big groups, with loud laughter and lively conversation, but lately I've been loving these stolen moments too.

I can be alone with my thoughts, away from the field. Away from my phone and focusing on nothing except the miles ahead of me.

I inhale and savor the first glimpse of the pinks and oranges and yellows signaling the start of what's going to be a beautiful day. I wave hello to the other runners I pass. I dodge a cyclist who apologizes for cutting a corner too close and almost crashing into me.

There's a pep in my step as I make my way onto a straight-away. I take a deep breath and let my legs get loose, settling into a rhythm that's just past comfortable. Just difficult enough where my lungs feel like they're putting in work and my heart starts to beat a little faster.

I tip my chin up to the sky and smile at the patches of clouds. It's almost like I can hear my dad up there, calling out to me, reminding me what a gift it is to be alive.

Sweat beads on my forehead and I push harder. I run faster, the last few weeks of work and life and *Reid* fading away until there's nothing but peace.

The quiet breaks with a roll of tires and the hum of an engine. I glance over my shoulder and spot a silver truck forty yards away. It's moving slowly, almost like it's creeping down the street, and I frown.

I cruise another half mile and check behind me again. The car is still there, and closer than it was before.

The hair on the back of my neck stands up. Panic claws at my throat, and I try to take a deep breath.

It could be nothing, I tell myself, shoving aside the worst-case scenarios racing through my head.

It could also be something.

I hang a left down a narrow street, heading away from the

river. I want to be visible to other people and I want to see if they'll follow me. When they drive up the wrong way on a one-way road, I know I have to make a split-second decision.

I fumble with my phone tucked in my sports bra. I pull it out and call the number at the top of my text message threads without a second thought.

It rings twice before I hear Reid's voice.

"Hello?" he answers, sounding like he's tucked away in a dream. Buried under a pile of blankets and dead to the world for another few hours. "Ave?"

"Hi." My heart hammers in my chest like a wild drumbeat. "I need your help."

There's the rustle of sheets on the other end of the line. The flick of a light switch and soft footsteps down the hall.

"What's wrong?" he asks, sounding more awake, his tone deeper. More forceful. *Safe.* "What's going on?"

"I'm on a run, and I think someone is following me." My shoulders shake and my eyes blur with tears, but I rein my emotions in. I take a deep breath, hold it for five seconds, and exhale. "I don't know what to do."

"Send me your location. I want you to keep moving while you talk to me. What's your closest landmark?"

I glance around and turn onto a busier street. I'm unfamiliar with the area, and I try not to let that raise my fear even more. Another deep breath, another hold, another exhale. "I see something up the road. A coffee shop, maybe. The lights are on."

"Great. I want you to make your way to it and go inside. That's where I'll meet you. I'm going to stay on the phone with you the whole time, alright?"

I pull the phone away from my ear and send him my location. My pace quickens and my breathing turns ragged and strained as I move closer and closer to the coffee shop. My muscles ache, but I keep going forward.

"I just sent you where I am."

"Thank you, Ave. You're doing so good, baby, and I'm so glad you called me. You're also really close to me, so I'll be there soon, okay?"

"I'm sorry I woke you up." I wipe my eyes and pick up my feet. I try to ignore the rumble of the truck behind me. I try to focus on Reid's soothing voice, the soft inflection of his words and how he's even and steady. "I know it's early and you like to sleep in."

"How do you know I like to sleep in?"

"You never answer my text messages before seven thirty," I say. "You post the majority of your content in the afternoon, except for the time you switched your routine at the conference in Vegas to piss me off. When I slip out of your apartment before work, you don't budge."

"I'd much rather stay up late. The sun and I don't get along."

"Are you a vampire?"

"Could be. I can't believe you're already out exercising. When do you sleep?" he asks.

"I got six hours last night," I say, proud of myself. "I shut down my computer at ten thirty and put my phone on do not disturb." I switch to speakerphone and tuck my phone back in my sports bra. "That's almost a record."

"You work too much. You need an assistant."

"I could say the same about you." The coffee shop is getting closer, and knowing Reid is on his way gives me a burst of adrenaline. "You reach for your phone in the night."

"I didn't know you saw me do that."

"I didn't see it. I felt it. You were holding me, then you weren't." I pause and swallow down the lump in my throat. Tears stain my cheeks, and this time, I let them fall. I'm so mad. So frustrated this is happening to me and so tired at the same time. "I always know when you're not touching me."

"I won't pick up my phone in the night again," he says, a promise there. "Not when you're with me."

"Where are you?" A quick check behind me shows more space between me and the truck than before. Four cars are in front of it now, a traffic jam building and giving me a chance to get away. The knot in my chest loosens. My shoulders sag, and I start to think I might be okay. "Are you close?"

"Three minutes. I ran a red light. If I get a ticket, I'm making Maverick pay for it."

"He wasn't the one who broke the law."

"No, but he's the one with a hundred million in his bank account. He could spot me a couple bucks."

I laugh. "Sometimes I forget how much these athletes make."

"I do too, until the rookie pulls up to the stadium in a Bentley, and I want to ask who his financial advisor is. Where are you?"

"Three stores away." I can see the neon sign out front. Can smell the sweet pastries and ground coffee beans. "I'm going to wait inside."

"Don't hang up, please. I want you to keep talking to me."

"If I didn't know any better, Duncan, I'd say you're obsessed with me."

Reid is quiet on the other end of the phone. I check to make sure our call didn't drop, and then he's saying, "What if I am?" so quietly, I think I might have misheard him.

It's the same tone he used at the bar two weeks ago when he told me he didn't like watching me give my attention to anyone else. Not when he was there. Not ever.

The same voice when he's wrapped around me, his arms banded across my waist, mouth on my neck and telling me I'm *beautiful.* I'm *perfect* and *wonderful.*

"I'm here," I say, breathless and overcome with emotion.

I yank open the door and tumble inside to warmth and heat

and someplace safe. I tuck myself into a table in the back and wait.

"I'm here too."

There's the slam of a car door and the jingle of keys. I blink, and the next thing I know, Reid is there, fifteen feet away from me, then ten, then five, and I burst into tears.

I leap to my feet and crash into him. "You came," I whisper around a sob.

"You called," he murmurs into my hair, his embrace an envelope of comfort. "Any time I see your name on my phone, I answer within seconds. My sleep-deprived, subconscious brain knows to answer too, apparently. Call me one of Pavlov's dogs."

He rubs my back. I sink into the press of his body against mine. It's fifty degrees outside, but his skin is like an inferno. I bury my face in his shirt and he doesn't pull away, letting me stay for far too long.

"I'm sorry. I'm sorry I woke you up. I'm sorry I asked for your help. I—"

"Hey." Reid cups my chin and tilts my head back so I'm looking at him. His eyes are bloodshot and red-rimmed. There's a crease on his left cheek from his sheets, and his hair is sticking up in different directions. I've never seen someone so beautiful. "Don't you ever apologize for asking for help, okay? Especially not to me. I wanted to, so I did. Simple as that."

"Thank you." I shiver, and he holds me even tighter. "I don't know why I'm so upset. Nothing happened. It could've been worse. Hell, it could've been a crazy coincidence I'm turning into a big deal."

"You're upset because you were doing something you enjoy, and someone tried to ruin it for you. You're allowed to be scared, Avery."

I nod and unravel myself from him. I stare at his feet and let out a watery laugh. "You're wearing two different shoes. And your pajama bottoms."

"I didn't stop to think," Reid says. "I needed to get here as fast as I could."

"I can't believe you're here." I touch his cheek to make sure he's real. My heart won't stop racing in my chest, and I think I'm going to cry again. "I'm so glad to see you."

"Did the truck pass?" Reid glances around, his head on a swivel and his eyes narrowing into slits. "Did you get any descriptions of who was driving? Did anyone come inside looking for you?"

"No," I admit. "I was so focused on getting away from them, I didn't think to get any information. I should've. That was stupid of me and—"

"It's okay." He hugs me again, tighter this time. "You didn't do anything wrong, Avery."

"I don't want to stick around in case they come back."

"Do you want me to drive you to your apartment? Or to the stadium?"

"No." I shake my head. "Can we go to your place?"

Reid smiles. I feel it in my heart and all the way down to my toes. He laces his hand through mine and I follow him to the door.

"Let's go, Sinclair. I'm going to fix you right up."

THIRTY-SIX

REID

AVERY WON'T STOP SHAKING.

I drew her a bath and set her up with my iPad so she could watch a show and relax. Ten minutes later, she asked if I would join her.

I did, obviously.

I'd be an idiot to say no.

After we climbed out of the tub, I gave her an old robe I found in my closet. I bundled her up with a pair of sweatpants and thick socks. I made her pancakes and sat by her side while she ate every bite.

An hour later, and she still won't stop shaking.

I'm so fucking scared.

Have I done enough?

Have I done too much?

What the fuck do I do now?

"What else do you need?" I tuck a wet piece of hair behind her ear. I can't stop touching her. I can't stop making sure she's okay. "Do you want me to grab your computer from your place? You can work here today."

"No." She shakes her head. "I emailed my boss and told him I'm taking a personal day."

"Good. I'm off today too. You can stay as long as you want. Or until I annoy the shit out of you."

"You always annoy the shit out of me," she teases.

"Figured as much. The feeling is mutual, Sinclair," I say, but there's no heat behind it.

"Thank you for letting me stay. It's nice to have some company."

"You're talking about the plants, aren't you?"

Her dimpled smile reassures me she's okay. "Did you have plans today?"

"A few errands to run. Maverick, Dallas, and I were going to get lunch, but we rescheduled. It worked out, though. June has a cold, and Dallas is staying with her while she's home from school."

"Oh." Avery frowns. She pulls her legs to her chest and rests her chin on her knees. "Part of our agreement is mentioning if someone is being too suffocating. Am I taking up too much of your time?"

"No fucking way. I'd tell you if you were. You know I'm blunt, Avery, and you've never taken up too much of my time."

Take up more of it, I find myself thinking. *Stay all day. Tomorrow and the next day, too.*

"Okay." She nods and bites her bottom lip. "I have a question for you."

"What is it?"

"It's something I've been wanting to ask for a while now, but I'm not sure how you'll take it."

I pause and squint at her. "It's anal, isn't it? I'm open to the idea, just as long as it doesn't hurt you or—"

She bursts out laughing, and it's the first time I've seen her relax since I found her in that coffee shop. "It's not anal, though I'm open to the idea. I'm surprised you haven't tried it yet."

"Uh, because common courtesy tells me that should involve a fucking conversation before it happens?" I say. "Seems rude to just… go for it."

"We're coming back to this." Avery reaches out and takes my hand. "Can I raid your comic book collection? I've been dying to read something from your shelves, but I wasn't sure if that was too forward of me. I'm sure you're protective of them and—"

I pull her into my lap and kiss her. I cup her cheeks with both of my hands and she hums against my mouth. She drapes her arms around my neck and runs her fingers through my hair.

"You didn't have to ask," I say. "No one's wanted to borrow one before, and the answer is an automatic yes."

"Really? But you love comic books," she says.

"I know."

"I have to tell you something embarrassing."

"Is *this* about anal?"

She shoves my shoulder. "I did some light social media stalking when I found out who you really were, and I couldn't find any photos of your exes. I'm imagining they're women you met at Comic Con. Big cosplayers who dress up like Harley Quinn and walk around with a baseball bat."

It's my turn to laugh. "Not even close. One is an accountant. The other is a kindergarten teacher, and neither are blond."

"They weren't interested in what you're interested in?"

"No. My first girlfriend, the one I dated out of college in my mid-twenties, told me she was fine with the collection, but I'd see her roll her eyes when I talked about a new issue I wanted to buy."

"What about your ex-fiancée? Am I allowed to ask about her?"

"Of course you are. I'm not going to hide anything from you.

She was more open to the idea of comic books being a passion of mine, at least at the beginning of our relationship. After I proposed, we started looking at houses. She kept asking me if I planned to bring my collection with me to the new place, and I could tell she was hoping I'd leave it behind."

"Is the kindergarten teacher the one you were going to marry?" she asks.

"Yeah. Sheila. We met at a fundraiser and dated for four years. I enjoyed our time together, but hindsight tells me she was the safe choice. What worked in that moment," I say. "If we hadn't broken up then, it would've happened eventually. I'm learning I need someone who challenges me a little bit. Who balances me out. Since you and I started this bet of ours, I've never worked so hard. Oddly enough, I'm also more comfortable with boundaries that prevent my professional life from bleeding into my personal life. Thanks for that."

"You're welcome." Avery grins. "It's the same for me. I used to struggle with boundaries too. I felt like if I didn't work myself to death, the job wouldn't get done. Turns out, I can shut my phone off in the evening and finish the tasks tomorrow. Who knew?"

"It takes some learning." I touch her chin. "What other questions do you have for me? The more you talk, the less tense you look. Might as well keep this rolling. Your well-being is my top priority."

"Such a selfless guy," she murmurs. "I'll come up with a list and send it your way. It will have bullets and subcategories."

"Now you're speaking my language."

She climbs off me and stands. "Take me to your lair, Duncan. I want to pick something good to read."

I jump up and sweep her off her feet. I throw her over my shoulder and walk down the hall, her laugh echoing in my ears.

In the grand scheme of things, this isn't a big deal. Avery and

I aren't dating. But given my past with women and their indiffer-ence to the things I like, it feels like this is important.

"They're organized by publication date," I tell her, kicking open my bedroom door and setting her down. "Oldest on the left to most recent on the far end. Graphic novels are mixed in there too, so pick whatever you want."

"Are there any that are off limits?" Avery asks.

"To you? No."

Her eyes hold mine for a brief second. She stands on her toes and kisses my cheek before stepping away.

She takes her time looking at the titles. Every time I think she's about to pick one, she moves on. She mumbles a few things under her breath, and *fuck*, she's pretty standing there like that.

"You're watching me," she says without glancing up from the issue she's holding. It's *Batman: The Long Halloween*, and one of my favorites. "And it's distracting."

"Talk about distracting. You've officially earned the title of First Girl to Read One of My Comic Books. I'm kind of geeking out right now."

"Can you shorten that a bit? It's far too long."

"How about I call you a brat instead?" I ask. I walk up behind her and wrap my arms around her waist. My mouth drops to her neck, and I kiss her throat. "Is that better?"

"Much. Say it again."

"I'll call you whatever you want after you pick something."

Avery shimmies her way out of my hold and sifts through all the editions I have. I'm not even this thorough when I'm deciding what I want to read, and I appreciate her commitment to detail. After twenty minutes, she settles on *The Amazing Spiderman*, and my tongue might be hanging out of my mouth.

"Done." She settles on the right side of the bed. It's become her side whenever she stays over, and she stretches out her legs. "Are you going to join me?"

"Do you want me to? Or do you want to be alone?"

"I don't want to be alone."

"I'm not going anywhere." I lean against the wall and bite back a smile. "But give me a minute. This is one of my fantasies and I'm trying to take a mental picture so I can remember it in six months. A beautiful girl in my bed and willingly reading a comic book? I can't make this up."

"Take an actual photo," she says, not bothering to look up. "It'll last longer."

"If you insist." I pull out my phone and snap a shot of her, laughing when she lifts her middle finger my way. "God, you're gorgeous."

Avery pats the spot next to her. I join her on the bed and grab the *Batman* comic I've been reading from the bedside table. She rests her head on my chest and curls up against me.

"This is nice. We should do it more often."

"Play hooky and read comic books?" I ask. "I'm down. Who cares about work anyway?"

"I know I already said it, but thank you, Reid. Thank you for showing up for me. Thank you for letting me stay here. I feel so safe around you, and today all I want is to feel safe." She pauses before adding, "You take care of me, and I can't tell you how much it means to me."

"I was scared." I hold her close. "I know you can take care of yourself, Ave. But *fuck.* I was worried something was going to happen to you. That I wouldn't get there in time. It terrified me."

"You did get there in time, and I'm so glad I can count on you."

"You can always call me. I'm always going to be there for you."

"Even in two weeks when our teams play each other again and our rivalry is in full force?" she asks.

"Yup."

"Even if it's two in the morning and I'm stranded on the side of the road with a flat tire?"

"Even then. *Especially* then. I swear to god, Sinclair, if you pull some independent woman shit and try to change it yourself, I'm going to be pissed."

"Wow." Avery tilts her head back so she can look at me. There's a gleam in her eye that wasn't there before, and my heart is in my throat when I stare at her. "Sounds pretty serious. Are you catching feelings for me, Duncan?"

I am.

Big, scary, terrifying fucking feelings.

Now that I have her in my arms, I don't want to let her go.

My chest feels impossibly tight when she smiles. Tighter still when she puts her hand over my heart.

"Guess you'll have to stick around to find out, Sinclair," I say. "Through Christmas at least."

Her smile is devastatingly bright. "You mentioned something about two Christmas gifts. That seems a bit excessive, and I don't appreciate you upstaging my one gift for you."

I laugh. "To be fair, one of the gifts I didn't have to do anything to get. Someone else made it happen, and I can't take all the credit."

"Do I get any hints?" she asks.

"Nope. Do you want to exchange them before we go to Maven and Dallas's place? It's always chaos over there."

"Is it rowdy?"

"It's gotten more tame over the years. The first time the three of us got together, we roasted marshmallows, drank scotch and watched *Die Hard*. When June came along, we had to make a few modifications. You've seen Maverick, though. He's a loose fucking canon."

"June probably would've loved a glass of scotch. It pairs

much better with *The Night Before Christmas* than cookies and milk," Avery says.

"I'm in agreement, but I don't think Dallas wants CPS called on him," I say.

"Responsible parenting." She sighs. "What a drag."

"Tell me about the Christmases you used to have." I trace over the freckles on her shoulders and connect them. "Before you moved up here."

"Oh, I love Christmas time. On Christmas Eve, I'd perform in The Nutcracker with my ballet class. On Christmas morning, we'd open presents as a family. My sister and I always got my mom a nice china plate and my dad a tie. The older we got, the more stupid the ties got. Ones with ducks. Ones with tacos. One year, we did one with our faces on it. I think he wore it for a week straight."

"He loved you," I say, and she nods.

"And, *god*, did I love him." She wipes her eyes and glances up at the ceiling. "In the afternoon, if the Orlando Blazers were good enough and got to play on Christmas, my dad and I headed to the arena for an NBA game. The night always ended with the four of us drinking hot chocolate around a fire, even if it was eighty degrees outside. We still do that, but it doesn't feel the same."

"Start some new traditions with us. It's nothing extravagant and no one wears leotards, but it beats being alone. And next year maybe your sister and mom can come up and join. There's plenty of room."

"Next year, huh? You see me in the picture that far away?"

"Yeah." I shrug. "I could do without the damn Thunderhawks song blaring on full volume when I pull up Instagram and the comments you leave on my posts, but you're there."

"The fans love my comments," Avery says. She runs her

hand up my chest and tugs on my shirt, her mouth inches away from mine. "They love to see us arguing."

"I know. They egg us on. Someone asked why you haven't been as snarky lately on a post last week, and it didn't feel right to tell them your mouth is busy doing other things these days."

"Wow." She kisses me and laughs. "Someone is sure of themselves."

"Only because you used your tongue to drive me wild two nights ago. My memory is too good to forget that, Sinclair."

"Maybe I'll tell them you haven't been as active on social media because your hands are busy doing other things. Like getting me off." She guides my fingers to the robe she's wearing and tugs on the knot. The terrycloth opens, and I find her naked. "Maybe we could do that right now."

"Are you feeling up for it?" I ask, tracing the underside of her breast. "You had a traumatic morning."

"I'm with you." She shrugs the robe off completely and settles back on the pillows. "I know I'm safe."

Thirty minutes later, once the adrenaline from the morning wears off and she comes on my tongue—twice—Avery curls up next to me. She laces our fingers together and closes her eyes, her smile soft and secret.

"Is it okay if I nap for a little bit?" she asks around a yawn.

"Yeah." I nod even though she can't see me. "I'll be here when you wake up."

I'm still looking at her long after she falls asleep, and I think I'd like to find a way to keep her here for more than a year.

I want to find a way to keep her here forever.

@dcfootball

Congrats on the win two days ago. What does that make you? 1-14?

@footballindc

Okay, asshole. As if you don't look at our schedule constantly.

@dcfootball

No idea what you're talking about.

@footballindc

You know exactly how many games we've won. It's seven, which means there's a high probability we're going to sneak in as the Wild Card team.

If we win that game, we'll play you all in the next round of the playoffs.

@dcfootball

I'm shaking in my boots.

THIRTY-SEVEN
AVERY

REID

You haven't talked about running since the day
you called me to pick you up.

I hate exercising, but I'd run with you if it made
you feel more comfortable.

ME

You're sweet. It's been too cold to run the last
week and a half, so I've been on the treadmill in
my apartment's gym. I did buy a whistle I'm
going to carry with me when I get back outside,
and I permanently shared my location with
Maven.

And you.

REID

You did?

Oh. I see it now.

Thank you for trusting me enough to do that.

ME

Thank you for being trustworthy. I'm on my way over.

REID

Can't wait to see you, beauty queen.

REID OPENS the door to his apartment before I can knock. I'm greeted with a shirtless chest and gray joggers that sit low on his hips. I look him up and down, and an appreciative sound works its way out of me at the sight of bare skin and lean muscles.

"Festive," I say. "I see the resemblance between you and Santa. Can I sit on your lap?"

"Obviously." Reid closes the door behind me. "Is it cold out there?"

I shrug off my coat and hang it on the hook on the wall. "It's fucking freezing. It took me forever to get here because of Metro delays. It's our third snow of the season and people still don't know how to act."

"That explains the snowflakes in your hair." He tugs off my beanie and touches the long strands I straightened before coming over. "We're driving to Dallas and Maven's, so you won't be stuck underground again today."

"Thank goodness. I was starting to feel claustrophobic down there." I unzip my boots and kick them off. "Merry Christmas, Reid."

"Merry Christmas, Ave," he says, dropping a kiss to my forehead like it's the most normal thing in the world.

He's been more affectionate lately, I've noticed. We used to only kiss when we were having sex. Now, he sneaks one in from time to time.

When I'm falling asleep. When he gets to my apartment late, caught up in a meeting and behind schedule. After he picks up our dinner plates and puts them in the dishwasher.

It's almost second nature at this point, and I've come to crave the physical contact.

The graze of his pinky when we're at Maverick's for team dinner. The way his knee presses into my thigh when we're out with our friends and squished together around a table. His palm on the small of my back when he passes me in the hallway. There's plenty of room to sneak by without touching, but he touches me anyway.

It's always small, subtle gestures, but they make my heart skip a beat.

He's whispered filthy things in my ear. Sent pictures of his hand wrapped around himself and using my underwear to get off. Fucked me in every position imaginable, yet the brush of his hand has me grinning like a girl with a crush.

"Is it present time?" I ask.

"Someone's eager. Let's go to the living room. That's where your gifts are."

I follow him through his apartment and spot an envelope on the coffee table. It's next to a small package with a red bow, and I wonder if Reid wrapped it himself. I sit on the couch and look up at him.

"You first," I say, smiling as I hand over the box I've been guarding with my life.

It's been hiding in my closet since it arrived last month, buried under a stack of coats and old pairs of jeans. He's never snooped through my stuff, but on the off chance he decided to rummage through my things, I didn't want him to find it.

Reid takes the present and peels back the tape. He's slow with his unwrapping, careful to not rip the paper. I wait with bated breath, suddenly nervous about what his reaction might be.

With all of the paper off, he stares at the large box. His

mouth pops up, and he holds up the gift, as if I haven't been staring at it for weeks.

"Is this—" He stares at the present and shakes his head. "Avery. How the fuck did you—I can't—where—"

"Malcolm is a huge LEGO fan too," I say. "When I did my interview with him, he spent fifteen minutes talking about some of his favorite creations. I mentioned I had a friend who was equally obsessed, and he asked about your dream set. He pulled some strings and was able to snag two Millennium Falcons for me before they went live to the public. I might owe him my first born child and a kidney, but it was worth it."

"I—I waited in the queue online, but I was too late," Reid whispers. He traces over letters on the box and clutches it to his chest. He lifts his chin, and his eyes meet mine. "I checked resale sites, and they were five times the cost of the original purchase price. I couldn't bring myself to splurge on one. You're telling me you have *two*?"

"I do, and they're both for you. I figured you could put one together for your display case and keep the other in the box. I'm not a collector, but that has to be worth something one day, right? Maybe not. I don't know, but—"

"Avery." His voice trembles when he cuts me off, and he blinks back tears. "How did you remember?"

"Oh. Um, you mentioned it the first time I came to your apartment. Before the smoke alarm went off," I say. "You lit up when you told me about it, but you shrugged it off like it was no big deal. Like you were embarrassed to show me your excite-ment. I could tell it was important to you, though. I told myself I was going to find a way to get you that set if it was the last thing I did. Everyone deserves things that make us happy, Reid, and I like to see you happy."

He carefully sets the box down and pulls me toward him. I

tumble into his lap and he cups my cheeks with both hands. His touch is warm on my skin, and he traces along the curve of my jaw. I sigh, relaxing into him, content and happy.

"You're the most magnificent woman," he says. He rests his forehead against mine, and a single tear hangs on his eyelashes. I wipe it away and he huffs out a laugh. "This is stupid. I'm thirty-four and emotional over a fucking LEGO box."

"Do you like it?"

"Like it?" His hands move to my hips and he holds me there. His fingers press into the waistband of my skirt and I straddle him. "I love it. I love it so much." He pauses like he wants to add something else, and I'd give anything to know what he's thinking. "Thank you will never be good enough, Avery, but I'm going to say it anyway. Thank you. Thank you, baby. Thank you so much."

He's never called me that outside of the bedroom, but it feels right.

Inevitable, almost, like we've been treading this way for a long, long time.

I lean forward and kiss him, because I think I might die if I don't. I put everything I have behind the press of my lips, and when he kisses me back, he leaves me breathless.

"You're so welcome," I say. I dip my chin to kiss his neck and he blows out a breath, his grip on me tightening. "My selfless boy deserves nice things."

"You deserve nice things too," he murmurs, husky and low. His hands move to my sweater and slip under the hem, splaying out over my ribs. "Why is your heart beating so fast?"

"Because I was nervous about your present. Because I like being here with you." I swallow, my next words shaky. "Because seeing you happy makes me happy."

Because I like you more than I should.

Because I'm breaking our rules, Reid.

Because I think I might be falling in love with you, and it's terrifying.

"Seeing you happy makes me happy too." Reid reaches around me and hands me my first gift. "I want you to open these before we go to Maven and Dallas's. Maverick can't keep his mouth shut, and he'll ruin the surprise."

I climb off his lap and settle against the cushions. I pull off the bow and stick it to his cheek, laughing when he plucks it off and puts it in my hair. I rip the wrapping paper and gasp.

It's a book.

A special edition of my favorite romance novel of all time, with an alternate cover and illustrated pages. Only three hundred were printed, and it sold out within seconds.

I've been searching groups on the internet, desperate to find someone selling their copy for an affordable price, but I've come up short for months.

Until now.

"How—" I turn the book on its side, examining the stenciled letters embossed on the spine. "I haven't told you how much I like this book. How much I *love* this book."

"Not directly, no. I've had to do some deductive reasoning and study my spreadsheets," he says.

"And what did you find?"

"Lots of evidence that supports my hypothesis. Your copy has been on your nightstand for months. Other books have come and gone, but this one is always there—and that doesn't include the two other versions you have on your bookshelf. When I asked for book club recommendations, this was your suggestion. Last year, when it was announced a production company was turning the book into a movie, you shared the post to the Thunderhawks' Instagram story for two minutes before realizing you weren't on your personal account."

"Last year? But that was before we even—"

"I know." He blushes and stares at the floor. "I can't get you out of my head, Avery, and I guess you could say I've been paying attention to you for a while now."

"This is the most beautiful gift I've ever received." My eyes prick with tears. "Thank you so much, Reid. I can't wait to show it off."

"We're not finished." He hands me the envelope. "This is your next gift."

"Is it your resignation letter? An admittance of defeat that I have the better social media account?" I ask.

"You'd like that, wouldn't you?"

"It would make my whole day." I tear open the envelope and burst out laughing. "Okay, hotshot. Fake tickets to the Ella Wright concert? Very funny."

"They aren't fake," he says. "They're real."

I whip my neck up to stare at him. "Holy shit. How—"

"Dallas," he says. "He and Theo Asher are friendly. Theo asked if he wanted a suite for the concert in DC. Dallas said yes, knowing Maven would probably divorce him if he turned down the offer. It comes with twelve tickets, and since you also like her music, I figured you'd want to go."

I launch myself at him and hug him tight. Reid laughs into my neck and hugs me back. "This is incredible."

"Is that a yes that you want to go?"

"Of course it's a yes. *Reid*. You got me VIP tickets to see my favorite artist with my friends. This makes the Millennium Falcon seem very underwhelming."

"Far from underwhelming," he says. "Exactly even, I'd say, because they're both things that are important to us."

"Are you going to come to the concert?" I ask.

"Are you going to wear a short skirt and dance to her music?"

"Obviously. Maybe I'll wear a sparkly dress. Some knee-high boots."

"You have my attention. Can I pull you into a dark corner and make out with you? Maybe feel you up when our friends aren't looking?

"Only if it's during one of my least favorite songs."

"You've got yourself a deal, Sinclair," he says, and I think my heart is dangerously close to falling out of my chest.

"When do we have to leave for Dallas and Maven's?" I ask. "Please tell me we have some time."

"We have to be there in half an hour, but we could probably push it to forty-five minutes. Maverick said something about Nerf guns, and the thought of him with any sort of weapon is fucking terrifying. Why? Did you have something in mind?"

"Yeah. A second present for you." I guide his hand to my leg and the top of my stockings. "They have bows. That's festive enough to count as another gift, right?"

"Are these—" He lifts up my skirt and groans. "Thigh highs? God. You're going to kill me. We're never going to make it to see our friends, and I don't care. Forget Christmas. Fucking you is going to be a new tradition."

"I think I've been good this year, right?" I ask, standing. I work the zipper of my skirt down slowly, and Reid watches me like his life depends on it.

"Yes," he rasps.

My skirt falls to the floor, and I kick it away with my toes. "Does that mean I can sit on your lap?"

"Take everything off but the thigh highs."

"Yes sir," I say, and his hand disappears in his joggers. I strip until I'm left in only the white stockings, and I watch him stroke himself. "Now what?"

"Come here," he says, yanking his pants down to his ankles. "Let me show you how good you've been, Avery."

"This might be my favorite part of Christmas. Ho, ho, ho, am I right?"

"Shut up and fuck me, baby," he says, and I do.

I groan when I sink onto him. I say his name when he presses his thumb into my clit. I lose my breath when he tips me over the edge, one orgasm than a second, and I don't give a damn we're almost an hour late to see our friends.

THIRTY-EIGHT
AVERY

"I'M BLAMING you for our tardiness," I say to Reid as we walk down the hall to Dallas and Maven's apartment. "This is *your* fault."

"Yeah, because you really hated the second orgasm I gave you," he draws out, and I blush. "I'll never do that again."

I elbow his ribs. "Don't withhold sex from me, Duncan. I like your dick too much."

He tips his head back and laughs. The sound echoes down the hall, and I laugh too. "We'll both claim responsibility. You, for your perfect pussy. Me, for being easily distracted."

"There's the holiday spirit." I smile. "Nothing says Christmas like a perfect pussy."

"Falalala, I want to eat you out later."

"There's the holiday spirit. Hey, speaking of holiday spirit. How are we going to act around our friends?"

"What do you mean?" he asks. "Are they aliens or something?"

"Are we going to be affectionate? Ignore each other? Send messages back and forth on our phones?"

"I can smell you on my hand, Avery. It's going to be impossible to ignore you."

"Okay, well." I blush and fix my skirt. "I haven't told Maven and Emmy we're sleeping together. Okay, that's not true. I haven't told them we're sleeping together again. Maven knows about the first two times before Vegas."

"Really?" Reid frowns and stops outside their door. "I told Maverick and Dallas."

"*What*? You did? When?"

"Months ago. The night you came over after book club, actually. Maverick could tell I was hiding something, and being honest about what was going on in my life was easier than trying to lie. I'm a shit liar. Is it okay that they know?"

"Of course it's okay. They're your best friends."

"Maven is your best friend, and you've spent time with Emmy. Why haven't you told them? I don't care that you haven't. I'm just curious."

"I don't know," I say, and it's the truth. "I'm not embarrassed of you or anything like that."

"You think I'm a nerd, don't you?"

"I'll tell you you're a nerd to your face," I say. "I guess I didn't want it to be this big thing. I wanted to have a sexual relationship with someone without all the meddling. Without people asking when it's going to turn into a relationship. I want to tell them now, though. I don't want to keep it a secret anymore."

"Yeah?" He grins and bands an arm around my waist. "I'd be shocked if Maven didn't already know. She and Dallas tell each other everything."

"I guess we'll find out soon." I nod to the bag of gifts he's holding. They're all for June, and there has to be close to a dozen in there. "Want me to take that?"

"So you get all the credit? Fuck, no."

Reid walks into the apartment and I follow behind him. We

take off our coats and shoes and head toward the laughter and loud voices coming from the living room. Our friends are gathered around a tray of nachos and pizza, and they all cheer when they see us.

"There you are!" Maven jumps up and hugs me. "I was starting to think something happened to you."

"Sorry," I say.

"We got caught up with work," Reid explains. He takes a seat on the couch next to June and hands over her presents. "It's Avery's fault. She lost track of time. Told me to keep going and she didn't want to stop."

I glare at him. His grin is beautiful, a wicked display of happiness that pangs in my chest, and I know I could never be mad at him. Not really.

"It's exhausting having to tell someone multiple times how to figure something out." I sigh and put my hands on my hips, smirking when Reid narrows his eyes. "They just don't get the hint."

"Let's get you a drink," Maven says, and she drags me from the living room. I flip Reid off before I round the corner to the kitchen. He pretends to catch it and tucks it away in his pocket. "What sounds good?"

"Anything," I say. I'm still on edge and turned on after he felt me up in the parking garage. He slid my underwear down my legs and tucked them in his pocket. He didn't give me a third orgasm, not yet, and I'm buzzing with anticipation and need after his teasing. "Alcohol. Lots of it."

"I'll make you a martini," Emmy says, joining us at the island in the center of the room. "Gin or vodka?"

"Vodka, please," I say, leaning against the counter. "A double, if you can."

She gives me a sly look and hums. "Any particular reason we're indulging so heavily in alcohol? Does it have anything to do with the mark on your neck and why your lipstick is smeared?"

Maven gasps and touches my cheek. "Holy shit. It *is* smeared."

I fumble with my purse and pull out a compact, groaning when I see the bright red streak across my jaw. "Goddamn him."

"Who is him? Are you seeing someone?" Maven asks, and I sit on a barstool.

"I'll tell you, but you cannot make this a big deal, okay?" I say. "Really. You're going to want to freak out, and there's nothing to freak out about."

"I promise," she says.

"Reid and I have been... we're..." I trail off, struggling to find the right words. "Sleeping together. We've been sleeping together. But we also spending time together outside the bedroom. And he bought me a special edition of my favorite romance novel for Christmas. We text a lot, and, well, I don't know." I shrug and brush a pile of crumbs into a hand. "Sex. We're having sex."

Maven looks at Emmy. "This sounds familiar," she says.

"Is it? Reid is a lot less obnoxious than Miller," Emmy says as she pours a generous serving of vodka into the shaker. "He also has the glasses thing going for him and he's not a total playboy with an ego the size of the state of Maryland. I don't see how they're related at all, actually."

"I'm confused." I drop my elbows to the counter and rest my chin in my hands. "Can someone fill me in?"

"This is exactly how Maverick and Emmy got together. They were at each other's throats, until one day, they kissed. Fast forward a few years later, and she's wearing his ring on her finger," Maven explains.

"Reid and I aren't... it's not dating," I explain as Emmy hands me my drink. "It's sex and then some. A friends with benefits arrangement with extras on the side. Like today. I get to come here and spend the evening with you all."

"Do you like spending time with him?" Maven asks, and I sip on my martini.

There's a moment of hesitation where I think about keeping these thoughts and feelings I've been having to myself, but I see them watching me, and I'm struck with how *badly* I want to spill my secrets.

Making friends as an adult woman is so fucking hard. It's nearly impossible when you add in a job with a heavy workload that requires frequent traveling. I'm constantly surrounded by men, looked at as *one of the boys* just because of my job, and I find myself craving the femininity that comes with talking with close female confidants.

"Yeah," I say. "Lately, it seems like all my free time is spent with him."

"What happened to never sleeping with him again?" Maven teases, and I groan. "I distinctly remember sitting in a booth with you when you said those very words."

"I thought that too. That was the plan. Then he kissed me, and, well, here we are. Having sex on a near daily basis."

"*Daily*?" Maven repeats, incredulous. "I didn't realize it was so serious."

"It's *not* serious."

"Spending almost every day with someone is teetering closer to serious than it is casual." She glances at Emmy and tilts her head to the side. "A little help, Hartwell?"

"I'm not sure I have anything to add. As long as everyone understands the rules of the relationship—and I use that term loosely—what's the harm?" Emmy asks.

"We're both well aware of what it is and what it isn't." I pause and trace the rim of my glass with my finger. "I might have a teeny, tiny crush on him, though, and that goes outside of what's allowed. It's not what we agreed on."

"Sex can go from detached to intimate real quick. It's nearly impossible to separate yourself from the person if you're consistently with them. A one-night stand is easy. You get what you want out of it then go on your way. Repeatedly seeing the same person allows time for those what-ifs to pop up. It's what happened with me and pretty boy," Emmy says, sounding matter-of-fact. Like she's talked about this a hundred times. "Take me and pretty boy, for example. One minute, it's all about each other's pleasure. The next, he's taking care of me when I'm sick and washing my hair. I'm not immune to romantic gestures; that's enough to sweep anyone off their feet. I think it's normal to develop some sort of emotional connection with someone who's seeing the most vulnerable parts of you."

"That's the thing," I say. "He *is* seeing the most vulnerable parts of me. It's not intentional, but he's putting together the puzzle of my life, and I'm afraid of what happens when he finds the final piece. What then?"

"Well." Maven takes my hand and smiles. "That's generally when people fall in love. It's not something you plan. It's something that happens along the way."

That word again.

The same one I tossed around earlier.

Love.

A hesitant and terrifying consideration.

Reid is the embodiment of the perfect man. Calm and patient and good to his very core. He's smart and funny and everything I'd look for in a partner if I were looking for one. Kind and full of hope.

It would be silly *not* to love him.

"We'll see," I say. "For now, we're going to keep doing what we're doing. Seeing where it goes and having fun."

"I'll drink to that," Emmy says, lifting her drink. "To good dick and men who treat us right."

I laugh, and we knock our glasses together. "Thank you so much for letting me join the festivities."

"We're happy you're here." Maven rests her cheek on my shoulder. "It's nothing special, but it's nice not to be alone this time of year."

"Don't sell it short, Mae," Reid says from behind us. I turn around and see him leaning in the entryway of the kitchen, his arms folded across his chest. "This is my favorite holiday because I get to spend it with you all."

"My expectations are low after Thanksgiving," Maven says. "The burnt turkey really brought the mood down."

"And Dallas and I were stuck out in Phoenix so we couldn't even enjoy it." Reid walks to the fridge and pulls out a water bottle, his gaze moving to me. "How are you doing, Sinclair?"

"I'm good." I smile and hold up my martini. "I have alcohol and friends. What more do I need?"

"Sounds perfect if you ask me. Did you tell them about the concert?"

"Oh." I brighten, looking at the women and beaming. "The Ella Wright concert? I'm so excited."

"I told Dallas our relationship hinged on him getting us seats," Maven says, popping a cherry from a bowl on the island in her mouth. "He made quick work of that."

"Maverick walks around our apartment singing her songs." Emmy smirks. "I think he likes her more than I do."

"I like her too," Reid says. "I put June's presents under the tree, Mae. Hope that's okay."

"That's perfect. She always loves what you get her." Maven stands and kisses his cheek, sneaking me a sly glance. "Will you help me clear the appetizer plates, Em? The ham will be ready soon and we need some space."

"Sure." Emmy finishes off her drink and sets it in the sink. "If you want a second, Avery, let me know. I'm happy to make you another round."

"I think I'm good right now," I say, crossing my legs and sighing. I feel warm. Content and surrounded by excellent company. "Thanks, though."

The girls disappear, leaving Reid and me alone. He brushes the hair away from my neck and kisses my throat.

"Did you tell them?" he asks.

"Yeah." I close my eyes and hum when he moves his mouth down my neck. "My smeared lipstick kind of gave it away."

"Whoops." He drops a kiss to my cheek. "Guess that's my fault. You're irresistible, Ave. I can't help it."

"A few months ago, you wanted nothing to do with me," I say.

"And look at me now. I'm bringing you to Christmas Eve dinner."

I spin on the stool so he's standing between my legs. I hook my fingers in the belt loops of his jeans and tug him closer to me. "I'm so glad I get to be here with you."

"Me too," Reid says. "I'm glad you get to celebrate with our friends."

It's funny to think we've cultivated a life that blends together so easily.

I felt like I've been muddling through the last couple of years. Grieving my dad. Adjusting to a new role away from home. Getting over a breakup and learning to love myself again. Branching out and trying new things.

These past few months, though, I've started to think I've found my place. The spot where I belong and where I'm most happy.

In all those shining moments, Reid is there. A constant pillar and the brightest star in the sky. It's almost like I was waiting for him to show up, and my life is better because of it.

"Should we help them set the table?" I ask. "If we stay in here any longer, they're going to start making sex jokes."

"Trust me. The jokes have already started. After we eat, I have one more surprise for you," he says.

"You've already done more than enough for me."

"This is different. I know how important your dad was to you. I also know it's not Christmas Day, and I know you're not there in person to watch like you normally would, but I wanted to include a part of him today. I, uh, might have downloaded last year's Orlando Blazers game so we can stream it later. It might be in a different language and it might ruin Dallas's television, but I thought we could give it a try."

"Y—you did that? For me?" I whisper.

"Yeah." Reid smiles. "There's no rule saying we can't do both old and new traditions."

A sob racks my shoulders. I throw my arms around him and hug him as tight as I can, afraid that if I ease up for even a second, he'll disappear.

I've been scared to admit it, but now I know with absolute certainty. If I let myself fall, Reid is the one I'm going to fall for.

I think I'm already halfway there.

@footballindc

@dcfootball

Congrats on the Wild Card spot.

We'll be enjoying our off week while you're in snowy Minnesota.

@footballindc

We get to live to play another day, and that's more than the team can say from the last three years.

Can't wait to blast the song on repeat when we win.

@dcfootball

Just do it away from me, please.

@footballindc

It's unavoidable if I win the bet.

@dcfootball

You're not winning the bet.

@footballindc

We'll see about that.

Attachment: 1 image

I swear. If I see one more duck in my office, I'm going to lose it.

@dcfootball

I'm playing the long game too, Sinclair.

@footballindc

And what's the long game? Driving me out of my mind?

@dcfootball

Stick around and find out.

"HOW ARE THINGS GOING WITH AVERY?" Maverick asks, leaning back on the couch in my living room and staring at the television. "Goddammit. Dallas. You need to go into the building on the left, not the fucking barn."

"Don't tell me what to do," Dallas says, and he groans when the game ends. "That's not my fault."

"It's not my fault. I was hiding behind a tree the whole time," I say, tossing the controller onto the coffee table. "What do you mean how are things going with Avery?"

"It's a pretty self-explanatory question, isn't it? You two are still hooking up, aren't you?"

I pull my glasses off my face and rub my eyes.

We are still hooking up. I had her twice last night.

Once again this morning before she had to leave for work.

Lately, though, it feels like *hooking up* isn't the right word to define what's happening between us.

The sex is still fantastic and the best of my fucking life.

We're still egging each other on through social media.

But there's something else under the surface too.

I felt it on Christmas Eve when she gave me my Millennium

Falcon present. I wanted to hug her and not let her go. I wanted to tell her how much she means to me and how special she is. I needed to let her know her attention to detail is one of my favorite things about her.

Instead, I fucking teared up.

I couldn't get the words out.

They got stuck in my throat, halfway between my heart and my mouth, and now I don't know what to do.

I *like* her.

A whole fucking lot.

I don't just want to put her arms above her head and fuck her while she's still wearing one of her leather skirts and heels, although that will never get old.

I also want to wake up next to her every morning.

I want to hold her hand when we're out in public.

I want to get her name tattooed on my thigh, under the butterfly tattoos, so she's always with me.

I want, and I want, and I *want* so many things with her, and I don't know how to ask for them.

In the past, it's been easy to have those conversations with the woman I've been seeing. It's easy to go from dating to serious.

How the fuck do you go from fuck buddies to something more? Do we just keep fucking each other from now until eternity? Is it going to be fifty years of this, of texts asking if she's free and her asking if I want to hang out?

"Hey." Maverick snaps his fingers in my face, and I blink. I didn't realize I'd sunk into a trance of dark brown hair the dimples on Avery's cheeks. "Earth to Plant Daddy."

"Sorry." I slide my glasses up my nose. "Yes, we're still seeing each other. It's going well."

"You know what this means, right?" He grins and nudges Dallas's shoulders. "Reid likes her more than he said he did at the bar. He's *obsessed*."

"I am not," I say.

"You so are, man. You're fucking blushing right now."

"I am *not*." I touch my cheeks, and they're warm under my fingers. "It's from the sun."

"The sun in January?"

"Is it bad if you like her?" Dallas asks. He clicks off the television and gives me his undivided attention. "It's obvious she likes you too."

"It's not bad. It's just not part of our plan. We agreed this was physical. Telling her I miss her when she's not next to me doesn't fit the bill of casual," I say, and I stand up, walking a lap around the room. "I do, though. I do miss her when she's not next to me. Like right now. Sure, I'm having fun with you all, but I wish she was here. And not just because of the sex. Because I want to hear her laugh and make her smile." I run a hand through my hair. "I have to tell her, don't I?"

"Uh, yeah, because you're halfway to being in love with her," Maverick says.

"I don't *love* her. That's a bold word."

"Fine. You don't love her—not yet, at least. But you do like her. You care for her, and it's not fair to either of you to feel this way and not let the other know," Maverick says. "Remember when I was sorting through my feelings for Emmy and didn't know what to do? You told me to tell her, and I think you should heed your own advice. You need to let her know."

It's funny to see Maverick like this—the doting partner. The family man. A one-woman guy who hasn't looked at anyone else in years.

I'm happy for him.

I'm happy for Dallas too. They both deserve that love. They fought for it and worked hard for it.

Deep down, I'm also jealous.

That's usually me, and I want it again.

I want it with *her*.

A sure thing in a confusing world of maybes.

"Okay," I say. I know it's the right thing to do, but it doesn't make it any less scary. "I'll tell her."

"Thatta boy." Maverick clasps a hand on my shoulder. "That's how you do it."

"I never thought I'd see the day when Maverick Miller was giving out relationship advice." Dallas laughs. "I like this new side of you, Mavvy."

We go back to playing video games, the afternoon passing with Maverick taunting the twelve-year-olds we're up against and Dallas handing us drinks. When it starts to get dark outside, Maverick stretches his arms over his head and swipes his phone off the table.

"I should get going," he says. "Emmy girl just landed from her road trip, and I haven't seen her in a week. I miss the fuck out of her."

"I'm heading out too. Mae and June are on their way back from a shopping trip." Dallas stands and pulls his hoodie over his head. "I can't wait to see the damage they did on my credit card."

"I'll sit on the couch and eat dinner by myself." I laugh and move the video game controllers under the television. "Thanks for hanging out with me. I appreciate when I get to see you guys."

"Aw, shit, Plant Daddy." Maverick tackles me in a hug and we fall to the floor. "I've only got a couple seasons left in me, then you can have me whenever you want."

"Christ." I groan, rubbing my arm where he ran into me. "Stop trying to proposition me, Miller."

"Enough with the dogpile, fuckers." Dallas helps us up and pats my shoulder. "I know it might be hard to be on the sidelines, Reid, but your person is out there. She's waiting for you."

My phone chimes in my pocket, and I pull it out, finding Avery's name on the screen. I smile at the three notifications from her, the ones rolling in from social media and the text messages waiting for me.

She must have finished work and is catching up. I like this time of day when she has different conversations with me across a handful of different platforms.

"What?" I ask, looking up at them. "Sorry. Avery texted me."

"Nothing." Dallas grins and shakes his head. "Forget I said anything. Enjoy your night, man."

"Yeah." I rub a hand across my jaw, grinning at the fresh wave of comments and likes she's spamming me with. "You guys too."

AVERY

Are you busy tonight?

ME

I'm free.

Want to come over?

AVERY

Yes, please.

I've missed you.

I haven't seen you since Christmas Eve.

ME

Come over and I'll show you how much I've missed you too.

AVERY

There's an offer I can't refuse.

"I brought pizza," Avery calls out from the foyer of my apartment an hour later. "I hope that's okay."

I jog down the hall and slide across the wood floor. She's pulling off her coat and beanie, the knee-high boots and the scarf around her neck. I take the box from her, the cardboard warm in my hands, and I smile.

"I was going to ask if you wanted food. I haven't eaten yet, and I'm starving."

"How was your day?" she asks, leading the way to the kitchen like she lives here too.

I think I'd like it if she did.

I think I'd be happy to welcome her home every night.

I'd pour her a glass of wine and listen to her talk about work. I'd nod along to the new ideas she has, teasing her like I'm going to steal them, but, really, I'd be in awe of her creativity. Blown away by how big and how beautiful her brain is.

Her sweaters could be next to mine in the closet. A toothbrush in the bathroom and the three pillows she insists she has to sleep with on the bed.

I could take my time with her. Fuck her on the kitchen counter. In the living room against the wall. Every room in here wouldn't just be *mine*. It would be *ours*, with fresh sunflowers in jars and our laptops in the home office.

"Reid?" she asks, and I snap out of my daydream of playing house.

"Hm?" I answer, and her smile tips into one that's bright and perfect.

"Where'd you go?"

"Sorry," I apologize, following her. "Lost in my thoughts there for a minute."

My eyes drift down her legs, to the swell of her ass and the shape of her hips. The skirt and tights she's wearing do little to hide her curves, and I have to bite my bottom lip to keep from groaning when I see little bows at the tops of her stockings.

I might actually be addicted to her.

I think she might be torturing me on purpose.

"Hopefully good thoughts," Avery says.

"Very good thoughts." I reach over her shoulder and grab two plates, setting them on the counter. "You want something to drink?"

"I probably shouldn't. There are only two days until we travel, and I know tomorrow is going to be long."

"If you change your mind, I bought some new whiskey," I say. "It got good reviews."

"You hardly ever drink whiskey."

I shrug. "But you do. Figured I should have some here so you can make yourself a drink whenever you feel like you needed one. And, with the end of your season approaching, the necessity is growing more inevitable."

"Asshole." She laughs and swats at my arm. "When they announce the winner of Social Media Account of the Year, you're going to look like a goddamn fool, Reid Duncan."

"You'd still fuck me." I crowd her space and rest one hand on either side of her hips on the counter, caging her in. "Wouldn't you, beauty queen? You'd still find your way over here because I know how to keep you satisfied. I know how to take care of you, don't I? Not just in the bedroom but outside it, too."

Her breath catches in her throat and she grabs my shirt. "Yes," she whispers. "I would and you do."

"How hungry are you?" I ask her.

"I can wait to eat."

"I can't." I lift her on the counter and shove her legs open, those damn stockings making my cock throb. "You know the question I'm going to ask you."

"Wet," she says automatically, adjusting her skirt so it rides up her hips. I see lace underwear—green this time—and the front of the material is already damp. "I need you, Reid."

"How much did you miss me?" I ask, my fingers moving to the front of her underwear. I grin when she lifts her hips and drops her head back, asking for more. "On a scale of one to ten?"

"Eleven. I missed you so damn much."

I feel that in the center of my chest.

It takes up all the space behind my ribs.

All the space in my head, too.

I know I need to talk to her about my feelings.

I know I need to ask if we're on the same page going forward, but it's too damn difficult to remember everything I want to say when she hooks her fingers in the waistband of her underwear and shimmies them down her legs.

When she tosses them on the floor and rests her hands on her thighs, spreading herself open for me.

When she looks at me with a mischievous glint in her eyes, the ball in my court.

"Fuck, baby." I drop to my knees and put my palms on her thighs. "That picture you sent me last night didn't do your cunt justice. You're so goddamn pretty."

"So hurry up and eat," she says urgently, one hand moving to the back of my head. She knocks my glasses off, and I don't care that I can't see. "Please."

"Fucking love when my beauty queen begs for me," I murmur, my beard grazing her bare skin. "I've never wanted anyone like I want you."

Avery tries to tell me something else, but I cut her off by licking a slow swipe across her entrance with my tongue. I push two fingers in her, then three, humming when she wiggles on the counter.

"There you go, baby," I tell her, my free hand reaching up under her sweater and cupping one of her tits. "Show me how much you want it."

She groans, and I fucking love that sound. I'd stay on my knees for the rest of my life if it meant I got to hear that noise on repeat.

"Reid," she pants. Her grip on my hair is sharp and stinging. She yanks on the ends and I nearly fall forward. "I like that."

"Yeah?" I circle her clit with my tongue and savor the taste. "You gonna come for me?"

"A little more. I can take a little more," she tells me, and I kiss her knee.

"You can, can't you? Deep breath, Ave. Let's get you nice and ready for me."

I add my pinky, careful to start slow. I listen to her breathing, to the glide of my fingers and how she starts to whisper my name. When she relaxes, I find the pace she likes. The rhythm that mimics how she likes to be fucked. Thoroughly, roughly.

Avery clenches around my fingers, and I pull my mouth away. She's blurry, more like a blob than the fucking knockout I know her to be, but I want to watch her come undone. I want to see the woman who's usually so put together, the face of professionalism and decorum fall apart, all because she's fucking desperate for me.

"Reid," she says again, and I swear I don't know if my name sounds more like a prayer or a curse. "I'm going to—"

"All over my fingers, Avery. You know I like it when you make things messy."

She's the only woman I've been so vocal with.

Avery unlocked a beast inside me.

Ever since that very first night we were together, back when she told me she was loud and enthusiastic, I wanted to match her. I wanted her to know I get off on getting her off. I wanted her to know I like being here with her. I wanted her to know I'll take anything she gives me.

I've never been greedy, but with her, I take what I fucking want.

And right now, I want her dripping down my hand.

"Shit," she curses, her fingers back in my hair. She presses me to the apex of her thighs, holding me in place, and she falls over the edge. "Fuck, that's—"

"All of it, Ave. Every drop."

She cries out and I feel her pulse around me. She gasps for a breath and I work her down from the high, slow to pull out of her. Her thighs shake, and with my clean hand, I rub up and down her leg.

"How—" She gulps down another breath. "How are you so good at that?"

"Am I good at it?" I ask.

If looks could kill, I'd be six feet under.

"You made me come on a kitchen counter, Reid. While I'm still wearing my clothes. You're fucking fantastic at it."

"Oh." I lick my lips and blush. I suck on my fingers, tasting her again, and she watches me with heated eyes. "Thank you."

Her gaze drops to the front of my jeans where I'm painfully hard. My cock aches and it wouldn't take long for me to finish, but her stomach rumbles. I laugh and stand, fixing her skirt and helping her to the ground.

"I want you," she says, pushing up on her toes so she can kiss me. Her tongue sneaks out of her mouth, brushing against mine, and I love that she wants to taste herself too. "So fucking badly, Reid."

"I want you too, but let's get you fed first. You can tell me about your day. I can watch you pull the pepperonis off your pizza before you take a bite. After, you can have me in whatever position you want."

"How do you know I like to eat the pepperonis first?" Avery asks.

"Been watching you for a while, Sinclair. It's about time you caught up."

"THAT PIZZA WAS DELICIOUS," Avery calls out from the bathroom where she's drying her hair. "Thanks for not judging me for eating five slices."

"Are you kidding?" I relax against the pillows on my bed and grab my *Watchmen* comic off the bedside table. I turn to the spot I left off on the other night and put an arm behind my head. "The cheese hanging from the corner of your mouth was hot as fuck."

"You're such a liar. Reading?" she asks from the doorway.

I hum and fix my pajama bottoms before slipping under the sheets and flipping the page. "Skimming. Someone posted an outlandish theory in a Reddit thread the other day. It's one I haven't picked up on. This is my forty-fifth read through, and I still don't understand what they're trying to say. It's infuriating."

"Anything I can help with?"

"Have you read *Watchmen*?"

"No. I promise I will soon, though."

The bed dips under her weight, and I barely look up. "You don't have to. It's long. It's not the short and snappy comics you've read before."

"You like it. I want to give it a try." Avery straddles me and rests her palms on my bare stomach. "I might like it too."

"You might." I rest a hand on her thigh. She's still warm from the shower we took after dinner, her skin soft and clean. "Don't hate me if you're bored to death."

"I'll survive." Her fingers curl around the spine of the book, blocking the page from view. "Reid?"

"Hm?" I try to nudge her hand out of the way, but she doesn't give me an inch. "What's up?"

"Can we put this down for a little while?"

I look up at her. Her cheeks are flushed, and she's staring at me. Her nipples are hard and pointed through the thin cotton of the T-shirt I gave her to sleep in. She rolls her hips in a slow circle against me. Her pussy brushes over the sheet covering my lower half, and I realize five seconds too late she's not wearing any underwear.

"Oh." I swallow, relenting my grip on the graphic novel without another thought. She takes it from my hand and sets it aside. "Yeah. Ah. Of course. Sorry. The world pulls me in sometimes. Please don't think I was trying to ignore you."

"I know you weren't. While I have your attention, I should tell you I haven't been completely honest with you." She tugs on the hem of her shirt and drags it over her head. I suck in a sharp breath at her naked body, and she gives me a wicked grin. "And it's time I come clean."

"What—" I swallow. My throat is dry, and I'm not sure I'll ever get over how beautiful she is. How lucky I am that I get to have her like this. "What are you hiding?"

"I know all about Doctor Manhattan and Edward Blake. Rorschach too."

I blink. "What?"

She leans forward, and her tits are practically in my face.

"After I left the bar the night we met, I ordered a copy of *Watchmen*. I read it front to back then I read it again. All because the cute guy who blushed when I complimented him said it was his favorite," she whispers in my ear.

My head is spinning. There's no way this is real life. There's no way she's saying these things to me.

I squeeze my eyes shut. I count to ten then open them, shocked to find her still on top of me. Still naked and beautiful and smirking with a sly little grin.

"You're messing with me, aren't you?" I ask.

Her smile falls. She sits back and I scramble for her, aching for her touch.

"This is silly." She folds her arms over her chest and shakes her head. "I'm so stupid."

"Whoa. Hang on." I stroke the space between her shoulder blades and frown, confused by her change in attitude. "You're the furthest thing from stupid. Where did you get that idea?"

"I wanted to surprise you by reading the story you like, but it's not that impressive. I don't know why I thought it was special and a big deal."

"That's not—Avery. Could you look at me, please?" I ask, and she lifts her chin. "I didn't mean that as a dig to you, and I'm sorry if it came off that way. I—" I huff out a laugh, embarrassed. "To be honest, I'm still in shock you're here at all. Add in the whole *naked and on top of me talking about comic books* thing, and I swear I'm having a stroke. You're—god. Calling you the girl of my dreams sounds so fucking cliché, but it's true. If I had to put together my perfect person, every part of them would be made of you."

It's not a confession to how I've been feeling about her, but it's close enough. It gets the point across, because one minute, she's blinking at me with wide eyes, the next, she's kissing me, her mouth on mine and a breathy moan escaping from her throat.

I touch her everywhere I can reach. Her legs, stomach. The hips I love to grab when I fuck her from behind. Her chest, my palm resting over her heart and feeling how our beats align.

Avery lifts off of me, pawing at my pajama bottoms, her intent clear. I switch our positions, guiding her to the sheets so I can strip down and be naked just like her.

"How do you want me?" she asks, slipping a hand between her legs and touching herself. When her slender fingers disappear inside her pussy, I can't help but groan. "You made me feel so good earlier, Reid. I want you to feel like that too."

"I feel like that every time you're with me, baby. It's always the best time of my fucking life."

She arches her back. "I want to fuck you. I want to be on top."

I try to speak, but I can't find the goddamn words.

I'm too mesmerized by the easy way she tugs me to the pillows. Her laugh when she straddles me again and goes to pull off my glasses, stopping when I shake my head.

"Want to leave them on," I rasp. "Want to watch you."

"Greedy slut," she murmurs in my ear, and I buck my hips into hers. "Look at you, Reid. Pre-cum already? You must really like what you see."

I think I might love what I see.

She spits in her hand and wraps it around my length, stroking me up and down. I grip the sheets, my head lolling back and my chest pinching tight. When her thumb runs over the head of my cock, I moan her name.

"*Avery.* You gotta get on and fuck me, baby, because the longer you touch me, the less time I'm going to last. And I really want to paint you with my cum."

Avery grins, the dimple on her cheek popping in the lamplight, and I make a decision right now to always wear my glasses when I fuck her. I like seeing the soft skin of her thighs. I like seeing her laugh when I practically grab for her, the giggle changing to a low moan when she sinks down on my dick.

"I almost forgot how full you make me feel when you're inside me," she gasps, rocking forward so her hands land on either side of my head. "Best I've ever had."

I grunt and grip her hips, slamming her down on my length then lifting her up. "Tell me how much you want me. Tell me how good I make you feel."

She licks my throat, and I hiss. Her mouth brushes against my ear, her breath hot on my skin as she dips her voice low.

"Do you know whose I am, Reid?" she whispers. "Yours. Only you can make me feel this way."

Fucking fuck.

I don't have any more self-restraint. I don't have any more patience. I have to have her, or I'm going to go out of my goddamn mind.

Mine.

I want her to be mine.

Totally and completely, in every sense of the word.

I want to put a ring on her finger and maybe have a couple kids.

I want to grow old with her and sit on a porch, talking about all the good things we've done together.

I want to argue and fight with her and let her push me out of my comfort zone.

I want to love her, and I want her to love me back.

Avery works herself up and down, her movements turning wild. Her hair sticks to her skin and her eyes flutter closed. The sheen of sweat on her forehead glistens. When she parts her mouth, I drag a thumb across her lower lip.

"You're mine," I tell her, letting the words slip free and she smiles. "Today. Tomorrow. For as long as you'll have me."

"Yours," she repeats, circling her hips in the way I like.

My breathing turns rough, and I know I'm teetering close to an orgasm. I drop my hand between her legs, touching her thigh. Her knee. Her clit and anywhere I can fucking reach.

"What do you need?" I ask. I close my eyes, afraid if I keep looking at her, if I keep watching her, I'll finish before she does. And that's not an option.

"You're enough." Avery sighs, pinching her nipples. She sounds happy. Content and satisfied. Because of *me*. "You're always enough, Reid."

Her pussy tightens, the same sensation I felt around my fingers in the kitchen I feel around my cock, and it's fucking fantastic. Heaven on earth. A place where I'd be glad to die. I groan and hold her in place, lifting my hips to thrust into her again and again.

I want to get her there.

I want her to be first.

What I don't say with my words I show her with my cock and my hands, and time stands still.

"*Yes*," she says. "I'm going to—"

"Fuck. Me too, Ave."

I follow her over the edge, moaning her name through my release. She tortures me, refusing to give me an ounce of relief until I'm whimpering. Until my legs shake and my hips buck, giving her every drop of the cum buried inside her and trailing down her leg.

"Holy shit." She puts her hands on my chest and eases herself off me. She settles on the mattress, her hair across the sheets and an arm thrown over her eyes. "You're the only guy who's ever made me come when having sex."

I'm weak.

My mental capacities are diminished and my limbs are heavy like lead. Still, I want to see her. I muster all of my energy and sit up. I grab her left knee and roll so I'm positioned between her legs.

"What—" She sputters out a string of curses when I rest my hands under her thighs and hold her open. "You—"

"Want to see. Want to feel." I push two fingers in her pussy, groaning when my cum coats my fingers. Warm, sticky, I pull out of her and drag my fingers over her skin. Up across her stomach and to her mouth. "Want to watch you taste."

"Greedy man," she whispers, sticking out her tongue. She sucks my fingers clean, a devilish gleam in her eyes that has my cock twitching again. That has me ready to go another round. "Such a bad boy."

I blush and climb over her, kissing her. "And to think, this was all because you started talking about *Watchmen*. About what you said earlier. I hope you never feel stupid with me, Avery. Not when you talk about the things you like. Not when you ask for things you might enjoy. I want... I want to be a safe space for you."

"You're something else." She kisses me again and laughs against my mouth. "A few minutes ago, you were fucking me within an inch of my life. Now you're over here waxing poetic. Where have you been hiding, Reid Duncan?"

"I don't know. Giving the wrong people my attention, I guess."

"Been there. Done that. At least, that's what some dude at a bar once told me."

I smile and rub my thumb along the curve of her jaw. "I want to clean you up."

"What else do you want?" she asks.

You here forever, I think.

"To hear all your *Watchmen* theories," I say instead.

Avery laughs again, softer this time. "I'll tell you all my thoughts in the shower. They're extensive, Duncan. I hope you're ready."

"Yeah." My heart is lodged halfway up my throat. "I am."

@footballindc

Guess what? Since we locked in the Wild Card spot, our ticket sales numbers have spiked.

When is the end of our bet?

@dcfootball

We didn't say.

Playoffs start next week. We should end it then.

@footballindc

Perfect.

FORTY-ONE
AVERY

REID

What are you doing tonight?

ME

Probably trolling you on TikTok.

REID

Cute. Want to hang out?

I only saw it through the photos you sent, but
that skirt of yours drove me wild today.

ME

I'm on my period and feel like I'm on my
deathbed.

RIP me.

REID

I'm sorry you're not feeling well. Is that a no to
hanging out?

ME

I'm going to be a monster.

REID

Get some rest, Ave.

ME

It's not a no.

REID

So it's a yes?

ME

I'm not in the mood for sex.

REID

That's not what I asked.

Do you want to hang out with me? With our
clothes on?

ME

Oh.

Yes. I do.

I WRAP my blanket around my shoulders and shuffle to my apartment door. I open it for Reid and grimace when I turn back to the living room and the nest I've made for myself.

"How are you feeling?" he asks, shutting the door behind him. "You look like shit."

"Nice to see you too." I sit on the couch and close my eyes, trying not to wince in pain. "Honestly? I'm miserable. The first day is always the worst, and being on my feet for eight hours didn't help."

"Cramps?"

"It feels like someone is taking a knife to my insides. Hacking up my small intestine and leaving me for dead."

"I brought you a few things. The internet told me they would help," he says. I open my eyes and watch him unload a bag of groceries on my coffee table. There's a heating pad. Aspirin and Gatorade. A gallon of water and a bar of dark chocolate. "In case you need them. The message boards are very divided on what works best."

I blink at the pile in front of me. "You brought all of this? For me?"

"Yeah." He unscrews the top of the Gatorade bottle and hands it my way. "You said you were in pain."

"That didn't mean you had to help."

Reid pauses and looks at me. His hand is halfway in the bag, and I spy more candy. His eyebrows are pinched, and he nudges his glasses up his nose.

"I wanted to help. Is that okay?"

My nose stings and my eyes blur with tears. I've been in so much physical pain all day. Walking from my bed to the couch was excruciating. I'm exhausted and hungry and so thirsty, but thinking about making myself food or getting a glass of water sounded like too much work. Work I don't have the energy to do.

And here he is, standing in front of me with everything I could ever need.

Asking if it's okay if he helps.

My heart nearly splits in two.

"Yes," I whisper, hiding my face under the pile of covers. Under here, he can't see my red-rimmed eyes or puffy cheeks. He can't see me at my absolute worst, and I don't have to see him being the selfless man he is. "It's okay."

"Hey." The couch sinks under his weight. I peel back the blanket that needs to be washed and look at him. "What's going on, Ave?"

"This is very nice." I sniff and wipe my eyes with the back of my hand. "I feel like garbage and you did something very kind for me. I'm overwhelmed, and it doesn't help that all my emotions are amplified by my cycle."

"Consider us even after you cleaned me up during the charity softball game," Reid says. "You stopped my nose from swelling. I'm helping your uterus... well. I'm not sure of the biological phenomena, but I'm trying to return the favor."

"I only stopped your nose from swelling so you couldn't complain I won our bet because you were holed up in the hospital."

Reid hums. "That's exactly why I'm here too. Though, I guess it's futile at this point. It's looking like you're going to be the winner."

We both turn quiet. He sits next to me and picks up one of the books resting on the arm of the couch. He opens it and reads the first page, then the second.

"Is it okay if I—" I ask, and he interrupts me by patting his thighs.

I rest my feet on his black sweatpants. This unbuttoned look of his is one of my favorites. The basic white T-shirt and the joggers that hug the curves of his legs. A pinch of exhaustion on his face and the hint of sunburn across his nose.

"Do you have dinner plans?" he asks after a long stretch of silence, and I realize I've been staring at him. Dozing off to the fiery red of his hair and the pink on his cheeks.

"Nothing besides crying in pain," I say. "Check back in a few days."

"I'll order us some food later. How does Thai sound?"

"Reid." I put my hand on his arm. He looks down at where we're joined, the smallest smile on his lips. "I was serious when I said we weren't going to have sex tonight."

He lifts an eyebrow. "And I was serious when I said I wanted to hang out with our clothes on."

"If you knew we weren't going to have sex, why are you here?"

"I told you." He marks his spot in the book with a long finger and taps my calf with his other hand. "I wanted to help. This is me helping. For the record, I have no problem fucking you on your period. I don't mind a little blood, and you know I like to clean you up after. But I can tell you're uncomfortable. You can barely keep your head up, and hanging out on the couch is just fine by me."

My body heats.

I imagine him on top of me, not a care in the world about getting dirty.

It would be intimate. Messy, and I like that he'd want to have sex with me when I'm vulnerable and not feeling like myself. I like that it doesn't turn him off.

I stare at him, lost for words, and everything sharpens.

This man.

This man is here taking care of me and getting nothing in return.

This man is reading my romance book and ordering food so I'm fed.

This man brought me a heating pad, for fuck's sake.

I should be on one knee asking him to marry me.

My breath comes out in short bursts the longer I stare at the hook of his nose. My chest hurts when I see his smile stretch wider.

It feels like a knot in me is pulling tight, some string I can't see tugging and tugging to the point of uncomfortable.

It's time for me to acknowledge the thing I've been trying so hard to fight.

I like him.

I like him so much.

I'd give him my heart if he asked.

I'd promise to treasure his in return, if he let me.

I think I might be a little in love with him too.

"Hey." Reid scoots closer to me and grasps my knee. His

fingers fold around my leg and his thumb rubs up and down my thigh, a touch that grounds and steadies me. "Are you okay?"

"I'm fine." I curse myself for being so obvious. "A little bit of pain. That's all."

He studies my face. When his eyes connect with mine, I *feel* it.

The worry.

The anxiousness.

The question on the tip of his tongue, ready to ask what else he can do to help.

He's looking at me like I'm made of stars. Something racing across a midnight sky made of hopes and wishes and wants. There's wonder when he parts his lips. Joy when I give him a nervous smile. Affection, too, when he moves his hand to my cheek, his touch as soft as clouds.

I'm falling for this man, and from the way my heart beats when he doesn't let go, I know I'm tumbling head first.

I wake up with a firm body pressing against my back.

I stir and open one eye, taking in my surroundings.

I'm in my bedroom. The window to the left of my bed is cracked and the curtains move in the light breeze. The lamp on the table to my right is on, a soft glow covering the sheets and blankets.

There's a heating pad against my stomach. Reid is wrapped around me, his arms resting on my waist and his mouth warm on the back of my neck. It's like he's holding me delicately, as if I'll break if he touches me too hard.

I hum when I stretch out my legs, delirious from a sleep I desperately needed.

"Hey," he murmurs, voice thick.

"Hi," I say back. "What time is it?"

"Not sure. Last I checked it was past ten. You fell asleep and I carried you in here. Fell asleep myself. I hope I'm not overstaying my welcome."

"You aren't," I say hurriedly, and I spin in his hold so I can face him. "Please don't go."

He yawns and rubs my back. "If you insist."

"I didn't realize I was so tired. My entire body aches. I feel like I got hit by a truck."

"Do you want me to run you a bath?" Reid slurs, and he sounds more delirious than me. "Might warm you up. Your feet are like fucking icicles."

"Because I normally sleep in socks. My equilibrium is all thrown off."

"You're a fucking weirdo."

"Yet here you are. Curled around me like a vine and making no effort to leave."

"Yeah, because you're my weirdo," he says.

I bury my face in his bare chest. He's warm and soft and smells like the soap I love—pine trees in the middle of a forest and the hint of rain. I blink back fresh tears, and I hate how exposed I feel right now.

"What hurts?" Reid asks. "I unplugged the heating pad before you fell asleep because the instructions said to not leave it on for extended periods of time. Let me get it set up for you."

"It's not the heating pad," I say, lifting my chin to look at him.

"It's not?" He wipes away my tears with his thumb and smiles. He blows out a breath and touches my cheek. "God. You're so beautiful."

"You told me I looked like shit earlier in the night."

"You're still beautiful even when you look like shit. Sometimes I—" Reid swallows and shakes his head. "Never mind."

"Tell me," I plead.

"You need to sleep. To rest and relax. I shouldn't be talking your ear off."

"I want to hear it."

"Sometimes I can't believe I get to be here with you," he tells me, and it's the softest he's ever spoken. "It's overwhelming, honestly. I look at you and…" he trails off, the words difficult to find, but I'm hanging on to every syllable he gives me. "I can't believe I get to exist within a four-foot radius of you. You're made of dreams, Avery, and I'm the guy lucky enough for even a few minutes of your time."

"Reid." The lump in my throat seems impossible to ignore, but I forge on. "I need to tell you something."

"Hang on." He fumbles behind him, reaching for his glasses, and slides them on his face. "There you are. I like you a lot more when you're not blurry."

"Speaking of liking things." I sit up, and the sheets pool around my waist. "I don't know how to say this without being direct, so I'm just going to go for it. Having you here tonight made me realize I haven't been completely honest with you."

"You haven't?" He frowns and props up on an elbow. "Is this another *Watchman* thing?"

"Not exactly. You've done all these wonderful things for me, and it wouldn't be fair to let you think you were operating under one school of thought, when really, it's something entirely different."

"I know I'm tired, but you're talking in circles, Ave." He puts his hand on my forehead. "Are you running a fever? Let me get you some water."

"I like you," I blurt out, and he gapes at me. "A lot. In a more than friends way. In a more than friends with benefits kind of way. I have feelings for you, and I can't let you sleep next to me thinking this is purely platonic for me. It's not. It hasn't been for a while, I don't think, but tonight solidified it. I'm so happy when you're around, Reid. I... I miss you when you're gone. I check my phone constantly to see if you've sent me a message. The time I get to spend with you is the best part of my day."

"Avery, I—"

"I know we said we weren't going to let our emotions get involved, and I tried really damn hard to not fall for you. I did my best, but I can't help it anymore. I'm sorry for misleading you. If you don't want to see me anymore, I understand."

Reid smiles. "Are you finished?"

"Yes."

"Good." He sits all the way up and draws me close to his chest. He kisses my shoulder and rests his chin on my head. "You're my most favorite person in the world, Avery."

"I am?"

"Is it not obvious?"

"I don't know." I shrug. "I don't like to get my hopes up, because you're my favorite person too."

"That means I need to do a better job of showing it. I wanted to tell you the other night when you came over, but you were on top of me and talking about comic books. It's hard to form any intelligent thoughts when you're wearing one of my shirts and grinding against me."

"Sorry for being distracting," I say, touching his arm. I know he's right next to me, but he's not close enough. I want to feel him everywhere. "Do you forgive me?"

"Yeah." His smile lights up his eyes. "How the hell did we get here?"

"Well, you asked if I wanted to hang out, I said yes and—"

"I don't mean literally here, smartass." Reid eases me onto my back. He hovers over me, stroking my hair, and even though I feel like the lowest of lows, I've never felt more beautiful. "I mean here. Having feelings for each other. Wanting to spend all our time together." He swallows down something else with a small shake of his head. "Five months ago, I hated you. I would've done anything to bring you down. Now I'm wondering how I lived so long without you."

"You've always had me," I say. I reach up and cup his cheek, my thumb running over the rough scratch of his beard. "In a way, I've always been yours."

I might love you.

I think I've been waiting for you for a very long time.

The thoughts ping-pong around in my brain. They cement themselves with certainty, a lightning strike in an open field. One second ago, it wasn't there. Now, it's all I hear.

I love you.

I love you, I love you, I love you.

When he kisses me soft and sweet, murmuring kind words until I drift back to sleep, I know there's a chance he might love me too.

@dcfootball

@footballindc

Are you nervous about the bet results?

@dcfootball

Nope.

Also, I'm taking you on a date tomorrow night.

@footballindc

You are talking to me, right?

Not one of the interns?

@dcfootball

Guess we'll see when you show up.

FORTY-TWO

AVERY

"YOU LOOK PERFECT," Maven says, unplugging the curling iron from the wall. "Like a total babe."

"Is it too much?" I run my hands over the front of the dark green dress and spin in a small circle. "It's just dinner."

Emmy tuts from where she's lounging on my bed. "It's never too much, no matter what the assholes who try to tell us to tone it down say." She looks up from her phone and grins. "Shit, Avery. You're going to make him lose his mind. That color is fucking gorgeous on you."

"Are you sure? He told me we're going somewhere nice, and I figured a dress from my pageant days might be borderline excessive," I say. "But I love this outfit so much."

"It's not excessive. Look at your *ass*," Maven says, and I burst out laughing. "How the hell are you so toned?"

"Running. Taking the stairs at work. Getting in twenty thousand steps on game days." I adjust the chain of my necklace and put on my earrings. "I want to start barre classes, but I don't want to go alone."

"I'll go with you," Emmy says. "I love cross training. I have a friend who teaches Pilates if you want to try that sometime."

"Yeah." I smile at my reflection and flip my hair over my shoulder. "I'd love that."

"Is he picking you up?" Maven asks, sitting next to Emmy on the bed. "Oh my god, I've missed this kind of girl talk. Being married is a real drag. This is so fun."

"Yes, he's picking me up."

Emmy lies on her stomach and gives me another once over. "What shoes are you wearing?"

"I was thinking black heels. I know they're not practical for this time of year, but I love them so much." I stick out my foot and show off the stilettos I bought on a whim last week. "Do you think they match the green?"

"They make your legs look fantastic." Emmy glances at Maven, giving her a small smile. "You're right. This is really fun."

"*See*? You're basically married too. You have Maverick's handwriting tattooed on your chest."

"Wait, *what*?" I put my hands on my hips and turn to face them. "I know I can't ask to see your boobs, but I kind of want to see your boobs."

Emmy chuckles and swings her legs to the end of the bed. She sits up straight and lifts her shirt, revealing a black sports bra. Pulling the left strap down, I see the word *mine* written in handwriting that looks like it belongs to a man across the top of her breast.

"I, um, like when Maverick touches my neck," she admits bashfully. "One time when we were together, he said he was going to get the word *mine* tattooed on the back of his hand so when we were together, I'd know who I belong to. I got one to match." She taps the letters, her skin turning pink under her painted fingernails. "It's right where his hand rests when he's... you know. Cutting off my air supply in a consensual, respectful yet depraved way."

"Why is that the hottest thing I've ever heard?" I say. "Good grief, Emmy. Not only are you and your boyfriend smoking, but you play in the NHL too? What can't you do?"

"The list is too long." She holds up her phone and taps the screen. "You only have a few minutes before he's here."

"Shit." I grab my purse off my dresser and shove a tube of lipstick inside. "Is it normal to be nervous? Reid and I have been sleeping together for months. If he told me to strip and lie on the bed naked, I'd be less anxious than I am right now."

"Because it's different." Maven walks toward me and adjusts the strap of my dress. "Now it means something."

"Yeah," I say faintly, rubbing a hand over my chest. There's a phantom ache there, a tightening sensation that's been in place since he took care of me while I was on my period. Since he held me to his chest and let me fall asleep in his arms. Maybe it's been there all along. "It does mean something."

I'm not sure I've ever been this excited about a date. Reid's given me no clues. No hints about where we might be going, but I like the idea of a surprise. I like thinking he probably spent an hour or two planning out the night. Crouching over his computer and creating a spreadsheet, and his quiet, careful consideration might be my favorite thing about him.

My phone vibrates, and I'm swiping my thumb across the screen before it finishes buzzing.

REID

I'm out front.

ME

Be right down!

"Can you all lock up on your way out?" I ask the girls.

"Of course we can." She hugs me and motions for Emmy to join in on the embrace. The two of them wrap me in their arms, and I laugh at their affection. "I hope you have so much fun, Avery."

"Me too." I smile and grab my coat off the bed. "I'll see you all later."

There are butterflies in my stomach as I take the elevator down to the ground floor. My throat is dry, and every step I take feels like the start of something important. Something poignant and bigger than me.

I shiver when I make it outside, the January air cool on my overheated skin. Up the road, I see Reid leaning against his car, and I stop in the middle of the sidewalk.

He's looking at the night sky, his head tipped back and his eyes cast upward. He's unaware I'm here, unaware I'm staring at him with my jaw almost on the ground, and I soak up the sight of him.

The tuxedo he's wearing is familiar, and I realize it's the same one he wore the night of the wedding. His bowtie is purple, and he's holding a bouquet of sunflowers close to his chest. A smile—the faintest hint of a grin—sits on the corners of his mouth, and I want to kiss it off his face.

"Waiting for someone?" I call out, and his neck jerks in my direction. His eyes brighten, sparkling under the stars, and he pushes off the hood of his SUV. "Disappointed it's me?"

"Ecstatic, actually." He closes the distance between us, a soft palm on my cheek as he bends his neck to kiss me. "You're way more fun than the interns."

"Hi," I whisper against his mouth, and he breaks out into a full beam.

"Hi." He dips his chin, eyes raking over my dress. I pull my coat open slightly to reveal my outfit, and a soft moan climbs up his throat. "You look beautiful."

"Thanks. So do you." I touch his tie and the scruff of his

beard. "Are you going to tell me where we're going so dressed up?"

"It's a surprise." He kisses me one more time then leads me to his car, opening the passenger-side door. "But I'll give you a hint. You've been here before. Both places, actually."

"Intriguing." I adjust my dress under me when I sit, trying to avoid any wrinkles. "You have my attention."

"Finally," Reid says once he rounds the car and slips into the driver's seat.

We make small talk on the drive, catching each other up on our days. He asks if I'm ready for the road game in Minneapolis. I ask how the Titans players are spending their bye week. It's easy and light and exactly how it always is with us.

I don't even realize he's shifting the car to park until he's unbuckling his seatbelt and turning off the ignition. I look out the dashboard and burst out laughing.

"Why the hell are we at this shitty sports bar again?" I ask.

"Why not?" he tosses back.

"Does the offer to hold back my hair if I get sick still stand?"

"Of course it does," Reid says. "But maybe we avoid the mozzarella sticks tonight. Just to be safe."

We're ridiculously overdressed for the location, and everyone stares at us when we walk in. Reid rests his hand on my lower back as the hostess leads us to a booth, and I shrug off my coat before sitting.

"People are looking at us," I say.

"People are looking at *you*," he counters, settling across from me. "I'm an afterthought."

"Not to me you're not."

Reid smiles and leans back. "Feel familiar?"

"This is the booth I sat in the night we met. The terrible memories of that date haven't escaped me that easily."

"You were sitting there. And I was—" He lifts his chin to the bar, the line of stools in the same positions as the last time I was here. "Sitting about ten feet away over there."

"You must have thought I was the world's stupidest woman."

"No." He shakes his head and pushes his glasses up his nose. "The opposite, actually. I kept trying to sneak glances at you to see what you looked like."

"When I walked up and asked if I could sit next to you, you were more interested in your phone than you were in me."

"So I wouldn't say something that made me sound like an idiot. The most beautiful woman in the world was six inches away from me, in my space, and I was trying to play it cool."

"You were my knight in shining armor," I tell him. "My hero."

"Well." Reid puffs out his chest. "I'm happy to have been of service."

We both order whiskeys and a plate of nachos to share, knocking our glasses together when the drinks come out. He gets the bartender to turn on the Orlando Blazers basketball game and moves to my side of the booth so he can wrap an arm around me while we watch the second quarter.

After a questionable plate of wings, our server brings over a slice of cheesecake and two forks. Reid cuts off a bite and holds it out to me.

"To not being allergic," he says, and I grin.

"And to good company," I say, leaning forward and eating the dessert. "This cheesecake is the best thing about this place."

"Really brings the average up to at least a C."

"What else did you have planned?" I ask. "You mentioned another place."

"Right." He dusts off his hands and grabs my coat. "Ready for the next stop?"

"But there's so much cheesecake left."

"We'll take it in a to-go box. You can eat it on the way."

"The best of both worlds," I say, and we slide out of the booth.

Back in the car, Reid puts on the new Ella Wright album, tapping his fingers on the steering wheel to the beat. We drive west on the highway, the city getting smaller and smaller behind us.

"Are we crossing state lines?" I ask, careful not to step on the sunflowers at my feet. "Do I need a passport?"

"It's just a quick jaunt up the road. We don't have to clear customs."

Fifteen minutes later, he's pulling into the parking lot at UPS Field.

"I'm confused," I say.

"It'll make sense in a minute."

He climbs out and hurries over to help me out. He swings our arms back and forth as we walk to the employee entrance, the door unlocked and open for him.

"Does the Titans staff frequently let nighttime guests in?" I ask.

"I got special permission. It helps that my best friend is married to the head coach's goddaughter."

We walk through the tunnel, and the stadium is eerily quiet. I've been in football stadiums thousands of times without fans, but never like this. Never at night without another soul around.

"Wow," I whisper when we get to the fifty-yard line. I pull my coat tighter around me and spin in a small circle, surveying the area around me. "I forget how big it is sometimes."

Reid takes off his tux jacket and spreads it over the grass. He sits down and pats the spot next to him. "Come here, Ave."

When I get close to him, I slip off my heels and drop them to the turf, getting comfortable beside him on the ground. I don't know what's going to happen next, but whatever it is, I know it's going to be perfect.

Because it's him.

"Thank you for tonight," I say, looking up at him. "It was the best first date I've ever had."

"No one puked, so I think we can consider it a win." He leans back on an elbow, his legs stretched out in front of him. I mimic his pose and scoot closer to him, a hand on his chest. "I had a motive for taking you there. For bringing you here."

"It wasn't to indulge in shitty food?" I ask. "I'm shocked."

Reid laughs, his breath warm on my cheek. "It was shitty, wasn't it?"

"The company made up for it. So why am I in enemy territory?"

"Because this..." He hesitates and takes my hand in his. He traces over my knuckles and down to my wrist, his touch resting on the pulse point he finds there. "This is where I started to fall for you, and I haven't been able to stop."

"What?" I whisper.

I know my feelings for him aren't one-sided; he told me as much the other night when he was taking care of me.

But *falling for you* sounds a lot like *falling in love with you*, and that might be my favorite thing he's ever said.

"You made work fun. You had me checking my phone every fifteen minutes, obsessing over what you might say and how I would answer. I made spreadsheets where I tried to figure out your schedule. My friends gave me so much shit. They said I had a crush. They said you were the only one who could hold my attention. I denied having any sort of feelings for you. You were the bane of my existence. My biggest pet peeve. My eye twitched when they mentioned you, but then it all made sense. Hating you felt a lot like—"

The rest of the sentence hangs between us, heavy and unsaid.

Loving you.

"And what do you think about me now?" I ask.

"I couldn't hate you if I tried." He rubs my arm and his smile is full of hope. "I took you to that shitty sports bar, Avery, because I... I don't want you to go on dates with anyone else. I don't want you to give your attention to anyone else. I've never, ever taken anything for myself, but with you, I want to. I'm greedy. I want more, and I'm going to keep being greedy for as long as you'll let me."

"You don't have to be greedy," I say, and he hangs on to my every word. "I'm giving you all that I have. Willingly. I want you to have it. I want you to have all of it."

The three blistering words remain unsaid, but I'm close to blurting them out. I'm close to *screaming* them.

But maybe tonight isn't about that. Maybe tonight is about sharing everything else. The smaller things that make up the big declaration. Like the way he kisses my forehead. How he pulls me into his lap, rocking me in his arms while whispering in my ear how beautiful I am and how lucky he is to be here with me.

When he takes me home and stands in the entrance of my apartment, his hand slipping under my dress and a tremble to his touch. I drag him to my bedroom and straddle him, desperate to feel him.

I fumble with his zipper and he struggles with my dress. When I sink onto him, nothing between us but the night sky outside the windows and the stars, I know this is different.

This isn't fucking.

This isn't strangers who don't know a thing about each other.

It's two people who know each other like the back of their hands.

Tender and quiet, a shift from normal.

Patient and slow, neither wanting to rush to be the first to finish.

It's indulgent and soul-crushing.

It's love, and when he cradles my cheek against his palm, the softest look of adoration in his eyes, I know I'll never be the same.

FORTY-THREE
REID

I WAKE up the morning of our playoff game against the Thunderhawks and the end of our bet with Avery wrapped around me.

Her hair is in my mouth. Her hands are on my waist. Her face is buried in my chest and I've never loved her more.

My eyes fly open.

Love.

Fuck, I love her.

This isn't a crush that's going to go away in a few weeks. This isn't something I can expect to fade away when the football season ends.

It's an all-in thing. It's big and important, and I can't ignore it anymore.

She stares in my arms and opens her eyes. She blinks and lifts her chin to look up at me, a smile curving on her mouth.

"Hi," she says around a yawn. "What time is it?"

"Late," I tell her. "You looked too comfortable to wake up."

"Why are you staring at me?" She sits up and stretches her arms above her head. The T-shirt she's wearing slips down her shoulder, and I see the bite marks I left on her neck last night. "You're looking at me like I have two heads."

"Sorry." I reach for my glasses and slide them up my nose. "You're really pretty in the morning."

Her smile melts into one that's beautiful and soft, and she kisses my cheek with a gentle press of her lips. "Are you being nice to me so it'll lessen the blow if the Thunderhawks lose today?"

"If I was going to do that, I would've called you gorgeous," I say, and she pokes her finger into my ribs. I laugh and bat her hands away, grabbing her wrists. "We've got the game and the bet to cover this afternoon. It's a big day."

"Promise you'll still like me after all of it?" Avery asks, her lips falling into a cute little pout. "Even if you lose?"

"At the end of the day, I still have you. That's not losing."

"Cheese award," she says, and I flip her off. "Did your sales manager send you the three-month report of ticket sales with all the numbers?"

"Yup. I haven't looked at it. Figured we could get Emmy to do the honors after the game. She doesn't have any stake in this feud of ours. What about the Social Media Account of the Year?"

"They're supposed to announce it tonight after the game ends. Do they usually call you beforehand?"

"It's cute you think this is a formal thing," I say. "They share the winner in a post on Instagram and that's that. I do know both of us are finalists, along with the Penguins out in Phoenix. But between you and me, they don't stand a chance."

"Right." Avery nods. "Got it."

I reach up and softly grip her chin, tilting her face to meet mine. "You know I don't care about any of this, right? I don't give a shit if I win or lose a stupid bet we made in the heat of the moment, Ave. I did in the beginning, but not anymore. It doesn't have any merit to how well we do our jobs, because I know for a fact you're a fucking superstar in your role."

"The flattery sure is nice this morning." She laughs and stands, the hem of her shirt riding up the backs of her thighs when she leans over to fix her socks. "I know it's not a big deal, and I really don't care which of us wins, but I'd love to prove that asshole Andrew wrong. My stats speak for themselves, but the accolade would be the icing on the cake. I love pissing men off."

"Thatta girl," I say, and she grins. "Can't wait to watch you in action today, Sinclair. You on the sidelines in those leggings of yours is my favorite sight. I can't even watch the game."

"Sorry to disappoint, but I think I'm going to be in jeans today. It's fucking freezing outside, and I hate being cold."

"Want to meet in my office at halftime? I could warm you up."

"Feeling nostalgic, Duncan?" is tossed over her shoulder as she saunters to the bathroom with a swish of her hips. "I can find some cellophane, if you want."

"Please, god, no. It took me three days to unravel the mess you made."

"Was it worth it?" Avery asks, leaning against the door.

I grin, never more sure of anything in my life. "Worth every fucking second."

<hr>

The game is a blowout, and I feel bad for Avery.

When the final whistle sounds and the Titans fans cheer, I look for her in the crowd, hoping she's doing okay.

I know she said it's not a big deal, but she pours her heart into everything she does. The season ending with an annihilation has to sting.

I congratulate the Titans players, clasping their shoulders

and laughing when the Gatorade cooler gets dumped on Shawn. We're one win away from heading to the Super Bowl, and with how the boys are playing lately, another ring seems inevitable.

"Nice job, man," I yell at Dallas. "Proud of you."

"You're coming out with us to celebrate tonight, right?" he yells back before messing up my hair. "Bring Avery."

"Not sure she's going to want to hang out with the guys who beat her team." I crane my neck, spotting her across the field. She's deep in conversation with one of the Thunderhawks players, and an idea comes to mind. "Text me the details. I'll see if she's down."

I move out of the way of the celebrations and kick off the confetti stuck to my shoe. I open Instagram and type out a post, adding an image of the team with their arms raised and jumping in the air. I hesitate for half a second then include a song on the post, uploading it before I can think twice.

I jog to the Thunderhawks' sideline and watch Avery pull out her phone. Her eyebrows wrinkle and her mouth pops open, her head on a swivel as she looks around. When she spots me, she storms my way, and I bite back a grin.

"What the hell is this?" She holds up her phone, turning the volume up so I can hear the Thunderhawks song blaring from the post I shared. "'Hell of a run, Thunderhawks. Looking forward to continuing the rivalry next year'?" She gapes at me. "You all destroyed us. Blew us out of the water. We're going to be a mockery on every sports show tomorrow morning."

"We did and you might be. But that's the thing about love, isn't it? You don't give up when the going gets tough."

"What does that mean?" Avery asks. "You're talking about football, right?"

"Maybe." I reach for her, and she takes my hand. "I might be talking about you too."

She blinks and steps closer to me. "I'm going to need some

clarification," she whispers. "Because I don't like to be confused."

"I spent three years talking to someone I pretended not to give a damn about, but the thing is, I love you," I say. "I love you a whole fucking lot, Avery, and it's the one part of our bet I didn't see coming. I planned for everything else except falling head over heels for you. And I still fell. Hard. I fucking smashed into the ground."

I thought this would be hard to say. Difficult to find the words, but when I look at her, it's the easiest thing I've ever fucking done.

I feel light. A little bit like I could fucking fly. Impulsive and reckless and happy—a kind of happiness I've never felt before. I thought I've been in love, but it was nothing like this. Like I'm on top of the goddamn world and nothing could bring me down.

"I love you too," she whispers, and my heart stops. It flatlines before jolting back to life when she takes my face in her palms. "I love you so very much, Reid, because you've made me believe in it again. I feel it when I'm with you. In every cracked corner of my heart that's putting itself back together again. Every morning when I open my eyes, and you're there. Sometimes it scares me how much I love you."

"You don't have to be scared with me." I wrap my arms around her and pull on the ends of her hair. "You know why?"

"Why?" Avery asks, a watery question that has her wiping her eyes and nose with the back of her hand.

"I've spent years learning everything about you. The things that make you happy. The things that make you mad." I pause, then add, "I have a spreadsheet on my computer for that one, actually."

"You're not serious."

"Dead fucking serious. It might be titled 'Thunderhawks girl', but it gets the job done. I know you. And you know me. Did we go about it in an unconventional way? Without a doubt. It doesn't change the fact that you are the most perfect person for me, Avery, and I'd be lucky if you tormented me for the rest of my life."

"The rest of your life?" Her palms move to my back, rubbing over my shirt and across my shoulders. The noise from the crowd quiets. The lights dim. In a sea of thousands, all I see is her. "I think I'd like that."

"Hey," Maverick says, interrupting us. I look to my right, and all our friends are there. Emmy. Maven and June. Dallas and his sweaty jersey. He waves an envelope in the air and grins. "Here's the ticket sales information."

"And I know who won Social Media Account of the Year," Maven adds.

"Do you want to know?" I ask Avery.

I don't care, to be honest.

Everything is moot now, but I want her to make the call.

"Yeah," she admits. "Just for bragging rights."

"Fair." I glance at Emmy. "What do you have for us?"

"I'm going to let Miller take this one," she says. "He's been giddy about it all day. He's treating it like it's the nuclear codes or something."

"I had no idea the NFL doesn't disclose ticket information. I like that this is a big fucking secret." Maverick rips open the envelope and huffs out a laugh. "Huh. Interesting."

"What?" Avery asks. "What is it?"

"I'm not sure how you all are going to determine a winner. The Titans had the higher season ticket renewal rate at 95%. But the Thunderhawks had the most *new* ticket sales. If we're looking at overall totals, though, the Titans are going to have forty-two thousand season ticket holders while the Thunderhawks only have twenty-six thousand," Maverick says.

"How many did you start the season with?" I ask Avery.

"Only thirteen thousand," she says.

"You *doubled* in sales? Fuck, Ave, that's incredible."

"That's not me. That's because the team is doing well. We're finally winning and signing big name players. A post on Instagram is *not* bringing in that kind of revenue," she explains.

"That's not true. You came up with promotions. Incentives to get people through the doors. Did your post eight Wednesdays ago encourage someone to buy tickets? Maybe not. But the payment plan idea you came up with did."

"Do you two want to hear who won the other part of your bet?" Maven asks.

"I don't know how I became so invested in this, but I have to know," Dallas says.

"Tell us," Avery says, and Maven grins.

"'The NFL is pleased to announce this year's Social Media Account and Marketing Department of the Year is the Baltimore Thunderhawks. With over a hundred million social media impressions and two hundred thousand new followers over six months, the Thunderhawks have cemented themselves as a fan favorite,'" Maven reads, and I scoop Avery into my arms.

"Congratulations," I say, my voice muffled by her hair. "You deserve it."

"I have to thank you." She laughs into my shoulder, and I fucking love that sound. I'd do anything to hear it again. "The Thunderhawks' account would be what it is without you. You made me want to work harder. Your DMs were the highlight of my day, and I love that you give me shit."

"Worth it," I tell her. "Worth it to see you happy. Worth it to see you get the recognition you deserve. Worth it to have been on this journey with you from the very beginning."

"Do you think I should send Andrew a care package with a note that says 'fuck you very much'?"

"I'll drive it to New York myself." I set her on the ground. "You really do deserve this, Ave."

"What happens to your bet?" Emmy asks. "You each won a part of it."

I look at Avery. There's a smirk on her mouth, and I bend down to kiss her. "Call it even?" I suggest.

"No way." She tugs on my shirt, lips on mine again. "We're just getting started."

"WHAT'S the plan for the Super Bowl?" Maven asks, cuddling up to Dallas on the couch in their apartment. She rests her head on his chest and smiles. "I know you all are taking the team plane to Pasadena, but what about the rest of us?"

"Never fear, Mae. Puck Daddy Mav is here," Maverick chimes in, and I roll my eyes.

"No one calls you that," I say. "No one has *ever* called you that."

"That's not true." He flips me off and drapes his arm around Emmy's shoulders. "There's a whole thread on the internet dedicated to my nicknames."

"Are you sure you didn't make the thread yourself?" Emmy asks. "Seems like something you would do."

"Fuck me, I guess." He pouts and scoots away from her. "I *was* going to mention the private jet I chartered to get us out west, but you assholes can get there on your own."

"Wait! What if I'm an innocent bystander? Can I still come on the jet?" Avery asks.

"Yes. Only Avery is allowed," he tells all of us. "And June Bug too. The rest of you can drive or take the train. Maybe the bus."

"Careful," I murmur in Avery's ear. "Being stuck in a metal tube with him for six hours might be a new level of hell."

"I can hear you, dickbag." Maverick throws a pillow at me, and I block it from hitting Avery in the face. "I hope you have to fly economy."

"Almost hurt my girlfriend again, and we're going to have a problem," I warn him.

"Oh." Avery tugs on my shirt. "That was hot. I didn't know I was into nerds who were protective of their women."

"Guess that means I need to do it more often."

My phone buzzes with a notification at the same time as Avery's. I look at her and roll my eyes. "You didn't tag me in something when I'm sitting right next to you, did you?"

"I thought we were past that, Duncan," she says, tapping her screen. "Holy fucking shit."

"What?" I glance over her shoulder. "What's wrong? What happened?"

"You know how Griffin Harrison announced next season will be his last year and inked a huge broadcasting gig that's worth more than he ever made playing?" Avery asks.

"Yeah. Ten years, three hundred million dollars. It's fucking insanity."

"That might be in jeopardy now." She turns her phone so I can read the alert she's showing me. "His OnlyFans account got hacked. Turns out he's been sending money to some girl for months now. She's the only one he follows on there, and one of the tips he left was four thousand dollars. Oh, shit. Some of their messages got leaked too."

"*What*?" Dallas jumps up and grabs the phone from Avery. "No fucking way. Griffin barely talks to anyone. I've seen him smile three times, and I've played next to him for months."

"Wait, why is this a big deal?" Maven asks. "Whoever this girl is, she's legal, right? Who gives a shit who the guy is sending his money to. I wish I had that kind of cash to dole out to hot women."

"The deal he signed is with a company that's very, uh, conservative, even though he's not. They're 'family oriented'. Whatever that's supposed to mean," Avery explains. "Finding out the guy they hired to talk about football for the next decade has an OnlyFans account is probably going to raise some questions."

"This is going to be a media shitstorm." I groan and drop my head back. "You're going to use this as content, aren't you? You're going to poke fun at it."

"I already have half a dozen ideas," Avery says, and she sounds fucking giddy. "There's no coincidence in this coming out right before the Super Bowl. Someone wanted to distract him."

"Wouldn't put it past the Pistons fans. They're ruthless. Anything they can do to take down an opposing player, they will," Maven says, and Dallas's phone rings.

"It's Shawn. I better take this." He slips into the kitchen, and Maven follows behind him.

"Do you want to head out?" Avery asks, and I frown.

"Why would I want to head out?"

"You've had a busy week at work, and now this news coming out? You know the comment sections are going to go crazy."

"I'm not on the clock right now," I say.

"You're a salaried employee. Aren't you always on the clock?"

"That's not what I mean." I pull her into my lap, ignoring Maverick's whistling. "I'm here with you and my friends right now. Is this a crisis? In a sense, yeah, but it's not *my* crisis. So a bunch of people flood the comments of our posts? Big deal. I'm not missing important moments in my life just so I can talk to some clowns on social media about a player's dick."

"Important moments?" Avery turns her chin to look at me. "We're just playing board games."

"Any moment with you is an important moment, Ave. I'm not risking this—" I gesture between us. "For this," I say, picking up my phone. "I've been there before, and it sucks. Nobody wins. Whatever is going to happen tonight can wait until tomorrow."

"I think I just fell in love with you all over again." She smiles and rests her forehead against mine. "You're a smooth talker, Reid Duncan."

"Whatever keeps you interested."

"What if I told you I'm wearing a new pair of lingerie and bought you a comic book today?" she asks. "Would that be classified as an important enough reason for us to head home?"

"We have to go," I announce, standing and setting Avery on her feet. She laughs next to me and pulls my hoodie over her head. "I have shit to deal with. Fires to put out."

"Girlfriends to fuck," she whispers in my ear, and I haul her by the waist to the door. "I'll see you later this week?" she adds to Emmy.

"I'll text you when Moneybags over here sets up all the travel stuff," Emmy says. "Maybe we can go shopping for some new bathing suits before we head out west."

"We're leaving too," Maverick yells, and Emmy rolls her eyes when he tosses her over his shoulder.

"Really, pretty boy? Do you want to make why we're leaving any more obvious?"

"Oh, like you didn't hear Avery tell Reid what she bought today," Maverick says, and Avery buries her face in my shoulder. "Enjoy your work, Plant Daddy. Don't let it keep you up all night."

I flip him off, and when we get to the elevator, I close the doors in his face. Avery laughs when we're alone, finally showing her red cheeks.

"That was so embarrassing," she says. "I can never see them again."

"Fuck it. We'll find new friends. I didn't like them anyway. Tell me more about what you're wearing underneath that sweater. Are we going to your place or mine?"

"Your place. It's red. And that's a shame, because I really liked your friends."

"Fine. We'll be friends with them again. Only because you said so."

She laughs again. "Reid?"

"Yeah, baby?"

"Is that what your nights looked like before we met? When we only talked through our phones?"

"Yeah." I rub my jaw, smiling at the memory of the late nights when I was in the guest bedroom, wide awake because I couldn't stop scrolling through the Thunderhawks' Instagram feed. Typing then deleting messages to her, too chicken to actually send them. "There was more cursing back then, though."

"I like being in your spaces," Avery says. "I like seeing the parts of your life I only had glimpses of. I like putting names to faces, and I like to imagine you were thinking about me in all the moments I was thinking about you."

"I was. Spitefully, of course, but I was. And I have no plans of stopping anytime soon."

"Good. You're going to include me too, right?"

"Baby. You're going to be fucking sick of me soon."

"Doubtful. I've always been a little obsessed with you, Duncan. It's about time you caught up."

"THANK you for letting me be here," I yell in Reid's ear as the players take the field. "I've never been to the Super Bowl before."

"Just wish I could've gotten you to wear a Titans hat," he yells back, knocking the brim of my Thunderhawks cap. "I'm still half afraid you're going to sabotage me."

I laugh and elbow his ribs. "No way. I'm so excited for you all. You might have lost one part of our bet, but *this* I hope you win. I hate the Pistons."

"There's my caring girlfriend," Reid says, dropping a kiss to my cheek. "Be honest: you're just excited to hear your damn song on our page again if we win. I really should've added stipulations to your victory earnings."

"I'm a little excited," I admit. "It's going to drive in so many new fans for us. I should be thanking you, really, for thinking you're better at your job than I am."

"You know I think you're fantastic. The best in the league." He tugs on the jersey I'm wearing, the oversized one with Dallas's last name on the back. Maven bedazzled it with jewels and rhinestones, and it felt wrong not to show up in at least *some* Titans gear. "I've never wanted to be an athlete before, but seeing you have some other guy's last name on your back makes me want to hit the gym and try out for a team."

"Is that jealousy, Duncan?" I ask, wrapping my arms around his neck. There are only a few minutes left to indulge in physical affection with him before he needs to buckle down and do his job, and I can't help but touch him. To let everyone in the stadium—all one hundred thousand people—know he's mine. "I like when you're possessive."

"Can't be jealous when I know you're going home with me." His hands settle on my waist, fisting the polyester between his fingers. "Thank you for coming out here. Thank you for supporting me and my friends. I know we're both competitive people, but it wouldn't be right if you weren't here to celebrate."

"We should be thanking Maverick. He's the one who chartered a private jet and flew us out here." I pause and tip my chin up, our eyes meeting. "You know there's nowhere else I'd rather be. I love seeing you in action, Reid, and I'm always going to support you."

"Speaking of which." He taps my hip and his hands fall away. "There's someone I want you to meet."

"What do you have up your sleeve?"

"Come here."

He leads me to the tunnel and the crowd of people congregated there. I see folks dressed in suits and slacks, their attire out of place in a stadium of football gear. We reach two women deep in conversation, and when Reid clears his throat, subtly trying to get their attention, they both light up at the sight of him.

"Reid," the first one exclaims. She bends down to hug him, her heels helping her tower over his six-foot-one frame, and he's careful to only touch the top of her shoulder with a friendly pat. "There you are."

"Sorry we're a few minutes behind schedule," he says, pulling away and smiling at me. "I was showing Avery around.

It's her first time at the Super Bowl, and I want her to get the whole experience."

"No apologies needed," the second woman says, fixing the collar of her blazer. "It's our first time here too. Knocks the NBA championship right out of the water."

"Sweetheart, this is Barbara Jones, the NBA commissioner, and Susie Cartwright, president of the Washington Ducks," Reid explains, and I beam.

"It's so nice to meet you all," I say, shaking their hands. "And congratulations on the championship, Susie."

"The first of many," she says, exchanging a look with the commissioner. "I'll admit we're here under somewhat false pretenses. I met Reid at a luncheon two years ago and spent forty-five minutes trying to poach him from the NFL over to the NBA. I wasn't successful, obviously, but the whole time we talked, he kept mentioning this woman who ran the Baltimore Thunderhawks' social media accounts."

I turn and look at him. "Two years ago?"

"I know," he says sheepishly. "When I ran into Susie a couple months ago, right at the beginning of our bet, she asked how you were doing. I admit I might have planted the seed of you switching leagues out of spite. But with everything that happened this season, with the goals you've told me about and the ways the NFL has made you feel like you belong in a box, I thought maybe there's something better out there for you. Something that doesn't shove your talent away, but welcomes it."

I swallow and glance at the three of them. "What are you saying?"

"We'd love if you came in and interviewed," Barbara says. "Either for the Chief Marketing Officer of the NBA, or, if you're not ready to leave the area, as head of marketing and social media for the Washington Ducks. We won't put you on the spot and set up a formal interview today; you have a lot to celebrate tonight. It shouldn't be about work. But if there's any interest on your end, give us your information. We can set something up later this summer after the season winds down."

"Oh, my god," I whisper. I take Reid's hand in mine and squeeze. I can tell he's beaming at me out of the corner of my eye, and I have the inexplicable urge to hug him. To throw myself in his arms and tell him *thank you, thank you, thank you.* "That would be—*yes.* I'd be honored."

"We love the work you're doing," Susie says. "Your inclusion of fans in your content and the spotlight series you do on players is extraordinary. You don't paint them as athletes; you show them as real people, and it's beautiful to see those walls come down."

"Thank you so much." I wipe under my eyes, hoping I haven't smudged my mascara before the game starts, and let out a watery laugh. I fumble with my purse and pull out my business card, handing it over. "That has my personal number on it too. I'll be back in the office on Wednesday, and I'd love to talk to you both some more."

"Perfect." The commissioner smiles and slips the card in her pocket. "It was great to meet you, Avery. We'll be in touch soon."

After a round of goodbyes, I stare at Reid, my mouth open and my jaw nearly on the floor.

"Holy *shit*," I squeal. I fling myself at him and he laughs, spinning me around. "Reid. I can't believe you did that for me."

"I was worried it was overstepping." He sets me back on the ground and smooths his hands down my arms. "I'd never want you to feel like I was trying to swoop in and be a hero. But after that conversation with Andrew earlier this season, I've been so *angry* thinking about how your potential is never going to be seen by a bunch of men who are intimidated by a woman's success. When you told me how much you love basketball— how much your dad loved basketball and that it was something you two did together—it got me thinking. Your talent deserves to be shown off somewhere bigger. Maybe the NBA could be that place."

"You *are* a hero." I stand on my toes and cup both his cheeks in my hands. "*My* hero. Thank you for thinking of me. Thank you for supporting me. Thank you for having my back."

"The NBA headquarters are in New York. If that's where you think you'd like to end up, I want you to know we'll figure it out. We'll figure us out. I'm in this for the long haul, baby, and if that means alternating cities every other week, so be it."

"I love you," I whisper, and his eyes light up. His smile melts into something beautiful, something precious. *Mine.* "I love you so much. I'm so glad I sent you that first message. I'm so glad I get to be here with you."

"What are you talking about?" Reid asks. "I sent you a message first."

"No, you didn't."

He barks out a laugh. "Are you shitting me, Sinclair? You commented first. I sent the first direct message."

"We're not arguing about this right now."

"Because you know you're wrong."

"No." I poke his ribs and he captures my wrist, kissing the tips of my fingers. "Because you have a job to do, and I have a game to watch."

"It's cute you think I'm going to be able to manage any productivity on the sidelines while I'm scrolling all the way back to our first interaction," he says.

"I have a screenshot," I blurt out, and Reid lifts an eyebrow. "I took a screenshot of the first time we interacted. I was afraid I was being too mean to you, but then you matched my energy and..." I bite back a smile. "Shit. We were inevitable all along, weren't we?"

"Yeah." He kisses me, and the fans watching us whistle and cat call. "I think we were."

"I don't know why I keep coming to these games." Maven peeks at the field through her fingers. "They take years off my life."

"Because your husband is the greatest kicker of all time and is about to win another Super Bowl on a field goal," Emmy says, jumping up and down. "What are the fucking odds?"

"Let's go," Maverick yells, holding up a bottle of champagne. "World fucking champions, baby!"

"Miller," Maven hisses, and she smacks his arm. "He hasn't kicked yet. Don't fucking jinx it."

"Swear jar," June says. "Swear jar, swear jar, swear jar."

I laugh and lean my elbows on the railing of the suite, watching the teams break from their huddles to take the field. I spot Reid on the sideline, pacing back and forth, his phones in his hand and his hat backwards on his head.

He must have spun it around during the timeout.

I grin, pulling out my own phone and sending him a message.

ME

> Could you wear your hat like that more often?
> It's hot as hell.

He reads the message and turns his attention up to the box we're sitting in. I wave, and he shakes his head, dipping his chin. His fingers fly across the screen, and soon my phone is buzzing in my hand.

REID

You're distracting me.

ME

Attachment: 1 image

Took that when you were in the shower this morning.

REID

You expect me to pay attention to what happens in the game after you send me a photo that looks like THAT?

Is that my Batman shirt you're wearing? With nothing under it?

I watch him drop his phone on the field before scooping it up and holding it close to his chest.

ME

Do your job, Duncan.

REID

Kind of hard when the woman of my dreams is sending me half naked photos of herself with a comic book in her hands.

If we win, can you wear that the rest of the night? Just that?

ME

You've been a good boy. I think we can make that happen.

Reid drops his head back, and I swear I can hear him groan from here. One of his assistants touches his shoulder, asking him something, and I burst out laughing when he shields his phone from view.

"Everything okay?" Maven asks, still covering her eyes.

"It's great, Mae. Stop hiding and watch the damn play. Your man is about to make history," I say.

She slowly lowers her hand. Her nails dig into my arm, and we watch as the Titans take the field. Reid is already halfway to the goalposts, phone poised and ready to capture the victory.

The players line up. The play clock reaches four. The ball is hiked, and Dallas kicks it through the uprights with yards to spare just as time expires.

The stadium erupts in chaos, and the cheers are so loud, my ears ring. Everyone is screaming and hugging each other, and I'm pretty sure Maven is crying. Security escorts us down to the field, and when we reach the grass, Reid is already hugging me.

"Hi," I say, the wind knocked out of me from how tight he's holding me. "Hi, sweetheart. Congratulations. I'm so happy for you."

"Hey, baby." A piece of confetti sticks to his forehead, and I peel it away. "Another Super Bowl win."

"I thought you didn't care about sports."

"I do when I get to celebrate with you," he says.

"You should be with the team. Filming the stuff you need for the next six months of content so you can tease me mercilessly."

"I know I should. But I'm learning to get better about a work-life balance, and right now, I want to be with you. The content can wait."

"You have your interns taking videos for you, don't you?" I ask.

"Yeah, but that wouldn't change a damn thing."

He presses his mouth to mine, and I kiss him. I kiss him like the world is going to end tomorrow and he cups the back of my neck, keeping me in place and kissing me back like I'm his salvation.

More confetti falls on our heads, a sea of colored paper that tangles in my hair, and I can't bring myself to care about anything besides his chest against mine and my heart in his hands.

"I love you," I whisper so only he can hear me. "I think I'm going to love you forever."

Reid grins, a smile matching mine. The adoration in his eyes makes me weak in the knees. "Wanna bet?"

I grip the collar of his shirt and knock his hat off his head. "You're on."

FORTY-SIX

EPILOGUE

Avery
Sixteen months later

I STRETCH my arms above my head and smile at the sun seeping in through the curtains of my bedroom. It's quiet and still, and I can tell I'm home alone.

I roll over and see a note stuck to the pillow on Reid's side of the bed. I grab it and smile at his handwriting.

> MORNING, SUNSHINE.
> I'M HEADING TO THE OFFICE EARLY TO DO SOME WORK.
> CAN'T WAIT TO SEE YOU LATER.
> CALL ME WHEN YOU WAKE UP.
> LOVE YOU.
> -R

I clutch it to my chest and sigh, still feeling like I'm living in some dream world even after a year and a half of dating.

It almost seems like a lifetime has passed with all the adventures we've had. With the trips we've taken and the work we've done.

A whole NFL season has passed, and even though my Thunderhawks gave the Titans run for their money in the playoffs again last year, Reid has another Super Bowl ring to add to the collection.

Sometimes he wears it to piss me off.

I throw back the covers and pop out of bed, a spring to my step as I walk to the kitchen and smell fresh coffee. I open the cabinet above the sink to pull out a mug and a rubber duck tumbles onto my head.

"What the hell?"

I pick it up off the counter and examine it, laughing when I realize it's the same kind Reid hid in my office last year.

This time, there isn't a number on the bottom, just a single question mark.

I take a picture and send him a text message.

ME

Didn't think I would be assaulted by rubber ducks first thing in the morning, but here we are.

What does the question mark mean? Am I missing something?

My phone rings, and I smile at the image of Reid that pops up on my screen. It's a photo I snapped of him two months ago during our trip to London. His eyes are half closed. His glasses are crooked on his face, but his grin is bright enough to light up an entire room.

"Hi," I answer.

"Hey." I hear the jangle of his keys as he enters his office. "Are you up?"

"Yeah." I yawn and pour myself a cup of coffee. "When did you leave?"

"An hour ago. I needed Dallas to help me with something, so I got to the field early. These one p.m. start times are fucking brutal," he says. "There's too much to do before kickoff."

"What are you filming? And can I steal the idea?"

"No, you cannot. I know you have something original up your sleeve, Sinclair. You're not the back-to-back Social Media Account of the Year because of my ideas."

"True. Man, I forgot how good it feels to win against you," I say.

Reid laughs, and I hear the roll of his chair. His computer powering on and the eyeglasses he's setting down on his desk, right next to the framed photo of us.

I know all of his idiosyncrasies by heart. The routines he likes and the order he has to do things in. Our lives have blended together so seamlessly, it feels like I'm right next to him, watching him run a hand through his hair and toss a Rubik's cube in the air.

A wave of love hits me.

It's there during all the big moments, a large swell that rises when he kisses me. When he fucks me nice and slow under the stars, a hand on my heart and the other in my hair. When we're with our friends and our eyes meet, a smile pulling at his lips the second he sees me.

It's more powerful in the mundane moments, though. That swell turns into a tsunami. A tidal wave of affection and adoration for the man who loves me wholly. Completely. With flaws and faults and beyond.

I feel it when he makes me coffee in the morning and sets out a fresh mug. When he does the crossword puzzle in bed, the cap of his pen in his mouth and his eyebrows wrinkled. Right now, as I listen to him mumble about algorithms and SEOs and a folder he can't find.

My chest is tight.

My feet are off the ground.

I never think it's possible to have any space left to love him more, but then another day happens, and I do.

"Enough with the showboating, sweetheart. Boasting doesn't look good on you."

"What's with the rubber duck?" I ask, leaning against the counter and sipping my drink. "I thought we left all the pranks in our past."

He laughs again, a deep rumble I feel behind my ribs. It expands and fills all the crevices I've long thought empty until I'm laughing too and missing the hell out of him. "It's a scavenger hunt."

"A scavenger hunt? For what?"

"I figured we needed a new tradition. Every time our teams play each other, there's going to be a scavenger hunt involved."

"This is my last season with the Thunderhawks," I say. "Next season I'll be an NBA girl with the reigning champions and the biggest market in the league. What are we going to do then?"

"We'll figure something out. We always do. When are you getting to the stadium?" he asks.

"I'll be there in an hour or so. I want to get some footage of the guys warming up and post it right before kickoff. You know fans love to see them having a good time before they need to get serious."

"Call me when you get here. I want to see you before I head to the locker room."

"Kind of sounds like you're obsessed with me, Duncan."

"Have been for a while now, Sinclair. Keep up." He pauses and clears his throat. "I love you, Ave."

My mouth splits into a wide grin. "I love you, too."

"Drive safe. I'll see you soon, pretty girl."

We hang up, and I down the rest of my coffee. I throw on my polo and leggings, pairing them with high top sneakers and a white ribbon in my hair. I shove my laptop and second phone in my bag, adding a water bottle to the mix and a hat too.

Ninety minutes later, I'm parking at UPS Field and jumping out of the car I bought last year. I wave hello to Bart, one of the security guards, and he tips an imaginary hat my way.

"Morning, Miss Avery," he says. "What's the prediction today?"

"Thunderhawks by fourteen." I sling my bag over my shoulder and grin. "And you can tell my other half I said that."

He laughs and swipes his keycard, giving me access to the tunnel. "If I see him, I'll make sure to pass it along."

With another wave, I head down the hall to the visitors' media room. I stop to say hello to a couple of other Thunderhawks team members then set up my computer at one of the long tables next to our sideline reporter.

Just as I'm about to sit down, I notice another rubber duck in my chair. I laugh and pick it up, the word *you* written on the bottom. I take another picture and send it to Reid, adding a half dozen question marks to the message.

"Good morning," Maven sings. She stands in the entryway of the room and throws a rubber duck my way. "I was told to give you this."

"What the hell is going on?" I glance at the underside of the third one, frowning when I see the word *me*.

"I don't know. Reid said I had to give it to you or face the consequences. I do not need him hacking into my laptop. There are way too many incriminating photos on there."

"Where is he?"

"He and Dallas disappeared a while ago, and they wouldn't

tell me where they were going. I love that the boys still have secrets."

"You want to head to the field for a bit?"

"Sure." She smiles and hugs me when I get close to her. "I feel like I haven't seen you in forever."

"Because the NFL and NHL schedules are a pain in my ass." I squeeze her tight. "Are you free for dinner this week? Emmy and June too."

"I'd love that." Maven tugs on my elbow and leads me down the hall. "How is your last season in the NFL going?"

I smile at her question. "Good. I love working for the Thunderhawks, but it's time for a change."

Switching leagues is the best thing for my relationship with Reid, too. We're putting space between our personal and professional lives. He got promoted to head of marketing with the Titans, and when I transition to the NBA, I'm not the one responsible for filming social media content. It also gives us more free time, which is exactly what we need.

"I'm so proud of you. And I'm so happy my friends are together," she gushes, and I laugh.

"Feels like yesterday I was wishing an anvil would fall on his head. Now look at me: I love that man too much."

"And he loves you back. I've never seen a man so down bad. I swear he's like a little puppy dog with you."

"I haven't dated someone who's been—what the hell?" I stop short of the field. There's another duck sitting on the fifty-yard line, and I charge toward it, the word *will* scribbled on the bottom.

I call Reid, tapping my foot while the phone rings.

"Hey, Ave," he says, out of breath. "What's up, baby?"

"What is going on with these ducks? Seriously. I'm afraid to know where else you're hiding them."

"Which one did you find?"

"Will. I have you, me, will and a question mark. Oh, for fuck's sake. You want to have a threesome, don't you? You could've just asked."

"You know I don't like to share."

"Who is Will?" I ask. "Do I know a Will? Are you signing a Will? Are *we* signing a Will?"

"Don't know. Guess you'll find out."

The line goes dead, and I curse him out under my breath.

"He's so obnoxious," I say to Maven, but when I turn around, I'm totally alone. "Mae?"

I blink, then the scoreboard lights up. Reid's face takes over the screen, and I stare at him, flabbergasted.

"Hey," he says, talking to the camera and starting a livestream on the Titans account. "My name is Reid Duncan, and for the last twelve years, I've been the social media admin for the DC Titans. You might know me from the videos I post. The memes I create and the captions I spend hours coming up with so you all laugh. I've never shown my face before, but today felt like the day to change that."

He pauses, and I walk closer to the screen.

"Almost five years ago, I got a notification that the Baltimore Thunderhawks' official Instagram account followed the DC Titans' account. In the moment, I didn't think anything of it. I was out at dinner with some friends and ignored the alert. Which is funny, because that's the day my life changed." He smiles and holds up a phone. "That follow turned into a direct message. A short and curt message from someone running the Thunderhawks account telling me to 'delete this' when I posted a comment about the Titans being the only decent mid-Atlantic NFL team."

I burst out laughing. He had to scroll through years of barbs and jabs and comments to find that message, and I wonder how long it took him to find.

"Thus began our feud. I wanted nothing more in life than to destroy the woman behind the account," Reid says, and he laughs.

"But then a funny thing happened. I fell in love with her instead. Slowly. Accidentally. Deliberately, now that I think about it. With every message. With every like. With every comment. With every late-night conversation that felt a lot like fighting, I lost my mind for this woman. And she's the total package. I'm talking smart. I'm talking knowledgeable about football. I'm talking smoking hot. I'm talking someone who likes to wear heels and Air Jordans and makes them both look good."

I blush at his compliment and see the number of viewers watching steadily increasing. We're well past the thousands and pushing five digits. The comment section is flooded with people chiming in, and the attention makes me squirm.

"I know what you're all wondering: what the hell is this nerd doing talking about love on a football account? Because, as silly as it is, this account brought me the most important person in my life. It brought me my dream girl. The person I've waited a very long time for. I thought I had it before, but I realize *this* is what I was looking for."

I wipe my eyes.

I wish he was here.

I wish I could see him and hold him and tell him how much I love him too.

"And now—you know what? Fuck it. I'll be back."

Reid stands and disappears. I frown when Maverick takes over the frame, a wide smile on his face and a shiny silver ring on his left hand.

That's new.

"I'm Maverick," he says, waving to the camera. "And I love romance novels. My buddies do too, and this is what we call the grand fucking gesture. If you're—Dallas. What the hell are you doing?"

"I don't know. Reid told us we had to follow him, and we're already behind. Let's go, Miller."

"Shit." Maverick picks up the phone, and I'm graced with a shot of his sneakers. "Avery, if you're watching this, you're supposed to go to the end zone. The one to the right. No. The left. Wait. Which is it?"

"This is why your job was to hold the phone, not give instructions." Dallas's face appears, and he looks irritated as hell. "The home end zone, Avery," he says, and the screen goes blank.

"What the hell?" I jog across the turf, the grass still wet from the late-morning humidity. I cross the forty and the thirty. I get closer to the end zone, and that's when I see another duck sitting on the uprights, right in the middle of the goal posts.

I shake the goal posts and nothing happens. I try kicking it, using the heel of my high-top sneaker to ram into the metal, and the duck finally falls. When I turn it over, I see a single word, and I stop breathing. I thought it might be leading to this point, but now I'm sure.

Marry.

"There's no Will," Reid says from behind me, and I turn around to face him. He's on one knee, a velvet box in his hand and his eyes on me. "Only me. I hope that's okay."

"What—" I sniff and look down at him. "What are you doing?"

"Tying my shoe. What does it look like I'm doing, Sinclair?" he teases. "How much of that video did you hear?"

"All of it," I whisper. "Every word."

"Good. Then you'll know I'm serious when I say the day you messaged me for the first time was the best day of my life. But then I met you at a bar, and that was the best day of my life. And again at a wedding. And again six months ago and again yesterday. Somehow, I keep having these *best days of my life* with you, Ave, and I know it's because you're it for me. You're always going to be it for me, and I want to keep doing this life thing with you. I know you're starting a new job. I know you have your eyes set on the next project that's bigger than what you created in Baltimore, and I want you to know I'm going to follow you. Wherever it is, I'm going too. I love you with my whole heart, baby, and with every fiber of my being. Will you marry me?"

I'm in his arms before he can finish asking the question. He laughs and holds me to his chest, his heart beating as fast as mine.

"Is that a yes?" he asks into my hair.

"Of course it's a yes." I wipe my eyes and kiss his chin. "Did you really think I might say no?"

"You can be a wildcard sometimes. Thought you might have one last prank up your sleeve, and I want to be sure."

"I'm saving the last prank. It's going to be something really good, and you're going to have to sleep with one eye open from now on," I say.

"I'll do it gladly." He helps me to my feet and kisses me. "Fuck, I love you."

"You told the internet that," I say, admiring the diamond he slips on my finger. "The entire internet. You can never hide from it."

"I'm going to have to deactivate the account for a while. I'm sure I'm going to get roasted online."

"You're used to that." I pat his chest, and the ring sparkles in the sun. "I've been doing it to you for years."

"Wow." Reid lifts me off the ground and throws me over his shoulder. I laugh as he walks us to the locker room, and I see all our friends waiting in the tunnel. "You better watch your back, baby. The feud isn't over just because I proposed. I only have a few months left to give you shit, and I have to make the most of it."

"You know, Duncan, I don't think I'm ever going to get sick of you giving me shit," I say. I'm not sure I've ever smiled this hard. I'm not sure I've ever been this happy. "In fact, I think our best work is yet to come, and I can't wait to kick your ass again. And again. And again."

"That many agains? You'll have to stick around for a while then, Ave."

I look up at him over his shoulder, and he's already looking at me. Pink cheeks, a grin that matches mine. A tiny hickey under his ear from where I kissed him too aggressively last night. The sun framing his face and a halo around his bright red hair.

Mine.

"There's nowhere I'd rather be," I tell him, and I've never meant something more in my life.

COMING SOON

Looking for more of my books?

The final book in the Love Through a Lens series will release in 2025 and will feature fake dating, a professional athlete x cam girl, and grumpy x sunshine.

Until then, make sure you check out the DC Stars series!

ACKNOWLEDGMENTS

This whole idea started because I'm a big fan of the Orlando Magic. A couple years ago, their social media team repurposed a song from their inaugural season. It became a smash hit in the NBA, and they use it on every post they share after the team wins.

It's CATCHY, y'all. Seriously. Go listen to it. Even YouTubers mention how catchy the tune is, so, naturally, I thought it would make a good romance novel.

And here we are, 450 pages later.

Thank you so much for reading Reid and Avery's story! I sincerely hope you loved them like I do. If you did, I'd be grateful if you left a review on Amazon

Amazon or Goodreads. Positive reviews do wonders for indie authors like myself!

Thank you to my wonderful beta readers who helped make this book the story it is now. Your comments shaped this manuscript, and I couldn't have done it without you.

Thank you, Hannah and Britt, for your wonderful editing. You all are superstars at your job, and I'm so lucky to work with you.

Thank you, Sam, for another beautiful cover! This series is gorgeous, and it's because of your brilliant brain.

Thank you to M & R, my two favorite guys, for believing in my dreams. I love you!

Thank you to the book community. I'm coming up on my

two year publishing anniversary, and I can't believe this is my life. Thank you for every review, every comment, every tag. Thank you for your enthusiasm for my words and for cheering me on. You all are what makes this job fun, and I love you endlessly.

ABOUT THE AUTHOR

Chelsea Curto is a flight attendant who lives in the Northeast with her partner and their dog. When she's not busy writing, she loves to read, travel, go to theme parks, run, eat tacos and hang out with friends.

Scan the code below to sign up for my newsletter where you can read bonus scenes and have first access to exclusive content!

instagram.com/authorchelseacurto

tiktok.com/@chelseareadsandwrites

amazon.com/author/chelseacurto

ALSO BY CHELSEA CURTO

Love Through a Lens series

Camera Chemistry

Caught on Camera

Behind the Camera

Off Camera

Camera Shy

DC Stars series

Face Off

Boston series

An Unexpected Paradise

The Companion Project

Road Trip to Forever

Park Cove series

Booked for the Holidays

www.ingramcontent.com/pod-product-compliance
Lightning Source LLC
Chambersburg PA
CBHW070401310726
48977CB00003B/515